Zigzag

And Other Stories

Philip Gambone

RATTLING GOOD YARNS
PRESS

Rattling Good Yarns Press
33490 Date Palm Drive 3065
Cathedral City CA 92235
USA
www.rattlinggoodyarns.com

Cover Design: Rattling Good Yarns Press

Library of Congress Control Number: 2024945614
ISBN: 978-1-955826-72-3

First Edition

Also by Philip Gambone

Fiction

The Language We Use Up Here

Beijing: A Novel

Nonfiction

Something Inside: Conversations with Gay Fiction Writers

Travels in a Gay Nation: Portraits of LGBTQ Americans

As Far As I Can Tell: Finding My Father in World War II

As Editor

Breaking the Rules: The Intimate Diary of Ross Terrill

Praise for *Zigzag*

"*Zigzag* is a wonderful marvel of the literary imagination. Gorgeously written but colloquial, witty but deeply felt, quotidian but wonderfully insightful – it is how gay men live today. Gambone is that person sitting next to you in a café observing, listening, and getting every detail, down to the smallest gesture and the slightest quivering of the voice, exactly right. These are men he knows, men that we know, and they come alive here as they grapple with love, loss, grief, and joy. Few writers can so accurately capture the tapestry of urban gay male life with such acuity and compassion."

—Michael Bronski, author of *A Queer History of the United States*

"People who complain that all gay fiction portrays hustlers, drag queens and sex machines have never read Philip Gambone, who writes with great clarity and fidelity about ordinary gay Americans."

—Edmund White, author of *A Boy's Own Story*

"In this collection of fully realized, fully fleshed portraits of gay men of a certain age, Philip Gambone reveals the rich, complicated, empowering history that defines a generation. These men are pioneers and survivors — but still growing and still learning. Storytelling at its best."

—William Mann, author of *The Men from the Boys*

"Gambone peoples his fiction as concisely in age and place as Updike and Calisher, and like them, he approaches his characters with a wry, yet mostly affectionate understanding. If all else was lost, future historians might be able to piece together a place and era from *Zigzag*. Readers will come away from this rich collection of stories with an entire world."

—Felice Picano, author of *Like People in History*

"Phil Gambone's powerful stories evoke the lives of gay men of a certain age as they grapple with loss and find fresh hope. By turns sexy, funny and poignant the result is a queer generational group portrait imbued with humanity and buoyed by a sense of joy."
—Raphael Kadushin, editor of *Wonderlands*

"Philip Gambone's gemlike stories are often as profound and multilayered as his full-length books. He sees the world with an empathy, both humorous and heartbreaking, and his characters are surprising, sometimes beguiling, but always complex."
—Scott Heim, author of *Mysterious Skin*

"Deeply observed, exquisitely precise, and elegantly told, Philip Gambone's stories in *Zigzag* explore the twists and turns of love, lust, regret, and hope in modern maturity."
—Joseph O'Malley, author of *Great Escapes from Detroit*

"These pensive, touching stories, told mostly from the viewpoint of older gay men, are post-AIDS stories. The principal characters are the ones who survived. Some have gone on to form couples or bands of friends; others find themselves alone. But all are looking back to the decades of gay life in which they came out, fell in love (or lust), broke up, stayed together, found callings or lost them, watched people they loved become sick and die. How moving they are, how honest with and about themselves! This is the book I would give a nephew or grandson, gay or straight, if I wanted them to know who I was and who I'd been."
—Reed Woodhouse. author of *Unlimited Embrace*

"*Zigzag* is vintage Phil Gambone—considered, humane, full of longing—but also something bracingly fresh: an intimate portrait of gay aging. He writes frankly (and wittily, and sexily) about men who find themselves reckoning with the perils and pleasures of having survived beyond what "gayness" signifies in the cultural imagination. A great choice for queer book clubs!"
—Michael Lowenthal, author of *The Paternity Test*

"Phil Gambone's new collection is the bitterest and the sweetest of the bittersweet. Such a glorious set of stories."
—Brian Bouldrey, author of *The Good Pornographer*

"Like the best work of Christopher Isherwood. This new collection contains slices of contemporary life among men of a certain age who've experienced enormous changes in the world. We see old wounds from the past, the games played by long-term gay couples, the delicate marriage of a high school French teacher, the challenge of illness, and a wild and witty account of a radical faerie wedding in rural New England. These stories are as unpredictable and real as the lives of our own friends"
—Christopher Bram, author of *Father of Frankenstein*

"The great short stories, from de Maupassant and Chekhov to Cheever, balance their authors' deep understanding of character with their fascination with place. The stories in *Zigzag*, Philip Gambone's touchingly real, tender, and sexy collection dealing with gay life in Boston, share those same qualities of being alive in a city he obviously loves and living through every crucial, telling moment with his thoroughly, humanly attractive characters."
—Lloyd Schwartz, Pulitzer Prize-winning critic

"In *Zigzag*, Philip Gambone deftly employs so many of the qualities I cherish in the best short stories: wit, frankness, economy, vulnerability. Every story in this collection erupts with the hopes and hungers of people you'll recognize, characters navigating through the high-stakes emotional landscape that lies beneath the drama of our everyday lives."
—K.M. Soehnlein, author of *The World of Normal Boys*

"*Zigzag* is a wonderful collection, an examination of and tribute to aging and community that is totally absorbing, beautifully written, and wise. Just when you think you know where a story is going, Philip Gambone makes a turn—sometimes startling, always satisfying."
—Patrick Merla, editor of *Boys Like Us*

For Isaac
con amor por siempre

Contents

But what can I do about the fact that, as far as I can tell, nothing, *nothing* is put to rest, however old a man may be?

—Philip Roth

Bar Story

When Dominik walked into Cru/Cuts—*zigzagged* was more accurate, the icy patches outside were such a treacherous obstacle course—Michael was already there sitting at the counter, a bottle of IPA in front of him.

"A man walks into a bar," Dominik said, taking the stool next to his friend. It was the standard, stupid line he always delivered whenever he met Michael for a drink. There was never anything more to it than that, no punch line. Just: *A man walks into a bar.* A way of announcing himself, Dominik guessed. Michael leaned over, presenting his cheek, and Dominik gave him a quick, friendly kiss.

"Apparently," Michael said, "we'll be the only men walking into this bar tonight. They've already closed the kitchen."

"It's the frickin' weather," Philip, the Sunday bartender, told them. He had already begun mixing Dominik's usual, a sidecar. "The temperature's keeping everyone at home." The "real feel," he said, was supposed to get down to single digits by midnight. Dominik looked around the bar. The place was empty.

"Looks like the 'real feel' in here is already single digits," he said.

"It doesn't help," Philip added, "that it's right after New Year's. Everyone's way partied out." He released a healthy measure of Cointreau into the cocktail shaker. Philip could be relied on for what Michael called a "gay pour." His drinks were always generous, if a bit on the sweet side.

Dominik wanted to say that *he* was hardly way partied out, that he'd been to exactly one holiday party all season, but he checked himself. He did not want Philip, who was somewhere in his late twenties, to think he was the kind of guy who stood on the sidelines of Boston's oh-so-fabulous gay scene.

Philip fit the lid onto the cocktail shaker, raised it high above his head, and shook vigorously. Dominik knew that it was a show calculated to flaunt Philip's lanky, athletic body to maximum advantage. When Philip mixed drinks, he looked like a go-go boy at a club pumping the jam. Was that still a thing, Dominik wondered, pumping the jam? And go-go boys? He had no idea. He hadn't been to a dance club in years.

Philip poured Dominik's cocktail into a martini glass, raising the shaker high above the rim in another bit of campy showmanship. Remarkably, the drink came just up to the lip without overflowing. He garnished it with an orange slice and carefully pushed it towards Dominik, who had to lower his head to the glass in order to take the first sip.

"How do you do that?" Dominik asked. "Get the drink to come right to the tippy top of the glass." *Tippy top.* It was the kind of phrase Jerome, his first boyfriend—Dominik's *only* boyfriend—would have hated, but then again Jerome would never have been caught dead in a place like Cru/Cuts. "Too frou-frou," he would have said.

Philip smiled, pleased to have been complimented. "Practice?" He inflected his answer with the upturned lilt of a question. Dominik found Philip's hint of studied dopiness charming.

Cru/Cuts featured wine and steaks—the "cru" and the "cuts," someone had had to explain to Dominik the first time he'd come here. In a neighborhood replete with establishments that catered to gay men of a certain income bracket or the pretensions to one, Cru/Cuts was known to be particularly gay, especially on Sundays when Philip tended the bar. On Sunday evenings, frou-frou drinks—lots of cosmos, margaritas, and flavored martinis—flowed freely, gaily, under Philip's sexy, flamboyant ministrations. At Cru/Cuts, frou-frou conversation flowed gaily, too. Whenever Dominik eavesdropped on the chatter around him, it always sounded like gossip and witty banter and verbatim accounts of other conversations that were full of gossip and witty banter. Laughter—chortling, hooting—often punctuated the barroom, which was lit by several candelabras dripping wax onto the granite bar counter. Without a doubt, Jerome would have hated this place.

Dominik wondered if Philip was keeping the place open merely as a courtesy to him and Michael. He felt guilty that Philip, who, on a typical

Sunday, would be sashaying up and down the bar, attending to three conversations and five drink orders all at once, was now reduced to straightening a pile of cocktail napkins. He watched Michael take a sip of his beer, eyes closed, the bottle tilted just so before his lips, in keen anticipation. It was one of Michael's many adorable mannerisms that Dominik doted on.

"Guess we didn't get the message that the party was somewhere else tonight," he said.

Michael leaned over and whispered, "But that means we get Philip all to ourselves."

Dominik laughed obligingly, but he couldn't help wondering how the guys who came here every Sunday evening, the ones who always seemed to know how to deliver a joke or what style shirt to wear, the kind of guys who'd have immediately gotten the "Cru/Cuts" joke, how *those* guys—every single one of them—had known to stay home tonight or go somewhere else. It was not the first time he imagined a secret cabal, some sort of insider communications network, among the alpha set of South End gay men.

"Maybe *you'll* get Philip all to yourself tonight," he told Michael.

Michael set his beer down. "You okay?" He gave Dominik a sweet, concerned look.

Dominik eased his sidecar over to Michael's beer bottle. "Just feeling old."

"Ah, yes, the ongoing woes of the modern, urban, post-liberation, post-ghetto, aging gay American male."

"Ouch!"

"Sorry, I take back the 'post-ghetto' thing," Michael teased.

They'd been friends for six years, having met at a pharmacology convention downtown. At the opening night meet-and-greet, Dominik had straight off noticed Michael. Tall and trim, with black-Irish eyes and luscious full lips, Michael was a stand-out. But who was the woman he was talking to? It would not be the first time he'd been attracted to a straight guy. It took him half an hour to work up the nerve to make his way over to them. When he got close enough to read their name tags, he discovered that Michael was also from Boston. *Can a fellow Bostonian horn in on this conversation?* he asked. He'd made up the line on the spur of the moment, something he rarely succeeded at, but this time it worked. They invited him into their tiny circle and introduced themselves.

Dominik was a pharmacist. The woman was a sales rep for a big drug company. Michael taught pharmacology at one of Boston's medical schools. As they segued from introductions to shop talk, Dominik found himself—another spur-of-the-moment delivery—saying he thought children were being over-medicated. This line did not succeed with the drug company sales rep. A few minutes later, she excused herself and drifted away.

Thank you, Michael whispered, bending his knees as if a heavy burden had just been lifted from him. The whisper and the cute balletic curtsy completely won Dominik over. They spent the rest of the cocktail hour hanging out, making conversation that circled around the gay thing but never quite landed there. When the party started breaking up, Dominik suggested that they go have dinner together. *Maybe Cru/Cuts?* he casually threw out, fishing for a reaction. Michael smiled knowingly, but said that he had dinner plans with his boyfriend. Despite the disappointment—or was it a thrill to have his suspicions about Michael's sexual orientation confirmed?—Dominik gave him his card; Michael followed suit. A mere polite formality, it seemed, but when Michael called the next week and invited him over to have dinner and meet the boyfriend, Dominik accepted. It turned out to be the evening that kicked off their friendship.

"So, nothing more than 'feeling old'?" Michael now asked. He moved his glass of beer away from Dominik's sidecar. He had broken up with his boyfriend over a year ago, but had made it clear that Dominik was still just his *friend*, not the one who was going to take Nick's place. "Nothing else going on, Pumpkin?"

Dominik took a deep breath. He hadn't planned on telling Michael the story. "Last Friday, I met someone."

"Nice."

"Well, kind of." He looked down at his cocktail. "We met on one of those hook-up sites," he said. "But we didn't hook up. It was just a conversation."

Michael waited for more.

"I mean"—he finally looked up at Michael—"for a texting back-and-forth conversation, it was pretty nice. We kept messaging for over half an hour. He told me he liked older guys. So we get to the point where I invite him over—you know, for a glass of wine and a we'll-take-it-from-there thing, and the next thing I know, he's texting, 'Oh, gosh, I didn't realize how late it was getting. Sorry, man. Later.' *Later!* Fucking later. I hate that word."

Philip returned to ask if they'd like another round. Dominik looked down at his drink. He had hardly touched it. He took a big sip and said sure, he'd have another.

"Dominik," Michael offered when Philip turned away to mix the cocktail, "maybe he really did mean later."

"The guy blocked me."

"Oh." Michael scraped his fingernail against a pool of candle wax that had hardened on the bar counter. "Look, Pumpkin, there are plenty of other guys out there. Guys who don't say *later.*"

Dominik drank down the rest of his sidecar. "Sure there are—lots of other guys—if you're twenty-eight, or thirty-eight, or even, God forbid, forty-eight. *Fifty-eight*, Michael, I'm fifty-eight. You reach your fifties and, as my dear departed mother used to say in the dear departed Czech of her youth, *Na shledanou.* Bye-bye."

Michael took another sip of his beer, set the bottle down, and looked Dominik directly in the eyes. "In my book, there's only one 'bye-bye'— the lights-out-forever bye-bye. Anything else is just a temporary setback."

"Michael, darling, fifty-eight is not a 'setback.' It's a calamity."

Michael shook his head in mock disgust. "Look, all I'm saying is that there are plenty of other guys, and plenty of other dating sites, out there."

"Like *what* dating sites? Michael, this is Boston, remember? College Capital of America. Twink Heaven. No one, *no one*, is looking to date a fifty-eight-year-old loser pharmacist." He pulled his cocktail glass back and tilted it to his lips. There was nothing left but the orange wedge, which he picked out and ate.

"*Ouch!* back at you," Michael said. "So tell me, Dominik, which part, exactly, is the *loser* part: that you're fifty-eight or that you're a pharmacist? There are, you know, lots of guys who are into older men. *And* pharmacists."

Dominik closed his eyes. At the moment, he couldn't face Michael's unrelenting good cheer, or his forty-two-year-old handsome, Irish-American face.

"The last date," he began, opening his eyes again, "the last *date* I went on was two years ago. Stuart—you know him, right? my lawyer friend?—he fixed me up with someone he'd met on one of your *dating* sites." He twisted the phrase sarcastically. "Apparently, the guy thought Stuart was too young. He was into *much* older men." Dominik crumpled up his soggy cocktail napkin. "So, having been passed on to me, the *much older* gay man, I called the guy up and we made a date, an actual date. Dinner. That cute Italian place on Shawmut Avenue."

"Good choice. Why haven't I heard this story before?"

"Um, maybe because it's humiliating?" Philip came over and set down the fresh cocktail. Dominik took a large sip. "So we order dinner, and I start asking him—damn, what was his name? Robert? Richard?—I start asking him what I thought were perfectly reasonable conversation-starter-type questions, you know: how was his day, where does he live, what were his plans for the weekend, stuff like that. And what does Ryder—*Ryder!* that was his name! Hallelujah, I'm not losing my mind!—so what does Ryder do but answer each one of my questions with a single-word answer. His day was ... *good.* Where does he live? *Cambridge.* Weekend plans? *Golfing.* Oh, does he like golfing? *Yes.* How long has he been golfing? *Since junior high.* Excuse me, that was a three-word answer. His *only* three-word answer. After ten minutes of this, I asked him if he was nervous. And you know what he says? *No.* Nothing more. Just no. Michael, it was excruciating."

"I had a date like that once," Philip, who had been hovering, said.

"Never again, right?"

"Never again." Philip picked up Dominik's drink and set down a fresh napkin. "So what about Silver Daddies?"

"Silver Daddies? What? Are you and Michael in cahoots now?"

"No, really. You'd be surprised how many guys on there would be totally into you."

"Totally into me, huh? And what do you know about Silver Daddies?"

"Hey, I've checked it out." Philip looked at Michael and winked.

Dominik turned to Michael. "Have *you* ever tried Silver Daddies?"

Michael took another sip of beer before he answered. "Once, but it seems I didn't quite fit the demographic. Too old to be a boy; too young to be a daddy."

"How old are you anyway?" Philip asked.

"Thirty-seven." Michael pushed his knee against Dominik's thigh, a signal that acknowledged he had subtracted five years from his age and Dominik should keep quiet.

"So really," Philip said, turning his attention back to Dominik. "If you're looking to date, you should try it."

"I don't know," Dominik said. "That last one … jeez, it felt like I was conducting a job interview."

"Damn!" Philip glanced at Michael again. "Sounds serious."

"Honey, at my age, *everything* is serious. Crossing the street is serious. Going for my annual physical checkup is serious. Having to take Viagra is serious." He couldn't believe he was telling Philip this stuff. He drank down the rest of his second sidecar. "And getting home at a decent hour so that I can get a good night's sleep is serious." He took his wallet out.

"It's on the house tonight," Philip said.

"You're sweet." Dominik pulled ten dollars from the wallet and put it on the counter. "That's for the good service and the friendly advice."

"Anytime." Philip looked over at Michael. "You going, too, or would you like another beer?"

"Heck, why not?" Michael said.

Dominik put on his coat, wrapped his scarf around his neck, and pulled on his knit cap.

He gave Michael another quick peck on the cheek.

"A man walks out of a bar …" he said as he moved toward the door.

When he turned back to say goodbye, Michael and Philip were feeding each other orange sections out of the garnish bowl.

❖ ❖ ❖

Outside, the temperature already felt like single digits, and the wind was bitter and dry. Dominik pulled his cap lower onto his head. There was still plenty of hair up there—the "silver daddy" kind, a salt-and-pepper blend that Michael was always telling him was quite handsome. Still, as it was a good fifteen-minute walk to his place, Dominik knew his ears (knit cap or no knit cap) would end up stinging in the deep-winter cold. Once again, he began to negotiate the patches of ice on the uneven brick sidewalks, those quaint Victorian sidewalks that were the South End's signature look.

On freezing nights like this, back in the days when he and the ex, Jerome, were together, they would lock arms as they made their way home from the bars, the straight, non-frou-frou bars his boyfriend insisted on. Jerome was usually drunk and needed Dominik's assitance. He was heavy and clumsy, and sometimes loud and abusive, too. But Dominik had put up with it, clinging to the idea of having a boyfriend. At least he'd loved it for a while. And then he hadn't. When they finally broke up, Dominik had just turned forty-two and was determined never to put up with Jerome's kind of shit again. There had been a lot of it with Jerome: Jerome's excessive drinking, Jerome's screaming fits, Jerome's comatose unresponsiveness in bed. There was the wrecked car, the unmanageable credit card bills, the loss of at least two jobs. On the day he moved out, in his final hysterical outburst, Jerome had screamed, "Who the fuck do you think is going to go for a forty-something drug store clerk?"

It was the push Dominik had needed. He got himself back into school, finishing the pharmacy degree that he had started years ago. His first job had been in Wilmington, Delaware, where he also began therapy. The therapist, an hour's drive away in Philadelphia, was a quasi-New Age ex-Jesuit, whom Dominik tried hard not to fall in love with.

One day, after they'd been working together for about a year, the therapist, whose name was Benny, said to him, "What about the possibility of living your life without the expectation of any particular outcome? Can you make a friendly place for uncertainty?"

"I think I made a big, friendly place for uncertainty with Jerome," Dominik told him. "He was one massive bundle of uncertainty."

"Is that what keeps you from falling in love again?" Benny asked. "Are you afraid it will always be that way? It's your choice, you know."

Dominik had immediately broken down crying, barely able to compose himself for the remainder of the session. All the way back to Wilmington, he kept chewing on that idea, that he could organize his life without the expectation of any particular outcome, and certainly not the outcome of permanence. It was such a healthy outlook. Why hadn't he been able to make it stick? What was the matter with him that he kept forgetting that kind of wisdom? And how, damn it, did anyone ever figure out that he could get away with feeding orange slices to a cute bartender?

A punishing blast of wind forced him to hunch over. He dropped his head to protect his face and eyes. And it was then, in that unguarded moment, that he found himself—bam!—flat on the icy sidewalk, pitched onto his right side. "Fuck!" he cried out. "Goddam it!"

He tried getting up, but an excruciating pain shot through his shoulder, leaving him gasping for breath. Wincing in agony, he tried to steady his breathing and eased himself onto his left side. Blessedly, nothing wrong there. When he tried to stand, his feet slipped again. He was on a patch of black ice. It had been an ambush waiting to happen.

Just don't let anything be broken. Please, not again.

Seven years ago, on the first day of a one-week vacation to Provincetown, he'd fallen off his bicycle and fractured his wrist. He'd spent five weeks after that in a cast. The day the doctor cut the cast off, what met Dominik's horrified eyes was a pasty, shriveled up wrist and lower arm. It looked like the desiccated limb on a mummy. Close to fainting, he'd turned so deathly white that the doctor had called Code Blue on him. Dominik never got on his bicycle again.

His cell phone was in his right pocket. He tried to get it, but the slightest movement of his right arm sent a harrowing punishment to his shoulder. Gingerly, every move a torment, he got to his feet. He tried reaching into his pocket with his left hand, keeping his right shoulder as still as possible, but the phone was too far down. And then, incongruously, he laughed—for the ridiculousness of the situation, the stupidity of it, and for the way life had of not ever letting you get too complacent before—*Na shledanou!*—it smacked you right back down again.

❖ ❖ ❖

Back in his apartment, he called Michael, told him what had happened, and asked if he wouldn't mind coming over to check things out. "Of course, of course," Michael said, though there was something in his voice, a trace of hesitancy, that made Dominik wonder if he was asking too much. "I'll grab an Uber. Hang tight. Be there as soon as I can."

As he waited, Dominik tried to make himself comfortable in his easy chair, but every time he leaned back, the slightest pressure to his right shoulder revived the excruciating pain. When the buzzer rang, he eased himself out of the chair, buzzed Michael in, and opened the door to his apartment, listening to Michael ascending the stairs.

Tucked in an alcove just outside the door was his old bicycle, its tires flat, the seat and frame dusty from seven years of neglect. Was this how it was going to be from now on—an accident every seven years or so, another part of his body broken, the playthings of his more youthful years tossed aside? A future of nothing but "Later"?

Two floors below, Michael said something, but Dominik couldn't make it out. When the talking continued, he realized Michael wasn't addressing him; he was talking to someone else, someone who was climbing the stairs with him. Jesus, had he brought the EMT people?

"I think I'm gonna live," he called down, trying to keep things light, embarrassed that emergency personnel had been summoned. But when Michael rounded the last turn of the staircase and appeared on the landing, his face as bright as a New Year's sparkler, the "paramedic" he was talking to turned out to be ... Philip.

"Look who I brought with me."

"Hey," Philip said. From behind his back, he produced a cocktail shaker. In his other hand, he was carrying a martini glass. "Thought you might need a painkiller," he announced cheerfully.

Dominik heard himself gushing thanks, when all he really wanted to say was, *Go away.*

"Let's take a look," Michael said. "Sit down." He pulled off his knit cap but kept his jacket on. Philip made a beeline for Dominik's coffee table, set down the martini glass, and began pouring out the cocktail.

"I don't think anything's broken," Dominik said, more wishful than certain. When Michael touched his shoulder, he flinched.

"Here?" Michael asked, touching again.

"Yeah, that hurts."

"What about here?"

"No, not so much."

Philip held out the cocktail. He, too, had kept his jacket on.

"Just put it down on the coffee table," Dominik commanded. He didn't try to disguise the nettled tone in his voice.

"I don't think anything's broken," Michael said, "but you've banged it up pretty bad. You're gonna have a hard time sleeping tonight. Ice it. And take something for the pain. What have you got in your medicine cabinet?"

"Everything. I'm a pharmacist, remember?"

When Michael went to the bathroom, Philip asked Dominik how long he'd had the apartment.

"Ten years," Dominik answered coolly.

"It's cute."

Dominik looked around. Six hundred and fifty-two square feet. He had moved to Boston with such high hopes: a better position, better benefits, a new condo, excited to put into practice all he had learned about how to be a healthy human being, a self-loving gay man. Now, these many years later, it seemed as if all he had to show for it was a "cute" condominium with twenty years of payments still to go.

Michael returned, holding out two capsules in the palm of his hand.

"I couldn't find a drinking glass in the bathroom. You can take them with the sidecar."

Philip had wandered over to the turntable and records across the room.

"Whoa, you've gotten into vinyl."

"I was never *not* into vinyl," Dominik snapped. He popped the capsules into his mouth and brought the cocktail glass up to his lips with his left hand. Some of the drink spilled onto the living room floor. "Fuck!"

Michael took the glass from him as delicately as if he were a priest removing a communion chalice from the lips of one of the faithful.

Meanwhile, Philip had pulled an album from one of Dominik's record shelves. "Etta James. She good?" He started slipping the record out of the dust jacket.

"Don't!" Dominik yelled. Philip froze, the record halfway out of the slipcover. "For your information, that record is almost fifty years old. It doesn't have a single scratch on it, and I'd like to keep it that way."

In slow-motion, Philip eased the record back into its jacket. Michael laid his hand gently on Dominik's good shoulder.

"I think I need to go to bed and be alone right now," Dominik told him. "Please."

Michael kept kneading his good shoulder. "Can I make up an ice bag? Help you get into bed?"

"Maybe an ice pack. There's one in the freezer."

Michael dashed off to get it and returned in less than half a minute. It was clear he didn't want to leave Dominik alone with Philip for very long. Michael laid the pack on his shoulder.

"Feel good?"

Dominik closed his eyes and nodded. A minute passed. No one said anything. It was only after they had left—a quick peck on the cheek from Michael, silence from Philip—that Dominik noticed the martini glass still on the coffee table. Easing up from the chair, he picked up the glass, brought it into the kitchen, and poured the rest of the drink down the drain.

In the bedroom, he sat on the edge of the bed. The wind rattled the window. Ever since he'd moved in, he had been meaning to get tighter windows installed. He bent over, unlaced his shoes, removed his pants. It was awkward using only his left hand. He felt like the old guys he occasionally saw at the Y—fifteen, twenty years older than he, with saggy asses and flabby muscles. They would take forever getting undressed,

12

stepping out of their loose-fitting gym togs with shaky, cautious movements.

When he went to remove his forest green pullover—he'd selected it purposely because Michael had once told him he looked good in that color—he realized he just might have to sleep with the sweater on. There was no way he could raise his right arm high enough to slip out of the sleeve. He was about to get into bed when the buzzer sounded. He shuffled to the intercom. It was Michael, asking if he could come up for a minute. "I'm alone," he added.

When they met at the landing, Dominik was holding out the martini glass. "You looking for this?" Playfully, he toggled it back and forth.

Michael didn't crack a smile. "I'm looking for *you*," he said.

"I was just getting into bed." Dominik moved back to the easy chair and eased himself down. "Would you mind helping me get out of this sweater?"

Michael slowly pulled the left sleeve over Dominik's good arm. Next he got the neck over his head, and finally, with the gentlest of touches, as if he were removing bandages, he unraveled the right sleeve.

"Michael, I was such a jerk tonight."

"You were a guy in pain. Philip got that. He's okay with what happened. The question is, Are *you*?"

"Am I okay?" Dominik echoed. "My whole life has been about looking for an answer to that question." He chuckled. "And I hope I get there before I die."

"That's what we all want, Pumpkin."

When Dominik shifted in his chair, his shoulder exploded in pain. "Can you help me up? Right now, the only thing this pumpkin wants is to roll back into his pumpkin patch."

Michael braced a hand against Dominik's back and guided him out of the chair. He walked Dominik to the bedroom and helped him onto the mattress. Fluffing the pillows, he made a nest for Dominik's bad shoulder. "How's that?" he asked. "Still hurts?"

"Yeah. You were right. It's going be a long night."

"Wouldn't be a bad idea to get it X-rayed tomorrow. Just in case. My game's pharmacology, not anatomy."

"I will."

"You need anything else? More pain medicine?"

"No, thanks. Honestly, I usually don't even take aspirin."

"You trying to be a martyr?"

Dominik shook his head. "Just trying to be in touch with what my body is telling me."

"And what's your body telling you right now?"

Dominik inched over in order to give Michael more room to perch on the edge of the bed.

"It's telling me ... this journey I'm on"—he let out a slow sigh—"it's telling me that I'm taking way too fucking *long*!"

Michael squeezed Dominik's leg. "But we keep on going, right?" He shot Dominik a smile. "Until one day, *Na shled* ..."

"*Na shledanou.* It was practically her motto. I suppose my mother had a right to think that way. Both her parents died before she came to America. One of her brothers committed suicide a few years after they got here. As you can imagine, my mother was the kind of person who held back on enthusiasm. It was her way of protecting herself."

Michael nodded, but there was more Dominik wanted to say:

"She came over here with so little, never trusted that life would hand her much. And it didn't. She became a very closed-up person. There are days when I'm terrified that I'm following in her footsteps. I see myself closing up just like her." He saw Michael studying his face. "And I hate"—he chuckled; it was so ludicrous—"I hate that I'm still learning that my future happiness—the twenty or perhaps thirty (please, God, make it thirty!) years I have left—that it all depends on whether I decide to close up or not."

"It's not a race, Dominik. You'll learn it when you learn it."

"At fifty-eight, I shouldn't still be learning it."

"Oh? And who made *that* rule?"

Dominik pulled the duvet up close. "So, are you and Philip going to start dating?"

Michael wagged his head. "Dating. Seeing. Sleeping together." He shrugged his shoulders. "Like I said, it's not a race."

"How did you get to be so wise?"

Michael leaned over and kissed Dominik on the forehead. "You think so?"

Dominik paused. "I never told you this, but I was crushed last summer, you know, when you told me you wanted to stick to us just being friends."

"I know."

"But I'm really glad you are my friend."

"I'm glad you're my friend, too." Michael kissed Dominik's forehead again. "And now," he announced, "it's time to call it a night. Sweet dreams, Pumpkin."

"Thank you, Michael."

After Michael let himself out, everything was quiet, though the wind kept shaking the bedroom window. Blessedly, the painkiller was kicking in. Dominik thought he'd be able to get through the night.

But half an hour later, he was still awake. Was it going to be one of those nights when his mind raced on, full of thoughts about the day just past and the day, and all the days, yet to come? On nights like that, he sometimes read or watched television or played solitaire on his smartphone. Sometimes he checked the postings on Grindr, though the guys he messaged almost never messaged back.

As he nestled deeper under the covers, Dominik pictured his bicycle, leaning against the wall in the vestibule, a piece of dusty junk that he still hadn't been able to throw out. That sweet, old bike. He'd brought it all the way up from Wilmington.

He began ticking off the things he had to do come morning: call in sick, get an X-ray, ask the condo trustees who they'd recommend to have replacement windows installed. Maybe he would even look up the address of a bicycle repair shop. Or ask Michael. Six years ago, it would have been so easy not to introduce himself to Michael at that meet-and-greet, but somehow he'd found it within himself to go up to him and say hello.

The window rattled again. He guessed that Michael and Philip must be glad to be sleeping together on a brutal night like this. Which one of them, he wondered had picked up that first orange slice and fed it to the other? Who had taken the first step?

As if it were an answer to his question, he whispered into the dark: "A man walks into a bar ..."

He had no idea what the next line would be. He never did. But perhaps there wasn't a need to know the next line. Perhaps there was something creditable in just taking that first step. *A man walks into a bar.* Just then, he remembered the Czech word for hello: *Ahoj.* Funny for a country that didn't even have a coastline.

"*Ahoj,*" he called out into the dark. "Hello." Hello to that first step. Hello to everything that would follow. And hello to making a place for uncertainty—yes, Benny, with no expectations—a place for uncertainty, again and again and again.

The Beautiful Game

"Yes!" Mitch burst out. And so did most of the other guys in the café. I looked up from my book toward the flat-screen TV, where something eliciting their delirious enthusiasm had just occurred. A point scored, a nice piece of footwork, a miraculous save by the goalie? Those are the only things I understand about this sport that Mitch tells me people around the world call "the beautiful game." Whatever it was that had caused such an uproar, it was already over. The tedious business of kicking the ball up and down the field had resumed. I turned back to my reading.

Mitch and I were at the Caffè dello Sport, a coffee shop on Hanover Street that, in addition to cappuccinos and cannoli, serves up international soccer matches in all their high-definition glory. Back in the days when we lived in Dorchester, Mitch used to watch the games at home, but after we moved to the North End, the café—which I like to call simply "the Sport"—became our regular Sunday afternoon hangout and Mitch's living room for soccer. Here, in the company of like-minded guys, he can sit for hours over a coffee, his eyes hardly straying from the screen, while I, one of those guys who was always picked last in gym class, dutifully keep my sort-of-husband company. He follows the adventures on the field and I follow whatever adventure is unfolding in the current book I'm reading. Mitch used to try to explain the game to me. But over the years, we've come to an understanding: I leave soccer to him, and he leaves reading to me.

Another cheer went up, then quickly subsided into a groan. Again I looked up at the screen—a failed kick at the goal—then went back to my book. That afternoon, it was Balzac's *Lost Illusions*. You would think a fellow sitting in a North End sports café, plowing through a nineteenth-century French novel, even a fellow as old as I am, would call the wrong kind of attention to himself with a book like that. But the Sport seems to be, thankfully, an equal-opportunity space: a post-dinner dessert bistro, a hangout for retired Italian-American men, a romantic date venue, a clubhouse for soccer fans, and, apparently, even a library for bookworms like me.

I got to the end of a chapter and took a break. Under the pretext of checking out the game, I gave the crowd a quick gander. Some of the guys who come to the Sport are quite good-looking, a few stunningly so. In addition to their physical appeal, the comradely excitement they share over soccer is a turn-on for me. But I always avoid eye contact with these regulars, who, to be honest, are a bit intimidating with their straight-jock swagger. Fortunately, at our age, Mitch and I do not look gay anymore. If there are people at the Sport who recognize us from week to week, they probably write us off as just a couple of old duffers enjoying a Sunday afternoon without their wives. Being in our sixties, there isn't much about us that fits the classic gay profile anymore. It's another reason, I guess, why I can get away with reading Balzac.

My gaze lingered a few seconds more than usual on a particularly attractive young man who was huddled in front of the screen. He looked to be about twenty-two, no older. A head of thick, dark chestnut hair— if I were painting his portrait, I'd start with burnt sienna as the base color—it crowned a sweet face that was fetchingly smudged by a scruffy beard, one of those self-consciously light-trimmed affairs, half stubble, half hair-salon fussy. Just then, he turned his head in my direction and we made eye contact. Immediately, I looked away. At the Sport, one keeps one's eyes on the screen, on the food at your table, or on your book, not on the boys. I miss old-fashioned cruising, but the Sport is definitely not the place to try that sort of thing. Besides, there's Mitch, my dear, soccer-loving partner. We've been together twenty-eight years. He's been the one steadiness in my life, a life that otherwise has been anything but steady. Don't get me wrong: a good-looking guy will still turn my head, but that's as far as it goes these days—here at the café, on the street, anywhere.

"Oh, my God! Did you see that?" Mitch asked, turning to me.

I grimaced. Whatever it was, I'd missed it again. Story of my life.

❖ ❖ ❖

We met at the Safari Club, a now-defunct bathhouse in the South End. It was never much of a bathhouse, not by the standards of the places I'd been to in other cities, and it didn't last very long. The city shut the club down when a gay man—someone who seemed to find it amusing to play Police Commissioner Louis Renault in his own Boston version of *Casablanca*—complained that he was "shocked, shocked to find that sex is going on in here!" As things turned out, the Safari was the last bathhouse to operate in Boston.

The night we met, Mitch and I fooled around a bit in the showers, but he cut it off, telling me he really hadn't come for sex. "I'm just here to unwind," he said. I didn't believe him for a minute. But I appreciated the delicacy, and decency, behind his rejection. He moved on, disappearing into the murkiness of that doomed hammam. Mitch was already out of my mind, when, an hour later, I happened to see him outside on my way home. Had he enjoyed "unwinding," I asked. It took him a few seconds to recognize me.

"Oh, hi," he said.

I had only seen him undressed under the shower. Now I studied what was covering that beautiful body of his: a new pair of jeans, a collared, button-down shirt, and a light vee-neck sweater. It was a look for a springtime stroll through Harvard Square, not a trip to the tubs.

"Did I enjoy it?" he asked and shrugged.

Yeah, I agreed; not much, was it? Perhaps, I ventured, he'd like to come over to my place? "A nightcap?" I suggested. Mitch looked dubious.

"It's kind of late, isn't it?" he noted.

"Tomorrow's Sunday," I said. The new jeans he was wearing were not flattering and certainly gave no hint of the magnificent dick I'd played with for a minute in the showers.

"Trouble is," he said, "I live in Dorchester, and the trains stop running soon."

"You could stay overnight."

The words were no sooner out of my mouth than I regretted saying them. I knew how freaked out some men get if you even hint at interest beyond a fleeting hookup.

Mitch studied my face. He was sizing me up. But sizing me up for what? I remember wondering what face I should present to him—hot trick? struggling artist? bookish nerd? I wanted him to see all three. But how do you put *that* look into your face?

"So, how far is it to your place?" he asked.

"A mere five blocks," I told him. "I walked here."

"A *mere*," he repeated, chuckling. "Okay, let's go."

All the way, I was silent. I was afraid that anything else that came out of my mouth would be the wrong thing to say. Plus, I didn't want him to pick up how excited I was. This handsome man whom I was about to bed. To fuck? To get fucked by? I didn't care. I just wanted him in any way I could have him. That was the year I was reading Alan Watts. As we walked to my place, I repeated to myself the lessons I was picking up from that Zen guru: Just be with whatever is now. Desire is impermanent; *everything* is impermanent.

Whatever reluctance Mitch had shown me in the dingy recesses of the Safari Club melted away as soon as I unlocked the door to my studio apartment and we tumbled into bed. Literally tumbled. He tripped over a tall stack of coffee-table art books that were piled up next to the mattress—just a mattress, set up Japanese style on the floor—and fell, face-down, onto the duvet. When I followed suit, throwing myself on top of him, I couldn't believe how amorous he became. He turned over, grabbed my ass, and started kissing me like crazy. What was real here, I wondered: the Mitch who had showed me so little interest in the shower room, who had hesitated going to my place that night; or this suddenly passionate lover who was ravishing me with tongue-probing kisses? And when I reached into the basket next to the mattress and pulled out a condom—*Who's gonna use this?* I asked—and he fucked me, with an attention to my pleasure that was almost too much to bear, I felt desired, *loved*, in fact, in a way I had never experienced before. I was thirty-five that year. Part of me had already foreclosed on finding love again. That night, I was stunned to discover that love might still be in the cards.

It was after four in the morning when we finally fell asleep. Or rather, when Mitch fell asleep. I was still too aroused for dreamland. And anxious about what I'd find in the morning. *Just be grateful for what is*, I reminded myself.

But over coffee, Mitch was relaxed and chatty. He seemed perfectly happy to linger at my tiny, two-person kitchen table, watching me toast English muffins. He told me his story: a childhood in rural New Hampshire, mom a school teacher, dad a postal worker. When I gingerly observed that I hadn't picked up much interest from him at the Safari, he told me he'd always been shy.

"Could have fooled me last night!" I teased.

He blushed, told me he'd opted for a small Catholic college over the University of New Hampshire for just that reason, his shyness. He'd majored in statistics, played club soccer, and, three years after he graduated, discovered he was gay. I decided not to tell him I'd been sexually active since I was sixteen.

When it came time to trade stories about what we did for work, the hesitation was now on my part. I never knew how to account for myself. By days, I was managing a photography shop. At night, I went to my studio to paint. I told him I was an "aspiring artist." *And you?* I asked. I was eager to divert the conversation away from my motley career.

Mitch told me he worked as an actuary for a company on Route 128. Risk assessment, he explained, when I asked what that was. Being an actuary was all about assessing the risk of potential events for his company's clients, predicting the cost of certain decisions and policies they might undertake. I tried to follow as best I could, but this kind of stuff—statistics, numbers, the mathematics of potential events—it's not my thing. And when he added that he worked mostly for insurance companies, my heart sank even further. I couldn't imagine falling for a man with such a dry and tedious job. How could this delicious lover, who only a few hours before had taken me to a level of passion I'd hardly ever experienced, spend his days crunching numbers?

Figuring I had nothing to lose, I braved a quip.

"And what," I asked, pushing the plate of English muffins toward him, "what does risk assessment say are the chances of us getting together again?"

Mitch's eyes went to the plate. He picked up a muffin, then reached for the jar of marmalade. Ah, I thought, so I guess I know the answer. I watched him spread some marmalade on the muffin. The way he did it—

so carefully, so deliberately—it was, I figured, the same kind of attention he must bring to his actuarial work.

At that moment, I understood that Mitch was *all* about attention. Love-making, buttering his muffins, calculating business risks—all of it, the same centered concentration of mind. I, who had spent the last few years flitting from job to job, trying to paint, trying to learn to meditate, trying to get the hang of how to run a photography shop, and getting nowhere with any of it, there I was, sitting across from this man who seemed to have mastered the art of happy, intentional living.

Mitch set down his knife. "Sure, why not?" he said. "I'd be happy to see you again, Christopher."

That's what clinched it for me: that he had remembered my name, an introduction I'd made in passing under the showers at the bathhouse.

Calm mind, I reminded myself.

❖ ❖ ❖

So there we were, twenty-eight years and the beginning of another spring later. Despite the slow, cold start to the season, a typical early March in Beantown, I felt renewal was in the air: the noticeably longer days, the city's resumption of street sweeping, and, most glorious of all, the blooming of the witch hazel trees. Their delicate chartreuse buds and that mysterious, arresting fragrance always remind me that Boston's winter dreariness is about to change.

Our table that Sunday was in front of the Sport's windows overlooking Hanover Street, away from the throng gathered directly around the television. The sun was streaming in, cutting a sharp line of light across our tabletop. It made me happy. All of it—the clean March sunlight, the steamy warmth and delicious aromas of the coffee shop, Mitch's pleasure in the game. And that chestnut-haired boy I stole another quick glance at. The past winter, our first in the North End, had been tough on me. From an eight-room house in Dorchester, affordably cheap when we bought it twenty years before, we'd gone to a four-room condo (*not* cheap!), and with that downsizing, I'd lost the painting studio I'd maintained all those years. "Maintained" is the operative word, because I actually hadn't done much painting there. The move finally confirmed what I'd been avoiding admitting to myself for a long time: I was lazy and had little talent. Though it was a relief to finally face a reality I'd been denying for years, nevertheless I was sad. And angry.

I'd almost not gone to the Sport that day. Mitch and I had had a fight that morning, a stupid squabble about what we should do with the small sofa in our kitchen that we were getting rid of. He wanted to leave it on the street for the city to pick up with the trash. I said we should call an organization that helps the homeless or people with AIDS. Why, I asked him, should we add to the already huge problem of overloaded landfills? Mitch acknowledged this, but countered that the sofa would never end up in a landfill. It was still in such good shape that, before the trash collectors came, someone would surely haul it away for their own use.

"Precisely!" I said, raising my voice. "Hauled away by some North End *yuppie* who can easily afford to buy a new sofa and would be taking this one away from someone who truly needs it."

Mitch gave me the look he always gives me whenever I get on my high horse. That morning, the look said, *And which North End yuppies might those be?*

"*We* are not yuppies!" I yelled. But Mitch just raised his eyebrows higher.

He was right, of course. Though we aren't young, we were certainly part of the influx of urban professionals who were gobbling up condos carved out of the North End's remaining cold-water flats. I was railing against ourselves. Maybe, I thought, *that* was what had been eating away at me all winter. Was I feeling guilty about being just one more intruder edging out the old-guard Italians in this grubby, congested, and totally charming Boston neighborhood? Was I feeling angry that I was, ultimately, no different from my neighbors, nobody special? Yes, all of that and also the reality, pressing upon me more and more, that I wasn't a painter after all.

"Okay," I conceded, "but if we have an opportunity to be certain that the sofa will go to a needy person, wouldn't that be better than just taking a *risk*"—it's a word I often throw at Mitch—"a risk that it might go to the right person?"

"Christopher, can't we just trust that the universe will bring the sofa to someone who needs it?"

I exploded.

"The universe! The fucking universe is not guiding anyone to anything," I yelled. Loud enough for our yuppie neighbors next door to hear.

I took a deep breath. It irks me that it's often Mitch who proves to be the one with the calm mind, he who gave up religion years ago and never looked back. At that moment, I hated myself: for the way I was treating him, for my abandoned pursuit of painting, for the anxiety I felt about our move to the North End, and for my years of expecting the universe to deliver some tranquility to my restless soul.

Which is why I decided to swallow my pride and join Mitch at the Sport that afternoon. I needed the comfort of his company, this man who has somehow managed to love me despite everything I have splattered all over the messy canvas of our marriage.

Mitch signaled the waiter to bring him another cappuccino. "How about you?" he asked.

"Just another glass of water," I told the waiter. These days, I'm trying to hydrate more.

What has kept us together all these years? At the beginning, it was the love-making. When we first got together, I was old enough to know that that kind of intensity did not necessarily portend a lasting thing. But in fact, after we'd been seeing each other for about a month—and the sex was still amazing—I concluded we were a match. I ignored all the differences: the math vs. art difference; the six-foot-two Mitch still soccer trim vs. the me who was only five-foot-nine with a nascent Buddha belly; the man who seemed perfectly content with his lapsed Catholicism vs. the confused spiritual pilgrim that was Christopher. Those differences seemed insignificant in comparison to what we had in common. There was something so incongruous—mysterious, really—in the fact that we should find each other so powerfully attractive. I decided to trust the attraction despite all the indications that we were, if you thought about it, actually pretty incompatible.

Sometime during the second month of our courtship, I invited Mitch to come to the Gardner Museum with me. I wanted to share some of my favorite paintings with him—the Fra Angelico *Assumption of the Virgin*, John Singer Sargent's *Jaleo*, and the Vermeer that was tragically stolen just a few months later. As we strolled from room to room, Mitch listened to my rapturous commentaries and gave each work a polite examination. But I could tell that none of these masterpieces hit him the way they did me. *It's not going to work,* I told myself again. So it was a lovely surprise when, during the break we took in the museum's coffee shop, Mitch bared his soul.

"I guess you can tell that I don't know a lot about art," he said, "but it was really fun listening to you talk about those paintings, Christopher. You make me realize how much more there is to, well, to *life.*" He told me how inexperienced he felt, how intimidated he was by art, by all the things he didn't know, and that he loved my enthusiasm and loved how I wanted to share that enthusiasm with him. "Sometimes I think the only things I'm enthusiastic about are my job and soccer." He paused. "Oh, and poker. Do you play poker?"

I told him no, but that I'd like to learn. But what was really going through my head was how nice it was to feel like I actually had something to bring to this relationship. That someone like him could actually be interested in *me*—the Christopher who hadn't a clue about soccer or poker, the Christopher who had flitted from career to career, who still hadn't managed to get a gallery interested in his paintings, who'd gone from trying to meet guys in gay bars to cruising the murky haunts of a second-rate bathhouse—*me,* Christopher, this sorry specimen of a gay man. Mitch actually thought I had something to give him!

Scenarios raced through my mind: of trips we might take to other art museums, of seats at the opera, of going to meditation classes together. And it wouldn't be just my enthusiasms that we'd share. I'd learn from him, too. I'd learn to love soccer and play poker, even to climb mountains in New Hampshire. Come the fall, we could help his mother, a widow now, with her vegetable canning projects.

All of those things we tried. Our one venture to the opera was a bust. As for museums, Mitch tried hard, but the paintings he cottoned to tended to be pretty, cheerful, and easy to read—stuff that bored me. The outings to New Hampshire were slightly more successful. Mitch, bless him, organized easy hikes, ones whose objective was more about the picnic at the end of the trail (assembled and packed by me) than strenuous exercise. And, yes, we even once helped his mom pickle string beans. *Once.* I couldn't believe how painstaking the whole process was. That was the beginning of our learning to make compromises: no soccer or vegetable canning for me, no opera for him. And for a while, the sex continued to be awesome.

"Some marriages are like cream," Balzac once wrote. "The temperature can turn them in a moment." *Some* marriages. Remarkably, ours has withstood the perilous temperatures that, from time to time, have threatened to curdle things between us. I give all the credit to Mitch, for the steady way he has met the challenges I have brought to our relationship. The biggest challenge has been my erratic, undependable job history. When we met, I was managing that photography shop in the South End. When the shop went belly up, I switched to managing a used bookstore that specialized in art books. That closed, too. The year we moved to Dorchester, I opened an upscale, handmade gift shop called Auntie Em's. Very cute, very gay, very doomed to failure.

Over the years, the catalogue of my ill-fated careers continued: manager of another book store, graphic designer, art gallery manager, children's after-school art program director. Most of these jobs folded through no fault of my own; a few I quit in protest over the company's policies. When COVID hit, I was doing web design, a lucky break that let me work from home.

As for the other major challenge—the waning of our sexual passion— Mitch didn't seem to mind. It was another risk he'd assessed and deemed feasible, work-around-able. I, on the other hand, could not imagine giving up sex. I was tempted to bail out, even though we had just bought that house in Dorchester. Instead, I strayed. At first, it was just after-dinner solo "walks" through the neighborhood, where I checked out parks where I thought guys might be cruising. Not much luck there. But the phone-sex lines had come in about then. Late at night, when Mitch fell asleep, I'd call and beat off talking to guys who told me how hot my voice sounded.

The really serious straying began one weekend when Mitch drove up to New Hampshire for the funeral of his best friend in high school who had died of AIDS. It was Mitch's first AIDS death. I'd already been to memorial services for three of my friends that year, and two more the year before. You would think that the shadow of an AIDS funeral would have squelched any temptations I was feeling to fool around. Just the opposite. I was angry. Angry at the virus, angry at the slowness of science to find a cure, angry at a God that would let this happen. Angry that I was now forty and still my painting career had not gotten off the ground, angry that I had lost another job. Sex seemed like a way to assert that all of this was not going to defeat me.

That night, I drove down to the Fens, where in the dark thickets of reeds along the Muddy River, guys had sex. Within ten minutes, I scored: a mutual jack-off session with a guy who would not let me kiss him. After I came, I wandered around, not yet ready to go home. I was amazed at how easy this had been, amazed at how many men were wandering around, amazed at how many were fucking.

Within weeks, I was down there every chance I had. I tried not to think too hard about what I was doing. Despite the specter of AIDS, despite a relationship I wanted to work, I told myself this is just what gay men in a long-term relationship did when sex died at home. I figured Mitch would want to stray, too. We'd met in a bathhouse, for Pete's sake. No matter his button-down shirts, he had a sleazy underbelly, didn't he?

The waiter brought Mitch his second cappuccino and me my water, which I drank down in one long, parched gulp.

❖ ❖ ❖

The team that everyone at the Sport was rooting for won the match. As soon as the game was over, most of the fans got up, full of winning-team good cheer and readiness to go home. They zipped up their jackets, anticipating the blustery March winds outside. The cute boy with the chestnut hair whom I'd checked out earlier got up, too—he seemed to be alone—and pulled on a handsome shearling-lined bomber jacket. Like his scruffy beard, the jacket was of a cut and style that seemed a little out of place for the Sport. A little too studied. As he eased himself into it, he again caught me watching. I immediately averted my eyes, but when I looked up again a few seconds later, he was still looking at me. He smiled—a quick expression of friendliness, flirtation, or both—and then he was off, out the door and down Hanover Street without the least look back in my direction.

"Shall we get going?" Mitch asked.

He'd missed whatever it was that had transpired between the boy and me. Mitch is more or less immune to the comeliness of the lads who frequent the Sport and who throng the streets of our new neighborhood.

"What's for dinner?" I asked.

"Hadn't planned anything. But there's some nice asparagus in the fridge that we should eat soon. How about asparagus spears over pasta? I'll throw together a pesto sauce to go with it."

Mitch has the knack of turning the almost-nothing in our larder into an exquisite meal, prepared with all the meticulous finesse that he brings to everything he does. Since we moved to the North End, he's been studying Italian cookbooks.

"Sounds delicious," I said. "I'm ravenously hungry."

"I need to stop at the salumeria first. We're almost out of olive oil."

Out on the street, people were strolling along, doing their late Sunday afternoon thing. It was a short walk to the Italian grocery store. Along the way, I glanced inside the windows of the restaurants that lined the street. Waiters were hustling from table to table, laying down gorgeous plates of food in front of hungry, happy patrons.

"What about eating out instead?" I suggested.

"I want to cook for you," Mitch said. "We'll go out next Sunday."

At the salumeria, he made a beeline for the olive oil shelves. I could tell he was eager to make the purchase and settle down to cook. He found his favorite brand, grabbed a bottle, and brought it to the counter, where the checkout boy—*Holy Extra Virgin, Batman!*—was the young man who'd smiled at me at the Sport.

We made eye contact again, but that's all. As Mitch and I walked back to our condo, I thought about how this conjunction of events would have affected me back when I was still actively straying. What would I have made of seeing Mr. Bomber Jacket twice in twenty minutes? Was the universe conspiring to bring us together? This is the kind of magical thinking I used to indulge in. No more. Professionally, artistically, physically, spiritually, I might still be a mess, but I'd *finally* decided that Mitch was the guy I wanted to spend the rest of my life with. Besides, the guys I was attracted to, younger guys, many years younger than I, just weren't showing me much interest anymore. I'd tried Grindr for a few years, but most of the boys I sent a "hey" to ignored me. Some wrote curt turn-downs—"Sorry, not into grandpas"; "Only looking for jock meat"—or responded with requests that turned me off: "Bareback?"; "Generous, daddy?"; "Got Adderall?"

"Why so quiet?" Mitch asked as we entered our building.

"Sorry, just thinking."

"Want to share?"

"That guy at the checkout counter, he was watching the game this afternoon. At the Sport." I tried keeping a neutral tone in my voice, as if I were just making a casual observation.

"He's cute," Mitch said. As offhandedly as if he were noting that the zucchini at the grocery store was good this week.

Back home, he opened a bottle of wine and poured each of us a glass. We clinked.

"Eye contact, Christopher," Mitch reminded me when I failed to look at him as we toasted.

He took a sip, then set about fixing dinner. I plopped down on that small kitchen sofa we were getting rid of. After dinner, we'd have to haul it down to the street for Monday's trash collection.

I watched Mitch, ever the conscientious worker. You could film him preparing dinner and air it on PBS without any edits, he was that exacting in the way he could prepare a meal. How does someone go through life so steadily? The same job for over thirty years. The same poker club. The same button-down collars and vee-neck sweaters.

During those times that I was thinking about bailing out of our marriage, I used to tell myself that Mitch was boring. Nowadays, despite my occasional irritation with him, I see Mitch with far more appreciative eyes. How did this change come about, I ask myself. Sometimes, I think it has to do with the distress I always feel reading about all the suffering in those nineteenth-century marriage breakups that Balzac, Flaubert, and Tolstoy write about. Why put either of us through that kind of pain?

Mitch took a scraper and gently began to trim the asparagus spears. The first time I ever saw him do that, I was flabbergasted. Who trims asparagus? But it's another thing I have learned to love about him.

The year I decided to give up Grindr, the COVID pandemic was in full swing. Mitch and I were still in the big house in Dorchester, hunkered down in semi-isolation: me doing my web design, Mitch in his thirty-somethingth year at the actuarial firm. My reading time doubled, and I started listening to some dharma talks that a Buddhist sangha in Cambridge was zooming. The dharma teacher talked a lot about the ways we keep falling into unmindful, and unskillful—that's the word they like to use—*unskillful* activity. Automatic pilot, you might call it in layman's terms. I began to see that that's what I had been doing with Grindr—or for that matter, with Mitch—just going on automatic pilot.

And so, while Mitch prepared dinner—me still a little pissed that we were going to leave the sofa on the curb—I reminded myself to bring more mindfulness to this moment: mindful of Mitch trimming asparagus, mindful of the lingering light in March, mindful that I was still pissed about the sofa. And mindful that Mr. Bomber Jacket and that sweet smile he shot in my direction were still on my mind.

After dinner, we washed the dishes (Mitch hates leaving dirty dishes for the next day), hauled the sofa out to the street, then got into bed to watch a movie. Usually, we settle on a film we both want, but that night, we just couldn't agree. In the end, Mitch conceded to my request, *The Seven Year Itch* with the fabulous Marilyn Monroe. We clicked it on and settled against the pillows to watch. I leaned my head against his shoulder, a sweet end to a day that had begun so acrimoniously. He put his arm around me. Within ten minutes, I was fast asleep. Sometime later, when I woke up, he was watching the film he had wanted to see, *Mr. Smith Goes to Washington*.

❖ ❖ ❖

Next morning, Mitch left for work. Every workday, he's out of the apartment at the dot of eight. That Monday was no exception. There are no exceptions with Mitch. A few minutes later, he called me.

"Just thought you'd like to know the sofa wasn't on the curb when I went out."

There was nothing snarky about his telling me this. He was genuinely happy to assure me that the sofa was not going to end up in a landfill.

I spent the morning working on a web design project. At lunchtime, I went looking in the refrigerator for something to eat. There were some leftovers from the night before, but I didn't have the appetite for pasta again. Instead, I had a hankering for a salami and cheese sandwich. But, aside from a few slices of provolone, there was no bread and no salami. The Sport makes a pretty decent soppressata panino, but something made me want to make my own sandwich. I'd have to go to the salumeria for the provisions. As I put on my jacket, I told myself that I wasn't going to the salumeria in order to see Mr. Bomber Jacket. And even if I was, it was just to be friendly.

When I walked in, he was there, serving another customer. I went to the deli section, examined all their salamis and chose one. Then, a loaf of good bread. He was still waiting on the other customer, so I browsed around some more, as if there were other things I wanted to buy, waiting for him to be finished. A much older guy—his boss, presumably—was free to ring up my purchases, but I told myself that I didn't want anyone else waiting on me because ... well, because it would be nice just to say hello. The customer left. I lingered another minute in the cheese section so as not to appear too eager. When I sauntered over to the counter, he greeted me with a broad smile and a *Hey!*

"Oh, hey." I wondered how convincing my fake surprise was. "That was a great game yesterday, wasn't it?"

He laughed. "But you weren't even looking at it. How do you know?"

I felt myself blushing. "Yeah, soccer's not really my thing." Out of the corner of my eye, I saw the boss mosey into the back room. That left the two of us alone. "Actually, it's my boyfriend who loves soccer." Pleased with myself for being up front with him, I studied his face, looking for a reaction. "I just go along for the ride."

"I figured that," he said. "I've seen you two there a few times. You always go on Sundays, right?"

"Aren't you the observant one."

"I used to work there." He shrugged his shoulders. "It was kind of my job to pay attention to who was there."

"Not a bad job," I teased, "spending the day checking out the guys."

He grinned. "It is kind of guy place, isn't it?"

His eyes were Bay of Naples blue.

"The wrong kind of guy place for me," I said. "A little too macho." I had no idea where this conversation was going, but it was fun. "I mean," I continued, "the kind of guy thing that goes on at the café is not really my kind of guy thing."

He chuckled. "Ah, you'd be surprised what kind of guy things go on there."

My imagination kicked into overdrive. Cruising? Sex in the bathroom? I'd never seen evidence of any of that.

"So," I ventured, "this guy thing at the café—is it your kind of guy thing? Or are you just, like, *curious*?"

"Curious!" He laughed again. "Um, no, I'm not *curious*. I'm way beyond curious, sir."

There's the "sir" that super polite shop clerks employ with their customers; and then there's the other kind of "sir," the one that twinks use to address their daddies.

"I'm Christopher," I said, holding out my hand.

"Tyler." We shook. His grip was firmer than I'd expected.

"Tyler," I observed. "Somehow I pegged you as Italian. Then again, with blue eyes like that, I should have known better."

"But I am Italian. And, as a matter of fact, lots of Italians have blue eyes." Playfully, he opened his eyes wide to give me a better look. "My parents named me Tullio, but I was not going to go through life with a name like that. In high school, I started calling myself Tyler. It stuck." He picked up the salami I'd set on the counter. "This for sandwiches?"

"Yes."

"Can I suggest another brand?"

Before I had a chance to answer, Tyler came from behind the counter and walked over to the deli case. Feeling like an obedient puppy, I followed, positioning myself next to him as he looked for the brand he wanted me to consider. I moved just close enough that our arms touched. He did not move away.

"This one," Tyler said, pointing another salami at me. It was impossible not to notice that it was thicker and a good four or five inches longer than the one I'd picked out.

"And what makes this one better?" I asked, taking it from his hand.

"Trust me," he said. "You won't be sorry."

When he rang it up, I saw that the salami was more than twice the price of the one I'd picked out. The thought crossed my mind that all his coquetry had been designed solely to lure me into a more expensive purchase. I racked it up to just another way that the old are toyed with by the young. When I handed him my credit card, he scrutinized it.

"Christopher Walsh," he read. He looked up, another impish smile on his face. "So you're Italian, too?"

I laughed. "Yeah, right off the boat from Kilkenny, Italy."

"Well, enjoy the salami, Mr. Walsh. Let me know what you think."

"I certainly will."

As it turned out, Tyler was right. The salami was delicious. He hadn't steered me wrong. I couldn't wait for an opportunity to give him my report.

❖ ❖ ❖

After that, I dropped in at the salumeria every few days, always under the pretext that I needed to buy something, and always delighted to shoot the breeze with Tyler, who seemed just as pleased to shoot the breeze with me. Sometimes his boss was there, too, but the boss seemed to understand that I enjoyed interacting with Tyler and let us have our time together as if it were nothing but another instance of customer-clerk friendliness. At first, our conversations were fairly inconsequential: the salami (amazing, we agreed), the weather (increasingly lovely, we agreed), the North End's cafés and restaurants moving onto the sidewalks (an unintended benefit of the pandemic, we agreed).

By my third visit, Tyler was telling me more about his life. During high school, he'd gone to the Arts Academy, changed his name, and become something of a star in the theater department, taking the male lead in several plays and musicals. He also became student convener of the gay-straight alliance. When I offered the opinion that this was very brave of him, he shook his head. "Chris, what city do you think we're living in? This is Boston."

It tickled me that he'd gone from addressing me as "sir" and "Mr. Walsh" to "Chris."

I asked him what he'd majored in in college. He told me he hadn't yet gone to college, that he was taking a gap year.

"Wait! How old are you?" I asked.

"Nineteen."

"I would never have guessed," I told him. "You seem far more mature."

Tyler beamed. "Thank you."

In a flash, I saw that this was precisely what he was aiming for—to cut loose from the world of high school theatrics and take his place on the stage that we adults were playing on. But why, I wondered. Why rush the already dreadful fleetingness of youth? *Don't!* I wanted to tell him.

In subsequent visits, I shared more about myself, too: my work, my interests, the challenges of the move to the North End. The challenge of downsizing and the challenge of having to give up my fantasy that I would become a successful painter. The challenge, I added—watching for a reaction—of being in a relationship with the same person for twenty-eight years.

"OMG," he said, "even my parents haven't been married that long."

Then one day—it was now April—I asked Tyler why he hadn't been coming to watch the Sunday soccer games. I hadn't seen him there since that Sunday afternoon back in March.

He came right out with it: "Because I don't want your boyfriend noticing how into you I am."

"*What!*"

"Chris, you're so hot."

"You're joking."

Tyler dismissed my skepticism with a laugh.

Just then, another customer walked in. "May I help you?" he called out and walked over to her. Their interaction lasted a good five minutes. It felt like an hour. Meanwhile, I sauntered around the store, trying to look like I was there for some other purpose than to moon over this lovely boy who had just told me he was, in turn, mooning over me. When he finally rang up the customer's order and she left, he picked up right where he'd left off.

"I've had a thing for older guys since I was, like, fourteen. Like, *really* older guys."

"Oh, so I'm just a fetish object for you?"

The radiant expression on Tyler's face dropped.

"I see you as a *person*, Chris—a really interesting person. And, yeah, really hot, too, but you are not some dumb-ass fetish object." He looked hurt. "Come on, dude, you come in here every other day, chat me up, listen to me. I love how much *experience* you've had, how much you know."

"My God," I protested, "I don't know anything, Tyler. If you only knew how"—I struggled for the right word—"how *bewildered* I feel a lot of the time."

Tyler shook his head in disbelief. "I don't see it, Chris. Unless you're putting on an act. I mean, come on, you're an artist, you've had all these great jobs, you *own* a condo, you have a long-term boyfriend!"

"Tyler, I think you're a bit starry-eyed."

Another customer came in. Tyler ignored her. "Just promise," he whispered, "promise you'll keep talking to me, Chris. I've never met anyone like you."

❖ ❖ ❖

And so we kept talking. First, across the counter at the salumeria, but soon enough over afternoon coffee—not at the Sport, which felt too conspicuous, but at another coffee shop in the hour before he had to go to work. Tyler kept telling me ever more intimate details of his life: his family life, his school life, and eventually his sex life, which always involved older men. He told me these stories matter-of-factly, but I began to pick up that he was trying to titillate me as well. He was, I figured, angling to get me into bed. And then one day, he came right out with it.

"So, when are you going to fuck me?" he asked.

I told him—reluctantly, I will admit—that he should let go of any notion that we were going to have sex. "I'm in a relationship," I reminded him. "That's enough for me." These felt like words in a script that I had memorized. Sure, I wanted to bed him, but I was afraid of the feelings that Tyler would unlock in me. I did not need any more upheaval in my life.

Tyler pushed back. He wasn't looking to get into anything serious with me, he said. After all, he'd probably be going to college in a year or so, but why couldn't we just fool around? What was the matter with just some casual sex once in a while? "I'm versatile," he whispered, leaning over his cappuccino. "I'll top or bottom for you."

I imagined it all in a flash: kissing those luscious Italian lips, running my fingers through his thick, dark chestnut hair, caressing that exquisite ass that I'd often admired when he turned to help a customer. I let myself imagine going all the way with him. I would have topped or bottomed for him, too. And how I would have loved to finagle a whole night with him, cuddled up in each other's arms.

Instead, I told him that ten years ago, five years ago, I would have jumped at the chance. "But now"—I paused, steeling myself for the big reveal—"Tyler, I'm *sixty-three*." No reaction on his part. "And I think it's time for me to"—*what* was the word I wanted?—"to simplify my life." I chuckled. Was that my major aspiration these days? I tried again: "I'm happily married. And an affair with you, that would really complicate things."

"It doesn't have to, Chris."

I shook my head no.

"Just once?"

"No."

"That makes me so sad, Chris."

"Sad! Tyler, you have your whole life ahead of you. The last thing you should be is sad."

He shrugged his shoulders.

"So, Thursday?" he asked. "Meet you here again at two?"

"Of course," I told him. "You know I love our conversations."

"I think you love more than that."

I shook my head, the kind of gesture that says, *What am I going to do with you, you little scamp?*

At each subsequent meeting, Tyler opened up to me more and more. He'd never had a boyfriend, he said. But he'd been having sex since he was fifteen—first with a couple of his high school classmates, and then, during his senior year, with older men he would meet on Grindr.

"You were eighteen by then, I hope."

"In Massachusetts, the age of consent is seventeen, Chris. I wasn't getting anyone in trouble."

"Still ..." I said.

"Still what? I wanted it; they wanted it."

There were more questions I wanted to ask him, but I held back. I did not want to appear to be too curious. Tyler, on the other hand, never hesitated to ask me personal questions: about what I liked to do in bed; about what it had been like to live during the AIDS crisis; about how gay men used to meet before there were hookup sites; about whether I'd ever been to an orgy; and how had I met Mitch?

"At a bathhouse," I told him.

"That's so hot," Tyler said. "There's one in Providence, right?"

"You aren't thinking of going there, are you?"

Tyler shrugged.

"Tyler, please! There are too many diseases going around."

"Chris, I know how to take care of myself."

"That's not the point!" I said, a little too loudly. But what exactly was the point? What did I want to say to this kid, this young man, this member of the rising generation of gay men?

"Come on, Chris, a visit to that bathhouse in Providence is not going to ruin my life."

"It could ruin your health. Tyler, a lot of guys at a bathhouse are going to have only one thing in mind—your cute ass—and they aren't gonna give a fuck about safe sex."

"I'm on PrEP," he said.

"Well, good. But that's not going to protect you against STIs."

"The way I figure it," he said, "older men are way more careful. They're less likely to be walking around with gonorrhea or syphilis or chlamydia."

He certainly knew his gay health lingo.

"What can I say, Chris? I'm really turned on by older guys. I love how I feel when I'm with them. I love how they make me feel about myself. Like I'm interesting, like I'm ..."

"You *are* interesting, Tyler! You don't have to seek a sense of self-worth through sex."

Oh, if there were a way to download my forty-plus years of gay experience into his head, to give him a virtual tour of all the dead ends I'd run into.

"I don't think I'm doing that, Chris." He shook his head. "It's like this: you like being married; I like being with older men. I'm not going to shame myself for liking that. It's just what it is."

"I just want you to be careful," I told him.

"I will," he said and picked up the check. "My treat." He reached into his back pocket for his wallet and pulled out a twenty-dollar bill, which he left on the table. It was a very generous tip he was leaving.

"Thank you," I said.

"No problem." As we stepped outside, he turned to me. "Do you really think I have a cute ass?"

❖ ❖ ❖

"So what's your condo like?" he asked one afternoon. Here we go again, I thought. I gave him an innocuous description, pitching my answer to be as bland as possible. As I described the size, the number of rooms, the view, Tyler kept staring at me, waiting for me to quit feigning naiveté.

"*What?*" I snapped.

"Can I see it?" he asked.

"I don't think that would be a good idea."

"Why?"

"You know why."

"Tell me again, daddy."

"For just that reason, Tyler." I lowered my voice. "I am not your 'daddy.' I don't want to be your daddy."

"But why won't you just have sex with me, Chris?"

We'd been through all this before, but I fired off the reasons once again: "Because I have a partner. Because you are *a lot* younger than I am. Because I like just what we have now. Because ..."

He interrupted.

"Don't you want to fuck my 'cute ass'?"

"It's not a question of whether I do or don't. It's a question of what's appropriate."

"So, you *would* like to?" He was grinning. "Chris, just once. Afterwards, we can go back to 'having what we have now.' Come on, just once."

As my dick got hard, I shook my head again, a gesture that said, *No*, but that gave me time to consider just how much trouble even one brief, delicious afternoon with Tyler would bring me. He must have been reading my thoughts.

"What time does Mitch come home from work?" he asked.

"Not until six." I took a deep breath and let him see the irritation on my face. Within three seconds, it softened to something like tenderness. "Come on, but I'm just showing you the apartment. Nothing more."

The tour lasted about thirty seconds, and then we were all over each other, kissing passionately, my tongue deep in Tyler's mouth, and his in mine. In another minute, we had tumbled onto the bed—dutifully made up by Mitch that morning, as he did every morning, before he left for work.

We tore off each other's clothes. Under his jeans, Tyler was wearing a pair of sexy underpants, the kind of brand that's marketed to gay men. When I slid them off, his dick popped up like a garden rake when you accidentally step on the tines—straight, hard, long. Dangerous. I had forgotten what teenage dick was like.

"Fuck me! Fuck me!" he yelled.

I slapped my hand over his mouth. "Not so loud!" It was then that I realized I had no lube or condoms. Those days were over for Mitch and me. "Damn!"

"What?" he asked.

"No condoms."

"Do me raw, daddy."

I have to admit it was the sexiest thing I'd heard in years. *Do me. Raw. Daddy.*

"Tyler," I pleaded.

"I told you, I'm on PrEP."

I raised his legs and ate out his ass, letting my saliva trickle all over his hole, and hoping that would satisfy him. Hoping it would satisfy me. It did neither. The next thing I knew, I was lubing up my dick with more spittle and then I eased in. I was a little alarmed at how easily he took me. Just how many times had he been fucked? Crazily, that turned me on all the more. If I was going to take a risk, then let it be this one!

Mitch and I had occupied this condo for almost a year. Apart from cuddling and the occasional blow job, this was the first time our bed had been used for any kind of carnal activity. A crazy baptism. As I pounded away, and as Tyler let me know with a litany of delighted moans and squeals how much he craved me, I thought about whether he and I would stain the sheets and whether there was a clean set of linens in the closet. I thought about what face I would present to Mitch when he got home that night. And then I reminded myself to let go of all that and just be with what was happening right now, which was ... It was more than delicious. It was—if you'll allow me a word from all those nineteenth-century novels I love—*sublime*.

No matter how hard I banged away—and I surprised myself that I still had that kind of stamina in me—Tyler kept asking for more. I grabbed his ankles; it made me feel like a porn star. My screams of pleasure were even louder than his. And when I shot inside him, it was—to borrow a word from the Gen Z kids—*awesome*.

Panting, I watched as Tyler finished himself off. When he shot, his spooge flew over his head and hit the wall.

"Holy fuck!" he said, collapsing on the mattress. I fell on top of him, snuggling up and cradling him in my arms. We kissed again, at first a delicate, after-sex kiss, and then more passionately. I kept trying to think of what after-sex words I should say. Nothing seemed quite right.

After another minute, Tyler untangled himself from my embrace. "Gotta get to work," he announced, pecking me on the lips one last time. In another minute, he was out the door.

❖ ❖ ❖

Pulling off a poker face with Mitch was relatively easy. It was my next meeting with Tyler that made me apprehensive. Because we had not made plans for another coffee klatsch, I would have to go to the salumeria to see him. I wished I could have texted him first, but stupidly, we had never exchanged phone numbers.

I went the very next day, so as not to suggest, by staying away too long, that I was feeling guilty, even though I was. The place was busy. He and his boss were both waiting on customers. The boss waved, but Tyler did not make eye contact with me. And no sooner had he rung up one customer's purchases than he was waiting on another. I picked up a basket and started browsing the shelves, filling it with things I didn't need.

At last, he was done with the customers. I went up to the counter.

"Hey," I said, shooting him a broad smile that I suspected was fraught with anxiety.

"Hey, Chris."

I glanced over at the boss, who was still busy with another customer, and then back at Tyler.

"So that was fun," I said, laying out my purchases on the counter. I hated the caution in my voice, the submission to waiting for whatever assessment *he* might make.

"Fun?" he whispered. "It was fucking hot, Chris."

I breathed a sigh of relief. But so many questions flooded into my head. They all boiled down to one: What now?

Tyler began ringing up my groceries. He seemed so cool and focused, just a counterboy doing his job. I saw why he had earned the lead in so many of those high school plays.

"So, we should probably talk," I ventured.

He looked up.

"Um, sure." He looked over at his boss. "But obviously not now."

Tyler went back to ringing up my purchases. I reached into my pocket and pulled out the scrap of paper I had prepared.

"Here," I said. "My cell. Text me when you get a moment."

Without a word, he picked it up and shoved it into his pocket. His jeans were so tight, he had a hard time stuffing it in.

"That'll be fifty-four ninety-seven," he said, once again in his cool, calm counterboy voice.

I had never spent so much at the salumeria before.

All that evening, I kept waiting for Tyler to call. It was Mitch's poker night, so I had the place to myself. I kept checking to see that the ringer on my mobile phone was turned on, the volume all the way up. At ten, Mitch came home, had a dish of ice cream, got ready for bed.

"Wanna watch a movie?" he asked.

I told him I thought I'd stay up and read a while.

"But go ahead," I told him. "I'll just shut the bedroom door so I can concentrate."

At eleven-thirty, I shut down my phone and went to bed. The sheets, which I'd changed the afternoon before, still smelled laundry fresh.

❖ ❖ ❖

The next two times I went to the salumeria, Tyler wasn't there. I went around the corner to check whether he was at the Sport, but he wasn't there either. The springtime weather was glorious. But I felt no exhilaration in the sunshine and warmth. Over the years, I'd been ghosted by many guys—Grindr guys were notorious for this—but I'd let myself believe that Tyler was not like them. Besides, it had only been three days since I'd given him my number. There could be a million reasons why he hadn't contacted me yet.

I tried to keep my sadness in check. I did not want Mitch to see how mopey I was. I became more affectionate with him, giving him lingering hugs when he came home from work, throwing my arms around him as he was working at the kitchen counter.

On my third try at the salumeria, Tyler's boss was behind the counter. Even though there was no one else in the store, I went through the pretense of browsing the shelves, picking up a few items first. It was only after I approached the counter to check out that I struck up a conversation, nonchalantly observing that I hadn't seen "the kid" who worked here in a while.

"Who, Tyler?" he said. "He's in New York." He shook his head in disbelief. "Went for a week to 'check things out.' He told me he's thinking about going to drama school in the fall. *Drama school!* Now there's a dead end."

"Well," I suggested, "if he's got talent and ambition and drive. I mean, why not? He could very well settle into a successful career."

The boss chuckled. "Settle? With an ass like that, there's only one thing that kid's gonna settle into."

A beat went by before I burst out laughing. All these visits to the salumeria and I'd never paid attention to this other guy behind the counter. Fifty-ish, slicked-back hair, a St. Christopher medal and a cornicello around his neck—I'd kind of dismissed him as a *goombah* type of guy. So much for stereotypes.

"He does have a beautiful ass, doesn't he?" I agreed.

The boss shot me a look that implied, *You don't know the half of it.*

"We should talk sometime," I said.

"We should have a drink sometime. Your boyfriend, too."

That took me aback, too. "Christopher," I said, holding out my hand.

"Johnny. Johnny Sinatra. No relation to Frank." We shook.

"Nice to meet you, Johnny."

"Same here."

And then, not knowing what else to say, I made a feeble observation: "There're a couple of good drama programs here in Boston. I hope he's looking at them, too." I couldn't bring myself to say Tyler's name.

Johnny Sinatra looked at me. There was sympathy—and I think a bit of pity—in his eyes. "Yeah, but Boston's not New York. *Capeesh?* You know what I mean?"

I did.

For the rest of the day, I didn't get any work done. I sat in front of my computer, staring at the screen. I wanted to be happy for Tyler. But I found myself hoping that this fishing expedition to New York might dissuade him from taking the plunge into a life in the theater. I was genuinely nervous for him. Too many risks for such an uncertain payback. In these uncertain times, shouldn't he be looking for something more stable? Like what, I wondered. Return to Boston and work at the salumeria the rest of his life? Fat chance. Tyler was on a safari for something bigger, that was for sure. What that bigger might be was anyone's guess. And what part I'd be playing ... I wasn't ready to let go of the notion that there just might be a part for me, even a bit part, though the indications weren't encouraging.

And then there was Johnny Sinatra. Mitch and I had gay friends back in Dorchester, and a few others elsewhere. But we'd yet to meet any members of the club in our new neighborhood. In truth, Mitch has never been as keen as I to have a large band of gay comrades. His poker buddies are pretty much his social orbit. How open would he be to enrolling Johnny as a friend?

That night, I made dinner. Mitch picked up on my subdued spirits.

"Something wrong?" he asked.

"You have no idea how such a simple question can be so complicated," I told him.

"Try me," he said.

"An unproductive day in front of the computer."

"Well, tomorrow's another day, right?" Mitch asked.

"Tomorrow's another day," I agreed.

I eased the fettuccine into the pot of boiling water. It was going to be a simple meal. I hadn't been inspired to cook. The sauce, simmering on another burner, was out of a jar. I'd chopped some mushrooms into it to gussy things up a bit.

Mitch uncorked a bottle of wine and poured for us.

"This is nice," he said.

I couldn't bring myself to agree, but I made the effort to clink my glass with his, making sure to make eye contact.

After dinner, after the dishes, after getting into bed and turning on Netflix, I snuggled up to Mitch. Even though I had picked it out, I couldn't get into the movie, another one with Marilyn Monroe.

"Change it, if you want," I told him.

He turned his head toward me. "Still in a funk?"

I shrugged, *yes and no.*

Mitch hugged me closer. Somehow, he knew there was nothing more that needed to be said at that moment. The hug said it all. He picked up the remote and tuned in to some sports channel that was airing highlights of great soccer matches. I leaned against him and tried to be interested.

I have often wondered what makes soccer "the beautiful game." I know all the "official" explanations, and, from time to time, I've tried hard to look for those aspects when we're at the Sport. But I know it's also a matter of getting my head out of all the *thinking* about it, the trying to analyze what makes it so beautiful. In that respect, soccer is like Zen. Thinking doesn't help. You just have to throw yourself into it, let the beauty happen.

"Yes!" Mitch burst out in his after-ten-PM voice, soft enough that our neighbors wouldn't be disturbed, but still exuberant.

Whatever it was, I'd missed it again. No matter. *Let the beauty happen*, I thought. All of it. This man and his crazy, inscrutable game. The boy and his crazy, inscrutable dreams. My new friend—*our* new friend, I hoped—Mr. Johnny Sinatra. *Let all the beauty happen.* Every last, crazy, messy, inscrutable moment of it.

"Yeah," I told Mitch, "this *is* nice." I gave him a light peck on the shoulder. "Really nice."

Gravity

That Saturday, Fred went out to the front porch to retrieve the newspapers, one of the courtesies he performed every morning for "our little family," as he liked to call himself and his fellow condo owners in their triple-decker on Elbridge Street. The early February sky was a dull gray, and the temperature, though not as brutal as February could often be in Boston, was nippy. Today he was turning sixty-five. The middling weather felt appropriate.

Fred had never met the paper deliverer. Gone were the days when someone came to "collect" every week, as they used to when he was a boy. But in tossing the papers that morning, Maria Ramirez—that was the name on the every-few-months solicitation for a tip that she inserted in an envelope with the papers—Ms. Ramirez had missed the porch. The papers had landed on the steps. Two copies of the *Globe* and two of the *Times* (one for him, one for Andy and Arthur, the guys on the second floor) and a *Herald*, the blue-collar daily, for Lynnette on the top floor. Lynnette had moved in in September. She was renting from Jack and Tony, the owners of the third floor, who had moved to Seattle. Andy and Arthur didn't like her much, but Fred thought Lynnette, who was a nurse at Boston City Hospital, was just fine. Arthur sometimes called Fred "Rose," after the character Betty White had played on *The Golden Girls,* because Fred was, Arthur contended, such a big-hearted softie.

He gathered up the newspapers and recinched his bathrobe. He'd thrown it on over his sleepwear, a pair of flannel drawstrings and a tee shirt, partly to ward off the cold and partly to present a "decent" look in case any of the neighbors caught sight of him. Although he'd lived on Elbridge Street for almost thirty years, he still took care not to offend anyone. It was, he supposed, another reason why Arthur called him Rose. Arthur never seemed to care whom he might offend.

Fred paused for a quick scan of the street. Snowdrops were already blooming in the front yard across the way. Ever since they'd moved here, he'd watched the transformation of this working-class neighborhood of triple-deckers and the occasional late-Victorian two-family into a gentrified—he was embarrassed by the word, but there it was—a *gentrified* enclave. It was the kind of street where the new owners tore off the vinyl or tarpaper siding, put in nice landscaping, painted the trim in several "period colors." Olive, cream, and mauve seemed to be particular favorites. During the Christmas season, the decorations tended to be modest and tasteful: no more inflatable Santas and painted plaster creche figures. In summer, when the porch furniture appeared, it was no longer upholstered in Naugahyde. The last Virgin Mary in a bathtub grotto had disappeared five years ago.

Fred knew he shouldn't take too much satisfaction in all of this. The old neighborhood families—firefighters, pipefitters, bus drivers, short-order cooks, those kinds of folks—had been displaced as the newcomers arrived. Still, Fred liked to think that he hadn't been personally responsible for uprooting anyone. They'd bought the building—he and Reuben, Andy and Arthur, Jack and Tony—from a family who was only too happy to leave Jamaica Plain for one of the white suburbs south of Boston. Fred liked to think that the purchase had been a win-win situation for everyone. He'd once said that—"a win-win situation"—to Arthur, who'd rolled his eyes and said, *Oh, Rose!*

They were lucky to have bought when they did. Twenty-seven years ago, Elbridge had not been a desirable street. A gang of teenage punks had held sway for years. But what he and Reuben had been looking for— a two-bedroom unit with a large kitchen, a dining room separate from the living room, space for an office—that kind of apartment was already out of their price range in the other neighborhoods they were considering. As soon as they saw the place, they knew it was the one. The owner was selling the entire building, three floors, all vacant and ready to turn into condos. There they were, six gay men, three couples—it was going to be such fun. It didn't matter that the house was fire-damaged and needed a lot of work. They were all young and ready to tackle anything.

Fred turned back into the building, leaving the other papers on the table in the common vestibule before returning into his apartment.

In the kitchen, he tossed his papers onto the table, set the tea kettle on the stove, and retightened the sash on his bathrobe. It was a chenille robe in seafoam green, intended as a gag gift from Andy and Arthur for his fiftieth birthday. It may have been a joke, but Fred had fallen in love with the thing and wore it all the time, especially on his weekend lounging mornings. The robe's soft, capacious embrace made him feel cozy and safe. It was threadbare in places, unraveling at the hem, but that made it all the more comfy. Comfy was what he was all about these days.

While he waited for the water to boil, he settled down to do the puzzles in the *Times*. He never had much trouble solving the KenKens and the Sudoku. A lifetime of teaching math had left him wise to the ways of numbers. Numbers made sense like nothing else in his life made sense. Though *sixty-five*, he thought. How the hell did that number make sense? In the last month, he'd had three medical appointments—one for back pain, one for a colonoscopy, and one to consult about getting off PrEP. "Since I'm not having sex anymore," he told his primary care physician, "I don't see the point." To his surprise, Dr. Gruver had agreed.

He filled in the last numbers of the Sudoku puzzle. A moment of satisfaction in an otherwise unsettled month. All these medical issues were the least of it. These days, everything seemed unsettled: the country's alarming swing to the far right, the murders of unarmed Black men at the hands of the police, climate change. (Those snowdrops across the street were up way too early.) He could hear Arthur criticizing him for saying "unsettled." *Unsettled, girl? Unsettled! Wake up, Rose. Things are totally fucked up.*

He folded the page over to the crossword. The Saturday puzzle was always a killer. In the old days, he'd needed the whole day to finish one, coming back to it at lunchtime and again while he was heating up dinner. But recently, he'd been finding it hard even to get a handle on the thing—a word here, a word there. Nothing else. He had begun to worry that he was losing his words.

When the kettle whistled, Fred made his tea, then fit the cozy over the pot—another gag gift from Andy and Arthur: merry olde Queen Elizabeth, the first one, in a quilted goose-turd green gown. He set the stove timer for three minutes and sat back down to work. A quarter hour and a cup of tea later, he was in trouble. He'd managed only one word.

GRAVITY. At least he *thought* he'd gotten that one. But the words that intersected with it eluded him. He suspected the puzzle maker of leading him astray with an answer that seemed obvious but was wrong.

He pushed the paper aside. Letting the puzzle alone for a while was, he'd learned over the years, a good strategy. Each time he came back to it, his mind was fresh, and new possibilities would suddenly reveal themselves. It was advice he gave his students at the Community College: if the solution to a math problem isn't immediately apparent, let it go for a while and then come back. Lines of thinking you've been stuck on will give way to new perspectives. This approach, he told them, was a good one for life, too. He liked giving these young people a bit of life coaching now and then. It was coaching that Fred thought he should be giving himself, too, because lately he'd been feeling stuck. It was time to look at his life in a fresh way, but nothing different was coming up. He retightened his bathrobe.

❖ ❖ ❖

Fred was deep into reading the editorial page, when he heard the familiar knock on his apartment door: Arthur from upstairs announcing his weekly Saturday morning visit. Fred looked up at the kitchen clock. Arthur was a half hour early. He got up, but Arthur was already letting himself in.

"Oo, girl, you is a fright!" Arthur said, picking disapprovingly at the sleeve of the chenille bathrobe.

"What do you mean? You guys gave me this robe."

"That's my point, Rose. *When* did we give it to you? Fifteen years ago!"

Arthur was something of a clotheshorse. This morning, despite the early hour, he was already impeccably dressed: charcoal gray slacks, a collared silk shirt in deep pink, and a light gray cashmere sweater. Despite his left-leaning politics, Arthur loved the preppy look. His mother had been a music teacher in D.C.; his father a doctor. They now lived in a nursing home in Virginia, close to Arthur's sister.

"Well, if you don't like seeing me in my robe, then don't come calling so early. It's seven-thirty, Arthur."

"*Come calling!*" Arthur cackled. "Girl, my 'come calling' days are over."

Arthur had inherited his Jamaican parents' good looks. He looked like one of the light-skinned Black models that L. L. Bean was using these days in its catalogs. From experience, however, Fred knew that the dreamy Harry Belafonte image was deceptive. As an assistant administrator of the city's Housing Authority, Arthur could be a terror.

Back when they were first getting to know each other, they'd gotten into a huge fight. Fred had made the observation—a harmless one, he'd thought—that fundamentally all gay folk were just like everyone else. Arthur had pounced. *Are you serious!* he exclaimed. *No, no, no, girl. Get that notion out of your head. We should be working toward transforming society, not mimicking it. You want to buy into that white patriarchal bullshit?* He'd given Fred a look of severe disdain, one that Fred never forgot and hoped he'd never see again. Over the years, Fred had become more "woke," as Arthur was wont to observe. At the same time, Fred liked to think that Arthur had mellowed a bit, but one never knew when his pique might surface.

"So, happy birthday, Miss Rose," Arthur said, giving Fred a peck on the cheek.

"Sixty-five," Fred ruefully reminded him.

"Goodness, the first of our happy little family to be eligible"—Arthur dropped his voice to a gossipy whisper—"*for Medicare!*" He slapped his cheek and rolled his eyes. "Child, you is old!"

Arthur loved throwing a little ghetto shade from time to time, though Fred had never figured out whether he was supposed to laugh at these stereotyped expressions or ignore them. Another way in which, he guessed, he was not quite woke.

Arthur walked over to the counter and opened Fred's cookie jar. It was in the shape of Little Red Riding Hood, another gift, this one from Reuben.

"You don't want those," Fred warned him. "They're stale, but yesterday I picked up some really nice biscotti from that bakery in the South End. Crumble."

Arthur made his fussy face. "I've had Crumble's biscotti. Oo, girl, scrumptious. But I just had dental work and I'm supposed to avoid anything too sticky-chewy-nutty."

Fred opened one of the kitchen cabinets, took out a package of store-bought madeleines, and set the package in front of Arthur, who had already seated himself at the kitchen table.

"What are *these*?" Arthur asked.

"Madeleines. Very soft."

"What happened to the biscotti?"

"I thought you said you couldn't have them."

"Girl, I can chew on the *other* side, you know."

The Saturday morning visits from Arthur had begun two years ago when Fred was going through a difficult spell: the first anniversary of Reuben's death. It had hit him hard. He had thought he was over it, but then, unexpectedly, at least once a day, he found himself breaking down in tears, a total mess. For weeks, it was all Fred could do to drag himself to teach his classes at the Community College. Weekends, he didn't leave the apartment. Andy was the first to notice, but characteristically, it was Arthur who rose to the occasion, marching down to Fred's apartment one Saturday morning and declaring, with his no-nonsense face on, that (a) he needed a cup of tea and (b) would Fred please stop playing the theme song from *A Man and a Woman*. "Girl, you do have the most sorry-ass white-boy taste in music!"

They had talked all that morning: about how much Fred missed Reuben, about how hopeless he felt now that he was in his sixties, about how teaching math courses—even to minority students, which he used to love—was beginning to get stale. Arthur had listened sympathetically, but sassed him when Fred got too maudlin. At the end of that first Saturday morning talk, Arthur suggested that Fred needed to shake things up: a gay cruise, some therapy sessions, perhaps a course at the Adult Education Center in Cambridge.

They had gotten together again the following Saturday and the Saturday after that. Arthur did most of the talking, emphasizing how important it was for Fred to find new interests, and how he should be "out there" dating guys. On the fourth Saturday, when Arthur didn't come down for tea, Fred called and asked where he was.

Girl, you told me you were going to Score! last night. I assumed you did not want me interrupting you this morning. When Fred told him that there was nothing to interrupt, Arthur had exclaimed, *Well, missy, you finally got some sense in that head of yours. Score! Score? That tired bar? No, girl, you do not want to be dragging none of those sorry-ass men back to this respectable house. Uh-uh.*

Fred took out the bakery box of biscotti and set them on the table. "I bought two kinds: pistachio and fig-almond."

Arthur peered fastidiously into the box. His right hand hovered, considering whether to take one or not. On his pinky finger was the gold-and-ruby ring he'd inherited from his mother. "I promised Andy I wouldn't eat much until your birthday dinner tonight, but that was upstairs." He let his hand reach into the box. "I'll have fig-almond."

Of late, their Saturday morning conversations were more light-hearted than they'd been in the past. Fred had eventually accepted Arthur's advice. A "triple whammy," he called it: therapy, medication, and an adult-ed class. (He'd taken Great Unsolved Math Problems.) The combination snapped him out of his depression. For a little while, he'd even dated a guy he met at adult education, but it hadn't worked out. After that, Fred announced that he wasn't looking anymore, a claim that Arthur always met with a withering *Who you fooling?* stare.

"So, who'd you shoo out of the bedroom this morning?" Arthur asked, helping himself to a second biscotto. "I sure hope he didn't see you in that bathrobe." Pinky erect, he dunked the biscotto into his tea and took a bite, waiting, like some regal diva—Jesseye Norman came to mind—for Fred to speak.

"Sweetheart, I've told you, it's not gonna happen," Fred told him. "If someone comes along, well, maybe. But I'm through looking. Honestly, I love the family I have right here. At this stage in my life, it's enough for me." A strange look came over Arthur's face. "What?" Fred asked.

"I've got news. About a member of the *family*." All the campiness had suddenly disappeared from Arthur's voice. "Bad news." And then he dropped a bombshell: Andy had fainted twice in the last week.

"What! Are you serious?"

"Girl, I do not joke about shit like this. The first time was last Monday night. He was getting out of bed to pee ... *bam!* Passed out in the bathroom. And then yesterday afternoon, when he was rummaging around under the sink, looking for scrub pads." He shook his head.

"Andy's father dropped dead of a heart attack at fifty-eight. His mother's diabetic. God knows what he's inherited from them."

Arthur went on to report on Andy's medical history: his fair skin that left him susceptible to skin cancer, his up-and-down PSA numbers, the seborrheic keratosis he'd had removed.

"Jesus, what's that?" Fred asked.

"A fatty lump on his head. You never knew about it because he always hid it under that damn baseball cap he wears."

"Was it ... "

Arthur cut him short. "No. It was benign. They usually are. But now this."

"Are you worried?"

Arthur shot Fred an annihilating look.

"Of course I'm worried."

"What does the doctor say?"

"*Yesterday*, Fred. He fainted yesterday. Have you ever tried getting in to see a doctor on twenty-four-hour's notice?"

Fred wanted to remind Arthur that he'd said Andy had fainted twice. Why hadn't they seen a doctor after the first episode? But he held his tongue. Scoring a point against Arthur—even if that were possible—did not seem appropriate under these circumstances.

"Look," he offered, "if you guys want to cancel dinner tonight. I mean ..."

"Don't be silly," Arthur scolded. "Andy has a fabulous birthday dinner planned. We want to experience the full thrill of watching you cross the Six-Five threshold!"

Fred let himself smile. It was good, he guessed, that Arthur was back to his campy sarcasm.

"So, just the three of us?" he asked.

"Four. Andy invited Lynnette."

"Lynnette? I thought she drove you crazy."

Ever since she'd moved in, Arthur had been griping about Lynnette: how she always turned her rent check in late, how the stairways smelled of her cigarette smoke, how she had once asked to set up a clothesline in the backyard, a request that Arthur had summarily vetoed. Even her weight—Lynnette had a beer belly—elicited his hauteur.

"Andy thought it would be nice to bring the whole—what's your word, *family?*—the whole family together."

"Since when have you thought of her as family?"

"Listen, girl, if it were up to me, it would just be the three of us, but Andy ... I guess the prospect of his imminent demise has uncovered a soft spot in his heart."

"*Imminent demise*. Oh, Arthur, please. Enough with the histrionics."

"Easy for you to say, Rose. Meanwhile, I'm the overwrought husband. Look, just show up at six-thirty. And don't be late. Andy has everything timed down to the minute." He got up to leave. "And never, *never* offer me one of those biscotti again." He picked a third biscotto out of the bakery box and waved it at Fred like a miniature wand before he let himself out.

Fred sat back down at the kitchen table. Before he was diagnosed with the aortic aneurysm that killed him, Reuben had fainted a few times. The first time he consulted their PCP, the doctor had dismissed it as nothing but heat prostration and dehydration. A year later, Reuben was dead.

Fred pulled the newspaper toward him again, then pushed it away. Arthur and Andy had been together forever, it seemed. From time to time, they sniped at each other, occasionally even fell into a mean verbal duel. Nevertheless, within six months of the state's allowing same-sex marriage, they'd gotten married. That day, Fred had never seen them more radiant.

At their wedding, Fred had read a sonnet by Shakespeare—"Let me not to the marriage of true minds"—a poem he would have asked someone to read at his own wedding if he and Reuben had had one. Instead, he'd read it at Reuben's shiva.

❖ ❖ ❖

Fred arrived for dinner a few minutes before six-thirty. Arthur met him at the door wearing a blousy West African print shirt. Even garbed like this, Arthur somehow managed to look preppy. African preppy.

"Darling," Arthur whispered, offering his cheek. As he kissed him, Fred couldn't help thinking it was the kind of gesture the bereaved one shows at a wake.

They went into the kitchen. It was warm and humid. Steam wafted from a pot on the stove. Fred had wanted some private time with the two of them before Lynnette arrived, but now he didn't know what to say.

"Smells wonderful," he said. He wondered if the steam and the heat were good for Andy's whatever-he-had.

Andy was bent over their butcher-block table, busily deveining shrimp. He wielded the knife as delicately as a surgeon. On another section of the butcher block was an arrangement of beautiful raku bowls: water chestnuts, sliced shitake mushrooms, wedges of lemon. A wet kitchen towel covered something that was the size and shape of a large loaf of Italian bread. Fred knew not to lift and peek. Andy approached cooking as if it were a religious ceremony, every step and movement choreographed with impeccable attention. Peeking would have been a sacrilege.

Back in his early twenties, Andy had dropped out of college and gone to Japan, where he'd lived for six months at a Zen monastery. Monasticism did not turn out to be his calling, but the Zen aesthetic stuck. Like the rest of the apartment, Arthur and Andy's kitchen was a study in simplicity: bare, polished hardwood floors; a steel-and-ash table; two sleek Bauhaus-type easy chairs. A small West African bronze statue of a warrior and a scroll with four Chinese characters were the only pieces of art. Andy, who worked at a bonsai conservatory out in the burbs, favored jeans and flannel shirts when he went to work, but always dressed crisply, like a Zen monk, for these evening get-togethers. Tonight, he was wearing all black: a black linen shirt and a pair of black drawstring pants. On his feet he wore flip-flop sandals made of hemp, and white socks. Incongruously, he also had on his baseball cap.

Andy gave Fred a quick, distracted peck on the cheek before returning to his work. Of the original six in the triple-decker, Andy had been the next-to-youngest. Even now, at fifty-nine, he was still boyish: tall, lithe, with milky-blue eyes and tousled (once blond, now silvery gray) hair. His thick, calloused fingers conscientiously worked one of his prized Japanese knives. Fred studied him carefully, trying to pick up any evidence of something amiss. Then he checked himself. He did not want to look like a man who is thinking, *What's wrong with my friend?*

He accepted a glass of champagne from Arthur, which he downed too quickly. Within a minute, he was feeling lightheaded. He poured himself a second glass.

"Save a drop for Lynnette," Arthur chided.

Fred shook his head. "I still can't believe you invited her." Arthur raised his eyebrows and glanced accusatorially over at Andy. "I mean," Fred continued, "we hardly know her." Andy turned from his work at the butcher block.

"I decided," he told Fred, "that we have never celebrated anyone's birthday, not since we bought this triple decker, without the entire house in attendance." There was, Fred thought, a mixture of challenge and melancholy in his voice.

During the few seconds in which no one spoke, Fred recalled all the many birthdays when it had indeed been all six of them, eating too much, drinking too much, raucously laughing at the mounting years. Those days had been such fun. He poured himself more champagne.

"Actually, I think it's really sweet that you invited her."

"Oh, Rose, stop!" Arthur scolded. "Gawd, next to you, even Betty White would look like Barbara Stanwyck."

"What? I mean it. I'm glad you invited Lynnette."

Arthur raised his eyes.

From the butcher block, Andy called out, "Fred, be a dear and hand me that pan." He motioned to the counter next to the sink. The pan was lined with small, polished black stones over which Andy had meticulously arranged a blanket of pine needles. In itself, it was a work of art. Fred gingerly brought it over and set it down. Andy lifted the wet kitchen towel from the bread-like mound to reveal a whole fish—head, tail and all—holding it out for admiration.

"Horaku-yaki," he announced. "Fish baked over pine needles." Arthur was already balling up the wet kitchen towel and removing it from Andy's altar. He often functioned as Andy's acolyte during food preparation.

"Now," Andy pronounced, as if intoning the next part of a ritual. Fred watched as he laid the fish in the pan and then arranged the shrimp, the mushrooms and the water chestnuts around it. He placed each piece down with attentive care. "The recipe says to cover it with aluminum foil, but"—he made a face—"can you imagine any self-respecting *okaasan* using aluminum foil?" As if on cue, Arthur produced a sheet of parchment paper, which he handed to Andy, who settled it over the fish. When Andy looked up from his final ministrations, there was an almost beatific smile on his face.

"*Ijo!*" He giggled. "That's Japanese for voilà."

Fred wanted to kiss him.

Just then, Lynnette arrived. "Knock, knock. Anybody home?" She was toting a bottle of expensive gin and a jar of blue cheese-stuffed olives. "Happy birthday, Fred," she called out a little too loudly.

Lynnette had gone through some trouble to dress for the party: a blousy silk top in a riotous pattern of purple and orange and a pair of nicely tailored black pants. There were little pearl studs in her ears, the first time Fred had ever seen her wearing jewelry of any kind.

As he went to accept the bottle of gin, Lynnette set it on the table, and Fred realized these provisions might not be a gift at all but just Lynnette's way of making sure she got what she wanted to drink.

"Champagne?" Arthur offered.

"You mind if I make myself a martini?" she asked.

"Be my guest," Arthur invited in a way that didn't sound at all inviting. "But I don't know if we have any martini glasses." He looked scornfully at the bottle of gin. "Andy and I don't drink gin. It gives both of us violent headaches."

"What about vodka martinis? I thought you gay boys drank vodka martinis—martini lites, I call 'em."

When she chortled at her own quip, Fred noticed her ample bosom jiggling under the purple-and-orange blouse. He didn't get how a woman who didn't wear a bra could also be a reader of the *Herald*. The cultural signals didn't match. Maybe this was one of the reasons she irritated Arthur.

Lynnette nodded toward an empty champagne flute.

"I'll just use one of these," she said. "Works just as well at dispensing the ethanol into the bloodstream." She unscrewed the cap. "So what're we eating?"

"We're starting with a little clear soup," Andy said. His tone was friendlier than Arthur's. "Garnished with bamboo shoots and *wakame*. Seaweed." To Fred's ears, Andy seemed unmistakably intent on being cordial. "It's good for the skin and hair." He slid the ice-filled champagne bucket over to her. "And for purifying the blood."

"For menstrual regularity, too," Arthur hissed.

"I'm way past that, honey," Lynnette said, and chortled again.

Lynnette fished an ice cube out of the champagne bucket, dropped it into the flute, and poured a hefty amount of gin over the ice. Twisting the lid off the jar of olives, she picked out two and plopped them into the drink. "I didn't bring any vermouth. I like my martinis dry and dirty."

"Like your men, I imagine," Arthur said.

"So what else is Andy making?" Lynnette seemed determined to ignore Arthur's barbs.

"It's a *Japanese* meal," Arthur snarled. He was challenging her to not like it.

"Andy lived in Japan for a while," Fred explained chirpily. He was summoning up all his Betty White, hoping to circumvent Arthur's snarkiness before it got out of hand.

"Awesome," Lynnette said. "I've always wanted to go to Japan. My dad was stationed there after World War II. He didn't much like it, but, hey, no accounting for taste, right?"

"World War *Two*?" Arthur attacked. "Your father was in World War *Two*? My God, Lynnette, you're older than you look. Why you're probably older than Fred is!"

"*After* World War Two," she said. "I'm the last of six kids. Born the last year of the Baby Boom. Nineteen sixty-four."

"Same year as Reuben," Fred said.

"Who's Reuben?" Lynnette asked. There was a century-long silence as each of the boys waited for someone else to speak.

"My partner," Fred said. "He died three years ago."

"Damn, I'm so sorry," Lynnette said.

"Thank you." Fred made eye contact with her. The compassionate look in Lynnette's eyes told him that she was probably a really good nurse. He lifted the lid off the pot of broth. "Hey, this birthday boy is famished. Is the soup ready?"

Arthur shot Fred a look, the look that said: *There you go again, Rose, trying to make everything light and gay.*

❖ ❖ ❖

The soup was delicious. Fred tried to eat slowly, savoring each spoonful. He knew Andy would notice and appreciate that. He saw that Lynnette was hardly touching hers. Surreptitiously, he glanced at Arthur, who, stony-faced, was staring at the still-full raku bowl in front of her.

"So what kind of a nurse are you?" Fred asked. She had told him when she first moved in, back in September, but he'd forgotten.

Lynnette burst into a breast-shaking spasm of laughter. "A damn good one, honey." Fred thought it was a clever rejoinder, but Arthur wasn't laughing. "I'm an oncology nurse," she said and took a gulp of her second martini.

Fred waited for someone to say something. It was Andy who broke the silence.

"Well, I'll bet that's no joy ride." Before she could answer, he got up to clear the soup bowls.

"I love my work," Lynnette said, twisting around to address Andy directly.

"*Love* it?" Arthur rasped. "Love it! What's to love about people who are dying—wasting away, puking from chemotherapy, walking around with—"

"Who said anything about dying?" Lynnette shot back. "I'm all about helping people live. Cancer is not necessarily a death sentence, in case you hadn't heard."

"Well, I *hadn't* heard!"

Fred gingerly pushed away from the table and went to help Andy, who was opening the oven.

"What can I do to help?" he whispered.

"Just hand me the dishes," Andy whispered back.

In silence, they plated the fish. Back at the table, Arthur continued to harange Lynnette. He went on and on: about the lousy system of health care in America despite Obamacare, the slow pace of medical research, the limited number of specialists in LGBTQ health. He was on one of his tirades, part moral outrage, part angry rant.

"We're going to garnish each plate with a few pine needles," Andy coached soto voce.

"How about adding one of these stones for garnish, too?" Fred asked, trying for a joke.

"No," Andy whispered, "the stones are for throwing at the two of them."

When they brought the plates to the table, Arthur and Lynnette were still at it. Now it was about inequities in access to medical care for people of color. Fred slammed a plate down in front of Arthur.

"Excuse me, but this is my fuckin' birthday party. Do you think we could change the topic of conversation?"

Arthur froze, looked up, and stared at him. Fred stared back, determined to win this one.

"My, my! What happened to Betty White?"

"I guess she quit, and they hired Eartha Kitt instead?" Fred snapped back.

Arthur burst into a cackle. "Eartha Kitt! Eartha Kitt! Oh, Fred, you *are* old!"

❖ ❖ ❖

There was no birthday cake. One of Arthur's favorite expressions was, "I despise cheap sentiment," and birthday cakes and candles and the Happy Birthday song all ranked as such in Arthur's book. Instead, Andy had made glutinous rice cakes and small pancakes filled with sweet bean paste. It was the only part of the meal that Lynnette seemed to enjoy, and Arthur made a snide comment to that effect.

What was it about Lynnette, Fred thought, that kept pushing Arthur's buttons? Why couldn't he cut her some slack? When she got up to make herself another martini—Fred had lost count—Arthur intervened.

"Ah, don't you think you've had enough alcohol?"

"Excuse me?" she fired back. "Like Fred said, this is a birthday party. And this is my fuckin' bottle of gin." Arthur had finally worn down her patience.

"And this is my house, bitch."

She slammed the bottle down on the butcher block table.

"You know what, Arthur? I don't need this."

Red-faced, she glared at him, daring him to open his mouth.

"Maybe," Fred began, not knowing what he was going to say. Lynnette shushed him.

"I lost two patients today, Arthur. *Two*. Okay? We all have problems. Every damn one of us. Whatever is stuck in your craw, you're not the only one who has a right to be angry." Without waiting for a reply, she turned to Andy. "Thanks for the party, hon. I gotta go." She picked up the bottle of gin. "Happy birthday, Fred."

Fred returned her good wishes with a feeble, apologetic smile.

After she left, none of them said anything. Arthur was the first to speak.

"Lost two patients today," he said. "But cancer 'isn't necessarily a death sentence.' Right!"

"Arthur, enough," Andy demanded.

"I think I ought to be going, too," Fred announced. Arthur started to protest, but Fred stuck firm. "It's been a long day, Arthur." He made sure there was not a whisper of Rose in his voice. "Andy, the dinner was fabulous. You went through a lot of trouble. I really appreciate it." He gave Andy a peck on the cheek. "Bye" was all he said to Arthur.

In the hallway, he made his way upstairs to Lynnette's apartment.

"I feel as if I should apologize for Arthur's behavior," he offered after she let him into her kitchen. Her décor was—even Fred had to admit it—atrocious. In addition to a Formica kitchen table and four wooden chairs draped with red-and-white check chairback covers, there were at least three other little tables pushed against the walls, on which were a clutter of appliances, jars, cannisters, utensils, bowls of candy. Café curtains hung over the windows, braided scatter rugs on the floor. Nothing matched. It was a Zen monk's nightmare. A gay man's nightmare.

"Not to worry, honey," Lynnette reassured him. She held out a bowl of jelly beans. "Want some?"

Fred shook his head. "It's just that Arthur's going through a lot right now."

She looked straight into his eyes. They spoke to him of long, hard hours of thankless work and motherly tenderness. Why couldn't Arthur have seen that? "I don't know if you know it or not, but Andy—"

"I know," she interrupted.

"You do?"

"When Andy called me up this morning to invite me, he told me."

"He did?"

"He had some questions about his fainting spells."

"So what do you think?"

Lynnette shook her head, brushing off his concern. "There are lots of reasons why he could have fainted. I went through the possibilities with him—dehydration, arrhythmia, diabetes, medications he might be on. All negative. My guess is he's just got low blood pressure, hypotension. It's common enough. You get up too fast and you pass out. Happens more than you might think. Especially with old people."

"Jesus, the way Arthur tells it—"

"Ha! The way Arthur tells it! He's something of a drama queen, isn't he?"

"*Something?*" And suddenly Fred was in her arms, hugging her, laughing, then crying, then hugging her even more tightly. "I was so scared, Lynnette. So scared."

"I know," she whispered. "I know."

But there was more Fred wanted to say.

"Oh, man. Getting old. There are days when ..." He pulled away so that he could look at her. "How do you handle it, all the sickness and death you see?"

"Hey, you handle it," she said. "Let me tell you something: you think you know how things will turn out, but the fact is, you never really do.

Strange to say, but that's what keeps me going. You actually never know. There's always something you didn't factor in—the patient's more of a fighter than you thought, the medications finally kick in, what looked super serious is just a fainting spell, or"—she paused—"or, well, the disease progresses a lot faster than it's supposed to. You never know. Keeps things interesting. Because—you know what?—I may be a nurse, but I'm not the one in control. It keeps me very, very humble." She chuckled. "Though I guess I wasn't very humble tonight, was I? Gee willikers, that Arthur. He got to me."

Fred managed a smile. "He can get to all of us."

Lynnette shrugged her shoulders. "And somehow we manage to love him anyway, right?"

"Unaccountably, yes."

"Because, like I said, you think you know the whole story, but you never do. Arthur can be a pompous son-of-a-bitch, but I bet you there's a lot more there than meets the eye. A lot more pain than meets the eye." She stepped back, put her hands on her hips and grinned. "Hey, there's a lot more to me than meets the eye, no?"

Fred laughed. "I'm really glad you came to my party tonight."

"Wouldn't have missed it for anything."

She held out the bowl of jelly beans again. "The purple ones are really good. Take some."

❖ ❖ ❖

Fred let himself into his apartment. He'd left the table lamp on in the kitchen, a practice he'd begun the night Reuben died. It had burned every night since then, fifteen watts, about the same number of lumens as a candle. He dropped the handful of jelly beans he'd taken onto the kitchen table. Then he went to the sink, poured himself a tall glass of water, drank it, and sat down. The crossword puzzle was still there. He was staring at it when there was a faint knock at the door. Arthur let himself in.

"Hey," he whispered.

"Hey."

"Sorry about tonight," Arthur said.

"I guess we all had a bit too much to drink."

"No," Arthur shot back. "Don't excuse it away, Fred." He looked exhausted. The West African print shirt hung on him like a tired costume.

Fred could guess at some of the reasons why Arthur looked so worn down—the medical scare with Andy, his fight with Lynnette—but he reminded himself of what Lynnette had said: there was always more going on that he didn't know. He supposed he couldn't even guess at the half of it. Arthur's position at the Housing Authority—straddling the Black and white communities, trying to address the concerns of tenants and management—it was not an easy one. Arthur's position as a professional gay Black man in this city was not an easy one.

"You want a glass of water?" Fred asked.

"Thanks."

While he went to the sink to fill a glass, Arthur sat down, picked up a pencil, and started working the crossword. By the time Fred set the glass in front of him, he had solved three more clues.

"I wish I had your knack for words." He sat down across from Arthur.

"I'm not sure I quite distinguished myself with my verbal brilliance tonight."

Fred twisted the puzzle over so that he could see what words Arthur had added, all of them working off that one word—GRAVITY—the only one he'd been able to solve this morning.

"Ha! I didn't see any of that. I kept doubting that 'gravity' was the right answer. Nice going."

Arthur took a sip of water, helped himself to two of the jelly beans on the table, and turned the puzzle back toward himself. Fred watched him. He seemed more composed now. The whole atmosphere—the dim kitchen lighting, Arthur quietly working the puzzle, the détente they'd managed—it brought a story to Fred's mind.

"Sophomore year in college, I took a physics course. There was a unit on gravity. It was fascinating. Did you know, the force of gravity never gets to zero? Our professor—Jeez, I can still dredge up his name, Dr. Savonen—he explained that, though that was mathematically true, eventually the pull of gravity would become negligible as far as any practical application was concerned. But I couldn't shake the notion that a body would never absolutely escape the pull of another body's gravity. There would always be, somehow, the whisper of a tug."

He took a sip from Arthur's glass of water.

"I remember after that lecture walking around campus in a kind of stupor, thinking about how everything was pulling on everything else, even if by an infinitesimally immeasurable amount."

Arthur filled in another word on the puzzle. "I'm listening," he assured Fred.

"For a week or so, I became kind of cuckoo, I mean like hyper-alert to every object in my environment: buildings, trees, books, my typewriter, my slide rule. God, remember slide rules?"

"Unfortunately, yes," Arthur said, looking up from the puzzle.

"My friends started worrying about me. They said that I would walk past them without even noticing them, like I was stoned or on an acid trip."

"Our Rose on an acid trip! Think of it." Arthur said. "So what happened?" he asked, returning to the puzzle.

"Eventually, I snapped out of it." He paused. "Well, the truth is, I met a boy." Fred took the pencil out of Arthur's hand. When Arthur made eye contact with him, he continued: "We were in that physics class together, and he kept inviting himself over to my room to do problem sets. He was an English major. Physics wasn't his thing, but he had to take the course to fulfill the science requirement."

Fred let out a little wistful laugh. "He loved Walt Whitman and would recite me poems he had memorized. At first, I didn't catch on as to what he was up to. Then one night, he told me that Whitman had written a poem about gravitational pull." Fred laughed again. I still remember one line: 'Does not all matter, aching, attract all matter?' *Aching?* I asked him. *Aching matter?* What does that mean? 'This,' he said, and leaned over and kissed me.

"That night, in bed together—it was my first time with another guy"—Fred smiled at Arthur—"and well, the problem of *gravity* suddenly felt very irrelevant. All the heaviness, all the worry I'd been dragging around ... *Poof!* I felt lighter than air."

Arthur waited for more.

"His name was Rafe. We only lasted a few months together, but they were a beautiful few months. I've never told you that story before, have I?"

Arthur arched his eyebrows. "You've been keeping secrets, Rose."

"I know not everyone our age had such an easy coming out," Fred continued, "but that was mine. No trauma, no guilt. Just feeling that everything was weightless. I suppose, for a little while, everything *was* weightless." When Arthur still didn't say anything, Fred turned the paper toward himself. "You know, when my students get stuck on a problem, I tell them to get away from it for a while and then come back with a fresh mind."

"Are you talking about me and Lynnette?"

"I'm talking about solving math problems."

"Rose, your trust in positive outcomes is one of your most endearing qualities. And one of your most infuriating."

Fred heard the automatic thermostat click off. Eleven o'clock.

"Actually, I thought you brought up a couple of good points with Lynnette tonight."

Arthur raised his eyebrows again. "Just 'a couple'? I think I raised more than a couple of points with her. But yeah, she's a fighter, that one."

"Do you ever wish I were more of a fighter?"

He watched Arthur studying his face. *Who do you see?* Fred wanted to ask. *Tell me.*

"Girlfriend, you just turned sixty-five. That means you *are* a fighter. No gay man gets to sixty-five without some fight in him."

"I don't feel like a fighter, Arthur. Most days, I don't feel the pull of anything significant anymore. My world is just numbers and puzzles."

"*Just* numbers and puzzles?" The impatient hauteur that Arthur had cultivated to perfection was back in his voice. "There's nothing else significant in your life?"

Fred felt himself blushing with embarrassment. "Okay, and this crazy family I have, Arthur, this crazy family. *Including*," he quickly interjected, "Lynnette."

Arthur opened his eyes wide and flashed him a sassy, skeptical look. "As long as she pays the rent."

"You know, she thinks Andy is going to be fine."

"Yes, that's what she told Andy today."

"When?"

"When he called to invite her to the party. He was concerned enough about the fainting spells that he asked her about them."

"Then why the hell ..." Fred was flabbergasted that Arthur had known about Lynnette's diagnosis and yet had chosen to indulge in so much emotional drama. "Arthur, you had me worried sick."

Without warning, Arthur burst into tears.

"I don't want to lose him, Fred," he managed to get out between sobs. "Andy is everything to me. When Reuben died ..." Whatever was going to follow was lost in another convulsion of tears.

"I know, I know," Fred soothed.

"When Reuben died," Arthur tried again. "I mean, he wasn't, he wasn't *supposed* to..." Arthur broke off, unable to finish his sentence.

Fred wished he had some wisdom to bring to this moment. The best he could find to say was: "A lot of things happen that we don't think are supposed to happen. But we pick up and move on." Still, he felt a twinge of resentment because, in Arthur and Andy's case, the thing that was not supposed to happen in fact, wouldn't happen. At least not for a while. Andy was going to be okay. Lynnette had said so.

Arthur sniffled and began to compose himself. "Sorry," he said.

"Nothing to be sorry about. We old birds have to face some scary shit."

"*We* old birds? *We!* Speak for yourself, Rose."

Fred got up and—fuck Arthur's aversion to cheap sentiment—planted a kiss on the top of his head. "I love you, Arthur."

Arthur pushed him away.

"Enough, girl, enough." He eased himself up from the kitchen chair. "Time for me to get my ass upstairs and help clean up the mess you folks done left us with." He was halfway to the door when he turned around and shot Fred a suspicious look. "Just don't go thinking that you'll make Lynnette part of our Saturday morning coffee hour. That time's for me and you, girlfriend!"

Fred grinned.

"And do me a favor, sugar." Arthur reached over and took another jelly bean. "Please get rid of that chenille robe you were wearing this morning. Oo, Lordy! Bad enough I done had to integrate the neighborhood. You don't want to go and scare away all them nice white folk movin' in, now, do you?"

The Bohemians

The four of us—Jake, Wilson, Henry, and I—used to call ourselves the "Crumble Crew" after Crumble, the café in the South End where we would meet every Saturday morning for coffee and conversation. But one day, about five years ago, Jake, who's the opera lover among us, pointed out that we four kind of approximated the roles of the four male bohemians in Puccini's opera *La Bohème*. He jokingly suggested we should call ourselves The Bohemians instead. We all laughed. We're hardly the type of guys you'd mistake for bohemians.

But, yes, opera-loving Jake is a musician, which qualifies him, I suppose, as the Schaunard of our group, and Wilson, his husband, who teaches English at a private school here in Boston, dabbles in poetry. "My Rodolfo," Jake calls him.

So there we had it, half the quartet: Jake/Schaunard, Wilson/Rudolfo. But that's as far as the bohemian comparison extends. None of us is a Marcello, the impoverished painter, or a Colline, the philosopher. More to the point, we are all just a bit too middle-class to think of ourselves as bohemians. And we're definitely too old. Henry, the youngest in our group, is forty-eight. I'm sixty-four.

All those objections aside, the nickname stuck. Even the staff at Crumble now calls us The Bohemians. They're amused, and charmed, by our longevity. We've been meeting up at Crumble for about ten years now.

At one time, back in our wayward gay youth, each of us was, I guess, a bit of a bohemian. Jake dropped out of music school, where he was studying the oboe, and took up with a rock band for a year before returning to finish his degree. Wilson studied poetry for a while with Allen Ginsburg at the Naropa Institute. And Henry, who is now a coordinator of child welfare services for the city, ran away from home at age sixteen, got himself to Provincetown, and became a much-desired busboy, eventually graduating to a much-desired waiter. Two years later, he was studying psychology at NYU.

Of the four of us, I had the least errant young manhood. There was no rock band or Naropa Institute or running away to Provincetown for me. About as bohemian as I got was the summer I worked at a refreshment stand in New London, dishing out ice cream to preppy kids, whom I secretly pined over. I was seventeen that summer. None of the prepsters paid me the slightest attention. I was a hireling; they, the future masters of the world. Instead, the guy who did pay me attention—the guy I ended up having an idyllic, if brief, affair with—was a cadet at the nearby Coast Guard Academy.

Like me, Rick was from a working-class family. I met him the night he came down to the stand for ice cream, handsomely dressed in his Coast Guard leisure wear. Some big-shot, preppy college kid tried to cut in front of him, and Rick shoved him aside and told him to wait his turn like everyone else. Words were exchanged. The prepster threatened to report Rick to his commanding officer for conduct unbecoming a military man. "Oh, really?" Rick fired back. "And let's see your draft card, you little fuck. Did Daddy wrangle a draft deferment for you?" More words were exchanged. The college kid's friends hauled him away, and that was the end of it. Rick moved up and ordered his ice cream.

"One day in the military and he'd be eaten alive," he said, looking me in the eye.

I was not a fan of the armed services. The war in Vietnam was still on. The next year, I'd have to register for the draft. Still, I liked this guy. Liked how he'd stood up to that entitled, self-important bully. When I handed him his cone, I told him it was on the house. I had no authority to do so, but I suddenly felt the urge to let him know that I admired him. He said he couldn't let me do that, but thanked me for the gesture. The next night, he came down to the stand again, just as we were closing up. I apologized, told him that the register was already cashed out. "I know," he said and smiled.

During the rest of that all-too-short summer, Rick taught me about things I was eager to understand: about sex, about responsibility, and, maybe most importantly, about privilege—about the obliviousness that too many advantaged people find as an acceptable way to move through the world.

The day after Labor Day, I returned home for my senior year in high school. Rick and I wrote to each other and met once more, when I drove down to Connecticut to interview at Wesleyan. He was graduating that year. The prospect of our being together in the future was nil, and the six-year age difference a concern for both of us. Still, knowing him had an enormous impact on my life. I ended up turning down an offer from Wesleyan and going to the University of Massachusetts, where I double-majored in international relations and communications.

Maybe all this qualifies me for claiming bohemian credentials. Certainly the fact that I've worked for non-profit arts organizations all my life feels a bit countercultural. Currently—and this will surely be my last job—I'm the executive director of a small gay theater company here in Boston. My role helps to keep an alternative voice alive in this city. I like to think Rick would be proud of the way my professional life has turned out.

Crumble opened about twenty years ago to much fanfare and not a little skepticism: an upscale business in a part of the South End that had yet to be gentrified. Planting a shop that serves expensive espresso drinks and fancy baked goods on Washington Street was, in its first year, tantamount to opening a meat market in the middle of a colony of vegetarians. Nobody thought it would fly. The old elevated that ran down the center of Washington Street had only recently been torn down. High-price condos were a developer's dream, not yet a reality. But the owner, an elegant middle-aged Lebanese woman, took a chance. Mrs. Mansour—eyes ringed with heavy mascara and ears bedecked with enormous gold spangles—has prospered. Her little Crumble has become a three-tiered cake.

I was one of her earliest patrons. Having newly broken up with my second boyfriend, I sought out the comfort of Mrs. Mansour's café. At first, I sat at one of Crumble's little tables, nursing my Saturday morning coffee and discreetly checking out the other patrons.

Instead, it was Mrs. Mansour who befriended me. She pronounced my name—and still does—"Da-*veed*," which I love. She's around my age, maybe a few years younger, but she treats me like a son. Only once, early on, did she ask me if I were married. When I told her no, she didn't press as to why. I figured she was getting hip to who a lot of her clientele were, where her cupcake was frosted, so to speak.

"Why the name 'Crumble'?" I once asked her.

She shook her head in bewilderment. "Crazy name, right? American friend tell me it's good name. I say, 'In my country, *crumble* is all around—the buildings is crumble, the business is crumble. I don't want to think about that when I look at my shop.'" Mrs. Mansour shrugged her shoulders. "My friend convince me anyway. 'Crumble is name of famous American dessert,' my friend say. She tell me it is also famous American saying: *This is way cookie crumble.* 'What means that?' I ask her. 'Means you have to accept the good with the bad.' 'Okay,' I say. 'That I understand.'"

It was sometime during the third or fourth year that I'd been going there that I noticed Henry, one of the current Bohemians. He was sitting at the long communal table, the table that Mrs. Mansour sets out with copies of the daily papers and a vase of flowers she changes each week. He was everything Boyfriend Number Two was not, at least in the looks department. Number Two was Greek: short, swarthy, a mass of curly black hair, black-olive eyes, and a perennially jovial outlook. I used to call him Zorba. Watching him dance at the weddings of three of his cousins, the nickname was not without its merits.

In contrast, the guy sitting at the table that morning was tall and lanky; smooth, clear skin; blue eyes and brown hair cut fairly close to the scalp. Maybe a bit too preppy. Still, I was intrigued.

I waited until the next Saturday morning to make my move. I'd already rehearsed my opening line: *Is the newspaper yours, or is it ...* He cut me off. *No, please, help yourself.* Our eyes met. We introduced ourselves. There was no more newspaper reading that morning.

Over the next few weeks, Henry and I got to know each other. We talked about our careers. We talked about where we grew up, the music we liked (classical for Henry, progressive jazz for me), favorite cuisines, movies, vacation spots, and which of Mrs. Mansour's confections was her pièce de résistance. I weighed in on the sticky buns; Henry said it was her *ma'amoul* cookies.

Crumble's sticky buns are legendary. The things are big, buttery, gooey, and ridiculously unhealthy, which doesn't dissuade their advocates from heaping praise on them as Boston's best. I wondered if, in praising Mrs. Mansour's sticky buns, I had revealed myself to be totally conventional. Or worse: if given a choice between Western and Levantine cuisine, was I declaring that I was someone who'd always opt for his own kind? The sticky bun as a vestige of colonial culinary hegemony.

I pegged Henry to be in his mid-thirties. In fact, he was thirty-eight that year. Already, I was calculating whether a fifteen-year difference in our ages would matter. Experience told me yes; my attraction to Henry said, *Maybe not.*

Our conversation moved on. Henry told me that he had recently broken up with his partner. But when I tried to steer the conversation toward the topic of the perfidy of ex-lovers, Henry made it clear that he would not badmouth his former guy. It was over; there was no more to say about it. That impressed me, too: he seemed a man of integrity.

We went on a few dates, but that's as far as it ever went. We never slept together. And, despite my giving him every indication that I wanted to take whatever was going on between us to the next level, we never talked about why we never became boyfriends. Henry has the ability to curtail a romance without cutting off a friendship. Over the years we've known each other, I've watched him do this a few times.

It wasn't much later, a few months or so, that Jake and Wilson joined the communal table. I watched Henry work his charm on them. I watched myself working my own brand of charm as well. But when it became clear that Jake and Wilson were a couple, I toned down the ardor. In the end, the four of us became good friends, the Crumble Crew, until Jake rechristened us The Bohemians.

❖ ❖ ❖

The story I want to tell begins on a gloomy, drizzly Saturday in November. Dutifully, we had all shown up at Crumble and ordered our coffee and treats, all except me, who now, in my mid-sixties, had sworn off Mrs. Mansour's pastry, both American and Lebanese.

It was one of those rare mornings when none of us had much to say. We'd gotten together for dinner the week before, so I guess we were all talked out, content now to grab a section of the newspaper and bury ourselves in yet another gloomy story about the way the world was going. All at once, Henry folded up his section of the *Times*, set it down on the table with a decisive thump, and cheerily announced, "Guess what. I'm adopting a baby."

In unison, the three of us looked up. Jake's mouth was open in a gesture of operatic stupefaction. Wilson spoke for all of us: "You're *what*?"

"Yup, I'm flying to Houston next month to pick him up," Henry said, a pleased-as-punch grin on his face. "It's a boy. Due in four weeks."

"How long has this been in the works?" I managed to get out.

"A while." Henry's grin died down, replaced by his serious, professional look. "I know it's a surprise, but I needed to work out this adoption thing in my head before I told you guys. I didn't want a lot of pushback." He chuckled. "I already *know* all the reasons I shouldn't do this."

And how, I thought. You're single, you don't make enough money to raise a kid, you love to go out to the theater. You're forty-eight. You're *single!*

"And this is a done deal?" Jake asked. "There's no way we can dissuade you?"

"Nope," Henry said.

"Henry, your whole life is going to change," I said, my tone wavering between incredulity and anger. "You're not ready for this!"

"I am," he said. There was a calmness in his voice that further irked me. "You know I've always wanted kids."

This was true. In the years that I'd known him, Henry had talked many times about wanting to be a father. But he'd always said it in the context of having a partner or a husband. During our abbreviated dating period, he and I had discussed the idea of gay men having kids. Telling him that I didn't see myself as ever raising children must have been a big factor in the demise of his interest in me.

"Talking about it is one thing," I said. "Actually doing it is another."

"Exactly," Henry said, looking me straight in the eyes. "Talk is just talk, David. It seemed to me it was time to put my money where my mouth was."

"You'll be seventy by the time he graduates high school!"

"Sixty-six," Henry said.

"Okay, sixty-six!" I snapped. "So what happened to the idea of a vacation home in Provincetown? What happened to the trip to Angkor Wat we once talked about? That was *talk,* too. Why aren't you putting *that* talk into action?"

Wilson interrupted to point out that I was raising my voice.

"David," Henry said, "I'm sorry, but this is super-important to me."

"What's going to happen to the Bohemians?" I asked forlornly.

"Nothing's going to happen," Henry said. "I'll bring the baby here on Saturdays." He was as nonchalant as if he were offering to bring beer to a picnic.

From behind the counter, Mrs. Mansour called out to him. "What baby? You have baby, Henri?"

"I'm going to adopt a baby, Mrs. Mansour!"

"*Alf mabrouk!*" she exclaimed.

A couple of the other patrons in the café started clapping. Henry's face turned as red as the rouge on Mrs. Mansour's cheeks.

When the hullabaloo calmed down, Wilson—peering through his tortoiseshell, English-teacher glasses—broached a practical question.

"So, I'm wondering about child care."

Henry had it all figured out. The wife of one of his colleagues—they were a childless couple—had offered to be the baby's nanny. And Henry's mother, who lives two streets over from him in South Boston, would also help out a couple of days a week. I was astounded that so many plans had been in the works without our knowing a thing.

Just then, Mrs. Mansour came from behind the counter bearing a plate of cupcakes.

"For Daddy Henri and the three uncles."

Uncle, I thought. *I've been looking for Boyfriend Number Three, and instead I'm supposed to be an uncle?*

❖ ❖ ❖

Three weeks before Christmas, the baby was born, and Henry flew off to Houston to pick him up. A week later he returned. He'd gotten a paternity leave from his job, so he had the rest of the winter to bond with the baby.

On his first Saturday back in Boston, he arranged to join us at Crumble so that we could meet the baby.

"And this is Brian," he said, setting the carrycot down on the communal table.

The baby was swaddled in a snowsuit and knit cap. Brian did not seem like an appropriate name for a half-black, half-Latino kid, but I held my tongue.

"He's so beautiful," Jake cooed. "And that adorable cap!"

"My mom knitted it for him," Henry said.

"Hey, Brian," Wilson said, bending his face down into the carrycot.

Mrs. Mansour came over, tears in her eyes.

"*Mignon!*" she exclaimed. In her rapture over the infant, she'd been transported to the language of her childhood, when she went to a French convent school in Beirut.

I was glad that the others were making such a fuss over the baby, because I couldn't think of anything generous to say.

Henry lifted Brian up and dandled him in his arms. "He's just had a bottle, so he's a little sleepy now, aren't you, Brian? Huh, sleepy baby?"

Everyone had questions: Did Brian sleep through the night? Had the nanny started her duties? What did Henry's mother think of her grandson? Where in his apartment had Henry set up the crib?

From somewhere, Wilson produced an envelope and held it out to Henry.

"Just a little something from Jake and me," he said.

Henry's hands were occupied with the baby. "Here," he said, offering Brian to me. "Take him."

"Ah, maybe Jake should hold him," I suggested. "I get nervous holding babies."

"Ooh, come to Uncle Jakey," Jake cooed again, holding out his arms. Henry transferred the baby to Jake's care and took the envelope from Wilson.

Inside was a gift card. "Oh, wow!" Henry exclaimed. "Thank you, guys." He held up the card. "A certificate for a half-year's worth of diaper service. Man, that will come in handy. Gosh"—he made eye contact with each of us—"you guys are great."

"I'm afraid I had nothing to do with it," I confessed. I was embarrassed that I had not shown up with a gift, and miffed at Jake and Wilson for not consulting me about what we were going to do during this first meeting with Brian.

Henry let out a laugh. "I've worked with kids all my professional life, but never with kids *this* young! Let me tell you, it's been a rollercoaster course in parenting."

So many snarky rejoinders were bouncing around in my head, but I held myself in check. Mrs. Mansour brought over pastries. They were on the house, she told us. This time, they weren't cupcakes, but a plateful of her most expensive creations.

I declined, but the others helped themselves, then resumed their goo-gooing at the baby. Left to fend for myself, I took a section of the paper and busied myself there. The headlines that Saturday morning were more alarming than usual. The President was at it again, issuing yet another executive order that repealed an environmental policy the previous administration had put into place. Not only were the Bohemians breaking up, America seemed to be falling apart, too.

"Look at this!" I said, holding out the front page to the others as if it were a dirty diaper. "Do you see what he's trying to get away with now?"

No one responded. Wilson was rearranging the baby blanket in the carrycot, while Jake handed Brian back to Henry.

"Time to go sleepy time?" Henry asked, nuzzling his nose into the baby's face.

Suddenly, he pulled away. "Oopsie! I *smell* something." In the two weeks that he'd had Brian, Henry had already adopted the sing-songy tone that parents of infants seem to think is de rigueur when addressing their kid. "Did we go poopie, little man?"

He reached into his carry-all bag and pulled out a clean diaper.

"You're not going to change him *here*, are you?" I snapped.

Henry grinned mischievously. "Sure, why not?"

"Because people eat on this—"

"Relax, David." The grin suddenly disappeared from Henry's face. "In case you hadn't noticed, there's a baby changing table in the bathroom." He picked Brian out of the carrycot, walked to the bathroom, and disappeared inside.

I turned on Jake and Wilson.

"Why didn't you guys tell me you were bringing a gift?"

Wilson gave me a guileless look. "I don't know. Guess we didn't think about it. Don't sweat it, David. Emily Post says you have a year to give a baby present."

"Fuck Emily Post!"

"Whoa!" Jake exclaimed.

I sighed. "Sorry, but this whole thing feels very uncomfortable."

"The 'whole thing' being ... ?"

"The bouncy-baby thing. All the paraphernalia Henry's toting around. The new-parent euphoria."

"It's what new parents do," Wilson said.

"You feeling left out?" Jake asked.

"I'm feeling ... I'm feeling like Henry's opted for a very hetero-normative ..."

Wilson cut me off. "Please, David. No jargon this morning. There's more than one way to be a gay man in the world these days."

"I know that," I snarled.

"Then let Henry be the gay man he is." Wilson took off his tortoiseshell glasses. "We grow, we change." I could imagine him saying that to his students in class.

❖ ❖ ❖

All winter, Henry hardly came to Crumble. From Jake and Wilson, I learned that the nanny had not worked out and that Henry had found a new one.

"Her name is Josephine," Wilson reported one Saturday in February. "We met her last week. She's terrific."

"You met her?" I asked. I saw Wilson flash Jake a quick look that said *oops*.

"It was a last-minute invitation to dinner," Jake explained. "Henry wanted to invite you, too, but ..." Jake was not good at fabricating lies. Wilson came to the rescue.

"He thought too many of us would overwhelm the baby," Wilson said.

"One more is too many?"

"Josephine cooks two nights a week," Wilson said. "I think she'd already prepared ..."

"Just conveniently happened to prepare dinner for three that night, but not for four, is that it?" I fired back.

Now it was Jake's turn to speak. This time, he did not mince words.

"David, I think Henry feels that you don't approve of his having a kid."

"*Don't approve?!* That's not true!" Jake and Wilson stared at me without saying a word. "Look, I think it's great if that's what he wants. I'm just not sure he thought through all the implications."

"Like what?" Wilson asked. So that he could make better eye contact with me, he pushed aside the communal table's vase of flowers. This week, they were an arrangement of three red amaryllis blooms, a nod to Valentine's Day. "What exactly are the implications Henry didn't think through, David?"

"Like how about loyalty to ... to this ten-year thing we had going?"

Wilson nodded. "So, yes, that's going to change."

"*Going* to change! It *has* changed."

"David, may I finish my thought, please?"

"Sorry," I apologized.

"The Bohemians have been a really important part of our lives—*all* of our lives—for quite a while. I cherish these Saturdays we've spent together. Our weekends in P'town, our dinner parties."

"Don't you mean, *your* dinner parties?" It was perverse of me to say that, but I wasn't feeling at all gracious.

"*But*," Wilson said, "circumstances change, what people want changes. You can't imagine how happy Henry is with this baby.

"Maybe I could imagine it if I saw him once in a while!"

"Have you called him?" Jake asked.

"The phone works two ways, you know," I countered.

"Yes, it does," Jake said. "*Two* ways."

"You probably should call him," Wilson added. "He's got some more big news for you." He glanced at Jake as if to ask permission.

"What?" I asked.

"He's dating someone," Jake said. "It's quite serious."

Wilson gave me a brief curriculum vitae: the boyfriend's name was also Henry, but he went by Hank.

"He's already gaga for Henry's baby," Wilson added.

"Hank's somewhat younger than Henry," Jake said. "He only came out a few years ago, but I think he's already gotten his trashy gay exploration out of the way. He's quite mature and quite in love with Henry. I think they're ready to settle down."

"How much younger?"

"Like about ten years," Wilson said. "Hank's thirty-eight, I think."

I remember a time in my life when thirty-eight felt very old. When twenty-four felt old. That's how old Rick, the Coast Guard cadet, was that summer we had the affair. Now even guys in their forties seem like twinks to me. Henry with a baby *and* a twink for a boyfriend. Jesus!

❖ ❖ ❖

In late February, the theater company put on a series of short plays by Tennessee Williams. Toward the end of his career, Williams had lost his way and ended up turning out one flop after another. But for our artistic director, these short plays, which featured twisted homosexual relationships, cryptic symbolism, and the flamboyant language of high gothic romance, were a brilliant new direction in the aging playwright's career. Never mind that they'd all been panned when first produced. Our production would reveal the true genius behind these late masterworks.

Even ten years ago, we might have found an audience for this production, but few people, even passionate theatergoers, were now interested in such misguided fare. It didn't help that the one review we got called our production "an evening of hot messes." From then on, the house was less than half full each evening. We were hemorrhaging money. Our principal backers, a rich gay couple, were threatening to pull out if we didn't change course. They suggested that we scrap the final play of the season. Instead of our announced spring production, which was to be a new play about hook-up sex, the backers lobbied for *Arsenic and Old Lace.* Played by male actors in drag. The board voted for the change. For me, the whole debacle was one more outrage in a winter full of them.

The next Saturday—it was now early March—I went to Crumble, still stewing about the substitution. Jake and Wilson hadn't yet arrived, but the communal table was already almost full. A couple of medical students were hunched over a laptop, studying anatomy. A handsome, nattily dressed Black man—he was wearing a purple V-neck sweater and paisley bow tie—was also sitting there, as were Henry and Mrs. Mansour, who was holding the baby in her arms. It was the first time I'd seen Henry in weeks.

"David," he said when I sat down, "I'd like you to meet Hank."

To this day, I pray that Henry didn't register the surprise on my face, because I suddenly realized that the attractive Black man was not some random patron, but Henry's new boyfriend.

"Oh, my gosh, it's nice to meet you."

Hank said it was nice to meet me, too. We shook hands. He looked even younger than thirty-eight. I looked at Henry. He was beaming.

Just then, Jake and Wilson walked in. The way they greeted Henry and Hank, I understood immediately that all four of them had already been socializing on more than one occasion. Mrs. Mansour got up to make room for the new arrivals and handed the baby back to Henry.

"Here, take him, honey" Henry said, passing Brian off to Hank, who seemed quite comfortable taking the baby.

"So," Jake announced, as if resuming a conversation that was already in full swing, "we've decided on Greece."

"That's awesome," Henry said.

"And look at this." Jake passed a magazine he was carrying to Henry. "The trip we booked is featured in here this month."

It was one of those slick, glossy magazines that promotes itself as the au courant source of information pertinent to the gay community, but is really just about self-congratulatory, middle-class gay consumerism. Henry started flipping through the magazine. "That's the article," Jake said, indicating the feature in question. I stole a glance. It was titled, "Gay Holiday in the Land of Apollo!"

"It looks gorgeous," Henry exclaimed.

Jake turned to me. "Wilson is retiring in June. We've booked a two-week trip."

I faked a smile and gave Wilson my congratulations.

"I think," Wilson added, addressing Henry, "that we'll add on that extra side trip to Mykonos I was telling you about."

I'd heard nothing about Wilson's retirement, nothing about a trip to the Land of Apollo.

I picked up the magazine and started leafing through it. I got to the article about Jake and Wilson's trip. In one photo, four Speedo-clad circuit boys in designer shades were lounging by a pool, sipping cocktails and admiring each other's gym-sculpted bodies. In another, an enormous crowd of bare-chested men was dancing the night away on the island of Mykonos. I flipped through more of the magazine. There were articles on other destinations as well. Lisbon was another new alpha destination, it seemed. In the so-called "culture" section, the book reviews featured a bunch of banal gay romances and a coffee table book on Liberace.

Wilson noticed that I'd dropped out of the conversation. "We heard," he said, turning to me, "that you guys changed the final show to *Arsenic and Old Lace*. Jake and I are looking forward to coming next month." I could tell he was trying to bring me back into the fold.

"Save your money," I snapped. "I can't believe we scrapped the hook-up play for *that*. We've totally sold our souls to the yuppies."

"What are you talking about?" Wilson said. "It's a wonderful play. And we heard you're going to do it with drag queens. What a hoot!"

"No," I corrected, self-importantly. "Not drag queens. Guys in gender non-conforming clothing. There's a difference, you know."

Jake chimed in: "I love the movie version with Cary Grant. Gosh, he was gorgeous."

"Gary Grant was a closet case!" I announced. I turned to Hank, who was feeding the baby. "You're probably too young ever to have heard of Cary Grant or *Arsenic and Old Lace.*"

Hank grinned. "As a matter of fact, when I was at Yale, my College put it on. I was Mortimer Brewster."

"*And,*" I added, trying to keep my deflated grievances pumped up, "he got to enjoy heterosexual male privilege—and the money that went with it—all the while he was sleeping with Randolph Scott."

My sudden outburst frightened the baby. He started wailing. Hank put down the bottle and started bouncing him in his arms, but to no avail.

"He's tired," Henry announced. "Honey, we should probably get him home."

All at once, everyone got up. They were fleeing, I knew, from the Fury of David. Quickly, scarves were twisted around necks, coats and caps were donned, the wailing baby was returned to its carrycot, and goodbyes were said. I saw how eager they all were to get away from me. Hank was the first one out the door, toting the carrycot. Jake and Wilson followed suit. Henry lingered behind, carrying coffee mugs to the bussing bin. He was stalling, waiting for a private moment with me.

"I'm sorry," I said when he returned to the table to get his jacket.

"David, David, David."

"I feel as if you've all left me behind."

"We haven't," Henry said.

"Then why does it feel that way?"

"David, what you're seeing is that I'm happy. This winter, two wonderful people entered my world. And suddenly, I feel like my life has started moving in a direction I'd forgotten was possible." He paused. "I want you to be happy, too, you know."

I nodded.

"You know," he continued, "we've known each other ten years, David, but in some ways, you're still a mystery to me."

"Some days, I'm a mystery to myself."

"I've missed you, David. We've hardly seen each other all winter."

"I've missed you, too." I was calmer now. "Look, I'm glad you're happy. And Hank seems like a lovely guy."

"So how about you come over for dinner next week?" Henry invited.

"I don't know. I'm up to my eyeballs in work for the company." I pulled a napkin from the napkin holder and blew my nose. "We almost lost our principal backers. I'm organizing a cocktail party in their honor." I shook my head. "They want the bartenders to be in drag."

Henry laughed. "Well, when you've packed up the feather boas, let us know. We'd love to have you over."

We gave each other a hug. Henry held me for longer than I expected. And then he was out the door. Through the plate-glass window, I saw that Hank had been waiting for him on the curb. The three of them walked off together, looking like a very happy little family.

I sat back down at the table. Mrs. Mansour came over holding a pot of coffee.

"Da-*veed*, you want fresh cup?" Before I had a chance to respond, she poured more coffee and sat down next to me.

"I think The Bohemians are dying, Mrs. Mansour."

"Maybe so. Maybe not."

"We've been together a long time."

"Long time," she mused, pushing the carafe of coffee to the side and folding her hands in front of her. "My husband—may God rest his soul—he and I had a café in Beirut. Long time, too."

I'd heard very little about Mrs. Mansour's life before she came to Boston.

"Then comes the war. You know?" Yes, I assured her, I knew. "We lose everything." She looked at me, searching my eyes to see if I understood. "*Everything.*"

"I'm so sorry."

"He and I, we bury our son, come here, start all over again. Then he gets cancer. I think I will lose my mind."

"Oh, Mrs. Mansour, I had no idea."

"It's okay," she assured me. "When he die, I start again." She looked at me. "What else you gonna do? And you see?" She gave a quick survey of the café. "I do all right. What you think?"

"I think you've done splendidly. Everyone says your sticky buns ..."

She unfolded her hands and raised them to the heavens. "Eh, the sticky buns! I never eat one before I come America. Now I'm Queen of Sticky Buns!"

We shared a laugh.

"Da-*veed*, the cookie crumble, but life, it go on."

"I know. It's just really hard sometimes to let go of what you've had."

She nodded. The dark kohl around her eyes made her look very old. And very wise. "You let go, but you start again. You start again. Understand, Da-*veed*?"

Yes, I told her.

Heavily, she eased herself out of the chair, picked up the coffee pot, and went back to the kitchen.

Jake's glossy magazine was still lying on the table. I pulled it toward me and began leafing through the pages. There was a photo essay on Russian sailors, blond, beautiful, rosy-cheeked mariners staring pouty-lipped at the camera. What is it with gay men and guys in uniform, I wondered.

I've always referred to Rick as Boyfriend Number One, even though, technically, we were hardly ever boyfriends. But he was my first experience with the aching understanding that each of us travels a different path. With Boyfriend Number Two, "Zorba," I used to think, *At last, someone on the same road*, but in the end our paths split as well. The Bohemians were a good compromise. Friendship, I told myself, gay solidarity—that's where I'd stake my claim. Jake, Wilson, Henry—they were the guys who would walk the farthest with me. But now there was Hank. And now there was Brian.

I tossed the magazine aside. There was nothing in that rag for me. *Uncle David*, I thought. Well, okay, so maybe that's the way the cookie was going to crumble.

The Hazardous Life

For the past several years, the Academy had not offered a fourth year of French. Three years of a foreign language were required for graduation, and that's as far as most of the students wanted to go. The one or two who occasionally opted for a fourth year were allowed to take an evening course at the Extension School down in Cambridge, for which the Academy gave them credit.

What a pity to send the students elsewhere, Mason Chastain always thought. As the Academy's senior French teacher, he knew these kids so well, knew what they needed, not only with regard to their studies but also in terms of their emotional growth. Their *spiritual* growth, he was tempted to say though he knew that sounded old-fashioned. As so often, his favorite poet, Rimbaud, had expressed it perfectly: "I would have liked to show children these sunfish, the fish of gold, the singing fish on the blue tide." Mason doubted that the students the Academy sent to the Extension School would be shown those golden, singing fish. They'd be treated like mere adult learners rather than the intense, eager, romantic young people they were.

Then, in the final year of his forty-three-year career, a surprise occurred. Six students, the minimum needed to justify offering the class at the Academy, signed up for French IV, and the dean of studies asked Mason if he would teach the course. It would mean, he said, that Mason would have to give up one of his sections of second-year in order to teach the seniors. Not a fan of the dean, Mason said he'd need a few days to think about it. Let him sweat it out, Mason thought. But when he drove home that afternoon, he was already putting together a reading list. The blue tide was swelling.

❖ ❖ ❖

As he circled the Back Bay looking for a parking spot, Mason knew it was petty to keep the dean in suspense, but there was something about Tony Krikorian that just rubbed him the wrong way. From the moment, six years ago, that Krikorian arrived as the new dean of studies, he had grated on Mason. It wasn't any one thing, but the whole package: Krikorian's youth (he was thirty-five), his good looks, his privileged Ivy League education. The guy wore his lucky breaks—good genes, good breeding, good schools—with irritating self-assurance. He had an easy way with the kids, an easy way with the faculty. Mason had turned sixty that year. Krikorian's arrival had put him on guard.

The *coup de grâce* came three years ago when Krikorian, who was straight, volunteered to be the faculty advisor to the Gay-Straight Alliance. The previous faculty advisor had moved to Baltimore with her wife, and Krikorian stepped in to fill the vacancy. In another one of his countless irritating moves, he renamed the club the LGBTQIA+ Discussion Group.

The damn know-it-all, Mason thought as he circled the blocks around Commonwealth Avenue, looking for a parking space. Krikorian prided himself on being so au courant, so right-up-to-the-minute on all the latest, politically correct views. Fifty years ago, when he, Mason, was in high school, it was just gays and straights—simple as that—with an occasional nod to the bisexuals, who no one really believed were bisexual at all. Now ... my God, being gay was as humdrum as coq au vin. LGBTQIA+ indeed!

It was the middle of April and the magnolias on the sunny side of Commonwealth Avenue were in glorious full bloom. If the weather held, these blowzy, delicate pink blossoms would be resplendent for a week or so. Every year since he and Mary had lived in the Back Bay, Mason looked forward to the appearance of the magnolias. And it saddened him to contemplate how soon they would disappear. Recently, he had been feeling the poignancy of disappearing things ever more acutely.

There were no parking spaces on Commonwealth. He turned left on Fairfield—none there either—and then right onto Marlborough. His daily circle around the neighborhood in search of a place to park. Every year it got worse.

Before Krikorian had taken over the Gay-Straight Alliance, the Academy's headmaster had approached Mason about assuming the role of faculty advisor. After all, the headmaster said, Mason was a senior member of the faculty, had relatively small numbers of students, and had in the past led other clubs—French Club, Opera Club, the Spring Trip to Europe. Besides, the only gay member of the faculty now, Frank Fidby, the obvious candidate, was already teaching an extra section of chemistry and had no time. The headmaster thought that since it was a Gay-*Straight* Alliance, the group should occasionally be advised by a straight "ally."

How extraordinary, Mason thought. The Academy had certainly changed since the day when he first arrived, a young French teacher right out of the University of New Hampshire. Forty-three years ago, there had been no Gay-Straight Alliance. There had certainly been no teachers who would have declared themselves gay or lesbian. But now, everyone wanted to get in on the act. The woman who had previously run the GSA had even invited her students to her wedding when she married her wife. And Frank Fidby, when it was his turn to chaperone, always brought his husband to soccer games and dances.

Even more remarkable, *students* at the Academy were now openly identifying themselves as gay and lesbian. And, it seemed, as every other variation along that rainbow spectrum—bisexual, transgender, non-binary, gender-fluid, genderqueer. The categories bewildered Mason. He suspected that many of them, certainly the younger students, weren't even sexually active. The labels they gave themselves described what were still, he assumed, just abstract concepts for them, hardly lived experiences.

There were no spaces on Marlborough Street either. Mason circled the block again.

He thought back to his own teenage years. In the eighth grade, his best friend had been a boy named Gordie Henderson, whose hobby was photography. One day, Gordie gave Mason a tour of his basement darkroom: the enlarger, the developing trays, the dim, film-safe red lightbulb. Then he pulled out his collection of photo magazines. Leafing through them under that dim red light, Gordie pointed out the various articles, which were full of technical information on things like lenses, composition, film speeds. Each issue always included a suite of art photographs. Mason remembered one such spread in particular: it featured a wholesome, rosy-cheeked young woman kneeling in an outdoor setting. Her arms were raised above her head in order to keep a wide-brimmed hat (the only article of clothing she wore) from blowing off in the wind, a pose that thrust out her ample breasts in fulsome, robust vitality.

Gordie told Mason that these were "artistic" shots, taken by a highly regarded professional photographer, but the next time they got together—it was always on Tuesday afternoons after Confraternity of Christian Doctrine classes—Gordie started rubbing his crotch, exclaiming how much the girls in these beefcake spreads turned him on.

"Yeah," Mason agreed, wanting desperately to feel what Gordie was feeling.

For the rest of the winter of their eighth-grade year, he and Gordie spent each Tuesday afternoon in the darkroom masturbating to the magazines. Mason's eyes always strayed from the photographs to Gordie's cock, ready at a moment's notice to shift back to the photo spread in case Gordie noticed that his friend's attention had drifted. Mason liked the tight quarters of the darkroom, which meant that his body—his arms and hips—often touched Gordie's body while the two of them indulged in their separate bouts of self-pleasuring.

The car behind him honked. Mason looked up and saw that the traffic light was green. He turned onto Newbury Street. A block down, he spotted a parking space, pulled up, and eased into it. A lucky break on a Friday afternoon. And now the car could stay there all weekend without his having to move it. Unbuckling the seatbelt, he grabbed his briefcase and headed off to the little market down the block. The street was crowded with end-of-the-week shoppers and café patrons.

And, for an hour, I fell into the hubbub of a Baghdad street.

He'd been reading Rimbaud again, fiddling in his spare time with translations that he hoped would capture some of the astounding lyricism of that boy genius. The older he got, the more Mason found himself drawn to Rimbaud, to the beauty of his words, the outrageousness of his vision, a wild but perfect harmony. How astonishing that Rimbaud had produced most of his greatest work when he was still a teenager. Younger even than the seniors he would teach next year!

The weather was warm enough that a few guys—Back Bay gym rats—were jogging down the street, their lean, beautiful bodies another declaration, like the magnolias, that the dash and brio of springtime had returned. Ah, yes, Mason thought, buttoned-up Boston was throwing off its winter weeds. Let the hubbub begin!

By May of that eighth-grade year, Mason was in love with Gordie. He loved the intimate playfulness of their darkroom antics, the physical closeness, Gordie's happy-go-lucky attitude toward sex. He tried to imagine more with Gordie—what would that be? Maybe they'd go on vacations together, just the two of them, without their parents. Or end up roommates at the same college. As he and Gordie whacked off in the darkroom, Mason imagined an entire life with his friend. Then one day, watching Gordie panting in pre-climax excitement, Mason leaned over and tried to plant a kiss on Gordie's cheek. Gordie recoiled. "Fuck, man, what are you doing?" he barked. "Gross!" Mason was never invited back again.

❖ ❖ ❖

The little Newbury Street market was crowded. Everyone there seemed to have the same idea on this beautiful springtime afternoon: prepare a nice meal, drink some wine, be with the ones you loved. Mason recognized at least one gay couple whom he often saw at the market. One was holding the grocery basket while the other picked items off the shelves—fresh pasta, a couple of artichokes, a quart of strawberries. Mason wondered what it would be like to feed a strawberry to another man, holding it to his lips, feeling his tongue touching his fingers.

The fall he entered high school, he and Gordie were blessedly not in the same classes. From the sidelines, Mason watched Gordie become quite the ladies' man, while he, in turn, buried himself, and his shame, in his studies. French—so foreign, so romantic, so beautiful—became his favorite subject. More than that, it became his refuge. He managed to stop mooning over Gordie, though he could not help having secret crushes on other boys, none of which he dared to act on. Senior year, his

French teacher assigned them Gide's *Symphonie pastorale.* The other students in the class weren't as proficient as Mason, and they labored over the book for months. Mason was bored out of his mind—with the story, with the pace, with their teacher's tedious droning on and on. This story of a secret, unrequited heterosexual love was not the story he needed to read.

That final year of high-school French had been so bad that Mason almost didn't take another French course when he got to college. But his advisor at the University of New Hampshire told him his French preparation had been so strong—and his Achievement Test so high— that he could pass into upper-level courses if he wanted to. Mason thought he'd give it a try. The poetry course he took turned out to be excellent. As did the other French course he signed up for that year, "Proust and His World." By June, he'd declared himself a French major. It was the first time in his life that he was absolutely sure he'd made the right choice.

He was less sanguine about his decision to join a fraternity, but fraternities were the way to go back then, and so he did it. At his first boozy frat party, Mason got drunk and then never again. He was afraid of what he might do if he let his guard down. At other parties, when his fraternity brothers told jokes about fags and homos, he responded with fainthearted smiles. The guys began to see him as the goody two-shoes of their house. They nicknamed him Chastity Chastain. "Chastity, isn't it about time you got banged in Boston?" they teased. By junior year, Mason was secretly wishing he could drop out of the fraternity. And then he met Mary.

She was five years older than he, a graduate student and teaching fellow in the course he took that year in abnormal psychology. Often after class, he'd linger to ask her questions. At first, she gave him only a minute or two of her time before she went off to do more research at the library. But one day, she invited him to join her for coffee. With guarded casualness, Mason brought up that week's topic: the recent decision by the American Psychiatric Association to depathologize homosexuality. With equally guarded casualness, Mary acknowledged that it was a "landmark readjustment," one that would have profound consequences for how *gay* people—he had already noticed how she preferred that word over "homosexual"—how gay people would think about themselves from now on. "Lesbians, too," she added. He remembered how she had looked down at her coffee cup and then back up at him, fishing for a reaction.

The next Saturday, they went to the White Mountains with the hiking club. It turned out that Mary was an outdoor enthusiast. Though she was a few inches shorter than he, Mary had a rugged, boyishly athletic body, and could hike at quite the clip. Mason had never been on a hike before, and had a hard time keeping up with her, but he enjoyed talking to Mary about psychology and French and their similar blue-collar backgrounds. When the weather got too cold for hikes, they did other things together—concerts, plays, trips into Boston for the museums (his choices); basketball games, skiing, bird watching (her choices).

One day—it was the spring semester and she was no longer his teacher—Mary told him her story: married at twenty-one, a child (now three years old), and a divorce about to be finalized. "I'm not sure there was ever much of a spark there," she told Mason. "Bob and I were just two people, much too young to get married, who happened to share a passion for psychology. Not enough reason to keep a marriage alive."

"What do you think *does* keep a marriage alive?" he asked.

She gave him another one of her sober, direct looks. "Well, for starters, the courage to make a go of it together, I'd say. I think in the end, Bob and I just couldn't muster that kind of courage."

Those sounded like such beautiful words—*courage, making a go of it*. He thought about what it would be like to share a long life with another person: keeping a house, raising a child, working side by side at the dining room table after supper, bandying ideas back and forth, trips to Europe. When he tried to imagine sex with Mary, he thought he could give that a try, too. Two weeks later, they slept together. He'd forgotten to bring a condom and Mary said she was not on the pill. So they just slept together, and this seemed fine with both of them.

"I think I'm a lesbian," she told him halfway through that night.

"I think I'm a gay man," he told her. Though tenuous, it was the first declaration of his sexuality he had ever made to anyone.

In the market's wine section, Mason picked up two bottles, a Merlot for himself, a Chardonnay, her favorite, for Mary. Then he put the red back on the shelf. Otherwise, he knew he'd drink the entire bottle over the course of the evening, and probably finish Mary's bottle of white. He was doing that a lot lately. He thought he should probably slow down.

A month after he graduated—by then, Mary's divorce had been finalized—they got married. It was a crazy decision, and yet it wasn't. He couldn't imagine another person who would ever know him—and *accept* him—as well as Mary did. They had grown fond of each other, enough to embark on an outwardly conventional partnership in a quietly unconventional way. Mary said that they were forging "a common front" against everything they hated—shame, theories of abnormality, the frat boys. Remarkably, they had been making a go of it together ever since. Mason's fiftieth high school reunion was coming up next year. He wondered if Gordie would be there and what he would say when Mason showed up with a wife.

Just before he got into the checkout line, he added a bouquet of tulips and a quart of strawberries to his basket.

❖❖❖

The building where he and Mary owned a condo was an elegant, late-nineteenth-century townhouse that had been broken up into apartments years ago, one of the first of these old Commonwealth Avenue mansions to go condo. He and Mary had lived in the Back Bay their entire married life, first in a cheap one-bedroom rental on Hereford Street, later in a nicer apartment on Beacon Street, and now, for the past thirty-three years, in this building, which the developers had christened "The Standish," a name that was supposed to connote, he guessed, Yankee history, decorum, and soberness. They purchased their unit with a down payment from Mary's parents. In those early days, three bedrooms were still affordable. One bedroom was theirs, another for the days when Mary's son Ben was with them, and the third they converted into an office for her therapy practice. Ben's bedroom was now Mason's study.

He took the elevator up to their floor and let himself in. Mary was at the kitchen table, working on her laptop.

"I hope you got outside today," Mason said. "It's positively glorious out there."

Mary looked up, peering over her half-frame reading glasses, and smiled. "I managed to get in a walk between patients earlier this afternoon." As Mason began to unpack his shopping bag, she noticed the flowers and berries. "How lovely!"

"A little something to celebrate the season. The strawberries are from California, of course, but ... well, I'm feeling festive." When Mary sent him a quizzical look, he explained: "Krikorian wants me to teach French IV next year." He went to the sink, turned on the tap, and began to rinse the berries. "I told him I'd think about it."

"But you will, won't you?"

As the strawberries were rinsing, he put the tulips in a vase and filled it with water.

"Mason, you've wanted to teach that course for years," Mary continued, "and next year ... well, it would be a lovely swansong."

"Dear me, 'swansong.' Sounds like I'm dying."

"Oh, stop!" she chided, taking the vase of tulips from his hands and setting it on the table.

Mason laughed—more to reassure her than because he saw the humor in her remark. He dumped the strawberries into a bowl, opened a kitchen drawer, and pulled out a corkscrew. "Want a glass?"

Mary glanced up at the kitchen clock. "A small one, Mason. I have a patient coming at five."

He opened the Chardonnay and poured glasses for both of them before sitting down across from her. They clinked.

"Simone Dugied was the last one to teach the fourth-year course. Which is probably why none of the seniors in recent years have signed up." He took a sip of the wine. It was cold and delicious. "Poor old gal. Simone stayed on at the Academy way past her prime. Her fourth-year course was a snoozer."

Mason took a strawberry from the bowl and brought it to Mary's lips. She pulled back and took it from his fingers.

"Mason, being a teacher at the Academy was Simone's whole identity." She bit into the strawberry. "She loved the school as much as you do. I suspect that staying on as long as she did kept Simone young."

"Ah, but there's the rub. Is that enough of a reason to keep teaching? I mean, it's supposed to be about the kids—right? I don't think it's enough of a reason to stay in the classroom just because it 'keeps you young.'"

"So is that why you're retiring next year? You think you're getting stale?"

He swirled his glass. "There are days when I do."

"And on the other days?"

He moved his attention from the glass to his wife. She was seventy-two and still going strong. Only last month, Mary had announced that she planned to keep her practice open until she was at least seventy-five.

"On other days, I think I still have it." He smiled at her. "That's why this chance to teach the French IV kids really intrigues me. I want to"— he chuckled—"I want to get revenge on the Madame Dugieds of the world! The ones who *should* have retired and didn't."

"Dear me, Mason. The poor woman."

He picked up a strawberry and bit into it. The juice ran down his chin. Mary picked a napkin from the napkin holder on the table and patted his chin dry.

"Do you think you might stay beyond next year?" she asked.

"No, I don't think so."

"You don't sound convinced."

"Convince me," he said.

It was Mary's turn to chuckle.

Convince me was their private joke. Five years into their marriage, Mason had begun having second thoughts. By then, both he and Mary were seeing other people: a casual love affair on Mary's part with a woman several years older than she; a more unsettling affair on his part with a twenty-one-year-old college senior. "Convince me, Mary," he had appealed to her one night, "convince me why we should stay together. I love you, but this is driving me crazy. I think I love Cameron, too."

That's when she'd said it: "Let's never ask each other that, for one of us to convince the other. That's not a responsibility I'll accept." She'd gone on to say that *she* was convinced that their marriage was the one she wanted. "What's going on between Rachel and me, or you and Cameron, has nothing to do with our *marriage*. But I don't want to be put in the position of having to convince you of that. Only you can decide whether you want this marriage. I can only tell you that I do."

In the years since, they'd each had other affairs. Mary always let her lovers know, from the start, that she was committed to her marriage; there was no possibility, she told these women, of their ever becoming a couple. Her husband and her son came first.

When he and Cameron broke it off—Mason using the same dictum: his wife and son came first—he thought that maybe he'd gotten it, whatever "it" was, out of his system. But about a year later, he found he couldn't beat down his curiosity: what might some other man offer him that Cameron had not, that domestic life with Mary did not? One afternoon, he stopped in at a gay bar near the Public Library for a cocktail before he went home. Just a drink, he told himself, nothing more. On his third visit there, he met Bill. Bill lasted about as long as Cameron, half a year. "I just don't want to be your mistress," Bill told Mason. "I understand," Mason said, "but my wife and son come first."

The third and last affair was with a guy named Loring, who was a civil rights lawyer. Loring said he was happy just to be Mason's occasional thing—he respected that Mason's family was important. But a year into their "arrangement," Loring told Mason he had tested positive for HIV. The news scared the hell out of Mason. Though they had been practicing safe sex, he was terrified he might bring something home to Mary. That was the year he and Mary bought their place on Commonwealth Avenue. Ben was sixteen, a junior at the Academy. Mason decided that his life was rich enough without the complications that Loring, or any other guy, brought into the equation. Still, he and Loring remained friends— dinner buddies on evenings when Mary was out with her bowling league, later a meals-on-wheels deliverer when Loring was too sick to take care of himself. When Loring died, he and Mary both attended the memorial service.

Mary picked another strawberry out of the bowl. "You don't *have* to retire, you know."

"I know," he agreed. "Sometimes it feels as if I've only made that decision because I think I'm supposed to make it." She waited for him to go on. "I've thought about delaying taking social security and continuing at the Academy a few more years." She waited again. "Mary, I just don't want to become another Simone Dugied!"

There, he'd said it; he'd confessed his deepest fear. He did not want to watch himself become a washed-up, has-been teacher. Teaching had been his whole life. What else did he have to show for himself? Plenty, he guessed: his forty-four-year marriage to this good woman, his stepson Ben, and now his two grandsons. Those were things to feel proud of, too. But in so many other ways—his desire to write poetry, his dream that they would one day own a house in France, those silly affairs and infatuations that had gone nowhere—there was so much *unfulfillment* in his life. Years ago, he had stopped his occasional pop-ins at one of the local gay bars. That was another thing to feel good about, too, though Mason sometimes wondered if his withdrawal from gay flirtation had more to do with the fact that gay bars in Boston were closing left and right.

"Mason, you could never become another Simone Dugied," Mary said affectionately. "Krikorian would never have asked you to teach the course if he had thought that."

He leaned across the table and kissed her cheek. "You're my greatest fan."

"Always have been, Mason."

They never had kids. Mary's son, Ben, whose custody she had shared with the boy's father, until he died of cancer, was the only child in their lives. Now forty-eight, Ben was a former rock guitarist who had become a successful agent for rock bands. Married at twenty-five, he'd given them two grandsons, who were—my God, the years were flying by!—nineteen and twenty-one this year. Becoming a grandfather—Boppy, the boys still called him—was another reason that Mason's passion for outside affairs had slackened. It just didn't square in his mind: the occasional Friday night forays into gay bars followed by the two of them babysitting the boys on Saturdays. Rimbaud had a phrase for the way that made him feel: "with this throat wrapped in a necktie of shame."

He poured himself more Chardonnay, and then went to add more to Mary's glass. She held her hand over the rim.

"My patient's coming."

He smiled affectionately at her. "We are both so levelheaded."

"Forty-four years of levelheadedness next month," she said. "*Imagine ça!*"

❖ ❖ ❖

At the end of the school year, Tony Krikorian called Mason into his office to finalize his teaching schedule for next year.

"Madame Dugied was the last one to teach the fourth-year class," he said, as if Mason didn't know this already. "We wrote to her—you know she's living on Cape Cod now—"

"Yes, the *Cape*," Mason interrupted. It irked him how Krikorian, who'd grown up in Fresno, California, had never learned the Boston way of referring to Cape Cod.

"She dug up her old syllabus," Krikorian continued, clueless that he'd been corrected. He handed Mason a sheet of paper on which was mimeographed a list of the fourth-year books. Mason glanced at it. Just as he suspected: a dull, unimaginative syllabus. An old lady's syllabus. My God, they were supposed to start with the *Symphonie pastorale!*

"And this," Krikorian said, handing him another sheet, is your class list. "Quite an impressive crew, I'd say."

Mason read the names. He'd taught all six of them back when they were sophomores: Sabrina Belknap, a good student and crack field hockey player; the twins Mary-Margaret and Margaret-Mary Donohue; another girl Chenguang Lee, whose American name was Dawn; and two boys, Nathan Lawrence, the least successful of the six back in his sophomore year, and—Mason tried to disguise his delight—Duncan Dietrich, one of the sharpest students at the Academy.

"Looks like a good group," he told Krikorian, handing back the list. "Though I'm surprised Nathan Lawrence signed up. He barely passed French II."

Krikorian smiled. "Sabrina Belknap," he said. "The two of them are an item. At least for now. I guess we'll see how things pan out over the summer."

"You'd be okay with my changing the reading list a bit?" Mason asked, irritated that Krikorian even knew the amatory background of the students. "I might want to make some tweaks." He intended to whether or not Krikorian gave the nod.

"No problem," Krikorian told him with that hang-loose amiability of his.

"*Eh bien, je vous souhaite d'agréables vacances d'été,*" Mason said, enjoying every delicious second of Krikorian's incomprehension.

❖ ❖ ❖

All summer, Mason read. And all summer, he cut books from Simone Dugied's syllabus, adding his own choices. The short story unit was easy—so many great ones to choose from. As for the novel, well, certainly not the Pastoral Symphony. Maybe Zola's *Nuits des Temps*. Or something by Balzac or Camus. For fun, during the doldrums of winter, he thought one of Sempé's Petit Nicolas books might work or Queneau's *Exercices de Style*. Then there was the question of poetry. Again, a world of choices. He had to admit that some of the poems on Simone's list weren't so bad, though she hadn't included a single poem by Rimbaud. Well, the poetry unit fell in the spring. He'd decide later, based on how the class was going.

At the beginning of August, he and Mary took their annual two-week vacation to Wellfleet. It was at the outer end of the Cape, an hour's drive from where Simone Dugied and her husband had retired. The thought occurred to him that he should drop in to see her and discuss the course. Just as quickly, he abandoned that idea. But among the books he packed to read, he threw in the *Symphonie pastorale*. He thought he should at least read it again before he officially dropped it from the reading list. Maybe, he thought, he'd dump the thing on Simone's front lawn on his way home at the end of the summer.

Each morning after breakfast, he and Mary went for a swim, then spent the rest of the time before lunch reading, he his French books, Mary her English mystery novels. Afternoons they went to the beach again or took walks or did some bird watching. In the evening, after dinner, they watched movies, played Scrabble, read some more. Mary's French was not nearly as good as Mason's, but a few days into the vacation, she picked up the Gide when Mason wasn't reading it and started making her way through the first few pages. The next morning, she went to the Wellfleet Public Library and took out a copy of *The Pastoral Symphony* in English.

On the last night of their vacation, one of Mary's friends came over for dinner. Priscilla was another therapist. She and Mary had had an affair back when they were in their fifties, but now they were just friends. Every summer, Priscilla rented the house next to theirs. Mason envied how these two women had remained close over the years.

Priscilla arrived with a potato salad and a bottle of Chardonnay.

"I would have made dessert," she told them, "but I spent the day in Provincetown." She joined Mary at the kitchen table. "It's Carnival Week." She raised her eyes in mock bewilderment. "Oh, those boys."

Mason was at the stove working on a bouillabaisse, wondering what in the world they'd do with Priscilla's potato salad, and delighted she hadn't brought dessert. Priscilla was a terrible cook. He turned and smiled.

"Those boys, indeed."

The last time he'd been in Provincetown, the last time he had seen *Carnival*, was fifteen years ago.

After dinner and dessert—Mason had made a tarte Tatin—Mary and Priscilla did the dishes. This was the unerring rule they'd followed their entire married life: whoever cooked left the dishes for the other. Mason counted it a good deal since he hated doing dishes and loved to cook. He left the ladies at the kitchen sink and went to the living room, where, under the autumnal glow of a reading lamp, he made his way through the final pages of the *Symphonie pastorale*. He was beside himself with impatience, boredom, and outright animosity. He'd never liked the novel, which he considered a piece of namby-pamby mushiness, and reading it again only confirmed his distaste. The symbolism of the physically blind girl and the morally blind pastor—it was trite and obvious.

"Done!" he announced, snapping the book shut. "I don't think I could have stood one more page."

He heard Mary explaining to Priscilla what he was talking about.

"I don't know why he bothered to read it again," she told her friend.

He heaved himself up from the chair and returned to the kitchen.

"Academic integrity," he explained. "Due diligence. I was hoping I'd find something in it that would convince me to change my mind."

"Did you?" Priscilla asked.

"Not a thing! Don't get me wrong. Gide's a beautiful writer, a great writer, and his basic message here—he brandished the book in front of her—it's one I can buy into."

"What's that?" Priscilla asked.

Mason opened the book, flipped through a few pages, and read to them:

"*Le mal n'est jamais dans l'amour.* There's never anything wrong with love."

"You think that's true?" Priscilla asked. "*Never?*"

"Well, in the context of the passage, Gide intends it somewhat ironically. The blind girl—her name is Gertrude—has just told the Pastor she loves him. It's an innocent remark. She wouldn't say that, she tells him, if he were not married. 'So, why shouldn't we love each other?' she asks. Of course, the Pastor is burning with undisclosed passion for her."

"And she doesn't know that?" Priscilla asked.

"No, not until the very end when ... Do you want to know how it ends?"

"You've piqued my curiosity," Priscilla told him. "So, no, don't tell me. I just might read it myself."

Mason shook his head in exasperation. "How such a great writer—and a homosexual, to boot!—how he could have written this ... this ..."

Priscilla looked at Mary. Mason knew that back when they'd had their affair, Mary had told Priscilla that her husband was gay.

(*And what did she say,* he'd later asked Mary. *She said she thought we were very modern,* Mary told him. *Is that the word for us?* Mason asked. *Modern?* Mary had smiled. *I told her we were just very us,* she said.)

"Why do you think Simone had *The Pastoral Symphony* on her list?" Mary asked. Her tone was the same one she used with her patients when she wanted to suggest to them the possibility of another point of view other than the one they were insisting upon.

"Well, I suppose because it's the right level of difficulty and the kind of story that appeals—or at least *used* to appeal—to impressionable teenagers."

"The love story, you mean?" Priscilla asked.

"The love *triangle*," Mason said, landing on the word with an emphasis he immediately regretted. He pretended to be interested in picking up a few crumbs from the half-eaten tarte, which was sitting on the kitchen counter. "The Pastor's *son* and Gertrude are in love."

"Well, that sounds interesting." Priscilla's laugh—deep, chesty, mannish—had always struck Mason as a dead giveaway that she was a lesbian.

Mary handed the last washed plate to Priscilla, who took it in her toweled hands, like a midwife swaddling a baby. Then she pulled the stopper from the drain and turned to Mason.

"I don't know, Mason, I think you're being a bit harsh. Granted, I didn't read it in French, but I liked it a lot. He's trying to get across that the only real sin is the one that tries to squash the happiness of another."

"That's beautiful," Priscilla said.

Mason was beginning to feel foolish. "It is," he conceded. "But Gide said it so much better in several other books."

"Then choose another of his books," Mary said. "It's your course now, Mason."

"Yeah, my swansong."

❖ ❖ ❖

On the Tuesday after Labor Day, Mason met his French IV class for the first time. Because the class was so small, it was held not in Mason's regular classroom but in the Hitchcock Seminar Room, a special privilege for seniors. This seminar room, outfitted with a large oval table and Windsor armchairs, had once been the former library of Hitchcock House, a fieldstone mansion located on the far side of the Academy's soccer fields. Hitchcock House was atypical of domestic architecture in this part of Massachusetts, but typical, Mason guessed, of the quirky family who had built it in the twenties of the last century and who, upon the death of old Mrs. Hitchcock, had bequeathed the mansion and an additional twenty acres of playing fields to the school.

Mason loved the seminar room. It represented so much of what he stood for as a teacher: a sun-filled, scholarly retreat from the noisy adolescent bustle in the main school building. He loved the relaxed give-and-take of discussions around that splendid oval table rather than the regimentation of the hideous stainless-steel-and-plastic desk-chair setups in the regular classrooms. He loved the sheer joy of the collegial intimacy he could create here.

He got to the seminar room early, took his place at the head of the table, arranged his books and papers, including packets of a handout that he had photocopied for each student. *My final year*, he thought. *Nail it.* As the six students drifted in, he greeted each one warmly. He still remembered the French names he'd given them during their sophomore year: the twins, who arrived together, were Marie-Margaret and Margaret-Marie, though he'd forgotten how to tell them apart. Next to enter were Sabrina and Chenguang.

"*Bonjour, Sabine et Aurore!*"

"*Bonjour, Monsieur Chastain*," they responded in unison.

Nathan was next. Two years ago, he'd rejected the French name—Nathaniel—that Mason had given him and chosen Claude, after his favorite French composer, Claude Debussy. Nathan was a pianist, a far better pianist than a French student.

Last to arrive was Duncan Dietrich, whom Mason had christened Dorian.

"It's lovely to see you all again," he told them, opting for user-friendly English.

All six assured him it was good to see him, too. They looked refreshed and eager, ready to tackle the challenges of their senior year.

But what was this, Mason thought, as his attention went to the book each of them had brought to class. To his consternation, they had shown up with copies of the *Symphonie pastorale*. After all the work he'd put in that summer to create a new syllabus, he had forgotten to send the revised list to Krikorian, and so the dean had mailed the students Simone Dugied's old syllabus.

"*Eh bien, mes élèves.*" He had always scrupulously avoided calling them by the more motherly, infantilizing *mes enfants,* which is how Simone Dugied had addressed her students. "I see you have all dutifully brought in *La Symphonie pastorale.*"

"Our brother read it when he took this course," one of the Donohue twins said. "Would it be okay if I used his copy? It's got his notes in it."

"It would indeed be okay ... *if* we were reading it this year."

A concerned look darkened the face of the twin—he guessed it was Marie-Margaret, who had always been the more fretful of the two.

"We're not?"

Mason took in a deep breath. He had to tread tactfully here. "The *Symphonie pastorale,* many say, is one of Gide's finest works. However, I regret to say that I do not share that opinion. Gide wrote several far greater books." He paused again, surveying the sextet of students assembled around the seminar table. He knew that, at the moment, he had their complete trust, but he was about to drop a bombshell. "In fact," he continued, "*je déteste ce roman.*" There, he'd thrown down the gauntlet. "I think it's rather ... well, a piece of sentimental hogwash."

He saw Sabine's eyes open wide. The twins tilted their heads together and confabbed in whispers.

"Our brother loved it," one of them declared.

"I'm glad he did," Mason said, "and I hope you'll learn to love the Gide that I'll be teaching this semester." He began distributing packets of the photocopied material that he'd brought to class. "So, we are *indeed* going to start with Monsieur Gide. But a very different Gide. These excerpts are from his first published work. He was twenty-one when he wrote it. Only three years older than you."

"I'm seventeen," Sabine said.

"Me, too," Aurore added.

"Okay, so *four* years older," Mason said, trying to strike a balance, which he hoped the two girls would detect, between amusement and annoyance. He'd intended to stress just how very young Gide had been when he brought out his first book, but Mason now realized that to these teenagers twenty-one was still light years away.

Aurore raised her hand, her head buried in the handout, already reading.

"No need to raise your hands this year," Mason announced to them all. "You're a small class and I want to run it like a seminar. Aurore, *as-tu une question?*"

"So, what is this? It looks like a diary."

"Precisely. These are passages from a book called *Les Cahiers d'André Walter. The Notebooks of André Walter.* André Walter was a fictitious character, but Gide used that character as a vehicle to present his own thoughts. He was trying to figure out who he was." He paused and looked at them. "It's his early psychological self-portrait. He wanted to discover what made him tick." He had their attention now, most of them anyway. Nathan was lost in staring at Sabrina. As for the Donohue twins, he wondered if he had laid to rest their brother's buildup of the *Symphonie pastorale.* He continued with his little promo spiel:

"Gide was an advocate for undaunted living, *la vie intense*, he called it. He said that everything happens deep in the soul. The polite surface we present to the world ... well, it's a lie. We suffer when we're unable to reveal our true selves." He saw that Nathan was now whispering to Sabrina. "Do you have something to share with the class, Claude?"

Nathan hurriedly broke off. "No, sir."

"Well, then. Pay attention. Today we are discussing literature, not the senior prom." Sabrina blushed; Aurore giggled. "So, back to Gide. Dorian, the first passage, if you please." Mason wanted to start off without any stumbling over words or syntax. He knew Dorian was his man.

"*L'air est si radieux ce matin ...*"

Dorian's accent was perfect. Mason listened with pleasure as the boy continued. When Dorian got to the end of the excerpt, Mason asked Chenguang to translate.

"This morning the air is so ... radiant?" she asked.

"*C'est exact.* Radiant, bright, clear."

"So clear this morning that ... *malgré moi,* in spite of myself, my soul hopes."

"*Très bien.* Continue please, Marie-Margaret."

"And sings, and adores with a desire for prayers."

"A desire for prayers," Mason repeated. "But how would we say that in English. Gide said it in his idiom; what would be ours? His soul is so elated by the radiant day that it sings and adores ..."

"With a desire to pray ... to God?" she asked timidly.

"I don't see God in that sentence, mademoiselle."

Mary-Margaret's sister came to the rescue: "Well, who else would the soul be praying to?"

"Ah, a profound question, my dear. So: *avec un désir de prières.* Anyone else want to hazard a guess?"

"A longing to pray?" Duncan/Dorian ventured. "A longing to cry out?"

"Indeed." Mason refrained from smiling too adoringly at Duncan lest it become obvious who his favorite one was already. The other night, he'd been finishing up a translation of another Rimbaud poem. It contained the phrase *pubescence d'or*—golden puberty. It was hard not to think of Duncan as enjoying that kind of radiant adolescence.

"As I mentioned, Gide once said that everything happens deep in the soul. What do you suppose he meant by that?" Mason had thrown the question out to anyone, but he now addressed one of the twins directly. "Margaret-Marie? *Que penses-tu?*"

"I think he means that God lives deep in our souls.

Duncan began to shake his head.

"Dorian? You disagree?"

"Gide was an atheist."

"Well, yes and no. He was raised in a strict Protestant family and, at least during his early life, struggled to live by Christian values. But, yes, he was a champion of what he called 'living mightily'—*vivre puissamment*—not letting himself be cowed, intimidated by life. *Que tout me soit une éducation.* 'Let everything be an education for me.' He believed that everything worth living for was worth going a little crazy for. Reason may keep us on the straight and narrow, but it makes the life of the soul *insupportable*, intolerable. He wanted to be open to all that life presented him; he wanted to be true to his own ..." Mason paused, realizing he'd been addressing only Duncan and not the rest of the class. "True to his own nature," he told them all.

"He was a homosexual, right?" Duncan asked.

"And *where* did you learn that?" Mason asked.

"Wikipedia."

"Ah, Wikipedia," Mason declared. "Yes, Gide was ..."

Marie-Margaret cut him short. "Gide was *gay?*"

"It's not the word he would have used," Mason told the class. "But yes. By the way, since we should be learning some new French vocabulary this year, does anyone know the modern French word for 'gay'?"

"*Gai,*" Duncan piped up, ever eager, in his charming way, to shine. "Also *homosexuel.* And I've also heard *pédé.*" Duncan was the student president of the Gay-Straight Alliance.

Mason raised his eyebrows. "Wikipedia has taught you a lot, *mon cher Dorian.*"

A look of pleasure and embarrassment bloomed on Duncan's face. "Actually, I learned that in the LGBTQIA+ Discussion Group. During orientation last week, Mr. Krikorian showed us a gay French film. It had subtitles. Not everyone in the Discussion Group takes French."

"I'm sure the LGB Etcetera greatly appreciates the linguistic advantage you bring to the club," Mason told him.

Everyone laughed. *Yes,* Mason thought, *I'm going to nail it this year.*

❖ ❖ ❖

Over the next few weeks, things happened fast. Krikorian called Mason into his office to report that Mrs. Donohue had complained that the *Symphonie pastorale* had been taken off the French IV syllabus. Mason gave him the same pitch he'd given the kids: there were better works by Gide. This seemed to satisfy the dean, but two days later, Mason was called in again. There was another complaint: Mrs. Donohue had decided that *The Notebooks of André Walter* were ... "Well, the word she used was degenerate," he told Mason.

"Oh, Christ, Tony! That's ridiculous."

"I know, I know," Krikorian assured him, but he sounded harried, caught between two competing concerns.

"Look," Mason said, "come sit in on the class, if you want. You'll see what horribly 'degenerate' things we're reading."

Krikorian said he would, but Mason could tell that observing the class was just one more task on the dean's already overburdened list of problems to solve. He actually began to feel a bit of sympathy for the guy.

Krikorian made his visitation the next day. "Twenty minutes," he said, "that's all I'll need." Mason took pains to select an excerpt that he thought would perfectly show off the beauty of Gide's thinking and, at the same time, send a virtual barb into Mrs. Donohue's timid, bourgeois heart. When the class got to the stinger passage, he deliberately called on one of the Donohue twins to translate.

"Margaret-Marie?"

"Something about minds," she began.

"*Narrow* minds," Mason suggested, swallowing his irritation that she didn't know the word.

"Narrow minds, which think that, um, that theirs is the only truth. Truth is multiple, infinite, as diverse as there are, um ..."

"As diverse as there are minds to think," Mason finished, now giving into his impatience. He glanced at Krikorian, who was standing in a corner, arms crossed. The expression on his face gave away nothing. "Truth is *multiple*, Gide says. What do you guys think of that?" His eyes scanned the six students around the oval table.

Margaret-Marie raised her hand: "My mother says that Gide ..."

"I don't give a ..." Mason caught himself. "Your mother isn't the one taking this course, my dear." He deliberately avoided looking at Krikorian.

No one spoke until Duncan said, "Monsieur, you said Gide wrote this when he was twenty-one. Did he know he was gay then? Because if he did, I see exactly why he'd say that truth is multiple."

"Go on," Mason coached.

"Well, gay people—I know Gide wouldn't have used that word—but gay people experience a whole different way of being in the world. I mean, their 'truth' is not the truth that straight people are handed—you know, the whole heteronormative script that says attraction to the opposite sex is the only way to be, that you have to get married and have two-point-five kids ..."

"Gay people can get married!" Sabine protested.

"What's 'heteronormative'?" Nathan/Claude asked.

"Let Dorian finish," Mason told them.

"What I'm saying"—Duncan addressed Sabrina directly—"is that gay people have to figure it out for themselves, have to find out what's right for themselves apart from what society says is right. I *love* what Gide said: 'Truth is multiple'! That's awesome."

Mason let Duncan's words ripple through the seminar room, like the slow dying out of a pealing bell. He had not intended to push a gay agenda today, but there it was. He hoped it all hadn't been too much for Krikorian. When he looked up, Krikorian gave him a thumbs up.

But the next day, Krikorian called him back into the office. It was Mrs. Donohue again.

"She called me last night," the dean said. "She's complaining that you're turning the French IV seminar into a propaganda piece for the—to quote her—'the homosexual agenda.'"

"I am *not* turning the French IV seminar into anything but what it's intended to be," Mason said, "the reinforcement and extension"—he held up one finger—"of the French studies they've done the past three years"—he held up a second finger—"studying some great literature"—a third finger went up—"and a preparation for the intellectual challenge they'll face in college. This class is not a catechism class, Tony. If Mrs. Donohue wants to keep her precious girls intellectually repressed, let her ..."

"Mason," Krikorian interrupted, "she's already decided to pull the twins out. They're going to take French at the Extension School."

Mason stood there, shaking his head in disbelief.

"I feel sorry for the twins."

Krikorian nodded in agreement. "It was a good class I saw yesterday, Mason. Those girls will miss out on a valuable experience. They'll miss out on *you*. Anyway, you've got yourself a class of four now."

Mason left early that day. He was eager to tell Mary what had transpired. But when he let himself into the apartment, she wasn't there. A note on the kitchen table told him she'd gone for a walk along the Charles with Priscilla. *Gorgeous afternoon*, she'd written. *Won't be many of these days left.*

It was the third week in September. Of course, there would be more beautiful days, Mason thought, right through October. The fact that Mary felt it necessary to justify her afternoon escape irked him. Two hours later, she called to say that Priscilla had invited her to stay for supper.

"Girl time," she explained.

"I need *wife* time," Mason said forlornly. He explained what had transpired that day. Mary offered appropriate consolation.

"You win some, you lose some, Mason," she told him. "If anything, this frees you up to make the seminar even more of what you dreamed it would be."

Mason chuckled. "What *did* I dream it would be?" At that moment, he couldn't put a word to what he'd been trying to accomplish. A protest, he guessed. But against whom? Simone Dugied was the obvious answer, but he knew he was railing against something much larger.

❖ ❖ ❖

In the days after the departure of the Donohue twins, the two girls who remained in the class, Sabine and Aurore, were subdued. Mason worked extra hard to rekindle their enthusiasm. So did Nathan/Claude, who alternately flirted with each of them.

Happily, Mason did not need to work at all to maintain Duncan's scholastic enthusiasm. The boy couldn't get enough of Gide. He would stay after class to pursue an idea or ask Mason's advice on what to read next.

"I just learned this," he told Mason one day after class, "but I'm sure you already knew it, that he married his cousin. A *woman*."

"Yes," Mason said. "And it turned out to be an unhappy marriage."

"I don't understand why—you know, if Gide was so unashamedly gay—why he did that."

"Oh, I suppose there are lots of explanations," Mason offered. "Social pressure mostly, don't you think?"

"My great uncle—my grandmother's brother?—he's gay, but when he was young, he married a woman. I guess *that* was social pressure." Mason tried not to look too interested. He'd never been comfortable when his students shared details about their families. "Then," Duncan continued, "when he was in his fifties, he finally came out. He's sixty-eight now. He's been with his boyfriend for eleven years."

"He has a boyfriend?" Mason asked. It was an idiotic question—Duncan had just told him so—but the question had popped out, and there it was, like an admission that he was curious for more.

"Yeah, his boyfriend is, like, twelve years younger. My grandmother won't even talk to them, but my mom loves them. We go see them every Christmas."

"They live around here?"

"No, Los Angeles. Mark—that's my great uncle's boyfriend—he's in television out there. Uncle Ralph's retired."

"So," Mason pursued, as delicately as possible, "are you"—a slight pause—"*out* to your great uncle?"

A smile blossomed on Duncan's face. "Totally. In fact, Uncle Mark and Uncle Ralph are the ones who coached me on how to come out to my parents."

"Duncan, that's *awesome*." Mason listened to himself using the vocabulary of his students' generation, something he'd avoided doing his entire teaching career. He wondered how much Duncan had figured out about his French teacher. Everyone knew that Monsieur Chastain was married, but he had never shied away from addressing issues of homosexuality when they came up in class. Sometimes, he'd even initiated those discussions. A sharp boy like Duncan ... maybe he'd already figured out the situation. Then again, what exactly *was* the situation? Mason had been trying to figure that out all his life.

❖ ❖ ❖

The surprises continued. By the end of October, Mary and Priscilla were seeing a lot of each other. Too much of each other, Mason thought. Tuesday nights had become their nights to have dinner together. And then there were long walks on Saturdays, Sunday afternoon trips to the Museum, the occasional afternoon coffee. He decided to ask Mary outright if they had resumed their affair.

"I mean, it would be okay with me if you were," he told Mary, "but I'd just like to know." The "okay" was tentative, a feeler he was casting out.

"Well, we aren't," Mary said. "Mason, Priscilla and I are both seventy-two. We each have a life that's working for us." She looked at him affectionately and smiled. "Working *very well*. And we're both quite aware of how unwise it would be to fall into a romance again."

"Sounds as if you've discussed this with her."

"I have. We have. We care deeply for each other, and *that*, Mason, is as far as we're going to take it."

"Levelheaded to the end," he said. There were days when he wished she weren't quite so sensible.

"To the end, Mason," she said.

In bed that night, Mason wondered what he would have done if Mary had told him that she and Priscilla were having a full-blown affair. What if she had said she wanted to leave him for her girlfriend?

He and Mary had chosen to make a life together, each for their own reasons, but ultimately, he guessed, because each of them had been a little lost, a little scared: Mary a young, soon-to-be divorced, lesbian mother; he a bookish, nerdy boy who couldn't imagine that there were guys out there like him, guys who might actually be attracted to him. *Chastity, isn't it about time you got banged in Boston?*

The first years of their marriage had been so happy: raising Ben together, building their respective careers, that quaint first apartment on Hereford Street. He was twenty-seven when he'd fallen into that first affair. He met Cameron, quite by accident, at a foreign-language bookstore in Harvard Square. They were both in the French section, Mason looking through a volume of Rimbaud; Cameron browsing through a copy of Cocteau's *Le Livre blanc*. Cameron began it.

"My guy," he said, holding up his copy of Cocteau, "thought he had to get from under the spell of your guy." He nodded toward Mason's Rimbaud.

"And why is that?" Mason asked. He'd just bought his first pair of granny glasses, which he liked, but suddenly he worried that he looked awfully strait-laced and academic.

"Cocteau thought Rimbaud's influence was more of an encumbrance than a boost to his own expression. I'm writing my senior thesis on Cocteau."

Mason, who had always been a bit intimidated by Harvard students, decided it was time to push back a little.

"Every author," he said in French, "thinks the writers who came before him are encumbrances."

Cameron followed suit in French: "It's surprising, though, that Cocteau, a homosexual, should not have found at least some encouragement in Rimbaud's example."

They'd ended up going out for coffee on Brattle Street, where they talked (in a strait-laced and academic way) about French literature. Every time Cameron raised the issue of homosexuality, Mason steered them back into safer waters. After an hour, he said he had to get home. "But you'll have to come to dinner some night. I suspect my wife and I can feed you better than they do at Harvard."

Cameron's face fell.

"Did I say something wrong?" Mason asked.

"No, it's just that I've been talking to you for an hour, all along assuming you were gay." He seemed utterly nonchalant, and utterly amused, at his mistake. "I was actually going to invite you to be my guest for dinner tonight at Adams House."

"Well ..." Mason said. He took off his granny glasses. "Well, I've never set foot in any of the august halls of Harvard. Do you suppose I could call my wife from your room?"

Their affair lasted four months. Mason was astounded by the intensity of Cameron's passion. Though he was only five years older than Cameron, he felt as if he belonged to another generation. What did this glorious boy find interesting in him, he kept fretting; when would

Cameron realize how much less vibrant, less attractive, less *gay* Mason was?

Once a week, they had dinner at Adams House, in a dark wood-paneled dining hall graced with huge Georgian windows and full-length oil portraits of important-looking Harvard men who looked down upon them with utter self-assurance. Cameron's friends would sometimes join them, mostly other young men but a few women as well. They were all smart, rapid-fire conversationalists, who seemed, for the most part, to be into the arts—drama, music, dance. Mason had no idea whether they knew what was going on between him and Cameron, though he suspected they did. It did not seem to make any difference to them. The casualness with which Cameron's friends accepted this prep school French teacher into their circle was another thing that astonished him.

Cameron came from a very rich, very broken family. He was accustomed to taking his spring vacation in exotic places, Europe mainly. When he found out that the dates of his spring vacation coincided with Mason's at the Academy, he invited Mason to join him in southern France. All expenses paid. That's when Mason got cold feet. His wife, his kid, he pleaded. He couldn't just leave them. Didn't Cameron understand the difficulties? *You only live once*, Cameron argued. Mason told him he was being impetuously romantic. In a flash, he decided the thing had gone too far. Ben was ten years old that year, in some ways a more mature kid than Cameron.

❖ ❖ ❖

In mid-October, the class finished the unit on Gide and commenced upon a study of French short stories. Since the students had already bought the anthology on Simone Dugied's list, Mason felt he had to assign it, and was happy to discover that at least three of the stories—the number he'd chosen for the unit—were totally acceptable to him. Aurore, Sabine, and Nathan/Claude enjoyed them, but now it was Duncan's turn to be subdued. He was clearly unhappy that they had moved on from Gide and kept bringing up far-fetched theories about what he called "queer undercurrents" in the stories they were reading.

The boy was hungry to keep pursuing the topic that had opened up when they'd read *The Notebooks of André Walter*.

One day, he stayed after class, trying to convince Mason of the homoeroticism—goodness, he had his gay lexicon down pat!—the homoeroticism in the stories by Maupassant and Camus that they were reading.

"You're reading too much into them," Mason told him. "You're projecting onto the text things that you *want* to see but that aren't there. These guys weren't gay, Dorian. There's nothing there to uncover."

"But what if, what if an author isn't aware of the homoerotic subtext that they've written into their story? I mean, come on, like *Billy Budd*? We just read that in English. Dude, it's a gay story whether Melville was gay or not."

"*Dude*," he playfully fired back, "Maupassant is not Melville."

"So what about Proust? Are we going to read him this year?"

Mason laughed. "I'm afraid not, Dorian." He was tempted to add, *Too difficult even for you*. Instead, he threw the boy a bone. "*Sois patient*. After this unit, we're going to do some poetry, including Rimbaud. I think Rimbaud's your man."

"Awesome!" Duncan yelped. "I've ready read a few of his poems. They're amazing."

Mason smiled. "He's one of my favorites. In fact, I've been working on translating some of his poems into English."

"Wow, really? Hey, if you'd ever like to show me ... I mean, I'm sure you have other people you ask to read your translations—like your wife, I suppose—but, I mean, I'd be honored to read your versions."

"Actually, poetry is not my wife's thing. She's a psychologist. Mystery novels are more her kind of literature." This was more information about his marital life than he'd ever let out to any of his students. "So, in fact, I haven't shared my translations with her, or anyone."

A brief, awkward silence fell between them.

"So which Rimbaud poems will we be reading?" Duncan asked. "I mean, in class."

Mason tilted his head from side to side. "I haven't decided yet."

"What about *A Season in Hell*?" The boy was not to be stopped.

Mason's eyes widened and he jerked his head back theatrically. "Jesus! Is that the Rimbaud you've been reading?" He had never sworn in front of a student before. "Nothing like starting with the most difficult."

It was Duncan's turn to laugh. "Comes from reading all those Wikipedia articles, right?"

❖ ❖ ❖

"The boy will not be stopped," Mason told Mary after he related the after-class conversation he'd had with Duncan. "He is so hungry for more. More Gide, more Rimbaud, more everything."

"Sounds like he has a healthy adolescent appetite for all that life has to offer," Mary said. "That's natural enough."

"Yes," Mason agreed. He went to the refrigerator, took out a half-opened bottle of wine, and held it out to Mary. She shook her head. He poured himself a glass and sat down at the kitchen table. "He seems curious about us, too. Keeps bringing you up. Today, he wanted to know if you were the person I showed my translations to."

"That's sweet."

"I don't know. I've never told a student so much about my personal life before."

"It makes you uncomfortable?"

"*Comme si, comme ça.* Maybe I *want* to tell him about my life."

"What do you want to tell him?"

"What do I want to tell him?" he echoed. "There's a phrase in a poem by Rimbaud—*Soyez fous!*—Be foolish, be crazy. That's what I'd tell him. *Sois fou, Dorian!*"

Their eyes met. "Any regrets, Mason?" she asked.

"About?" She didn't answer. "Well, it's a little late for regrets, no?"

Mary laughed. "That's not much of an answer."

He studied his glass of wine. "Let's put it this way, darling: I think I've been as *fou* as"—now it was his turn to laugh—"as it was ever reasonable for me to be."

❖ ❖ ❖

In November, Duncan approached Mason after class and told him about a reading that was going to take place the following Friday at the French Library in the Back Bay. A visiting professor from the West Coast would be debuting excerpts from a new Gide translation he was working on. Duncan could hardly contain himself, he was so excited at the prospect of attending the event. Mason said it might be an interesting outing for the whole class. And since the reading would take place at five o'clock, perhaps afterwards, they could all go out to a French restaurant for dinner.

It turned out that none of the other students could attend: Sabine had a tennis lesson on Friday evenings, Aurore said her mother—"my Chinese helicopter mom," she groused—wouldn't allow her to go into Boston at night. Nathan just said he couldn't make it, giving no particular reason. Mason wasn't sure about the propriety of a solo outing with Duncan, but Krikorian told him he saw no harm in it—even the restaurant afterwards sounded like fun, he said—as long as Duncan had his parents' permission and he didn't drink any wine at dinner.

"Technically, I don't need my parents' permission to go," Duncan said when Mason outlined the provisions. "I'm already eighteen."

"Okay, but you're not free to drink wine," Mason told him.

"Hey, Rimbaud wrote *The Drunken Boat* when he was sixteen," Duncan said.

"You are *not* Rimbaud!"

"And I'm not sixteen." Mason couldn't read the expression on Duncan's face: it looked almost like a lascivious leer. He hoped the boy was teasing.

A few days before the reading, Mason decided to invite Mary to join him and Duncan. The program would be in English, he assured her. "And I think you'll enjoy meeting my star student," he added.

There were other reasons, too. Krikorian's permission notwithstanding, Mason knew he'd feel more comfortable if he didn't go to the lecture—and out to dinner—with only Duncan in tow.

"Sure," Mary said, "but when you originally told me you were taking the class out on Friday, I made plans with Priscilla for us to do something together. Would it be alright with you if I asked her to join us?"

"The more the merrier," Mason said.

❖ ❖ ❖

The Professor's reading was prefaced by a short talk that he titled "*La Vie Hasardeuse*: Gide's Courageous Journey." He began his remarks with a quotation from *The Notebooks of André Walter*—"The young poet believes it is the Muse that inspires him when, in fact, it is puberty that leaves him aroused."

He looked up from his notes and smiled. The lecture room, which was being held in the French Library's parlor, was small enough that Mason could see the faces of several people in the audience. It appeared that half of them were gay men. Somehow, the word had gotten out that this lecture would be of particular interest to them.

Or maybe it was the Professor himself who was the big draw. He was young—Mason guessed in his early thirties—and strikingly handsome. Tall, svelte, athletically sexy. Cascading over his forehead was a plume of tousled hair, which, from time to time, he would nonchalantly comb back with the fingers of his right hand. Instead of a suit or even a sports jacket, he wore an open-collar shirt left untucked over a pair of close-fitting slacks. Despite the fact that it was now November, he was not wearing an undershirt. Maybe, Mason whispered to Mary, that's how they all dressed at California universities these days.

The Professor said that his research, and his translation work, were focused on the younger Gide—"that is," he clarified, "the Gide up through 1903, when he published *The Immoralist*." It was this Gide, he said, who, "already unabashedly, *courageously*, set up the case for his defense of homosexuality, which he magnificently articulated in *Corydon*."

Out of the corner of his eye, Mason saw that Duncan was fiercely scribbling away in his notebook.

After delivering his introduction, the Professor launched into his translation. "I'm going to read from Part II of *The Immoralist*," he announced. "In this scene, the narrator, Michel—he's a kind of "blind-folded scholar," Gide says—is giving one of his Thursday evening at-homes with his wife. He knows his friends come because they are attracted to his wife's charm and conversation. For himself, he is bored with the entire bourgeois social scene."

Mason saw Duncan close his notebook.

"In this first scene, Michel's friend Ménalque shows up at the Thursday evening at-home. Ménalque, whom Gide modeled after Oscar Wilde, lives a rather scandalous life. With a 'face like a pirate' and a drooping moustache, he disdains respectability and 'good society.' *J'aime la vie hasardeuse*, he tells Michel. 'I like the hazardous life, and I want it to demand of me, at every moment, all my courage, my wellbeing, my health.'"

The Professor began to read from his translation. Mason had last read *The Immoralist* during college. He'd forgotten just how outrageous a book it was. And how fresh, how, yes, courageous. He smiled to think what Mrs. Donohue might have said had he assigned his class excerpts from this novel.

He was sitting in the aisle seat of a row of gilded, faux-antique chairs. To his right were Duncan, then Mary, and last, farthest from the aisle, Priscilla. Mason wasn't sure how it happened that he had ended up seated next to Duncan. He guessed because Priscilla had taken her seat first, and Mary had slipped in next to her.

As the reading continued, Mason began to have the uncomfortable feeling that, whenever he glanced up from his paper, the Professor was making eye contact with him. He glanced over at Mary. All her attention was on the speaker.

The Professor wrapped up his first translation: "'What we feel is different in us from other people is precisely what is most exceptional.'" He looked up from his paper and, in a pretext of surveying the audience, once again made eye contact with ... *My God,* Mason said to himself. *He's cruising Duncan!*

In the second scene that the Professor read, Michel visits Ménalque at his Paris hotel, and their conversation continues. "Here," the Professor told them, "Gide lays out even more explicitly the life philosophy he'd been developing. Michel asks his friend why he doesn't write his memoirs." He looked down at his manuscript and began to read: "Regrets, remorse, repentances: these are earlier joys, backward-looking prospects ...."

As the Professor continued reading, Mason let his mind wander ... back to the eighth grade and Gordie's darkroom, back to his days at the

University of New Hampshire and his fraternity brothers, back to meeting Mary. As much as he loved Gide, he couldn't imagine ever behaving the way Gide had: consorting with Arab boys, cruising the boulevards and swimming pools, the restless traveling, the shabby pulling away from his marriage. No, he had chosen a very different path from that one. He'd made it work. Perhaps he'd even nailed it.

The reading ended, the audience applauded, and in turn, they were thanked and invited to ask questions. Duncan's hand shot up.

"What do you think Gide would say about the LGBTQIA+ movement today?"

Several people in the audience turned to see who had asked such a goofy, bold, adolescent question. Mason glanced over at Mary, who raised her eyes surreptitiously.

"It's an excellent question," the Professor said. He went on to give his opinion. Mason heard none of it. All he heard was the flirtatious ardor in the Professor's voice.

"Thank you," Duncan said when the Professor had finished.

"*Mon plaisir,*" said the Professor.

There were a few more questions, and then the audience was invited for champagne and hors d'oeuvres in the salon.

Mason glanced at his watch. It was six-fifteen. Their dinner reservation at the French restaurant was for seven. He looked at Mary and Priscilla.

"Shall we stay a few minutes?"

"Why not? But keep an eye on the boy," Mary said, nodding over to the refreshment table, where Duncan had already wandered. "We don't want him getting soused on free champagne."

They made their way to the table. Duncan had already been approached by a few of members of the audience—all men of a certain bent, Mason noticed—who seemed to want to talk to him. When one of them offered Duncan a glass of champagne, Mason was relieved to see that Duncan shook his head no.

The three adults—Mary, Priscilla, and Mason—stood around drinking champagne and talking. Priscilla said she had found the lecture fascinating. It had renewed her interest in reading *The Pastoral*

Symphony. Mason again told her not to waste her time, that she'd be better off reading *The Immoralist*.

Priscilla laughed. "I feel as if I should start with the 'less dangerous' one first." She made air quotes around "less dangerous."

"Why the hell do that!" Mason snapped. It startled him, the combative tone that had suddenly arisen in his voice. "Weren't you listening? *La vie hasardeuse:* living hazardously, living with all your courage." He realized he'd probably had too much champagne.

"There are many kinds of courage," Priscilla said.

"Yes, *many* kinds," he fired back, still unable to curb the disagreeable note in his voice. "And Gide's kind strikes me as exceptional."

"That's the word, isn't it?" Priscilla said. "'Exceptional.' Not everyone is capable of that degree of bravery"—she paused—"that degree of recklessness, I'd say." A frostiness had crept into her voice. "It's okay, you know, for people to live their lives, well, more *moderately* than your darling Gide did, yet still live with integrity."

"Yes, I'm quite aware of that, Priscilla." Now it was his turn to pause. And then to let out a snicker: "I guess I didn't realize I was coming here for *two* lectures." Mason felt himself getting red in the face. Here was his wife's former lover spouting to him his very own life's doctrine, and it was pissing him off. "Yes, my dear, not all of us can be exceptional, can we?"

Mary gently touched his arm.

"Mason, it's getting late for our reservation." She made brief eye contact with Priscilla. "I think we should probably get going."

Mason took in a deep breath. At the moment, going out to dinner, especially with Priscilla in tow, was the last thing he wanted. As for what he *did* want, he couldn't say. This whole outing was suddenly feeling like a bad idea. Or maybe he should have stuck to the original plan: just inviting Duncan and no one else. He looked toward the hors d'oeuvre table. Duncan had disappeared. Sourly, he told Mary and Priscilla he'd go find the boy.

As he made his way through the crowd, he caught snippets of conversations. *The Dorothy Bussy translation is still my favorite,* he overheard one man say. Another exclaimed, *What a cutie.*

Who? Mason wanted to ask. He felt his animosity rising again, now directed to these pretentious gay men and their tittering prurience. But where the hell was Duncan? He was about to return to Mary and Priscilla when he caught sight of the boy. He had gone back to the lecture room and was talking to the Professor, who was packing up his briefcase. As Mason approached them, Duncan saw him and called out.

"Monsieur Chastain!"

Introductions were made, handshakes exchanged, compliments from Mason received by the Professor. Mason hoped the men back in the salon were noticing the exclusive little trio he had formed with these two beautiful young men. *That's* what he wanted right now: someone to be jealous of him.

"Um, sir, would it be okay with you if I skipped the restaurant?" Duncan asked. "The Professor has asked me to join him and his husband for dinner on Beacon Hill."

Before Mason had a moment to recover from the surprise, Mary and Priscilla wandered over. More introductions. The Professor looked at Mary and Priscilla and smiled knowingly. *There's nothing to know,* Mason thought.

"It seems that Duncan won't be joining us for dinner," he told Mary.

"Oh!" She searched Mason's face, trying to gauge his stand.

"I was just about to tell him that it was okay with me." Mason turned to Duncan. "As long as you have a way to get home."

"Of course," Duncan said. "I'll take the T."

"And ..." Mason added. This was awkward, but he had to say it. "You will remember that the drinking age in Massachusetts is twenty-one."

The Professor laughed and patted Duncan on the shoulder. "We'll see to it that he remembers."

"We'll miss your company, Duncan," Mary said. She turned to Priscilla. "But I guess these three old folks can still have a good time, no?"

"Absolutely!" Priscilla said in her husky, mannish voice.

"Well, then," Mason said, "may everyone, each in his own way, have a lovely evening."

"*Bon soir.*"

"*Bon soir.*"

It was a mild evening. As they left the Library, Mason made sure to position himself between Mary and Priscilla. He took Mary's hand. In return, she squeezed his, her way—she had been doing it all their married life—of saying, *Yes, I'm right here.*

Mason wondered if he should have insisted on Duncan's staying with them. But, yes, the boy was eighteen, technically, *legally*, an adult and able to make his own decisions. He was choosing to be among those "singing fish on the blue tide." And why not, Mason thought. Why not?

The magnolia trees along Commonwealth Avenue were dropping their yellow leaves. The sidewalk was strewn with them. They made a crinkling sound under his feet. Years from now, Mason thought, Duncan would come to cherish this evening. To see it as something exceptional. And to feel, Mason hoped, a touch of gratitude for his old French teacher, who had, in his own modest way, allowed the boy a taste of the hazardous life.

Silently, he reached over and took Priscilla's hand. Startled, she looked over at him, smiled, and said nothing. They entered the restaurant, the three of them, hand in hand in hand.

The Portrait

The month I turned forty-three, I moved to the South End. It was the beginning of June, one of those radiant early summer days that make you fall in love with Boston all over again. When I went down to the curb to meet the moving truck, there was sunshine, blue sky, birds twittering like crazy. It felt like all of nature was smiling at me, applauding my decision to return to single—*available*—gay life.

My "marriage" to Lincoln had ended two months before, finalized by the selling of my half of our Roslindale house to him. I'd spent the spring looking for a new place, packing up my stuff (five times as much as when we'd moved in together), and sleeping in the guest bedroom, which, truth be told, had been my bedroom for most of the final years Lincoln and I were together. I was eager to extricate myself from our fourteen years of coupledom, from the domestic monotony of Roslindale, from everything that had made Lincoln so contentedly (and I so unhappily) entrenched there—endless house repairs, Saturday nights at home, boredom, boredom, boredom.

"Patrick, what do you *want*?" he'd pressed me during one of our sessions with the couple's counselor.

"Not *this!*" I fired back. My angry vehemence was, I knew, a way to avoid answering because I couldn't have said what I actually wanted. Not in any definitive way. The best I could say was that I wanted a life that felt more exciting than what we had, more stimulating, and a lot less cozy.

"More dangerous?" our counselor asked provocatively.

"Not exactly," I said. But, in fact, maybe yes. At least more dangerous than life with church-going, dahlia-growing, needle-pointing (yes! needle-pointing) Lincoln. Other couples we knew went clubbing on Saturdays, vacationed in Provincetown, shared guys they picked up on the beach or in the bars. We gave tasteful, fussy dinner parties for our tasteful, fussy friends. Perhaps it *was* danger that I craved, but by then, I had so little experience pinpointing what I wanted, saying what I wanted, that I was at a loss to find the words. "Just less comfortable," I managed to tell the counselor.

I'd deliberately chosen the South End as my new home. While not exactly New York's Chelsea or Chicago's Boy's Town, it was Boston's muted version of a gay ghetto. Leafy Victorian squares, fun cafés and bistros, lots of churches now mostly converted to condominiums, and brick everywhere—the sidewalks, the townhouses, the borders around the trees. Okay, so still the *Gemütlichkeit* we'd had in Roslindale but with the heady erotic buzz of male-on-male desire always in the streets.

Lincoln and I had briefly considered the South End as the place to start our life together, but he quickly put the kibosh on that idea. He wanted nothing to do with gay ghettoes. I was twenty-nine that year and totally in Lincoln's thrall. He was a few years older than I, was better looking, and, most impressive of all, knew his mind. He announced that he did not want to live in a neighborhood that "was all about one thing." By "one thing" he meant street cruising, gay bars, rainbow flags in shop windows, the Pride Parade running down Tremont Street. By "one thing," he meant sex.

So here I was, fourteen years and hundreds of dollars in couples counseling later, finally in the neighborhood that, I hoped, would resuscitate my gay life. Resuscitate may be the wrong word, because, in so many ways, I didn't think I'd yet had a gay life. I'd had an unofficial gay marriage and, before that, a few years of tepid gay exploration. But none of that felt like the real thing. Only when I walked into The Rainbow Café, a week after I moved in, did I sense that the real thing was finally about to get underway.

❖ ❖ ❖

Wanting to look my best that morning, I'd put on a pair of shorts and a short-sleeve jersey. The shorts, I realized, were bland and preppy (my standard look during the Lincoln years), but at least they showed off my calves. Penny loafers without socks completed the meet-the-gay-neighborhood ensemble. It was, alas, a fashion statement more appropriate for attending the Head of the Charles Regatta. As for the tonsorial details, my hair was cut short. It was a look that my barber decided would be the best option now that I was thinning on top.

The Rainbow Café was on a tree-shaded corner just off Union Park. It was only a few minutes' walk from my place, but I had to use the GPS on my mobile phone to find it. I didn't know the neighborhood yet, but I'd heard The Rainbow was a good place to go for coffee and pastry. I'd heard it was a good place to meet gay men.

When I arrived, there was a line extending out the door. True to The Rainbow's reputation, there were lots of gay men about, inside and out, mostly in twos and threes, waiting to be served. Most were chatting away in all the ways that Lincoln hated, those witty, supercilious, catty voices that gay men who pride themselves on being witty, supercilious and catty can affect. Most of them were in their twenties and thirties and better dressed. None of them paid me any attention. For a fleeting second, I panicked—*moving here at my age was a mistake!*—but then I reminded myself to "put on my Big Boy pants," as my friend Bruce had advised me when Lincoln and I split up.

"With the Saturday traffic, we're not gonna get to Crane's until noon," one of the guys in front of me said to his friends. Even with my limited knowledge of gay venues, I knew that Crane's Beach up in Ipswich was a favorite summer destination for gay men, a place Lincoln and I, you can be sure, had never gone.

The line moved up. The Crane's Beach boys put in their order, paid, and turned to leave.

"Enjoy the beach, guys," I said. It was my feeble attempt to make contact with the denizens of my new neighborhood. One of them smiled and thanked me; the other two said nothing. That didn't seem like such a bad batting average for my opening-day outing.

I ordered my coffee and—despite my recent resolve to avoid sweets—asked for a raspberry muffin. Comfort food.

Outside, all the tables were occupied, so, back inside, I grabbed the one table that was free. Three guys, much older than the Crane's Beach boys, were seated nearby. The oldest, a swarthy, bald guy with a salt-and-pepper goatee and black-frame glasses, was holding court. He reminded me a little of the "ethnic" types I used to see running pizza joints or selling groceries at mom-and-pop stores in Roslindale.

I will confess that I eavesdropped. His name was Harry, and he was reporting to his tablemates on his latest sexual escapade. From what I could piece together, it had taken place at a highway rest stop and featured quite a cast of characters, mostly truckers. One was "a hairy guy with a big belly," whom he had blown in the woods; another he'd done in the cab of the guy's truck. This was definitely not typical Saturday morning banter in the Roslindale Square café I used to go to when I was with Lincoln. I continued to listen, trying to look as inconspicuous as possible, half wallflower, half spy.

One of Harry's two tablemates was a slight, soft-spoken guy, about my age, nattily dressed in pressed slacks and a button-down shirt, who simpered and *Oh my*'d at his friend's stories. "Harry, you *didn't!*" he exclaimed after Harry wrapped up his tale with the claim that he'd blown two truckers at once.

"Well, back and forth," he corrected. "I mean, come on, I couldn't possibly get both those gorgeous dicks in my mouth at the same time!" He let out a jubilant cackle.

Harry's other tablemate was completely different from the simpering friend. He was a dirty-blond, butch type, a bit overweight in an outdoorsy, blue-collar kind of way. I guessed he was around my age, somewhere in his early forties. Though it was a warm morning, he was wearing a flannel shirt. He looked a little bored, as if he'd heard all of Harry's stories before.

Mr. Flannel Shirt caught me eavesdropping and smiled. I smiled back. Harry saw this exchange and looked over.

"Come join us," he invited.

I panicked. "Thanks, but I was just about to leave."

"Really?" Harry said, his eyes straying to my uneaten muffin and almost full cup of coffee. The cackle metamorphosed into a chortle. "Well, we're here every Saturday. Next time, park yourself at our table. We don't bite." He looked over at the soft-spoken one. "Well, not usually. Right, Vardan?"

Right on cue, Vardan tittered.

I got up and left, promising I'd see them next week. Outside, the temperature had already risen another five degrees.

❖ ❖ ❖

All week, I kept recalling Mr. Flannel Shirt's smile. During my years with Lincoln, as our sex life dwindled and finally stopped, I'd let myself flirt with guys—guys I'd see at the gym and the supermarket, and the occasional cute waiter. Most of these flirtations were tepid dalliances, more wishing than doing. Once, however, for a period of about three months, I carried on a secret and tortured affair with a nurse I met on an AIDS fundraising walk. But as gaga as I was for Noah, and he for me, I couldn't bring myself to tell Lincoln I wanted to end things. Not even in couples counseling could I say those words. By the time Lincoln and I broke up, Noah was long gone.

But now I was free to flirt to my heart's content. No more holding back, no more playing coy. No more sneaking around. That smile from Mr. Flannel Shirt—it felt like I was being acknowledged, given permission. All week, I kept thinking about how I would see him again when I returned to The Rainbow. And what I might say.

Sure enough, on the following Saturday, he was there, sitting with Harry and Vardan at the same table as the week before. Harry was the first to notice me when I walked in.

"Well, well!" he called out. "Our young man from the provinces. So, are you going to join us this week?"

"Thanks," I said, making a special point to smile at Mr. Flannel Shirt. (It was unbuttoned this time, worn loosely over a tight white tee.) When I returned to their table with my coffee—this time foregoing the muffin—Flannel Shirt looked at his watch and got up. "Off to climb more telephone poles," he said to Harry. He hoisted a heavy backpack over his shoulder and walked out the door. He had a lovely ass.

"I've got to be going, too," the mousy one declared. He held out his hand. "Hello, I'm Vardan."

"Patrick," I said. "Nice to meet you."

"Likewise, I'm sure," he said, his eyelashes fluttering. "Harry, I'll see you later."

"Watch you don't grope any mannequins," Harry chortled. When Vardan left, Harry turned to me. "He's a window dresser at Macy's."

"And the other guy?" I asked, trying to sound as nonchalant as possible.

"Who, Jeff? He works for the phone company." A sly smile came over Harry's face. He'd seen right through me again. "Why? You interested in him?"

"No, just asking."

Harry laughed. "Sure you are! Well, you're out of luck. He's already got a boyfriend. A doctor, no less." He laughed again. "The butch, blue-collar dude who never went to college and the Harvard Medical School doctor. A match made in heaven, right?"

I'm an environmental rights lawyer; Lincoln is a dean at a junior college. That should have been a "match made in heaven." It wasn't.

"So, you're new here," Harry said.

Without giving too much away, I delivered a capsule summary of my recent history: the break-up, the move, the fact that I'd always wanted to live in the South End.

"Well, a good-looking guy like you is going to make lots of new friends here." Harry let out that cackle again. "Look at me. I'm eighty-two, and *I'm* still making"—he raised his eyebrows suggestively—"*friends.*"

"You're eighty-two! Wow, Harry, you look amazing." Addressing him by name was my way of telling him we could be friends if he wanted.

All of a sudden, he pulled up his shirt to reveal his abdomen. "Huh? What do you think?" he invited. Soft tufts of salt-and-pepper hair covered his belly, which he slapped twice. "Not bad for eighty-two, eh?" It was no washboard stomach, but it wasn't a mass of blubber either. He was remarkably fit. He slapped his stomach one more time. "Tuesday, I had three dates with guys I met on Silver Daddies. Ten o'clock in the morning, two in the afternoon, and seven at night. The concierge in my building congratulated me."

All I could do was laugh. The scene he was describing seemed both ludicrous and just what I'd imagined the South End was all about. I was definitely not in Rozzie Square anymore.

❖ ❖ ❖

Throughout the summer, I returned to The Rainbow Café every Saturday. Soon I was enrolled as the third courtier at Harry's Saturday morning table. He was never at a loss for another story about his "frolics," as he called them. Sometimes they took place at his favorite rest stop along Route 2. Other times, he met guys on Silver Daddies, hook ups that took place at his apartment, a ritzy, high-rise condominium in the Back Bay.

"And the concierge, he really knows what's going on?" I asked one morning.

"Of course!" Harry crowed. "They've seen everything. And not just from me. There's an old broad on the sixteenth floor whose nephew"— he made air quotes with his fingers—"*nephew* comes to visit her every Friday afternoon."

"Tell him," Vardan coaxed, "about the time ..."

Harry laughed. "Once, when one of my tricks came by, the concierge rang me up. 'Ah, Mr. Dukov,' he says, 'there's a Black gentleman here to see you.' Then he drops his voice and whispers, 'Looks like rough trade, Harry.' 'That's the one!' I said. 'Send him right up.'" Harry burst into another one of his cackles. Vardan looked at me, raised his eyes, and shook his head.

Some Saturdays, Harry told stories about his earlier days—his teens and twenties—when he would spend hours cruising the movie theaters in long-gone Scollay Square or pick up men in the long-gone Combat Zone bars. I was fascinated by his endless inventory of adventures. And taken aback. Had he never worried about venereal diseases; had he never thought about attacks and entrapment and blackmail?

And every Saturday, I was back at The Rainbow, ready to hear more. This modern-day Alexander the Great—it turned out Harry was of Macedonian extraction—kept rolling out his tales of conquest.

Harry's earliest story took place the year he was seventeen, when he worked in the periodical room at the Boston Public Library in Copley Square.

"The bathrooms were so cruisy back then," he told me, "and a lot more reliable than the football players I was blowing in the locker room at West Roxbury High." He took off his black-frame glasses and wiped them with a paper napkin.

"The periodical room looked out onto the courtyard," he continued, putting the glasses back on. I noticed a spot of something—it looked like dried paint—on one of the rims. "Whenever my boss—I thought he was such an old queen—whenever he would see a cute number crossing the courtyard, headed for the men's room, he'd say, 'Go get that one, Harry.'" Harry chuckled. "He was sort of my pimp. I loved that job."

But even the reliability of the library's restrooms was not enough for young Harry. He wanted a place where he could, as he put it in an uncharacteristically delicate mode, "entertain my partners at greater leisure."

"So," he continued, "I rented an apartment—really just a room—here in the South End. In what was then the Lebanese section. I furnished it with a folding canvas cot and not much else."

"You were *seventeen*?" I asked.

"By then I was eighteen," Harry clarified. "The landlord didn't care as long as I came up with the rent. I'd pick up guys and take them back to the flat, where we'd have a great time." He laughed. "It was a little uncomfortable because that canvas cot was so flimsy."

I thought back to when I was eighteen, how I'd mooned after boys but would never have done anything as brazen as cruised a men's room, let alone rented my own apartment for sex trysts.

"I don't think I paid more than forty dollars a month for the place," Harry continued. "But that only lasted a few months. Then I met a guy on Beacon Hill and he started inviting me to his fancy Sunday evening parties. *Soirées*, he called them." Harry put a finger to his lips, playfully mocking the effeminacy of a word like soirée.

"Adolphe was a Russian dance instructor who claimed to be a deposed Romanov count," Harry continued. "His parties were these piss-elegant affairs: gentlemen of a certain age and lots of pretty boys. Aspiring ballet dancers." He raised his eyebrows. "There would be canapés and champagne and someone playing cocktail tunes on the piano. Guys would pair off into one or another of the count's bedrooms. I may not have been an aspiring ballet dancer, but I was really cute back then and very popular."

Harry's most infamous story concerned a far less classy affair, an orgy he was invited to in Bay Village when he was nineteen. It was not, he made it a point to emphasize, his first group sex party. "I was giving this hunky sailor a blow job when the cops raided the place. A couple of guys jumped out a window, but the rest of us were hauled off to the police station. My father had to come and bail me out."

He was a freshman that year at Massachusetts College of Art, he told me. His arrest on morals charges might well have ended his college career, but his father, who was a tailor and used to make suits for one of the college's deans, somehow finagled things so that Harry was allowed to stay.

"It was bad enough, my father thought, that I'd chosen to go to art school. He wasn't going to have it be known that I was kicked out because I'd been caught blowing some sailor. But he told me I could not major in fashion design, which is what I'd been aiming for. He didn't want me hobnobbing with those fairies who made dresses. So I switched to painting." He cackled again. "Guess my father thought painting was more manly. Turned out to be one of the best decisions of my life. Life drawing classes, especially when we had male models ..." The chortle came back. "I must have gone to bed with half of those models. The male ones anyway."

"Harry, you are irrepressible!"

"I don't know what the fuck that means, but thank you, I guess."

After Mass Art, Harry embarked on a long career as a medical illustrator. It wasn't particularly interesting work, he told me, but it provided a good income and left him with plenty of free time to do his own artwork on the side. His passion was portraiture. By the time he was in his thirties, he was doing quite well for himself. He would only paint men and only if his subjects posed for him in the nude, even if they just wanted a bust portrait.

"The nude body," he told me one rainy-slushy Sunday morning in January, "the way a man *thinks* about his nude body—it's written all over his face."

It was just the two of us that morning. On Sundays, Vardan went to see his mother; Jeff and his doctor boyfriend slept in. Often, I learned, with a third guy they'd picked up on Saturday night.

"If I can't see the whole body," Harry went on, "then I can't get the face right. I have to see how my sitter *feels* about his entire body. Get them to take their clothes off, and you see who they really are. Sometimes, the prettiest guys just hate their bodies. The discomfort, the shame, it's written all over the face."

"And do you show that?" I asked. "The shame?"

"Well, I don't do vanity portraits, if that's what you're asking. I'm all about telling the truth, Patrick."

My parents were both French Canadian. The pale, washed-out look of Nova Scotia is written all over my face. I have one of those noses that you will never see in Abercrombie ads or on the porno sites. My eyes are an indistinct shade of hazel; my lips are thin. Even now, you can still tell I suffered from bad acne as a teenager. The first crow's feet are appearing at the corners of my eyes. If Harry ever painted my portrait, I thought, he wouldn't have to get me naked to see the self-consciousness—and yes, maybe even shame—written all over my face.

"I imagine," I said, "that lots of guys turn you down when they learn your precondition about posing naked."

Another chortle exploded from Harry's mouth. "Not as many as you'd think." I gave him a puzzled look. "Don't you see? They're looking to *me* to love their bodies. They want me to show them that they have nothing to be ashamed of."

"And do you?"

"I do my best," he said. "I do my best." He paused. "Why? Are you interested in having your portrait painted?"

"Um, I think not, Harry. I'm going to pass on that."

"Oh, you 'think not,' eh? You're 'going to pass'?" He laughed again. A few crumbs, which were stuck in his goatee, bounced up and down.

❖ ❖ ❖

It wasn't until February that I felt relaxed enough with Harry to accept an invitation to visit his studio. It was in an old factory building in Egleston Square in Roxbury. He took pride in telling me that he would never deign to have a studio in the "fancy-schmancy" artists' district in the South End. Roxbury was fine with him, he said. I had the feeling he was illegally occupying the space, another mischievous, risky act in a life of mischievous, risky acts.

It was a freezing afternoon when I met him outside the building. A few days before, we'd had some snow. It was now shoveled up along the curbs in dirty gray mounds. In the eight months that I'd been living in the city, my life had started to feel like those miserable piles of snow—all the brightness and brio of those first days on my own had given way to something that felt more like slush. I'd not had much luck in the dating department. A few coffee dates, a couple of hookups. Nothing had panned out. I told myself it was because I was so busy at work. There was a lot of construction going on in the city, and we had a mound of environmental impact cases to review.

Harry ushered me into the vestibule, which was lit by a single, naked bulb. We climbed up a flight of dark stairs to the second floor. My breath condensing, we made our way down a long, unheated corridor toward his studio. Even before he unlocked the door, I could smell the oil paint and turpentine.

Once inside, I had to revise the story I'd been telling myself about him. Harry was neither a dabbler nor a pornographer, but a surprisingly fine artist. Drawings and sketches covered the entirety of one wall. Several paintings rested against another wall. A large painting was prominently displayed on an easel. It was of a handsome middle-aged man. I didn't know much about painting, but I knew enough to know Harry's work was really good. His style was somewhere between realistic and expressionist. On our last trip to New York, Lincoln and I had gone to the Alice Neel show at the Metropolitan Museum. Harry's style was a little like hers—bold, bright, warts-and-all truthfulness—but with his own distinctive touch: sexier, you might say. And decidedly focused on men.

Next to the easel was a table crammed with paint tubes, rags, cans of brushes, and bottles of solvents. On another wall, Harry had pinned photos he had taken of nude men, preliminary studies, I assumed, for future paintings.

"Harry, this is ..."

"Eh?" he asked, an invitation for me to admire even more. "What do you think, kiddo?"

"Wow, I had no idea you were so good."

"Of course I'm good!" I had never seen him so radiantly pleased.

There was not a clothed body amid the scores of sketches, drawings, photos, and paintings in the studio. And while not every one of those bodies was an Apollo, I saw how Harry had unveiled the individuality, the sensuality, the *dignity* in each of these men who'd posed for him.

I was full of questions that afternoon. Did he only work on commission? Yes. Did he get a lot of commissions? More than he could handle. And what kinds of guys commissioned these works?

"Almost all my clients are gay." He smiled mischievously. "Well, there's the occasional 'straight' man, the one who tells me he wants to have his portrait done for his girlfriend." He laughed. "Yeah, right!"

"So they're not really straight?"

"Well, they sure don't mind posing in the nude."

"And do you ... you know, I mean, like, fool around with them?"

"Patrick, I have *never* fooled around with any of the guys who pose for me, gay or straight."

"Seriously?"

"It wouldn't be professional. Business is business, and play is play. That's what Silver Daddies is for."

My questions mounted. How much did he charge for a portrait?

"Depends."

"On what?"

"Size, length of the sitting." He let out another cackle. "Doesn't it always depend on size and length?"

I turned the conversation back to art. "How much for a drawing in pencil?"

Harry quoted a figure that seemed reasonable. "For you, I'd do it for less."

Right then and there, I was not ready to make a commitment. But a few weeks after my initial visit to his studio—it was now mid-March—I gave Harry the go-ahead. It felt a little like telling a surgeon he could operate on me.

"Full-length. And you don't have to give me the discount," I added. "I'm happy to pay your going rate." I wanted to be clear, even though I knew I didn't have to be, that this was to be another of his professional arrangements. No favors, no goodies in return.

❖ ❖ ❖

Two days later, I showed up for our first session. It was a mild, early spring day. I'd put on a pair of jeans, a tee shirt, and my old Holy Cross varsity jacket. It was over twenty years old, but still fit and had the comfortable feel of a well-worn piece of clothing. Harry took one look at me, shook his head, and chuckled.

"What?" I asked.

"The jacket," he said. "You trying for the college-boy look? Is that what you want the portrait to convey?"

"Well," I teased back, "considering it's going to be a nude, I don't see how that'll be possible, right?"

Harry smiled. "Like I told you, out of your clothes, we'll see who the real you is. There's the screen." He motioned to a three-panel room divider. "Go get undressed, Mr. College Boy."

When I came from behind the screen, I hoped Harry would take note of the good shape I was in. He gave me an up-and-down gander.

"Is your dick that small because the room is cold, or aren't you glad to see me?"

"Like I always tell you, Harry, you're incorrigible."

"Fuck you very much. Look, just sit there," he said, directing me to a high-top stool. "And take a pose you think you'd like."

"I have no idea. Isn't that your business?"

Harry shook his head incredulously. "You want a full-length portrait, but you don't know how you want to look? Okay, how about with your feet up on the rungs, legs spread open a bit. That's it. Nice."

He moved behind his easel, on which he had already set up a large sheet of drawing paper, pushed the black-frame glasses further up his nose, and began to study me, directing me to twist my torso a bit.

"And take your hands away from your dick!" he yelled. "If we're going to do a nude, we're going to do a *nude*. Cross your arms over your chest. That's it. Now relax. And try not to move."

As Harry sketched, he started asking me questions. How was I enjoying living in the South End?

"It's good," I told him. *Good* seemed mild enough so as not to be a flat-out lie.

"Lots of straights moving in," he noted, "but I'm sure you've managed to find plenty of hot men."

"Well, not *plenty*."

"What does that mean, 'not plenty'?" he challenged. "Patrick, what the hell are you waiting for?"

"I guess I just need more time."

"My God, at your age—how old are you anyway?"

"Forty-three."

"At your age ..." He shook his head in astonishment. "I was such a whore."

"I think you were a whore long before my age," I joked.

Harry cackled. "That's true!" he said. "That's so true!"

He resumed drawing. In the silence that followed, I thought about how far away from being a whore I had always been. Altar boy, Eagle Scout, Catholic college, Catholic law school. I know that not every guy who grew up Catholic ended up as timid about sex as I was—far from it—but there it was. The previous week during coffee at the Rainbow Café, Jeff—Mr. Flannel Shirt—had told us about how he and his doctor boyfriend had arranged a three-way with someone. *But the guy turned out to be way too vanilla for us,* Jeff reported. *Vanilla,* I thought. I was relieved that I'd never given Jeff an opportunity to see just how vanilla I was.

"Chin up, just a bit," Harry directed.

"So exactly how young were you when you first started having sex?" I asked.

"Thirteen."

I was glad that I had to hold my pose. Otherwise, I might have jumped out of the stool.

"I seduced an older cousin," Harry continued. "He was a soldier, just back from Korea. One day, we were alone at his house and I asked him to put his uniform on for me. He said sure and began to take off his civilian clothes. I saw his dick underneath his boxer shorts, and that was the end of the uniform change."

"Harry, you've been a practicing homosexual since you were *thirteen*?"

"I have *never* been a 'practicing homosexual,' Patrick. I've always been very good at it! Right from the start."

I couldn't help laughing, and apologized for shaking so much.

"But really, what's so funny?" he asked. "I love sex, Patrick. That animal energy, that ..." He held out both his hands, gripping the pencil with his right, clenching his left. "That hunger, that intensity, that primal ..." He stopped again and suddenly shot me a look that I can only describe as one of concern. "You never had that with Lincoln?"

"Not like what you're describing. I don't know, maybe I threw all my passion into my work."

"You like being a lawyer?"

I told him I loved my work. But why environmental law, Harry wanted to know.

"I love nature, Harry, ever since I was a kid. There's something so ..." Now it was my turn to struggle for the right word. "So majestic, so spiritual about nature."

I told him I considered it my solemn duty to do whatever I could to protect the natural world from the depredations of polluters, developers, climate-change deniers.

"Solemn duty," Harry echoed. "Patrick, you *are* a serious one, aren't you?"

"I had Jesuits for teachers."

"You know what Macedonians say about Jesuits?" he asked.

"No."

"You don't want to know."

"In high school," I told Harry, "the guys nicknamed me St. Patrick because of how I never got into any trouble. Everyone assumed that I'd go into the priesthood."

"Why didn't you?" he asked.

"I think I just had that feeling that it would have been a disastrous decision."

"It would have!" Harry affirmed. "You know that, right?"

"Of course," I said. "I'm quite happy being a gay man." I did not sound fully convinced, even to myself.

Harry put down his pencil. "Come on, let's take a break."

I looked around for a robe—wasn't there supposed to be a robe? Harry took no note of this, whether deliberately or not, I can't say.

"Can I take a look?" I asked, standing there naked, not knowing what to do with my hands.

"No!" he barked. "I don't want to be influenced by your opinion." He paused to survey what he'd drawn so far. I saw him frown. "Besides, I'm having trouble with it." He studied the portrait again. "But with a little work, it's going to rival the nudes on the Sistine Chapel ceiling."

"I doubt that," I told him. "In any event, it's chillier in here than in the Sistine Chapel. Can I put something on?"

"What? You need a fig leaf?" He laughed. "There's a robe here somewhere. Over there"—he motioned to a corner of the studio—"right where my last model left it."

I was a bit squeamish about putting on a used terry cloth robe, one that had been discarded on Harry's unswept floor. But as soon as I did, I felt a shiver of titillation. This soft, comfy fabric that had touched another male body—there didn't seem to be anything about Harry's studio that didn't give off the smack of hyper-sexuality. During my years as a swimmer, I'd often been tempted to steal guys' Speedos or underpants from out of their lockers—to imagine the illicit touch of those garments against my skin when I snuck them home in my gym bag. But, good Catholic boy that I was, I never did anything like that.

"So, how old were *you* when you first had sex?" Harry asked, lighting up a cigarette.

"Twenty-two."

"And was it good? I want details."

"Actually ..."

"Actually what?" he pounced. I heard a twinge of panic in his voice, as if he were steeling himself for some sort of feeble, pathetic reveal. Which I guess it was.

It happened during the summer between college and law school, I told him. I'd gotten a job waiting tables in Wellfleet on Cape Cod. Two towns farther up, at the tip of the Cape, was Provincetown, which I'd only vaguely heard about. Halfway through the summer, on my day off, I'd hitched a ride there, thinking I'd poke around.

"'Poke around.'" Harry chuckled and took another drag on his cigarette.

"I certainly hadn't intended to get into anything sexual," I said.

"Of course not."

"I got a ride almost right away. His name was James. He was a few years older than I and had a job playing cocktail piano all summer at a club on the waterfront. He later told me that when he saw me hitching, he immediately pegged me for gay."

"Don't know why," Harry joked.

"When we got to P'town, he invited me to come to the beach with him. I told him I hadn't brought a bathing suit, and he told me it would not be a problem. By then, I should have figured out what was going on. Anyway, we get to the beach. And we keep walking and walking, even though there were lots of places we could have parked ourselves."

"He took you to the gay section," Harry said.

I nodded. "It was all guys, and they were all naked. I'd never seen anything like that before."

"And?" Harry prompted.

"Oh, my God, I was so nervous I didn't even take off my shorts."

"Jesus, Patrick, what did those Jesuits do to you?"

"I know. Pretty pathetic, right?"

"So, get to the good part. When did you and James do it?"

"Well, after a while, I told him I was hungry, and could we go get something to eat? I wasn't really hungry, but I wanted to get off the beach. We drove back into town and James suggested we go to his place. He said he had some leftover pizza. By that point, I knew something was going happen. And I decided I was okay with that."

"Bravo!" Harry cheered.

"Well, not so bravo. We got there, but I couldn't go through with it."

"Couldn't go through with what? Details, Patrick, *details*." Harry threw his cigarette butt on the floor, stomped on it, and lit up another.

"James wanted me to blow him, but I was shivering like a leaf. It was all just too overwhelming, I guess. He ended up jerking himself off."

"And that's it?"

"I'm afraid so. I spent the rest of the day browsing in a used book shop. You know, Harry, sometimes I think I'm still browsing in used book shops."

Harry stubbed out his cigarette. "Patrick, you know what Auntie Mame said?"

I smiled at him. "Why do you think I like hanging out with you, Harry? I love watching you at the banquet table."

"It's not about *watching*, Patrick!"

"I know, I know," I said.

❖ ❖ ❖

During my first semester in law school, with the memory of James burning in my mind, I went to my first gay dance. I wanted so badly to meet a guy, *connect* with him, get the whole gay hunt thing over with. I wanted to skip right to the settle-down part. I went home with a guy that night and fell in love with him. He must have sensed that, because I never heard from him again.

Later, I started going to gay bars, picking up guys. And falling in love, again and again. I wasn't experienced in the repertoire of sex play. I would have bristled at the notion that what I was doing was "playing." I wanted it to mean more than that. As Saint Augustine said, I was in love with loving. With *falling* in love.

Then I met my friend Bruce—Put-your-Big-Boy-pants-on Bruce— the summer we were reviewing for the bar exam. He was lighthearted and flirtatious—a guy with an easy, almost ironic attitude toward sex. I was immediately attracted to him, but he had a boyfriend. Still, we became friends. It was Bruce who introduced me to Lincoln. There are times when I think that I decided to date Lincoln only because I wanted to please Bruce.

The first time we went to bed, Lincoln went down on me. After years of masturbation, I knew exactly what I liked, what would arouse me. *No, I wanted to tell him, not like that.* But I couldn't cough up the words. That would have meant describing things that I couldn't bring myself to articulate. To use words, to actually name those actions—it seemed vulgar, obscene, pornographic. It took him forever to bring me off.

"And that's pretty much how our sex life continued," I told Harry. It was my second posing session with him. Not even with the couples' counselor did I feel as comfortable as I did with Harry, revealing the sorry details of my sexual life. Not even Bruce knew most of this.

"Every time Lincoln and I had sex," I told Harry, "I became tongue-tied. The best I could do was wriggle a bit, indicate with my body what was going right, what was not. To direct him with words felt so unromantic. Wasn't it all supposed to happen magically?"

Harry chuckled. "Magic, huh? Patrick, the last time magic entered into sex was when the Virgin Mary got pregnant. *That* was magic. Baby, sex is messy and sweaty and earthy. It's carnal, Patrick. And, yes, vulgar. You need to find someone who will help you unleash your inner pig."

"I'm not sure I have an inner pig, Harry."

"*Everyone* has an inner pig." I shook my head *no*. "So instead, you put up with milquetoast sex for twelve years?" Harry challenged.

"Worse than milquetoast. By our second year, we were hardly having sex at all. Just dinner parties for our friends."

"My God, he turned you into a lesbian!"

"Harry, that is so politically incorrect."

"Okay, Saint Patrick, I stand corrected. He turned you into an *old* lesbian."

"Come on, Harry, give me a little credit. I did finally get out."

"And what have you got to show for it?" he snapped. He sounded genuinely impatient with me, as if I were a college student who'd taken a gap year and done nothing with it.

"Not much," I admitted. The plaintiveness in my voice sounded pathetic.

Harry took off his black-frame glasses and wearily rubbed a hand over his eyes. He stood back and studied the drawing. "This is shit," he pronounced. Tearing the drawing off the easel, he crumpled it up and tossed it away. "We'll try again next week."

❖ ❖ ❖

All that week, I wondered if I should cancel. I could tell Harry I didn't think things were working out. *It's my fault*, I would assure him. *I think I'm holding back.* I would insist on paying for the portrait no matter what. But the days went by and I didn't call him, and then it was time to show up again, and I did. Which is, come to think of it, pretty much the way I conducted those fourteen years with Lincoln: showing up but not much else.

When I emerged from behind the changing screen and took my place on the stool, I noticed that Harry had moved his paint table next to his easel. On it was a box of colored chalk.

"Oil sticks," he told me. "I think working with a pencil was inhibiting me. I want to try this out instead, see what happens." He looked at me hard. "Don't worry. No extra charge for color."

He immediately set to work, attacking the new drawing with intensity and relish. For the longest time, neither of us spoke. After a while, trying not to move my head, I let my eyes wander around the studio. Naked men everywhere. This time, I was struck by the diversity—old and young, buff and flabby, hairy and smooth, Black, white, Asian, big dicks and little, cut and uncut. No matter who they were or what kind of body they had, Harry had revealed the unique beauty in each of these guys. No, not the beauty exactly, but the *worthiness* of each of these bodies, each of these faces, their right to exist proudly, unabashedly in the world.

"Yes, this is better," he said, pausing a moment to examine the oil stick in his hand. "Much better. Now we're getting somewhere."

"You know, I was close to canceling our session today," I confessed.

"Because?"

"I think I felt I was wasting your time. I mean, you seemed so disappointed in what was coming out. I don't think I was giving you what you were looking for."

For a minute or so, Harry said nothing, just kept working away. He would make a mark with the oil stick, pass the stick into his left hand, select another color from the box, make a mark, then transfer that stick to his left hand as well. Sometimes, he'd go to the box for another color; sometimes, he'd return to the sticks he was already holding. His movements were rapid, deft, agile, intuitive. At last, he broke the silence.

"*Anything* you give me is what I'm looking for. As long as it's *you*, Patrick, and not some idea of who you think you should be."

"Is that what I was doing?"

Again, he didn't answer. Instead, he continued to work, studying me for a second, then selecting a color, attacking the drawing with the oil stick, looking at me again, selecting another color. I decided to turn the conversation in another direction, one that might get him talking.

"So that large portrait over there, the one on the easel."

"What about it?" He considered the box of oil sticks again, selected one, and made another mark.

"Is it finished?"

"As finished as it will ever be."

"The guy didn't want it?"

Harry tossed the four or five oil sticks he was holding back into the box and made eye contact with me.

"The guy is dead."

I said something polite and innocuous to the effect that I was sorry to hear it.

"That's Walter."

"Walter?"

"He was my lover. We were together for thirty-nine years."

No one—not Jeff, not Vardan, certainly not Harry—had ever mentioned that he had had a lover.

"Harry," I began, but he interrupted me.

"He died fifteen years ago," Harry said. "Lou Gehrig's disease."

"Harry, I'm so sorry."

"Stop fidgeting!" he commanded, picking up another oil stick. "I've got something good going on here."

For the next hour, Harry continued to draw. Every now and then, he would volunteer a little more information about Walter: how they'd met when Harry was twenty-eight and Walter thirty-two. "At a bar called Sporter's," he said. "You wouldn't know it; you're too young." The night they met, Walter took Harry back to his place. "And that was it. Thirty-nine years."

He told me that Walter had been the vice-president of a bank. It was Walter's salary that made it possible for them to buy their place in the Back Bay. Walter had been the domestic one: four nights a week he would cook dinner. On weekends, they went out. Harry chuckled. "And we graduated from Sporter's to the Napoleon Club. You don't know that place either, but it was the swanky bar in town. We'd spend hours around the cocktail piano belting them out. Walter knew all the old songs."

"Thirty-nine years," I said. "That's a milestone I'll never reach."

"Not at the rate you're going," Harry affirmed. "Hold still!" He was drawing like crazy now.

"So ..." I didn't know how to put this delicately. "Did you ... I mean, were you, you know, gallivanting about all those years you were with Walter?"

Harry looked up from the easel. "Gallivanting! Oh, Patrick, you are a word queen, aren't you?" He went back to work. I waited, but the answer to my question didn't seem to be forthcoming.

"So did you?" I pressed. "Fool around when you were with Walter?"

Harry looked up again. "Of course! You think one guy would ever be enough for me? But let me tell you: there was not one single night in all the years we were together when I ever woke up in the morning with anyone else in my bed."

I wanted him to elaborate more. How had he and Walter struck that balance between Harry's adventures outside the marriage and their commitment to each other? The thought occurred to me that I might have asked for the same from Lincoln, but I couldn't imagine ever bringing myself to have broached a subject like that with him.

Harry went back to work. The concentration he brought to his drawing was intense. Finally, he stood back, studied what was in front of him, and tossed his crayons into the box.

"Done," he announced.

"Really?"

"Want to take a look?"

"Of course."

I was so eager to see what he'd done that I didn't even bother to put on the robe. As I moved toward the easel, Harry stepped away.

What I saw jolted me. Revolted me, in fact. The colors were bright—garish—and did not conform at all to those pale, Nova Scotia flesh tones in my body. They weren't even flesh tones. Green, purple, yellow, fire-engine red. He'd gone whole hog with his box of oil sticks. *Hideous*, I thought.

"So?" he prompted again.

"I don't know, Harry. It's ... it's a little wild."

"Oh, 'a little wild,' huh?"

He'd taken liberties with my body, too. My feet, my hands, my ears—he'd exaggerated the size of all my appendages, and had painted in an erection. The first thought that came to my mind was where the hell was I going to hang this thing. I let out a nervous little laugh. "So, this is how you see me?"

"Get used to it, Patrick. This is how you *are*."

I laughed nervously again. "I don't know, Harry. It sure isn't how I ..."

Suddenly, he grabbed an oil stick from the box and streaked it across my chest. When I looked down, an obscene red slash cut across my body. "What the hell, Harry!" But he lunged at me again, this time attacking my belly. "Quit it!" I yelled. I turned away and made for the robe, which was lying on the floor a few yards away. Harry slashed at my ass. I whipped around. "What the fuck are you doing!"

A mad wildness lit up his eyes.

"You know what the fuck I'm doing. And you love it, don't you?" he taunted.

"No, I do not love it!" I bent down to pick up the robe, but Harry stamped hard on it. Standing there, naked and streaked in red slashes, I stared him down. "Harry, I don't know what you think you're up to, but it's not funny."

"Well then, what *is* funny, Patrick? Huh? Tell me that. What'll put a tickle into that prissy, uptight body of yours? Maybe I should take you down to the Fens, just like this—butt naked—turn you loose in the reeds? Our environmental lawyer communing with nature. Would that do it for you? Is that the fantasy you haven't been able to speak?"

"No!" I shouted.

"A dungeon, then? Is that your secret? Chains, flails, paddles? Or maybe you want to get pissed on? Double fucked? Fisted? Is that what you weren't able to tell Lincoln?"

"Harry, you're being gross!"

"Gross? Really? I don't think so, Patrick. No, I'll tell you what's gross. Repression is gross."

"I am *not* repressed!"

"You tell me you have a 'solemn duty' to protect the environment. How about your *solemn duty* to love who you are?"

"This is not who I am!"

"Okay, fine, but then who are you, Patrick? Huh? Tell me. What exactly did you hope you'd learn coming here?"

"Not this!" I shrieked. "You once told me that you were all about telling the truth. You think this"—I nodded toward the easel—"you think this, this *atrocity* is the truth?"

We were only a few feet apart. I could smell his cigarette breath.

"Atrocity, eh?" He glared at me. "Go get the fuck dressed." He kicked the robe toward me. "We're done."

In angry silence, I picked up the robe, went behind the screen, and got into my clothes as quickly as I could. The oil stick marks rubbed off all over my tee shirt. It looked like I was bleeding. I didn't care. When I emerged from the screen, Harry was puttering around as if everything were fine, as if I wasn't even there. I felt bad about my outburst. Maybe I'd overreacted. I looked at him, trying to come up with something to say. He continued to ignore me.

I had never, not for a minute, ever thought of Harry as attractive. But just then, that old-man look I'd always dismissed—the bald head, the salt-and-pepper goatee, the paint-splattered glasses—he seemed, I don't know, weirdly magnificent to me, a fighter, an Alexander the Great, pushing the boundaries to the end. I was actually relieved to see that he hadn't torn up my portrait. It was still on his easel.

"Harry?"

He didn't answer, just kept cleaning up. Tomorrow was Sunday, the day when just he and I went to the Rainbow. I hoped by then we'd both have calmed down enough to talk about what had happened today.

"See you tomorrow?"

"I'll be there," was all he said.

I let myself out, walking the dark corridor to the staircase and down to the street. It was late afternoon, the sun just falling behind the buildings in Egleston Square, that time of day when the birds set up one final riot of chirping before nightfall.

Why do they do that, I wondered, that last burst of frenzied commotion at the end of the day? Are they settling themselves down for sleep? Bidding goodbye to the sun? Is it panic or elation that I hear in their manic, cheeping cries?

I could have taken the Orange Line home, but I decided to walk all the way down Washington Street, about two miles back into the South End. I was wearing my varsity jacket, but the air was mild enough that I unbuttoned it. My tee shirt was splattered with the oil stick marks. I reached underneath, rubbed my belly and chest, and pulled out my hand. It was smeared in red. I studied the greasy paint on my palm, brought it up to my nose, smelled it, then ran my hand all over my face, my nose, my lips. Around me, the air crackled with the sounds of ecstatic birds.

Even Dough Needs Time to Rise

At the end of his first day of high school, Matthew Zalenski, following his mother's instructions, took himself to his grandmother's house to start his homework. "*Od razu*," she told him. "No stops to buy candy or look at magazines in the drug store." She would pick him up after she got out of work. Dutifully, he told her yes.

As he walked to Babunia's, Matthew thought about what it had been like, the opening day. He'd been a little nervous, but everything had turned out fine. All his teachers were laymen and laywomen, not nuns like at Saint John Kanty School. And new subjects—algebra, biology, and Latin, already his favorite, where, in his first class, he learned *puella* and *agricola,* words he hadn't encountered before in the Latin of the Mass. New classmates, too, ones who hadn't been to parochial school with him. Matthew had wanted to linger after school and talk to them, but he knew not to disobey his mother. Disobedience was a sin, though he couldn't remember whether mortal or venial.

There wasn't much homework that first day, but there was a glass of milk and a slice of Babunia's homemade szarlotka. All these years later, he could still remember how happy he'd been: just turned fourteen, a high school student now, and ceremoniously presented—like the little prince his grandmother always said he was—with a plate on which she had carefully arranged a piece of that delicious, sugar-dusted apple pie. Her secret, Babunia used to tell him, was the pinch of *goździk,* clove, which she added to the recipe. "But only just a pinch," she emphasized. Like his mother, Matthew's grandmother had always exercised restraint in everything.

She set down his snack that afternoon, then said something that left him puzzled.

"*Uważaj, Mateuszu.*" He looked up at her, wondering what he was supposed to be careful about: not spilling the milk? not eating too fast?

Then came the punch line: "Even dough needs time to rise. You understand?"

Matthew understood Polish quite well—it was the language in which his mother and grandmother always spoke to him—but this business about the rising dough. Had the apple pie not turned out the way Babunia wanted? Or was she talking in parables, like Jesus, telling him something about this new life he was embarking upon: that success would not come as quickly as it had during his elementary years? Okay, he thought. He knew he needed to guard against too much self-confidence. Up through the eighth grade, the nuns had taught him that being too self-confident was a sin. Pride, a mortal sin. Matthew did not think of himself as prideful, though he knew that a few of his friends thought it odd—maybe even prideful—that he asked them to call him Matthew and not Matt.

"*Rozumiesz*?" his grandmother asked again. You understand? There was a look in her eyes that told him she would not explain further. It was a look that said, There are things I know, and that you will know someday, too, but a grandmother doesn't talk about them. Just remember, Matthew: Even dough needs time to rise. He nodded.

All through those September afternoons, Matthew went directly to his grandmother's after school, his bookbag slung over his shoulder. (He'd learned back in eighth grade not to clutch his books to his chest, the way the girls did.) He would sit down at her kitchen table and do his homework. Without any fuss. And every once in a while, accompanying his snack, she would lay down that mysterious admonition again. "Don't forget, even dough needs time to rise." And every time she said this, he promised he would heed her, though he had no idea what she was talking about.

His mother, who worked as a bookkeeper for a department store downtown, would pick him up at 5:30. He could just as easily have walked home on his own. Babunia lived only five houses away. But his mother insisted on their walking home together. Their side of Milwaukee wasn't particularly dangerous, but she wasn't taking any chances. Married at twenty-five, widowed at thirty-two when Matthew was six, she'd had enough loss in her life already, she told him. Matthew wondered if she would ever marry again. He guessed she wouldn't.

It wasn't until early November—his grandmother's kitchen was in semi-darkness that afternoon—that Matthew finally screwed up the courage to ask her what it meant exactly, dough needs time to rise. Exasperated, Babunia threw up her hands. "*Ojej!*" she exclaimed. "Matthew, *love*—girls, dating, all that foolishness—don't rush it. You have plenty of time. Concentrate on your studies." Now did he understand?

Yes, he said. He did not add that "all that foolishness" was not, in fact, anything he was interested in. Not like the other boys. Already, two months into their freshman year, they were showing a lot of "foolishness" toward the girls. They would walk them home from school, carrying their books, or take them to the drug store for sodas. Some of them were the same boys he had known back at Saint John Kanty, the ones who until then had hardly given a girl a second glance. Lo and behold, over the summer, these boys had mutated into unfathomable creatures. Whoever they were, Matthew knew he was not one of them. But what *was* he then? There was a word his grandmother had once used the time he'd asked her if she would teach him how to make a szarlotka and she had refused, telling him such things were not for normal boys, only for ... It was not a pretty word.

❖ ❖ ❖

"What was the word?" Bobby McMahon asked him. They were driving west from Boston along Route 2, headed for an apple orchard that Bobby had read about in the *Globe*. A trip to pick apples and a picnic lunch afterwards might be, Bobby had suggested, a nice way to get to know each other.

"In Polish it's *ciotą*," Matthew told him. "I don't know if it's the word that's still in use." He hoped he wasn't coming across as too pedantic. Did he sound like the retired reference librarian he was? "Mind you, my grandmother's been dead more than thirty years."

"What's it mean?" Bobby pressed.

"I guess the closest is something like 'faggot.' Like I said, it's not pretty."

Their outing to the apple orchard had gotten off to a late start. Bobby was supposed to have come by at ten-thirty, but at quarter to eleven he'd texted to say he was way behind schedule, and could Matthew chill for an hour. *No problem*, Matthew texted back. But it *was* a problem, because the cheeses he had packed for lunch had to be put back into the refrigerator along with the cold bottle of soda water that he'd wrapped in a kitchen towel. Two more text messages and an hour-and-a-half later, Bobby had finally shown up in a very expensive car—a Mercedes or a BMW, Matthew guessed (he was clueless about cars)—toting a backpack with the wine, his contribution to the picnic

The day was warm and October-blue, the foliage at its peak. Against the deep azure sky, the yellows, reds, and oranges of the trees along Route 2 blazed brilliantly. Matthew remembered autumns back in Wisconsin—a half century ago now. They were full of color, too, but ever since he'd moved to Boston for college, the colors of a New England autumn had always seemed more splendid.

"I wonder just how obvious it was that I was a little *ciotq* in the making," he continued, chuckling at the memory. "In high school, I used to go to the sock hops. They were agony. I tried to do everything I was supposed to do: ask girls to dance, make friendly conversation with them. But every time the DJ put on a slow number, I made sure to be somewhere else: the boy's room or in line to get a glass of punch. Anything to avoid that kind of intimacy. I'm amazed no one noticed how I never got all tight and clingy with a girl. How I never had a steady girlfriend."

Bobby laughed. "Oh, I'll bet some boy noticed." He flashed Matthew a suggestive smirk, which emphasized the surprisingly handsome wrinkles in his craggy Irish American face. "Come on, at least one cute boy was checking you out."

"Not in Milwaukee," Matthew countered. "Not in those days."

Bobby let out another raunchy laugh. "Oh, yes, Matt, even in Milwaukee! Even in *those* days!"

Matthew had already corrected Bobby twice about his name: Matthew, not Matt. He decided to let it go this time. He wondered if Bobby would ever get it right.

They'd met only a few weeks before at a sports bar in the South End—it was called Score! (ending in a suggestive exclamation mark)—where they'd both gone on the Sunday of Labor Day weekend for brunch.

Matthew didn't care about sports, and gay bars had never been his thing, but he'd woken up that morning feeling slightly panicked that another summer had gone by and nothing had changed. He was sixty-six. His last boyfriend, Joe, had died of a heart attack ten years ago. Since then, he'd spent each August reading and doing watercolor sketches at a cottage he rented on a lake in Maine. This summer had been no different. But with summer over and his friends away for the holiday (Richard and Julian to Provincetown, Paulie to Ogunquit), he had felt very alone. He'd stayed in bed that morning, reading *Memoirs of a Dutiful Daughter*—he was making his way through Simone de Beauvoir—until even the company of a good book gave him little pleasure. Around noon, he'd roused himself to go to brunch. The sports bar was air-conditioned; his apartment was not. That was the excuse he gave himself.

Score! was packed, and the host, a big bear of a guy, had asked if he wouldn't mind sharing a table. The table was occupied by Bobby and a friend. Matthew immediately thought he was out of his league. These two—one with rugged good looks and a thick crop of beautiful gray hair; the other, younger, more conventionally handsome—he figured they'd just ignore him, let him eat his food in peace. But after introductions, he was surprised when his two table companions engaged him in friendly conversation. He was quickly won over by the garrulous personality of the older one, who regaled him with stories about the gay softball team he played on.

He was relieved that he'd worn his tweed golf cap that day. It made him look younger and more jaunty, he thought. And hid the fact that he was balding. Happily, his three-times-a-week jogging regimen kept him in pretty good shape. In fact, he was trimmer than Bobby. His skin, too, was in better shape—not coarsened by too much sun and, he guessed, a bit too much alcohol. Still, Bobby had sex appeal. Matthew wondered if Bobby would consider *him* at all sexy. It turned out Bobby was sixty. It also turned out that the younger one was just a friend, nothing more.

Over eggs Benedict and bloody Marys, they talked. Besides sports, Bobby's other topic of conversation was city politics. He seemed to be quite tight with the Boston Democratic establishment. At the end of their meal, the friend put thirty dollars on the table and excused himself, saying he had to get going. Matthew wondered if he was deliberately giving him and Bobby a chance to get better acquainted.

During a second round of bloody Marys, which Bobby ordered without consulting him, the conversation moved to the matter of growing up Catholic, the Irish versus Polish variety. "No one's as strict as Irish Catholics," Bobby declared, and then he let out another of his loud, unbridled laughs. "Lotta good that did me!"

Matthew fancied that, under the right circumstances, he might be able to get something romantic going with Bobby, but during their conversation, Bobby made it clear—whether intentionally or not, Matthew couldn't tell—that he went for younger guys. Still, after brunch he handed Matthew his card—ROBERT ADAM McMAHON, Attorney at Law—and told him to stay in touch. Matthew had waited a week before calling.

"The point," he now told Bobby (taking his eye off the autumn foliage to check the speedometer, which was way past the speed limit), "the point I'm making is that the dough seemed to be rising fast that year for all the boys but me. I watched myself not being interested in girls, in *most* of the stuff the guys were into, and I felt so ... I don't know, so out of it. So unable to be a part of that world."

He considered quoting a sentence from de Beauvoir's memoirs—"I was an industrious pupil, a good little girl, and nothing more"—one that had stuck as soon as he'd read it that morning. But something held him back. Through the windshield, he could see a hawk idly hovering in the October air. This conversation seemed to be hovering, too, circling around and around, going nowhere. He tried again:

"I remember in Latin class one day, our teacher told us about the satyrs, you know, those half men and half goats, who—"

"Oh, I know all about the satyrs," Bobby chortled. "I've been called one on a few occasions."

"Mr. Ćmielowski—that was our Latin teacher—he loved to tell naughty stories about the Greeks and Romans. When he told us about the satyrs, all I could think of was my girl-crazy classmates." He shook his head in amusement. "The way they acted toward girls seemed that foreign to me. Whatever they were feeling, I just didn't feel those things. Not for girls anyway. Jeez, I was slow on the pick-up back then!"

Bobby laughed. "Was that Milwaukee slow, Polish Catholic slow, or just Matt Zalenski slow?"

Matthew laughed. It was becoming clear that Bobby, who had grown up in New Rochelle, had not been a slow-on-the-pick-up teenager.

"A bit of each, I guess." He shook his head again. "Oh, man, another thing I was naïve about: Mr. Ćmielowski. He must have been gay, but it never dawned on me. I mean, he never married, and he was always telling us these off-color stories about the ancients and their sex practices. Mind you, he never touched anyone or did anything like that."

Bobby exploded with a belly laugh. "*Mind you*? You've said that twice now! I haven't heard that expression since they made us read Charles Dickens back in high school."

Matthew had no idea that *mind you*, which he guessed he did use a lot, was old-fashioned.

"*Mind you*," Bobby said, twisting the phrase like a finger in the belly, "senior year in high school, I *did* fool around with one of my teachers."

"You're kidding, right?"

Bobby slowed down and turned off the highway onto a country road. "Not kidding."

"Like how 'fooled around'?"

"It was senior year." Bobby checked the GPS on his smart phone and swung the car down another road. He was still driving too fast. "There were only three of us in fourth-year Spanish. One Friday, our teacher organized a trip into Manhattan for us to see a Spanish-language flick. Only two of us kids went. After the film, the other student headed off to her grandmother's on the Upper West Side. So the teacher and I went out to dinner. I was eighteen. Back then, you could drink at age eighteen. And we ended up too tipsy to drive back to New Rochelle, or so Señor Moreno claimed, so he offered to pay for a hotel room. And, well"—Bobby burst out laughing—"I guess the dough rose early that year."

"Jesus! What did your parents say?"

"They weren't home that weekend. I think they'd gone to the Poconos. My dad loved the Poconos." Bobby turned to him and smiled that suggestive smile again. "I remember making sure Señor Moreno *knew* my parents weren't home."

"You did?"

"Of course! I mean, come on, Matt, I *wanted* him to seduce me. The guy was *hot* ... not even thirty, I think." He turned to Matthew and grinned. "Besides, this was—*mind you*—over forty years ago. Parents trusted teachers back then. When my folks got home, all they wanted to know was how was the movie and did it have subtitles."

❖ ❖ ❖

They arrived at the orchard. Bobby pulled in and parked the car. As he unbuckled his seatbelt, Matthew tried to picture Mr. Ćmielowski doing something like that. He remembered how Mr. Ćmielowski had always smelled of sandalwood aftershave lotion. The clean, but slightly exotic smell of repressed sexuality, he now guessed.

They got out of the car. Matthew took the picnic basket from the back seat. It had been his parents' picnic basket back when they were first married, one of the few keepsakes he still had from them. The lunch he'd packed—a French baguette, the bottle of soda water (imported), some plums, and three kinds of cheese, expensive cheese—was meant to be a little special, even though he knew this outing was not a date.

The air was fragrant with the aroma of apples warmed by the October sun. It reminded Matthew of the smell of his grandmother's apple szarlotka. It was turning out to be a day for recollecting the aromas of his youth: Mr. Ćmielowski's aftershave, the incense at St. John Kanty Church, his Babunia's pastry. The aromas of his innocence.

The orchard was spread over many acres. The trees nearest the cashier's booth had already been picked clean, but if they walked farther in, the attendant told them, they'd find plenty more. Bobby led the way, toting his backpack. Matthew had to hustle to keep up. The picnic basket was heavy.

"My grandmother loved apples," he called out to Bobby. "She used to reminisce about ... Hey, slow down." Bobby slackened his pace just a bit, but not enough for Matthew to catch up. "She used to reminisce about the varieties they had back in Poland, varieties she never could find in America. I still remember some of the names: Kosztela, Złota Reneta." Bobby was now several yards ahead of him. "Jeez, Bobby, what's the rush?"

Bobby stopped and turned around. There was a hint of impatience on his face. Back in Boston, Richard and Julian had invited Matthew to go shopping at Ikea that afternoon. Perhaps that's what he should have done—stuck to the familiar, the tried-and-true—but, no, he had decided to "break out of his comfort zone," something his other good friend—single, on-the-make Paulie—was always encouraging him to do.

"Sorry," Bobby said. "I guess I just like to keep moving." Whatever impatience he might have been feeling was already gone, replaced by his Irish American good cheer. "My grandfather used to pinch apples from the pushcarts in New York and then run like hell. It's in my genes, moving fast." He laughed.

Matthew caught up. Back when he was in his twenties, new to Boston, new to his finally-acknowledged gay self, befriending gay men had been so easy. It would just happen, without his having to work very hard at it. Not with every guy he met, but with the ones who eventually became his friends—first Julian, then Paulie, later Richard, who wasn't yet coupled with Julian—they had all just fallen in with each other, excited to have found kindred spirits. These days, it was a different story. Even though gay men were now a dime a dozen, making friends was harder now. The young ones didn't seem much interested in friendship, and the older ones were all coupled, busy, or depressed. This outing was a perfect example: it had taken them days to find a mutually free weekend afternoon, and another week to plan the thing: the orchard, the route they'd take, who'd bring what for the picnic lunch. Matthew was beginning to wonder if all the effort would prove worth it.

"How about this one?" Bobby asked, motioning toward a tree a few yards in front of them. "Looks good, no?"

"Sure," Matthew agreed.

Setting down his backpack, Bobby reached up and tore a piece of fruit from its branch. The force of his pulling knocked two other apples onto the ground. He picked another apple and held it out to Matthew.

Matthew accepted the fruit and took a bite. It was delicious. And suddenly, the riotous fecundity of nature, here at its peak—apples bending the boughs, apples rotting on the ground, their sweet, vinegary perfume stinging his nostrils—all this profligate fruitfulness left him extravagantly happy. Could he share these feelings with Bobby? He knew he could have with Joe. Dear Joe, gone ten years already, Joe had always listened to everything he'd had to say; had always had time for indulging any of Matthew's enthusiasms: his love for discovering out-of-the-way used book stores, his tales of growing up in Milwaukee, his yearly Polish-themed Christmas party. With Joe, it had always felt as if there would be time for everything, way into the future.

"I'm done," Bobby suddenly announced. His bag was heaped high with apples. A mess of leaves and twigs were sticking out of it, too. "Let's go eat. I'm starving."

Matthew looked down at his own bag. It was only half full. "Hold on a sec," he said. "Let me just get a few more."

"I'll go grab us a table," Bobby called out, already moving toward the picnic area.

Matthew gathered a few more apples, still not a bag full, and hustled after this guy who was feeling less and less like even a potential friend.

❖ ❖ ❖

It was late enough in the day that several of the picnic tables were free.

"Let's take this one," Bobby announced.

Matthew noticed that it was close to a table occupied by two guys who were also picnicking. They were obviously a couple, or at least on a date.

He set the picnic basket and his bag of apples down on the bench and began unpacking what he'd brought. First, a linen tablecloth. It was one his grandmother had embroidered, with a running border of farm girls in peasant costumes, staves in hand, herding a flock of geese. He spread the cloth out on the table.

"My grandmother made this," he said. Bobby did not respond. He was rummaging in his backpack, pulling out one bottle of wine and then another.

"Two?" Matthew asked.

Bobby still didn't respond. He was now frantically digging deeper into the bag looking for something else. "Fuck!" he said.

"What?"

"I forgot the corkscrew."

"Oh dear. That's a problem, isn't it?" But considering how fast Bobby drove, Matthew thought it wasn't such a bad idea if they had a non-alcoholic lunch. "I packed a bottle of cold seltzer water," he offered. "Lime."

Bobby shook his head. "Hey, I'm sorry. I was in way too much of a rush this morning. We shouldn't have tried to leave so early."

Matthew took out the water, unwrapped it—happily, it was still cold—and set it on the table cloth, then laid out the rest of picnic: the baguette, the plums, which he emptied into a ceramic bowl that he'd also packed, and the three cheeses. When he saw the plums, Bobby chortled.

"You brought *fruit*?"

Matthew felt himself blushing again. "I mean, I just thought ..."

"Hey, dude, I'm teasing," Bobby said.

From the basket, Matthew brought out plates for the cheeses, three cheese knives, and juice glasses. He poured them each a glass of the flavored seltzer water.

"Well, cheers."

Bobby clinked glasses, drank his down in one gulp, and then went for one of the cheeses. Matthew watched him cutting a large piece without first putting it on a plate. The knife sliced through the wedge of cheese and into the tablecloth. Inwardly, he grimaced, hoping his grandmother's heirloom had not been damaged, then deliberately made a show of unwrapping the other two cheeses, folding the paper to use again later, and arranging the wedges on plates. Just then, Bobby called his attention to the nearby picnic table.

"Hey, look. Those boys have a corkscrew."

Matthew glanced over at the table. One of the guys, a handsome, auburn-haired man wearing a shawl-collar sweater, was in his late forties or early fifties—definitely not a "boy." The other one was. In fact, he was practically a twink. Twenty-five max, Matthew thought. He was wearing sunglasses, flip flops, and raspberry-colored shorts that hugged a pair of firm, gym-toned buttocks. Even with his ass on a bench, the twink's tight butt was noticeable.

Bobby got up from the table and walked over to them.

"Hey, boys. Can we borrow your corkscrew?"

The twink immediately handed it over to Bobby with what seemed to Matthew an inordinately friendly smile. "Come join us," the twink said, taking off his sunglasses. "We've got some pretty great cheese here."

Bobby waved Matthew over to the table. Reluctantly, Matthew got up. It annoyed him that Bobby was about to change the direction of their afternoon. He walked over to the other table. Introductions went around. The twink was Jared; the older guy Dave.

"I'll bring our food over," Matthew said. Bobby did not offer to help.

Returning to their picnic table, Matthew grabbed one of the cheese plates and one of the two bottles of wine. When he returned to Dave and Jared's table, Bobby had already sat down, cozying up next to Jared and already singing the praises of Jared's "pretty great cheese." Dave held out his hands, offering to take Matthew's contributions.

"Thank you," Matthew said, handing over the wine and cheese.

"No problem," Dave said. He motioned for Matthew to join him. Matthew was only too happy to put a little distance between himself and the other two, who were already lost in what seemed like mutual fascination.

"You guys come here every year?" Dave asked him.

"No, neither of us has ever been here before," Matthew said. He hoped the "neither" would clarify that he and Bobby were not a couple.

"We haven't been here before either," Jared called from his end of the table. "Actually, Dave and I just met." He looked at Bobby and grinned. "Like last night."

Bobby gave him a thumbs-up.

Matthew glanced at Dave. During their half-second of eye contact, Dave raised his eyebrows. Matthew flashed him a quick, conspiratorial smile, then helped himself to a piece of Jared's much-touted cheese. It had no flavor whatsoever.

For the next fifteen minutes, two conversations went on simultaneously: Matthew and Dave talking together; Jared and Bobby doing the same. Dave was an architect, specializing in converting deconsecrated churches into condos. He expressed surprise when Matthew told him that he was retired.

"You don't look old enough to be retired," he said. "Is Bobby retired, too?"

Matthew said no, he didn't think so. Was Dave not registering that they weren't a couple?

"So, what do you like to do when you're not architecting?" Matthew asked.

Dave said he loved to cook. Pastry was his specialty.

"Well then, I'll have to give you my grandmother's apple szarlotka recipe," Matthew said. "Polish apple pie."

Dave smiled. "Sounds good." Dave had a lovely smile.

As they continued talking—the story about going to Babunia's every afternoon came out again—Matthew listened out of one ear to what Bobby and Jared were talking about. Bobby was as garrulous and entertaining as the day the two of them had met at Score! His conversation ran the gamut from where to go in the South End for great drinks to the latest bingeing of TV shows he'd done. When Matthew realized that by eavesdropping on their conversation he was missing some of what Dave was saying, he brought his attention back.

"Did you and Jared really just meet?" he asked, lowering his voice so only Dave could hear.

"I'm afraid so," Dave whispered, shaking his head in a heaven-help-me gesture.

Matthew flashed back to his own hookup experiences. Six months after Joe died, he had downloaded a few hookup apps, but the guys he met, well, they just weren't Joe. Paulie had encouraged him to stop looking for another Joe—another bit of his "break out of your comfort zone" counseling. But Matthew couldn't get into it, especially the disengaged sex the guys wanted as soon as they entered his apartment. He was still working then—the library was adding a new wing—and that became his life. For the most part, working made him happy. He felt needed at the library. Then came retirement, and suddenly there had been no more feeling needed.

"Kind of a big mistake," Dave whispered. "I mean, Jared was pretty drunk when we hooked up last night. Passed out five minutes after he arrived. I let him sleep. This morning when he woke up, he wasn't in any rush to go home. And pretty hungover. I proposed this outing. Anything, just to get him out of my apartment. Stupid, huh?"

Bobby and Jared got up from their end of the table. "Guys, we're going for a little stroll," Bobby announced. He winked at Matthew. "If we get lost, don't come looking for us." Beyond the orchard, there were some woods. He and Jared sauntered over and disappeared into the trees.

"Wow," Matthew said, "that was fast."

Dave laughed. "There's a dog park near where I live. I don't have a dog, but I sometimes go there just to unwind after work. I watch these pooches running around all over the place: one minute one of them will be chasing one dog, and the next minute he's off chasing another." He poured some wine into his glass and asked if Matthew would like some.

"Sure. Just a little."

They clinked glasses and drank.

"So," Dave said, "you're not boyfriends with Bobby."

"Gosh, no!" The words came out a little too emphatically. Matthew tried again. "We're just ... acquaintances, I guess." He smiled. "Dogs sniffing around in the park."

"You a *dog*?" Dave asked. The smile on his face was more playful than prurient.

Matthew chuckled. "Actually, I'm about as far from a dog as one could be. I met Bobby when we got seated at the same table at Score! last month. There's nothing more to the story than that."

"And what about the pre-Score! story?" Dave asked. "Ever had a boyfriend?"

"Three," Matthew said, and suddenly the stories began to pour out: about Joe, and before him, Terry, a designer for a florist on Newbury Street. He'd met Terry while he was working on his master's degree in library science. Together they witnessed the devastation wrought by the AIDS epidemic, the ongoing transformation of the South End into a gay neighborhood, the death of Matthew's grandmother, for whose funeral Terry handled the flowers long-distance. A year later, they agreed to go their separate ways. "Terry wanted to move to a place where flowers grow outside year-round. California." When Dave didn't say anything, he added, "I guess by that point, I was more attached to Boston than to him."

"Happens," Dave said. "And Number One?"

"Byron. My first love. The shortest relationship of the three and, in some ways, the one it took me the longest to get over."

Dave nodded in recognition.

"He used to call me Kościuszko because of my Polish nose." He saw Dave transfer his attention to his nose, checking it out. "Didn't matter what he called me—I was crazy about him."

Dave smiled the kind of smile that said he'd been there once, too.

"When we'd been together four or five months"—and as Matthew began the story, he thought, *mój Boże*, I've never told this to anyone!—"I found his stash of porno magazines tucked away in his closet. A box full of them."

Dave laughed. "You were snooping around in your boyfriend's closet?"

"Kind of. He lived in Cambridge, I was living in a dorm at Boston College. We always slept at his place."

He described Byron's studio apartment off Harvard Square: the main room that hardly accommodated a nine-by-twelve rug, the alcove that counted as a kitchen, a bathroom that both of them couldn't occupy at the same time except when they took a bath together in the claw-foot tub. "I was twenty-two that year, a senior. I thought it was the height of sophistication, being boyfriends with him, staying overnight in a real apartment. Byron was six years older than I; he was an electrical engineer."

Usually, on the nights he stayed over at Byron's, they would leave together the next morning, early enough for Matthew to make the ride out to Boston College, first to Park Street on the Red Line—was the subway even called the Red Line back in those days, he couldn't remember—and then switching at Park for the long trolley ride out to Chestnut Hill. But that morning, he had slept in when Byron left for work.

"It must have been some Catholic holiday. My classes were canceled." He noticed that Dave was listening intently. "In any event, I remember getting up pretty late."

"And you went looking for his porno?" Dave goaded.

Matthew took a deep, theatrical breath. "Okay, so here's the story. I liked to wear Byron's underwear, and I think I went into his closet to find a pair."

"He kept his underwear in the *closet*?"

"Sometimes, I liked to wear his *used* underwear." Matthew said this without blushing, with no shame or embarrassment. Talking to Dave felt different than talking to Bobby. "I went looking in his dirty laundry pile. It wasn't as kinky as you might think. I really just wanted to be that close to him. The porno was tucked away, behind his dirty laundry."

The box had been stuffed with magazines, scores of them, each Technicolor page lurid with another overt image, and each image a variation on that year's version of Adonis—blond, smooth-chested, well endowed—the fallen angel look.

"I kept flipping through the pages—pages and pages of sucking, fucking, jerking off—*Is that what he wants?* I kept thinking. Where's the love? Where's the affection?"

"Oh, Matthew," Dave said.

"Naïve, huh?"

"But kinda sweet, too."

Matthew began to feel the effects of the wine. The alcohol and the heat of the afternoon were making him a little too talkative.

"I was so hurt, that someone could prefer that stuff to ..." He broke off and began again. "My grandmother had this expression. *Even dough needs time to rise.* She used to tell me that all the time. When I found Byron's porno collection, I thought to myself, Okay, so this is going to take time. But we'll make it work. The dough just needs time to rise."

"Did you?" Dave asked. "Make it work?"

"For a little while, but ... well, from then on, every time I slept over, I snuck a peek into that closet, and every time there was a new porno magazine. I couldn't get beyond the feeling of being cheated on and, like, I don't know ... devalued. Like I wasn't enough for him."

"Or maybe he wasn't enough for *you*, Matthew." Dave was staring directly into his eyes.

Matthew shrugged. Dave kept studying his face. To break the eye-lock, Matthew picked an apple from one of the bags—was it Dave's or

Jared's stash?—and took a bite. "You think they're going to be gone a while?"

Dave cast a glance toward the woods. "Your guess is as good as mine." When he turned back, he was smiling. "Some of those dogs I see in the park, they just love to play for hours."

Hours, Matthew thought. He wondered how he would get home, but held his tongue. He didn't want Dave to think he was fishing for a ride. Still, he thought he should say something.

"Look, I've got some 'pretty great cheese' over at our table. And a nice French baguette. Want to go have a taste?"

"Sure," Dave said. "That cheese Jared bought. Ouch, not 'pretty great,' was it?"

"Um, pretty uninspired, if you ask me."

They got up and headed for the other picnic table. The ground was littered with apples, many with a just bite taken out of them and then tossed away. When they got to the table and sat down, Dave looked at the spread before him.

"Nice table cloth," he said. "And the plates. I guess you were out to impress him, huh?"

"Was it too much?" Matthew asked.

Dave sat down and rested his elbows on the table, cupping his hands in front of himself and leaning forward. "You were just showing him who you were, Matthew. That's never too much."

"Thank you," Matthew said, looking at Dave's hands, which were framed by the generous material of his shawl-collar sweater. He felt the urge to reach over and touch them, and he saw how Dave was watching him, waiting—wasn't he?—for him to make a move.

"So, how about some cheese?" Matthew asked.

Dave uncupped his hands.

"Promise it's better than the stuff Jared bought this morning?" Dave asked. "He got it at the Seven-Eleven."

"Promise," Matthew said. He tore off a piece of the baguette, cut a slice of cheese, and arranged it on the bread before handing it to Dave, careful to make sure their fingers did not make contact.

Dave took a bite. "Wow! You really *were* out to impress him."

"Oh, my God!" Matthew said. "And to think I was also going to bake a szarlotka for him, too. Fortunately, even I knew that would be overkill."

Neither of them said anything else. He watched Dave finish the piece of bread and cheese, before breaking the silence.

"Some more?"

Dave patted his stomach. "Oo, I couldn't. I've already eaten a lot today."

Matthew was already feeling like he'd run out of things to say. But he tried again:

"So, pastry, huh? It's really your specialty?"

Dave made a gesture with his head that indicated he guessed that was a fair assessment.

"I'm okay at it," he acknowledged, and then added with a smile directed squarely at Matthew, "I mean, I don't think I'll win any blue ribbons, but, yeah, I like to bake. How about you?"

"I've got a few Polish recipes I pull out from time to time."

"Like *charlotta*?"

"Szarlotka," Matthew corrected, putting every pinch of luscious Slavic articulation into the word.

"Szarlotka," Dave repeated.

"*Dobra wymowa.* Good pronunciation!"

"Before I went to architecture school, I majored in French in college. At one time, I was pretty good at languages."

Now what? Matthew thought.

Uważaj, he heard his grandmother warning him. *Be careful.* Ah, that Old World cautiousness of hers. She'd had it until the day she died. Except for the flower arrangements that Terry had handled long distance, her funeral at Saint John Kanty Church had been a passionless affair. A cautious, play-it-by-the-book Mass. Even the priest seemed weary.

"So, I guess it would be overkill to invite you to come over to my place tomorrow so that we can make a szarlotka together, right?" Matthew asked.

"Actually," Dave said—a hint of pleasure blooming on his face—"yeah, that might be fun."

"Really?"

"Yes, *really*," Dave said, laughing now. But then he added, "Just not tomorrow, though. I can't tomorrow, but another day? Sure."

Matthew knew all about "another day." The polite postponement that disguised a kiss-off.

"Sure, another day then."

They hadn't exchanged any information about how to contact each other. Matthew decided he'd wait for Dave to offer.

He glanced down at Dave's hands resting on the tablecloth. *Caution*, he thought. Well, Terry had hardly exercised caution in his choice of flowers that day. If anything, he'd gone way overboard. *You ordered these?* his mother had asked when she saw the avalanche of flowers being delivered to the funeral home. When he returned back to Boston, he'd gotten into a fight with Terry about how ostentatious the arrangements had been. He was still ashamed of his ungratefulness, which, years later, he saw had only been a way to mask the discomfort and embarrassment he felt over Terry's impetuous, *faggy* extravagance.

Another day, he thought. *No*, a voice deep inside him said. *Now.*

He reached over, touched Dave's hands, and began to massage them, just a little, just a *pinch*, as Babunia used to say about the clove in her apple pie. Without flinching, Dave left his hands where they were. Matthew didn't know what that meant, but he hoped Jared and Bobby would stay in the woods a long time.

Big Boy

It had been a day of record-breaking temperatures and was still brutally hot when Daryl and I finished dinner. A cold salad was all we'd had the appetite for. After tossing the dirty dishes into the sink, we weren't ready to go to bed, even though the one air conditioner we owned was in the bedroom, doing its feeble best to cool down the place.

We decided to take ourselves out to the stoop. Although we'd bought our apartment the previous winter, it was only since the middle of May that we had discovered the pleasures of sitting outside after dinner. The other unit that was for sale that winter had a deck in the back, but the price was more than we could swing. Daryl is a graphic designer who also dabbles in creating websites; I'm a letter carrier. It helped that my mom, who had died the year before, left me some money, just enough for the outrageous down payment these Boston condos are going for.

I say "stoop," but it's really just a rise of three steps up to the front door. Nothing like the grand staircases on many of the other buildings in the neighborhood. We live in the least fashionable part of the South End, though these days, every street here seems to be regarded as desirable. The realtors like to call buildings like ours "townhouses," but this block was always just working-class apartment buildings—"infill housing" built to put something, anything, into the empty lots that remained once the Victorian building boom petered out. The apartments are small enough that people like us can afford one. When we first moved in, I joked to Daryl that we were one of the "infill gays," not wealthy enough or fabulous enough for a piece of elegant real estate.

The truly chic properties are several blocks away. They're in the area everyone thinks of when you say "South End"—the nineteenth-century bow fronts and brownstones. Postage-stamp gardens surrounded by wrought-iron fences. London-type residential squares. Lots of little parks, too, with fountains and even an occasional statue. Every few blocks, there's a neo-Gothic church. Most of them are now condos.

The South End fizzled as the fashionable new place to live when the Brahmins developed the Back Bay and all the fancy folks up and moved there. That's when the working-class Catholics moved in. And eventually the Lebanese, the Greeks, the Chinese, the Blacks. After we gays discovered it, back in the sixties, the neighborhood began to come back. Though a lot of the old timers here would tell you that it wasn't a question of coming back. I talk to them sometimes when I'm out on my mail route. The old South End was just fine, they say. It didn't need to "come back."

So there we were, sitting on the steps in the unrelenting heat, nursing the rest of a bottle of white wine we'd opened at dinner. True to our unfashionable locale, we'd added ice cubes to our glasses. If it had been even ten degrees cooler, Daryl might have taken himself to the Eagle for a beer, to shoot some pool, or maybe to find a little "fun." That's what we call his occasional hookups with other guys. A few years before we bought our place, we'd agreed to open up the relationship. It was Daryl's idea, but I went along with it. Daryl, who turned forty this year, is a lot younger than me. It was only natural, he explained, that every once in a while he would want some "play time"—another of his terms. Our rule is no overnights, never more than two hookups with the same guy, no bringing him into the apartment, and no falling in love. Daryl, bless him, treats this open relationship thing as responsibly as he treats our own relationship. That's the kind of guy he is.

Shortly after our agreement, I tried a little something on the side myself, but I wasn't into it. I was happy with Daryl. Content, you could say. He's smart and clever, sweet-tempered and attentive. A great husband, even though we aren't legally married. When we agreed to open things up, Daryl assured me that I was his guy, but that he'd be more comfortable if he didn't feel penned in.

I was thinking about all this, and half-heartedly sipping my wine, when I saw these two guys slowly making their way up the street. I'd never seen them in the neighborhood before, although, as I said, we were new to the area and new to hanging out on the stoop. Still, they were distinctive enough that if I'd ever seen them before, I would have remembered.

Both of them looked to be over sixty, one of them well over sixty. That one, the older guy, was wearing a pair of shapeless khaki shorts, a short-sleeve collared shirt (tucked-in), one of those braided belts, and deck shoes over pale yellow socks that rose to mid-calf. On his head, he had a Panama hat that looked like it had been made back when they built the Panama Canal. His eyeglasses were the round, tortoiseshell type. The whole look—it said "geeky professor." The other guy was at least ten years younger, somewhere in his early sixties, I figured. Close to my age. And he wasn't dressed like a professor. More fashion-conscious.

When they reached us, the frumpy, older one stopped and said hello.

"You two fellows look like you're staying cool." I couldn't remember the last time I had been called a "fellow."

"As cool as a cucumber," Daryl said, rattling the ice cubes in his glass of wine.

"Come on, Monroe," the younger friend coaxed. "Let these gentlemen finish their wine in peace."

I piped up and said they weren't bothering us at all. Being so new to the street, I was always looking to meet my neighbors. And these two intrigued me. The older man's name alone, Monroe—I mean, who names their kid Monroe anymore? I'd already pegged them as a couple. I figured they had a good story to tell.

"We've got another bottle of cold wine in the fridge," I said. "Happy to share it."

Monroe turned to his companion with a what-did-he-think look.

"That's really nice of you," the companion said. "But really ... maybe just a glass of cold water? And if you don't mind, I think Monroe could do with a bit of a rest on your stairs."

Monroe chuckled. "Richard thinks this old geezer won't make it back to Worcester Square without the assistance of an ambulance."

Worcester Square was on the other side of the South End. On a sweltering evening like this, it was a long way for them to have walked.

"Please, come sit," I invited, scooting up one stair to make room for them. Monroe gingerly eased himself down and then patted the place next to him.

"You, too, Richard," he said. "These kind gentlemen have rearranged the living room furniture just for us." Once more, he chuckled at his own quip.

We introduced ourselves. *Monroe and Richard*, I thought. Yes, they must be a couple. I turned to Daryl.

"That bottle of cold water in the fridge. Can you get it, babe?" The "babe" was deliberate, a way of establishing for our guests that we were a couple, too.

After Daryl went inside, Monroe kidded me: "You have that one well-trained."

His playful observation that Daryl, maybe as the younger of us two, was at my beck and call irked me. I like to think that we have a more mature relationship than that, less about roles and more about ... well, mutuality, I guess you'd call it.

"Oh, he has *me* well-trained, too," I assured him.

It's taken a lot for me to get over the shame I used to feel about my attraction to younger guys. I've always gone for younger. Even when I was in my twenties, it was what they now call twinks who turned me on. But until Daryl, I'd never felt at ease about my wanting a younger partner. The fact that none of my earlier infatuations ever worked out only seemed to confirm for me that something was wrong with my feelings.

That changed with Daryl. We met twelve years ago, when guys still met in bars. In our case, it was at Fritz, the South End watering hole that had such a neighborhoody feel—friendly dart games, the Celtics on TV, guys from the softball team they sponsored dropping by. Cruising almost seemed beside the point. *Almost*. I was there to cruise. Daryl was, too. He smiled at me almost as soon as we made eye contact. I walked over and told him—cheekily, flirtatiously—that he was a lot more fun to look at than the guys at the stamp club meeting I'd just left. Daryl grinned, thanked me, and then brightly launched into stories about his own stamp collection when he was a kid. We ended up talking for almost two hours.

Around eleven, I invited him back to my place. He said no, that he had an early conference the next morning. But he might be able to meet me for coffee after my mail run, he offered. The following morning, I showed up at the appointed place. Daryl was right there waiting for me, another big, bright Boston Irish smile on his face. Waiting for *me*, I thought. *Me!* Over coffee, we talked again for well over an hour.

Along with his boyish good looks and good-natured disposition, there was something else about him that got my attention, something I realized I'd always been looking for. Yes, he was a "boy"—fair-faced, light-hearted, sweet, unaffected—but in so many ways, he behaved like a mature man. I mean, it was easy to see how responsibly he took his job, and how responsibly he was conducting the opening salvos of this thing, this *pursuit*, we were negotiating. That combination—boy and man—completely won me over. To this day, I call him my Big Boy.

Daryl returned to the stoop with the bottle of water, ice cubes, and four tumblers, which he'd arranged on a tray. He has always had more of a sense of style and presentation than I do.

"I thought we *all* could use some ice water," he said.

Monroe took off his Panama hat and fanned himself. He had a gorgeous head of thick, silvery white hair. I began pouring us all glasses of water.

"So, Worcester Square," I said, a way of opening up the conversation. "That's a good long walk on a hot evening like this.

"Long, indeed," Monroe affirmed. "*Più di be' la cacheremo.*"

"I'm sorry?" I said.

"Italian," Monroe explained. "From Boccaccio." He chuckled. "A bit of scatological distance reckoning that's hard to translate."

Richard intervened: "I think we bit off more than we could chew this evening. Most nights after supper, we take a walk, but tonight we got a little carried away. Monroe wanted to see the Pride Lights on Tremont Street, and then we just kept going."

This piece of information—a stroll to see the Pride Lights—clinched what I had already guessed: they were a couple.

"This is our first Pride in the South End," I offered. "We only moved here in January." I handed Monroe a tumbler of water.

"Well then—it's Daryl and Jim, right?" Monroe said. "Welcome to the neighborhood!"

"Sam," I corrected. "Daryl and *Sam*." I finished pouring the waters and we all clinked glasses.

"*Salute!*" Monroe toasted. "Sam and.... Dear me, I have such trouble with names these days."

"Sam and Daryl," Richard reminded him.

"Sam and Daryl," Monroe repeated. "Yes, of course."

"How long have you guys been in the South End?" I asked.

"Forty-three years," Monroe proudly announced, chuckling once again at the thought of it. "Forty-three years."

"*Both* of you?" Daryl asked.

"Oh, yes. The whole time together." Monroe's attention momentarily drifted away as if he were recalling the significance of that span of years.

I tried again to gauge their ages. Late seventies, I guessed for Monroe, though he had that crusty WASP handsomeness that could put him anywhere between sixty and ninety. Richard, definitely younger, had probably been a real beauty in his day, but now—was he sixty? sixty-five?—he had definitely aged, though he was still good-looking. The hint of blond in his hair suggested he'd once been the Surfer Boy type. A pair of black-framed glasses rested halfway down his nose, not without charm. The years have not been as kind to my face, one I inherited from my German-Scottish ancestors.

Monroe returned from his reverie. "We must reciprocate your kindness and have you gentlemen over for drinks some evening." He twisted around to look at me. "Our garden is quite lovely this time of year."

"Wow, your unit comes with a garden?" Daryl exclaimed. Daryl's unaffected sense of delight tickles me every bit as much as it did when we first met.

"Our *unit*?" Monroe smiled. "In a manner of speaking."

Richard took over again. "We actually own the entire building."

And so their story came out, told in tandem, back and forth, each of them adding another detail. They'd bought the townhouse two years after they met.

"At the old Napoleon Club," Richard told us.

"He was twenty that year and *quite* the cutie!" Monroe said. Even the word "cutie" sounded highbrow when he spoke it.

"I'm sixteen years younger than Monroe," Richard said.

"Oh, yes," Monroe confirmed. "I was quite naughty in those days, chasing after the lads."

"Well," I said, "if that was naughty, what do you make of Big Boy and me? There's a twenty-year difference between us. He's forty; I'm sixty."

Monroe let out a hearty laugh. "Big Boy! Oh, that's marvelous. *Bravissimo!*" He raised his tumbler of water again. Was he toasting our longevity or me alone, a fellow satyr in the world of intergenerational attraction? "Ah yes," he continued, more subdued now. I could hear the whisper of a nostalgic sigh in his voice. "The Napoleon Club. I had taken myself there to celebrate my elevation."

Richard interrupted again. "Monroe had just been made a full professor. You know, he taught Italian for almost forty years."

So, I thought, I wasn't wrong about the professorial look.

Monroe picked up the story. "So, as I say, to celebrate my ascension to Parnassus, I asked two of my favorite graduate students to join me at the triumphal festivities. But Fortuna upended all that, for no sooner did we enter that iniquitous drinkery, than I espied this one."

"We *espied* each other," Richard said, twisting Monroe's piss-elegant verb with affectionate mockery. "In he walks, this very distinguished-looking gentleman, accompanied by a bevy of boys."

"Hardly a bevy, darling!" Monroe protested. "There were two. My intention had been to *attaccare l'uncino* with one or the other of them later that evening,"

"Rope one of them in," Richard translated.

"You speak Italian, too?" Daryl asked.

"Hardly a word," Richard said, "but Monroe loves that expression. He uses it every time he tells the story." There was such sweet affection in his voice.

"Ah, yes, naughty I was!" Monroe reminisced. "Of course, you could get away with that sort of thing back then. And those two ephebes—they were only too eager to be, well, shall we say, 'inducted into a little fun'? As eager as any young swain in Boccaccio." He shook his head in amusement. "I'd taken them to the Napoleon a few times before. To lubricate their libidos, so to speak." He paused, confusion suddenly darkening his face. "It's closed now, isn't it? Richard, the Napoleon—it's gone?"

Richard confirmed that the Napoleon had closed several years ago. Then he shot a quick, private look at Daryl and me. *Do you catch what's happening to him?* he was asking.

"Pity," Monroe said. "Such lovely times there. Such lovely times."

"I still remember the handsome tie he was wearing that night," Richard said, bringing the conversation back to a cheerier pitch.

Monroe brightened, too. "Italian silk. It came from Canali in Rome."

"I wanted him to take me home that night," Richard continued. "But he played hard to get."

Monroe chuckled. "But not for long."

"I wrote down my telephone number on a book of matches," Richard said. "He called me the very next day."

Before they headed back to Worcester Square, we also exchanged phone numbers, but not on a book of matches. Instead, we entered the numbers directly into our mobile phones.

❖ ❖ ❖

A few days later, Richard called to make good on Monroe's promise for drinks. He made sure to emphasize that this was an after-dinner thing. That seemed about the right pace—nothing too elaborate for our first formal get-together. They must have been testing the waters with us, checking to see if we were good candidates for a deeper friendship. Daryl said that made sense. In the twelve years we've been together, he still takes things carefully.

The following Friday, we showed up with a bottle of wine. Monroe graciously accepted it, glanced at the label, said nothing, and then set it down on a table in their foyer, which was almost as large as our bedroom. Then he disappeared—I couldn't help but imagine it was to his wine cellar—while Richard gave us a quick tour of the parlor level.

The only place I'd ever seen rooms like these was in the copies of *Architectural Digest* that I deliver along my mail route. It was a place ready to be photographed: overstuffed, gorgeously upholstered sofas; oriental rugs; hassocks that looked Moroccan or Egyptian; walls covered in ornate Victorian wallpaper. (Daryl later told me it was imitation William Morris, which, he explained, meant top-notch and expensive.) On the walls hung several paintings, drawings, and etchings, some fairly large, others small, in interesting groups and clusters. Most of them were colorful, sunny landscapes. Italy, I guessed. But there were also portraits (mostly of naked men) and some abstracts, a lot better, I could tell, than the kind you see in hotel lobbies.

I thought about the kind of confidence you have to have to mix and match like this—different periods, different styles, and nothing symmetrical. As a graphic designer, Daryl has some of that flair, too. You get it partly from training, but mostly, I think, from fearlessness, from knowing that more things than you might imagine can actually go well together. "William Morris and Moroccan. Think of it," Daryl told me later.

There were piles of coffee table art books, but stacked up on the floor, not on the coffee tables. The double parlors were separated by dark walnut pocket doors. Venetian blinds, not the usual kind you can find in any hardware store, but blinds with real wooden slats covered the windows. The slats were closed almost all the way, letting just a trickle of light in. It was another hot summer evening, but these dark rooms were elegantly cool, even though there was no air-conditioning that I could detect.

The back garden was as magnificent as the house. The last of their bearded iris were still in bloom, and the lilies, clematis, and roses were coming into profusion. There was a small fountain, too, of a naked Cupid, one arm akimbo, pissing water into a stone basin.

"It's all Richard's doing," Monroe said after we returned from the garden tour. He poured us a glass of wine from the bar cart. I couldn't see the label, but I was guessing it was a better bottle than the one we had brought. "Richard's got the green thumb." And once more, he let out that pleased-as-punch chuckle of his. "He should, I suppose. It's his profession."

"I'm a landscape gardener," Richard explained.

"And you've been in this house the whole time?" Daryl asked.

Richard nodded. "Forty-three years. It should have been forty-five, but it took two years from the time we met for me to convince Monroe that I was what he was looking for."

"Forty-three years," Daryl echoed. "That's amazing."

"Forty-three years in the same neighborhood, in the same house," Monroe said. "We were pioneers back then."

"Monroe means that we were practically the first non-African American folks on the street," Richard explained.

I tasted the wine. It was complex, delicious, and expensive. And, of course, served without ice cubes.

Monroe resumed the tale: "We started taking our after-dinner walks the first week we moved in."

Richard followed up: "To reconnoiter the neighborhood."

"Reconnoiter indeed!" Monroe said. "We wanted to see what the hell we'd gotten ourselves into."

"What we had *gotten into*," Richard continued, "was pretty dicey at first. Junkies, hookers ..."

"It was as bad as the Quartieri Spagnoli in Naples," Monroe added with a gleam in his eye. "We got to know them all—the denizens, the demented, the dowagers, and the damned."

"Except for nights when it was raining hard or during blizzards, we've never not taken our walk," Richard said. "The Elevated still ran down Washington Street the first years we lived here."

Monroe turned to Richard. "It *did*, didn't it? I'd forgotten that."

❖ ❖ ❖

That summer and fall, we saw Richard and Monroe quite often. Drinks soon gave way to dinner parties, just the four of us. Early on, Richard explained that Monroe got confused if there were too many folks around the table. Which was another reason why they always insisted that we come to their place: it was just easier for Monroe, who sometimes became thrown off in a new setting. This was fine by me. The cool retreat of their dark parlors and dining room (we were never shown the rest of the house) was a pleasure.

Over these meals, Monroe kept up his storytelling. He was a born raconteur. There were stories, surprisingly interesting, about his scholarly research—Boccaccio was his specialty—and rapturous, ribald tales of all the "mischief" (his word) he had gotten himself into in prep school, in college, in graduate school, on an archaeological dig in Sicily one summer, and with a few of his students when he was a junior professor.

"Once they made me a full professor and I met Richard, well, that kind of hanky-panky stopped."

Most of all, Monroe loved telling stories about his years with Richard and the house—the many renovation projects, the creation of the garden, the famous scholars and writers they'd entertained. And the story of a trip to Italy—"our *third* trip to Italy," he emphasized—when Richard fell into a Venetian canal as they were disembarking from a gondola. "A proper Italian baptism for this Indiana Methodist!" Monroe laughed every time he told us.

By that winter, Daryl and I had heard several of Monroe's stories at least half a dozen times. When I first realized what was happening, I used to make quick eye contact with Richard just to let him know that I was aware of Monroe's memory lapses, but Richard never seemed that concerned. And so, after a while, I went along with it, too, letting Monroe reminisce—and repeat himself—to his heart's content.

But one night last February, I brought it up with Daryl as we were walking home from another dinner at the "Casa Boccaccio," as I had jokingly dubbed the Worcester Square place. We were having one of those Boston winters when there was plenty of cold but no snow.

"Richard seems to be in denial about Monroe's ..." I didn't know what word to use. "About the way he keeps repeating himself."

"I think Richard is just trying to postpone the inevitable," Daryl suggested.

I looked over at him. Even bundled up against the cold, his face barely showing, Daryl was still so handsome. He's a few inches taller than me and a bit on the burly side. A "bear" is how he describes himself when he's trolling for something "open" on the hookup apps.

"The inevitable?"

"I mean," Daryl said, "it's clearly the beginning of Alzheimer's. Pretty soon, Richard's going to have to make some major decisions about Monroe's care."

"You mean, like, a facility?"

"No," Daryl said. "Richard told me he'd never put Monroe in a facility."

"When did Richard tell you that?" I asked.

For the briefest moment, Daryl's pace hesitated.

"We need to talk," he said.

❖ ❖ ❖

Back in the apartment, which suddenly seemed very, very small, it all came out. Daryl and Richard had been seeing each other, just the two of them, since early December. Nothing serious, he assured me. Just a friendship that had "opened up a bit."

We were sitting on the sofa. I'd deliberately positioned myself as far from Daryl as possible. I was full of stern-faced questions, but I let Daryl tell me in his own way.

"One night," he began, "Richard and I got together for a drink. You weren't around. I think you were at your stamp club. He called, said he wanted to talk about Monroe, how worried he was about Monroe's memory loss. Honestly, Sam, he was hoping that both of us could come over."

I could see how eager Daryl was to convince me that this thing with Richard—I still had no idea how much of a thing it was—this "dalliance" with Richard, to use a Monroe word, had all come about rather innocently.

"So," Daryl continued, "I went over. Monroe had already gone to bed. Richard and I sat in the parlor and talked. He was really upset. Monroe had made dinner the other night and forgotten to turn the broiler off in the oven. In the middle of the night, the smoke detector went off. Richard doesn't know what to do. There's plenty of money for an in-home caretaker, but with Monroe slipping away more and more, well, live-in help really isn't much of a consolation."

As Daryl was telling me all this, the only thing I heard was his knowledge of some pretty personal details about Monroe and Richard's life—their financial situation, the discussions about live-in help—stuff Richard had never brought up with the two of us. It was obvious that Daryl had been let into Richard's life in ways I hadn't.

"So, there's Richard, pouring his heart out to me," Daryl continued. "We're sitting on the couch, drinking wine. And at one point, he just started crying, Sam."

He looked up at me, an expression of utter helplessness on his face.

"And you decided that you would provide some consolation," I said frostily.

"Sam, he adores Monroe."

"Then why ..."

"Honestly, Sam, I just wanted to give him a hug—that's all—he was so worried and confused. But the next thing I know, we're making out ..."

The way he trailed off set my imagination racing.

"How does it go from 'just wanting to give him a hug' to making out? Making out is not about comforting him, Daryl. It means you were attracted to him. And you acted on it."

"Attracted to him," Daryl echoed. "Sure. He's a really lovely guy, but I always held it in check. I mean, he's with Monroe; they're a couple; we're their friends. I got caught off guard. Richard was so utterly heartbroken, Sam. He showed me a side of himself that was so ... so unprotected, so naked."

"And?" I prompted.

"Sam, do you know they haven't slept together in years? They have separate bedrooms upstairs. Richard has strayed a few times, but he's too devoted to Monroe ever to abandon him."

"So, is that what this is? Just another of Richard's little 'straying' episodes?"

"God, Sam. I don't know."

"Yes, you *do!*" I demanded. "He was so heartbroken that you decided to take advantage of his vulnerability."

"And he took advantage of *mine*," Daryl fired back.

Across the four feet of safe space between us, we stared at each other.

"*Your* vulnerability?" I asked.

"Sam, I love you, but sometimes I need something more."

"And I've given you more, Daryl. You've got your damn open relationship, but ... Jesus, *this*?" And what exactly was "this"? I needed more details. "So, you're sleeping together now?"

"Not *sleeping* together," Daryl said. "I mean, not overnight or anything. But ..." His voice trailed off. "Yeah."

"How many times?"

"Christ, Sam. Why is that important?"

"Ah, because we have a no-more-than-two hookups rule? Because we have a no-falling-in-love rule?"

"I'm not in love with him, Sam."

"Then what are you?"

Miserably, Daryl shook his head. "I don't know."

Daryl's words, *I love you, Sam*, echoed in my head.

"You know one of the rules is no bringing the guy into the apartment," I said. Daryl began to protest, but I cut him off. "You may not literally have brought him in here, but we both *know* the guy, Daryl."

"I know, I know, I know," Daryl pitifully agreed.

He leaned over for a hug, but I pulled away.

❖ ❖ ❖

The next time we got together with Richard and Monroe, I could tell that Richard was trying to assess my disposition. Over dinner that night—it was delivered pizza, the first time Richard hadn't cooked for us—the conversation was pleasant but stilted. At least, that's how it was between the three of us. Monroe, on the other hand, was his garrulous, jovial, and repetitive self. I kept hoping he would retire to bed so that Richard, Daryl, and I could have a talk, but Monroe just kept telling stories. It was Daryl who finally announced that we should probably be going. Richard agreed and saw us to the door.

"Thank you," he said, directing these words toward me.

"For what?" I asked. I'd been slightly frosty all through dinner. This was supposed to have been the reconciliation get-together, but I wasn't quite ready for a thaw.

"For ..." It was Richard's turn to be at a loss for words. "For not hating me, I hope. And for not hating Daryl. It was a mistake."

I nodded my head, the most I could show him in the way of empathy.

"Yes, I suppose mistakes happen," I said. A dry, deadpan cliché was all I had in me to give him that night. Before Richard had a chance to say anything more, I opened their front door and let myself out.

It was a mild evening in early March. For most of the way home, Daryl and I were silent. When we got to Shawmut Avenue, he turned to me.

"Are you ever going to have sex with me again?" he asked.

We had not been together that way since the night of his big reveal. Though we were still sleeping in the same bed, I didn't feel anything affectionate when I was with him. Not that in the previous few years, we'd been having much sex anyway. (It was one of the reasons for Daryl's wanting to have an open relationship.) In truth, I think he had always turned me on more than I had turned him on.

"Do you want that?" I asked. "You want to have sex again?"

"Yes, of course. I still love you, Sam."

As much as I wanted to tell him the same, I couldn't bring myself to say the words. We walked the rest of the way home in silence. When we got to our place, I turned to him. I couldn't help wanting to rub a little more salt into the wound.

"Well, here's where it all started, right here on these steps."

Daryl said nothing.

❖ ❖ ❖

As the days went on, I found excuses to stay up late, not wanting to take myself to bed at the same time Daryl did. I made sure he was asleep before I crawled in with him, scrunching up on my side, practically in a fetal position. This was as far as I was willing to go: to sleep with him as if he were nothing more than a buddy I'd been forced to share a bed with. I was waiting for some shift to happen, but I had no idea what that would look like.

In the morning, I'd get up first, make the coffee, but leave early, even though I didn't have to be at the post office until late. And I took my good old time delivering the mail, so as not to return home until well after dinnertime. On top of the stove, Daryl always left me a plate of food, covered in tin foil.

One night, Richard called. He said he had to work the Flower Show all the next day and wanted to ask if the two of us would take Monroe on his evening walk.

I was suspicious. Was this some sort of ploy to get me and Daryl to spend more time together? Had Daryl told him about my coolness? I knew they were no longer seeing each other "that way," but I was sure that Daryl was still filling Richard in on what was going on in our domestic scene.

"Well, if there's no one else to do it," I told him.

"There probably is," Richard said, "but Monroe really enjoys you two."

You two. Was there still a "you two" there to enjoy?

We showed up the next evening at the appointed hour. Richard had already left for the Flower Show, but Monroe was ready to go. He was wearing a woolen car coat, a silk scarf, and a homburg. We gingerly helped him down the grand set of steps to the sidewalk. It felt like we were babysitting a child, a child who was oblivious to the fact that his parents were on the verge of a divorce.

Once we got to the sidewalk, Daryl and I walked on either side of him. The uneven brick sidewalks, which had heaved up in places after a winter of freezing and thawing, were treacherous. I noticed that Daryl had crooked his arm into Monroe's to help him keep steady.

"We were pioneers here," Monroe said. "Astonishing to think of that now. Do you know how long Richard and I have been in the neighborhood?" I'd heard the figure a dozen times. "Someone ought to give us a medal, don't you think?" He chuckled. I'd never met a man who chuckled as much as Monroe. Either life completely amused him, or his dementia was more advanced than I suspected.

As we continued walking, I thought about the first generation of South Enders—the post-Civil War generation, who had absconded to the Back Bay as soon as things looked better over there. I'd always copped an attitude toward them—fair-weather citizens, ready to quit the neighborhood because things had suddenly turned more attractive elsewhere. They never returned. As for the South End—well, like an abandoned lover, it fell on hard times, though in the end, after several generations, it recovered. I've been acquainted with enough couples who've broken up to know they recover, too. They move on—yes, hurt, wounded, angry—but they find themselves again. Usually separately.

After about fifteen minutes, Monroe slowed his pace. "Where are we going?" he asked.

"Wherever you like," I offered. "We could go to Blackstone Park and sit on the benches for a bit."

"No, I mean after this?" He sounded flustered. "When *this* is over."

"We'll take you back home," I assured him.

"No, dammit!" He stopped dead in his tracks. "When this, this *life* is over? Where do we go then?"

I looked at Daryl, at a loss as to what to say. Neither of us is religious. I knew that Monroe and Richard attended services at Trinity Church—the blueblood Episcopal church in Copley Square—"but only for the music," Monroe once told us. Now, tentatively, as a feeble attempt to comfort him, I suggested that, well, maybe we "go to Heaven."

"Bullshit!" Monroe snapped. "You don't believe that cockamamie fairy tale, do you?"

I looked at Daryl again. The expression on my face said, *Help me.*

"Well, Monroe, what do *you* think?" Daryl asked.

"What do I think!" Monroe grunted, linked his other arm in mine, and pulled us along, resuming the walk.

It was another minute before he piped up again. "They must have thought they were so important." He stopped and looked around, taking his bearings. "The people who once lived in these lovely houses. They must have thought they were so important—with their careers, their families, their domestic dramas. All the bustle and brouhaha of their lives. Then—*poof!*—gone." He tugged at us to get walking again. "And then others took their place, other families, other people, with their own bustle and brouhaha."

"This neighborhood has certainly had its fair share of history," I offered.

Monroe stopped and stared at me.

"History? I'll tell you about history," he said. There was more than a tinge of irritation in his voice. "When I met Richard, that night at the Napoleon, I thought he'd be just another trick." He paused. I tried to get him moving again, but he sloughed me off. "But as we got to know each other better, I saw something in him I'd never seen in any other stud I'd ever had the hots for." *Trick, stud*, and *hots* were not words I'd ever heard Monroe use before.

"What did you see in him?" Daryl quietly asked. He was trying to ease Monroe's agitation.

For a moment, Monroe didn't say anything. He seemed to be struggling to find words. "There's a story in Boccaccio," he said.

Oh, God, I thought, he's already lost the thread of what he was saying.

"In the Decameron. There's a story about a man—his name is Galeso—but he's such a clod—coarse, dull, uncouth—that everyone calls him Cimone. A brute, an ignoramus. It's only when Cimone falls in love, Boccaccio says, that *amor l'avesse di montone fatto tornare uomo.* Love turned him from being a *montone*—a ram—into a man." He looked at Daryl and then at me. "You understand? I was a full professor, at a distinguished university, but I didn't become a man until I met Richard."

Out of the corner of my eye, I saw Daryl nodding his head.

"But what does that mean, Monroe?" I asked, perhaps a bit too combatively. "What does it mean to be a man?"

Before he answered, Monroe held my gaze for longer than I was comfortable.

"It means you let go of whatever it is that's keeping you from being a man—your arrogance, your pride, your *fucking* stubbornness."

"But ..."

"Exactly," he said. "Butt, butt, butt. That's what a ram does, isn't it? Butts his head, again and again, the stubborn brute. And for what?"

"To defend himself," I shot back.

"*Humpf,*" Monroe snorted and tugged at us to move on again.

By now, he was practically shuffling. I'd never seen him move so faintly. Then he stopped again.

"It means you come back, over and over again."

"Even if..."

"Stop!" he commanded. "What the hell are you, a ram or a man?" Monroe was breathing so hard, I thought he might be having a heart attack. "Answer me, dammit. Has love not yet turned you into a man?"

Helplessly, almost in a panic, I glanced over at Daryl. *Help me*, the look on my face said. And the look on my Big Boy's face—so steady and patient—he was standing by, waiting once again for me to be his man.

Sleeper

When Joseph opened his eyes, Donald was already gone. *Friday*, he thought. The beginning of another one of Donald's four-day weekends. Four days off, three days on—a pattern Donald had set as soon as he turned sixty-five. That was three years ago, and it still left Joseph envious whenever Friday rolled around. Fridays were one of *his* most intense days: piano students beginning at nine, an hour's break to practice the organ at the church (and grab a quick sandwich), and then more students in the afternoon before meeting his husband for dinner. That was another routine, the "Friday night date," that Donald had established when he began his semi-retirement. Donald was a therapist. Routines, he told his patients, were healthy anchors, especially for older gay men.

Lying in bed, New England spring sunlight tenderly playing on the windows, Joseph recalled Donald's words when he first proposed the weekly Friday date: *It's important to set aside some "special time" each week. So that we don't take each other for granted.*

They'd been together fourteen years now. And, yes, Joseph did not want to take his marriage for granted, even though there were days when he didn't want to take it at all. Donald was a good man, by far the best relationship Joseph had been in. Still, if he were honest, he'd have to admit that Friday night dates weren't quite accomplishing the desired effect anymore. He was a little bored with Donald, a little bored with everything: his piano teaching, his church gig, their sex life, which had pretty much turned into snuggling, spoon-style, and some tame caressing. Joseph was the big spoon, and sometimes Donald pushed him off. He knew Donald didn't mean anything by this. Donald just needed plenty of undisturbed sleep. Joseph was careful not to wake Donald whenever he got up to pee, which these days was about three times a night. *Ak, vecumdienas!* his grandfather used to say. Joseph had never been able to understand much Latvian, but he knew that *vecumdienas,* old age, was not something anyone in his family had ever taken pleasure in. *Ak*, indeed.

It was going to be a warm one, this April day, warm enough, Joseph guessed, for Donald to spend all of it doing his gardening. One of the bedroom windows was cracked open. It faced the backyard. Joseph listened now for the sounds of Donald raking up the muck of winter or pitching a shovel into the muddy soil to dig holes for new plants. But outside, it was silent.

As silent as the house itself. Even now, a month after they'd put Buddy to sleep, Joseph still felt the hushed absence of their beloved dog. Everything this morning felt hushed—the house, the early morning light, his breathing—a tranquility that Joseph would have liked to nestle into a bit longer. He twisted over to check the clock radio. Seven-forty. He should have been up ten minutes ago. Still, five more minutes in bed wouldn't do any harm. Five minutes to lie there, stare at the ceiling—it badly needed repainting—and contemplate the day he was not quite ready to begin.

But wait, what was *this*? Under his flannel pajama bottoms, Joseph felt a slight stirring. Nothing exactly imperative—"morning wood" was a thing of the past—but there it was, the unmistakable *hello* of his old friend, just letting him know he was still around in case Joseph wanted to pay him a visit. He reached down into his pajama bottom, cupped the dear fellow, then thought of the time. Not enough to get anything started. He took his hand away and hunkered down under the covers. These days, curling up in bed was almost as pleasurable as choking the chicken.

Who says "choke the chicken" anymore, he wondered. It was right up there with words like *gizmo* and *hootchy-kootchy*. Words his father had used and that Joseph still knew and occasionally used himself. *Gizmo!* He bet the hottie he had struck up a conversation with last week in the sauna at the gym had no idea what a gizmo was. His name was Jared, and he was in "IT." *Of course you are*, Joseph had thought. *Who isn't in IT these days?* He'd made the mistake of asking Jared what exactly he did in IT, and within two sentences of Jared's explanation, Joseph was lost. The world today was full of new professions and new words that he didn't know a thing about. What the hell was an "interface" anyway? Or a "bug-out bag"? *Clueless,* his friend Charles had said. *Joseph, how can you be so clueless?*

Perhaps his greatest feat of cluelessness had been to go through four years at the Conservatory, not realizing that a quarter of his male classmates were gay. And afterwards, when he moved to the back of Beacon Hill (in those days still the affordable side), clueless again, about the kind of young men who were drawn to this neighborhood and about the nature of the nameless bar on Cambridge Street that he walked by every day. Or rather, not so much clueless as simply not wanting to know.

The tiny studio apartment he'd rented that year was on the top floor of a grungy, walk-up building on South Russell Street, just another of the warren of grungy streets and homely, walk-up buildings on the "back side" of the Hill. There was linoleum on the stairs and fluorescent lighting at each landing. Grim, but still, it was his first adult apartment—no more living at home or in a dormitory. There were days when he longed to be living in such bohemian, romantic quarters again. When he longed to be that sweet kind of clueless again.

Given his limited resources, Joseph had decorated the place as best he could. The furniture came from Goodwill; a print of Van Gogh sunflowers mounted on foam core was the only piece of artwork on the walls. He'd had to leave his baby grand piano at his parents'—it wouldn't fit up the apartment building's narrow staircase—so he used to practice at his girlfriend Marilyn's place in Cambridge. She was a bassoonist he had met at the Conservatory and was renting a room from a family with a lovely Steinway and no musical talent.

He twisted over once more to check the time. *Up,* he told himself, and then hunkered down even deeper under the covers.

Where was Donald? If not in the garden, and not in the kitchen—he couldn't hear any noises coming from downstairs—where had he gone? Perhaps to the garden center in the part of Dorchester that Joseph wished they lived in, instead of the section they did live in. He considered again whether to get something going with the chicken, but tonight was their date night. Though that rarely led to sex, Joseph figured he should at least hold off in case Donald was feeling amorous.

He threw off the covers and went downstairs. There was a note on the kitchen table: *No more half-and-half.* (Here Donald had drawn a frowny face.) *Have gone out for coffee. Will probably still be gone when you leave. Have a great day. See you tonight.* (And here a smiley face.)

They were both "cream whores," as Donald liked to say. Coffee with just plain milk, even whole milk, wouldn't do for either of them in the morning. Joseph loved this shared detail in their lives. Whenever the staleness of their marriage surfaced, he'd remind himself of "the little things," as Donald put it. The little things. Like their mutual love for morning coffee with half-and-half (and no sugar). Another of those little things had been the dog. They still hadn't been able to bring themselves to get another.

Buddy, Buddy, Buddy. It pained him to think just how little he'd paid attention to him when he was alive. Buddy had always just been there: Donald's puppy first, and then their dog together. He was fifteen when they'd put him to sleep. Fifteen: a good life for a dog, the vet had said. Fifteen. A year older than Joseph's relationship with Donald.

❖ ❖ ❖

He and Donald had met at a New Year's Day brunch in the Fenway given by a guy Joseph occasionally ran into, and chatted with, at concerts. When the guy—his name was Mark—invited him to the brunch, Joseph had wondered whether Mark was perhaps interested in dating. But over the phone, Mark had made it clear that he was just being friendly. At which point, Joseph had come close to not going. All that week, he'd been fighting the blues. A combination of a bad cold, his church choir singing wretchedly, and the fact that he'd recently turned fifty-five. Turning fifty had been trauma enough. But fifty-five was halfway to sixty. *That* had really freaked him out. Still, he roused himself to go. It would be better, he figured, than moping around doing nothing but listening to the New Year's Day concert from Vienna on the radio.

At Mark's party, he'd noticed Donald immediately: tall, kind-faced, and wiry like the runner he was. Like Preston, Boyfriend Number One, and Patrick, Boyfriend Number Two, Donald was a blond. It was one of Joseph's weaknesses. Boyfriend Number Three, Lee, had been a redhead. Three blonds and a redhead. That was going to be the tally, he figured.

There wouldn't be any more boyfriends, whatever color hair they might have.

Over a plate of ham and black-eyed peas, he and Donald got to chatting. Joseph hoped he wasn't coming across as a nerd, though he was aware of how much he kept talking about classical music. But Donald seemed interested in everything he said. That afternoon, as the sun faded on the first day of the new year, Joseph vowed not to fuck this one up.

❖ ❖ ❖

In the bathroom now, lathering up his cheeks, he looked at his face and wondered how, fourteen years ago, he'd ever thought fifty-five was old. He finished shaving, took a thirty-second shower, toweled off, dressed, and went back down to the kitchen, where he read Donald's note again. One of Donald's domestic rules was that if either of them used something up, he wrote it down on the shopping list. Joseph had finished the half-and-half during his afternoon coffee break yesterday, but had forgotten to write it on the list. Dear, sweet Donald. He was not one for punishing. The frowny face was about as far as Donald would ever go toward chastisement. Joseph could only imagine how Preston—nasty Boyfriend Number One—would have reacted in a similar situation.

On Fridays, his first piano lesson was always demoralizing. Nathan was a senior at a private high school. On Fridays, because of "senior privilege," his first class didn't start until eleven, so he had time for a nine o'clock lesson with Joseph. The boy had some talent, but he never practiced anymore. "His interests have shifted," Nathan's mother told Joseph apologetically as she wrote out that week's check. "It's the young ladies now. He's on the phone with them constantly." Joseph saw the helplessness on her face. "Nathan's my first teenager," she explained. "I don't know who I'm dealing with anymore."

Joseph knew just how thrown off you could become when romance entered the picture. He wanted to reassure the mom, tell her that Nathan's distraction from the piano was just a passing thing, that with as much talent as Nathan had, he'd never lose his interest in music. He would have liked to tell her his story, about the major distraction that Preston had been. But this was a story he never told anyone.

❖ ❖ ❖

It was a story that began three months after he'd moved to Beacon Hill. By then, his post-Conservatory life had settled into a pleasant-enough routine of giving lessons during the week followed by Friday nights with friends (never Saturday nights because he had to get up early to play the organ at a parish out in the suburbs). The Friday outings, which always included Marilyn, were usually for pizza and beer, which is what, in those days, any of them could afford.

Marilyn had been a diehard Catholic and had taken a vow of celibacy before marriage. This suited Joseph just fine as he, too, was a Catholic. Celibacy before marriage seemed like a good idea. In truth, sex with women was another thing he'd wanted to postpone knowing anything about for as long as possible. When he went to Confession, which was every other week, he always confessed that he'd had "impure thoughts and actions with himself." The priest never asked for details. A relief, because whenever Joseph used to masturbate, he always imagined men.

One night—it was a mild Friday night in November, the end of his teaching week—walking down Cambridge Street toward his apartment, he found himself slowing down as he approached the bar he'd always previously, *deliberately*, ignored. His lessons had gone well that day, but something was eating at him. The weekend pizza group was not getting together that night, and Marilyn was playing a gig for two weeks in Cleveland. What was he going to do with this free Friday evening? Practice? A movie? Neither of these options had appealed to him.

He slowed down a bit more. The entrance to the bar—a nondescript door in a wall, nothing more—was a block away. Joseph studied the men who were loitering and smoking outside. Some were chatting and laughing; others looked intent, ominous, even predatory. All of them— there must have been a dozen on the sidewalk—were wearing jeans. More than a few of those jeans were extremely tight. He thought about what he was wearing that night—baggy corduroys, a long-sleeve jersey, a woolen carcoat his mother had given him as a graduation present. With his head lowered, not making eye contact with anyone, he turned into the bar. He'd spent a long time not wanting to know. A peek wouldn't kill him. He wasn't even sure he'd have to confess this.

For the first half hour, he stood in a dark corner, nursing a beer and trying to look as inconspicuous as possible while he studied the crowd of men in the smoky, dimly lit room. To his amazement, they all looked so *normal.* There was the occasional swishy one, which he didn't like, but the rest—several with moustaches, others clean-shaven—they were as attractive as the former classmates he'd admired at the Conservatory.

During his second beer, he sensed that someone was standing next to him, and staring. When he turned to look, the guy flashed him a broad grin. "Come here often?"

They introduced themselves. The guy's name was Preston. Joseph guessed him to be a few years older than himself, maybe twenty-six. He was wearing an Oxford cloth button-down shirt and chinos. His blond hair was almost as white as his shirt. Unused to the protocol in gay bars, Joseph gave his full name. Joseph Guletajs.

"What's that? Italian?" Preston asked.

Joseph watched as the guy studied his hair, a nondescript cut in nondescript brown that could pass for any nationality from Icelandic to Greek.

"Latvian," he told him. "My dad's side of the family was from Latvia."

"And your cute looks?" Preston asked, running a finger along Joseph's aquiline nose. "Did you get them from the Latvian side, too?"

Joseph figured he must look as frightened as a chihuahua among pit bulls. He blurted out the first thing that came into his head, something about how his name meant "Sleeper" in Latvian.

"Mm," Preston purred. "I hope you're not always a sleeper." And then he laughed. "Sorry, I'm not always this forward."

It turned out that Preston was in town for a math educator's conference. "But actually," he explained, "I'm going to graduate school next year." He flipped his head so that the blond hair falling over his forehead was momentarily brushed away. "I've had it with teaching. It's a profession for losers."

Joseph wanted to protest that teaching was not a "profession for losers," but held his tongue. He was so grateful that he was actually talking to someone and not just standing there wishing he were talking to someone.

"And you? What do you do?" Preston asked. The lecherous grin appeared again. "I mean for work."

❖ ❖ ❖

"At first, I didn't get why he said that," Joseph told Donald. They were on their Friday night date, at a favorite Vietnamese restaurant on Dorchester Avenue. He'd never told Donald the whole story of Boy Friend Number One. It had been such a long time ago. He thought he'd erased that painful chapter from his memory, but all day—during piano lessons, practicing the organ, while he was swimming his laps—he couldn't stop the memories of Preston from coming back.

The waiter brought them their appetizers, fresh spring rolls with peanut sauce. When he left, Joseph continued the story.

"I told him I was a musician. Without missing a beat, Preston said, 'Why don't you tell me all about it back at my hotel?' Against my better judgment, I went."

"Or maybe," Donald offered, picking up a spring roll, "maybe it *was* your better judgment."

"You haven't heard the rest of the story," Joseph told him.

It went like this: Once they got to the hotel room, Preston fixed Joseph a bourbon and water, which Joseph prudently nursed, waiting for what would come next. "You've never done this before, have you?" Preston asked. And when Joseph told him no, Preston said, "Just relax," and moved in to kiss him hard on the lips.

"And what was that like?" Donald asked.

"Like a sledgehammer. Pretty soon, we were on the bed. He was undressing me, kissing me—*rough!*—fondling me. Oh, my God. I couldn't believe what was happening. He told me I wasn't like those other 'losers'—it was one of Preston's favorite words—those losers in the bar." Joseph dropped his voice. "He told me he wanted to fuck me, but I didn't want to go that far. The rest of it, though—I couldn't believe how exciting it was."

Donald smiled. Joseph couldn't tell whether this was a smile of happiness for his coming-out experience, or a smile of tender empathy for how "exciting" those early sexual experiences could be. Maybe a little of both.

"Afterwards, Preston told me he didn't usually like to have guys sleep over, but that he'd 'make an exception.' And the next morning ... well, what I wasn't keen to do the night before, we did then."

"And?" Donald coaxed again. He was going into therapist mode.

"I can't believe I'm telling you all this. Preston is so *not* the memory I've ever wanted to share with you. With *anyone*."

"Up to you," Donald said.

"So, yeah, overnight I went from uptight virgin to ravenously in love. Or in lust. Or something. Whatever it was, we started seeing each other. Twice-a-month bus trips between Boston and Hartford. Always me going there, but that was okay because I couldn't get enough of him. Not just the sex. There was something else about the guy that I was in awe of. His self-assurance, I guess. Or what I saw as self-assurance. Preston seemed so adult, so confident, in the ways that I longed to be." He chuckled. "I never went back to Confession again."

"And Marilyn?" Donald asked.

"Well, at first, after I told her what was going on, she said I was going to go to Hell." Joseph chuckled again. "And then she met a trombone player and fell in love. That was the end of her vow of chasity. But she never did like Preston. She told me he was a mistake."

"Because it was a gay relationship?"

"No. Because he could be so negative, so scornful of everything. Of the teaching profession, of Hartford, of Boston, of classical music. I should have known right then and there that it wasn't going to last."

"But it did," Donald said.

"Well ... by February, we were planning the rest of our lives together." Joseph shook his head. "I guess I was just so hungry for the something that I'd put off—that I'd *ignored*—for so long, that I was willing to overlook the warning signs. I was even willing to uproot myself and move to Lawrence, Kansas, of all places. Preston had been accepted into a doctoral program out there."

"Kansas," Donald mused.

"When I tried to picture the place, I saw cowboys in chaps and flannel shirts sauntering down Main Street." He shook his head.

The waiter came by and took away the spring roll plate.

"For Preston," Joseph continued, "the move was kind of a going-home odyssey. He'd grown up in Topeka. About half an hour west of there."

The waiter returned with the main courses: a plate of sautéed fish with spring onions on rice noodles (Donald's choice); and another of grilled pork strips with herbs and a sweet-and-sour dipping sauce (Joseph's). Donald's choice, Joseph knew, was the "healthy" one.

"I remember how hot it was when we drove out to Kansas." Joseph picked up his chopsticks and helped himself to the pork. "Three scorching days in August. Preston leading the way in his VW; me following in a ten-year-old Oldsmobile I'd just bought, my first car. We found an apartment the afternoon we pulled into Lawrence. Preston insisted on two bedrooms—'for propriety's sake,' he said, even though it cost us an extra thirty-five bucks a month."

Donald picked up a fork and took a piece of the fish. "You wouldn't have been comfortable telling the real estate agent you guys wanted a one-bedroom?"

"You are being *so* Mr. Therapist tonight!" Joseph teased. "Nope, no one-bedrooms for two guys in those days, honey. Back in those days—if you recall—it was *all* about maintaining 'propriety.' Besides, Preston used to make it clear that he was the one who knew better. He used to play the age card: four years older, smarter, wiser, more experienced. Jesus, how I put up with it!" Donald still didn't say anything. "What are you thinking?" Joseph asked.

"I'm just listening to the story," Donald said.

"So, the weekend after we moved in, we 'apartment-mates' paid a visit to Preston's mother in Topeka. When we got there, before he even introduced me, he started complaining to her about how the neighbors hadn't taken in their barrels after trash collection that morning. I remember how his mother turned to me and said, 'Pay him no mind. He's been this way since he was five years old: the neighborhood busybody.' When she found out I was a musician, she invited me to play her turn-of-the-century harmonium. She called it a pump organ. I took to her immediately. She was cheerful and homey—almost folksy—with a golly-gosh kind of openness to everything."

Joseph felt tears welling up in his eyes. "Sorry," he said, and took another piece of the pork. "It's just that she was so welcoming, so reassuring. And I was so scared. My life was suddenly moving at such a clip. I felt—I don't know—immediately *accepted* by her." He made eye contact with Donald and smiled. "Just the way I did with you."

As they ate, Joseph continued the story. The Topeka house was an eight-room Victorian that Preston's mom had turned into an arts-and-crafts palace. Despite arthritic hands, Mrs. Sedgwick threw herself into her projects—braiding rugs, decorating ostrich eggs, refinishing furniture, doing tole painting—projects that she set up in the house's former bedrooms, now turned into her various "studios." She had also cobbled together an in-home beauty salon in the front parlor. There, in slippered feet, she did shampoos, cuts, and permanents for a gaggle of middle-aged Topeka women who often lingered afterwards to chat and eat slices of the lemon teacake that she managed to bake between everything else she was doing. All these years later, Joseph could still summon up the aroma of those teacakes and the salon women's twangy Kansas accents as they gossiped away around the claw-foot refreshment table.

"I remember so much about that Topeka house," he told Donald. "Mission-style plant stands topped by pots of begonias and Swedish ivy, panels of framed stained-glass hanging in front of the windows, macramé everywhere. And the bathroom! A pull-chain toilet, walnut wainscoting, a marble sink. She had a huge collection of Victorian kitchen gizmos, which she actually used when she cooked." He paused. "You know what a gizmo is, right?"

Donald smiled. "Yes, Joseph, I know what a gizmo is."

"And her bedroom. It was decorated with pink-flocked wallpaper and plaster cherubs hovering over the headboard. It was the only bedroom that still functioned as a bedroom, the one she turned over to us 'boys' when we stayed overnight."

"Where would she sleep?" Donald asked.

"On one of the sofas downstairs, but I'm not sure she ever did sleep. I think the most she ever got were catnaps. She was a dynamo, Donald. She once told me that when her husband died—she always referred to him as Mr. Sedgwick—when Mr. Sedgwick died, she decided she would just have a try at anything that would keep her going. She didn't want to give up. She was so unafraid. While that son of hers ..." Joseph shook his head. "He could be such a pill: complaining about his graduate program, complaining still about the two years he'd spent in Hartford, complaining about his father, who was *dead* for Chrissake! I think it's why I loved those visits to Topeka: there was such positive energy in that house. I remember once telling Preston how much I loved visiting my 'mother-in-law,' and he snapped at me: 'Don't you ever call her that in public!'"

Joseph looked at the plates in front of him. Donald hadn't touched the pork.

"It wasn't long before I actually liked her better than Preston. A *lot* better. When Preston and I broke up, what really made me sad was that I wouldn't have a relationship with his mother anymore." Joseph watched as his husband took another bite of the fish. "Why aren't you eating the pork?"

"Why aren't you eating the fish?"

Joseph took a piece of fish.

"You never came out to her?" Donald asked.

"But that doesn't mean we didn't have a relationship! We did. It was 'the best relationship that I was capable of at the time.'" Such sweet retribution, to give back to Donald one of the tenets of his therapy practice: that as young gay men, each of his patients had done the best they could do at the time, whatever it was they had done. Most of the men Donald saw were middle-aged to older gay men, and this was an observation that seemed to speak volumes to them.

Donald laughed. The crow's feet around his eyes came into full prominence.

"Oh, my God!" Joseph burst out. "Another thing I remember"— suddenly it all came flooding back—"Mrs. Sedgwick's border. Edwin Fleck. Jesus, I haven't thought about him in decades."

"We *are* going down memory lane tonight, aren't we?" Donald said.

❖ ❖ ❖

Edwin was a graphic artist who worked for an environmental organization, one of the first in the state of Kansas. Somewhere over thirty, pudgy, pale, and prematurely bald, he illustrated the booklets and annual reports that the agency published: "prettying up pages of statistics," he once told Joseph through delicately pursed lips. Then, raising his eyes in mock self-importance, Edwin had added, "I make clean water policy sexy."

One Saturday afternoon, Edwin had invited the two of them, Joseph and Preston, down to the basement apartment—his "subterranean abode," as he called it—for tea. Preston hadn't been enthusiastic about the idea, but Joseph, who was intrigued by Edwin, said it was only polite to accept the invitation.

"I was curious," he told Donald. "He was the most exotic gay man I knew." He laughed. "He was the *only* other gay man I knew!"

"Exotic?" Donald asked.

"His 'abode'! You should have seen it, Donald. It was all Japanese lacquered screens, table lamps draped with fringed shawls, peacock feathers arranged in his collection of vintage Rosewood pottery. The walls were covered in framed drawings from the nineteenth century, French mostly, of milkmaids, society women, and Carmelite nuns in mystical swoons. When we walked in ..." Joseph paused, trying to summon it all again. "I thought to myself, *This is the son Preston's mom really wants.*"

"You think?" Donald asked.

"Preston was always saying snide things about Edwin. I used to think it was because the prissy-faggy stuff turned him off, but I think it was really because his mom liked Edwin so much."

"He was jealous?"

"I think."

"Or maybe," Donald offered—and Joseph could hear the therapeutic deep dive coming into play—"maybe Edwin's style reminded Preston of something in himself, something he didn't like."

"Well, there *was* a bit of the queen in Preston," Joseph acknowledged, "but, oh, he kept it tamped down." With his chopsticks, he helped himself to a large clump of rice noodles. It gave him a moment to screw up the courage to say what he was about to admit. "I'm not proud to tell you this, but whenever I was around Edwin, he kind of made me uncomfortable, too. After that first visit to his cave, I went into shutdown mode. I mean, here was this guy, an artist, an antiques collector, a classical music lover—another gay man!—and I just shut down. I didn't want to admit I had anything in common with him."

Donald winced.

"Yeah." Joseph acknowledged. "Oh, man, I was such a closet case back then. Poor Edwin, I wonder what ever happened to him."

"He lived his life," Donald offered.

"Probably better than I lived mine for most of my life." Their eyes met. For a moment, neither of them spoke.

"No, darling," Donald finally said. "You lived …"

"I know, I know! 'The best life I was capable of at the time.'" Joseph took a sip of tea. "Donald, it's just that there are days when it astounds me how shut down I was. Not only with Preston, but later with Patrick and Lee as well."

"And now … do you feel less shut down?" Donald asked.

"Of course," Joseph insisted, a little too swiftly.

❖ ❖ ❖

On the way home—Donald was driving in his maddeningly slow, meticulous way—Joseph pulled out his cell phone. There were no text messages, and the new e-mails were all junk. When he looked up, the light at the intersection was just turning yellow. Donald stopped. Joseph counted to himself: it took three more seconds for the light to turn red.

"Stop it," Donald said.

"What?"

"You're counting."

"How can you tell?"

"Fourteen years," Donald reminded him.

"What I'd like to know," Joseph asked, letting a tone of amusement take over the annoyance he felt, "is how you manage to get on my nerves more than Preston did."

Donald looked over at him, smiling. "Because, sweetheart, you weren't in touch with your feelings back then. And now you are." Joseph couldn't tell if the look on Donald's face was one of amusement, exasperation, or sarcasm.

But it was true, he guessed. Back then, there was still so much he hadn't wanted to pay attention to. He'd wrapped himself in a cocoon of numbness: numbness not only to his growing dissatisfaction with Preston, but to his unresolved feelings about a host of things—living in the Midwest, fraternizing with Edwin, even being gay.

The light turned green and Donald drove on. When they'd first moved to Dorchester, this stretch of the Avenue had been an unsightly mélange of modest storefronts, shabby two-family houses with asphalt-shingle siding, a few working-class bars, several empty lots, and no restaurants to speak of. The one bakery specialized in First Communion cakes and oblong loaves of soft, unsliced bread, which they called "Italian."

Back then, Joseph had tuned out the neighborhood, too. It was another thing he hadn't wanted to deal with. Dorchester had been Donald's thing, not his. It had taken him two years to agree to move in with Donald, another year for them to buy the Dorchester house together. When the Supreme Court allowed same-sex marriage, Donald proposed. Joseph hesitated for another year before saying yes.

He looked out the window. Over the years, the neighborhood had improved: there were now decent restaurants; the dreary grocery store in Fields Corner had been replaced by an upscale supermarket. There was even a gay bar-cum-bistro. Crime was down and people kept up their property. So why was he still so ambivalent about it all? Right now, about the only thing he wasn't ambivalent about was that it was Day Light Savings Time again and there was still light in the sky.

"Why don't we stop at the garden center to pick up tomato plants," he suggested.

Donald looked over at him. That smile—amusement, exasperation, sarcasm—had returned to his face.

"What tomato plants?"

"Aren't we putting in tomatoes this year?"

"Of course, we're putting in tomato plants this year, but what do I tell you every year, Mr. Jump-the-Gun? You don't put tomatoes in until Memorial Day. There's still a chance of frost."

"Donald, we're in the middle of Global Warming. There is no more frost in April."

"Do you remember April last year?"

"Last year? Donald, there are days when I can't remember what I had for dinner last night."

Donald didn't respond right away, and then he asked, "Are you worried about that?"

"Global warming?"

"Memory loss."

"No!"

"Okay. Just checking."

They drove on while Joseph silently stewed: about Donald's fastidious timetable for planting tomatoes; about his husband's annoying habit of paying attention to every little thing Joseph said; about the day when memory loss would become an issue. For either of them.

"Why so quiet?" Donald asked.

"No reason."

"You sure?"

"I'm sure."

But he wasn't sure. Not sure about this house they owned that was always in need of repair; not sure about his forty-plus-year career in church music, a church and a religion he had stopped believing in years ago. Not sure about the occasional dalliances that he allowed himself to fall into, nothing more than a mutual wank in the steam room at the gym, though on a couple of occasions, he'd lingered so long that he'd been late for dinner back home.

"So, what about pansies?" he asked, letting a mildness return to his voice. "Couldn't we at least put in some pansies this evening? They do well in cool weather."

"And these pansies you want to plant?" Donald asked. "Are we going to turn around and drive all the way to the garden center?"

"We can pick up a flat of pansies at the supermarket, for Chrissake."

"The ones they're selling aren't very good."

"Donald, I just want to plant something. Besides, we need to stop to buy half-and-half."

❖ ❖ ❖

In the fading light, they turned over one of the flowerbeds, preparing it for the pansies that Donald had agreed to buy at the supermarket, pansies that even Joseph knew were inferior to the ones they could get at the garden center in Lower Mills. He watched how the rich loam crumbled under his pitchfork, releasing earthworms that wriggled out of their winter somnolence.

When they bought the house, the backyard had been a sunless, weed-infested plot of land. Now, every summer, it erupted into a lush, fertile garden. They'd cut down three obnoxious Norway maples, whose roots were robbing the soil of nutrients. Every year, they added copious amounts of compost. They'd pulled out the previous owner's cement-anchored clothesline poles; sifted the earth nearest the old coal chute for fragments of coke; marked off a central plot, which they divided into four beds: two for vegetables, two for Donald's dahlia collection.

Donald had immediately fallen in love with the house, especially for the possibilities the backyard afforded. Joseph—on whom the irony of its being another eight-room Victorian was not lost—liked the fact that the parlor was big enough to fit both his baby grand piano and his harmonium (a purchase inspired by Preston's mom). As for the rest of the house, they'd slowly transformed the "charming fixer-upper," as the realtor euphemistically described it, into a home, one that also nicely accommodated Donald's counseling office.

Joseph stuck his pitchfork back into the loam. A half hour's work and he was winded. "I swear, every year this garden gets bigger and bigger," he called out to Donald.

Donald didn't answer. He had moved to the other end of the garden, and his hearing was getting worse.

During the initial months of their house hunting, Joseph had hoped for a smaller place, maybe even a condo. They'd squabbled about it. But in the end, Donald had been so enthusiastic about the prospect of a big house and a big garden that Joseph went along.

"I sure hope this works out," he told Donald the afternoon they decided to make an offer.

"No," Donald had said. "Not hope, Joseph. *Make.* Choose to *make* it work." And then he'd added, "It's all about behaving like you actually want to be in a relationship."

That was the year that Joseph had been mildly flirting with a young tenor in his choir. A conscious decision to turn away from all that, to make this relationship with Donald work—it had seemed so adult. A different kind of adult, he'd hoped, than Preston's kind.

❖ ❖ ❖

The breakup with Preston was ugly. All that spring, Joseph had found it increasingly hard to ignore the anger that had been brewing inside himself: a poisonous broth of resentment over how little sex they were having, exasperation with Preston's now constant complaints about the doctoral program, and—the tipping point—fury over a comment Joseph had overheard one of the salon ladies making about Edwin Fleck. Something about Edwin's being "as queer as a three-dollar bill." The other ladies in the salon had clucked and shaken their affronted heads in agreement. Preston's mom had been out of the room at the time.

The afternoon of the snide remark, he and Preston were at the Topeka house, fixing dinner. In the kitchen, chopping vegetables for ratatouille, Joseph had suggested they invite Edwin, too. Edwin may have been a queer one, but, all in all, he was a sweet guy, certainly not someone who deserved to be maligned by the assembled flock of self-important, self-righteous women in the front parlor. It infuriated him that these paragons of middlebrow Topeka society should take it upon themselves to ridicule poor Edwin. It infuriated him that Edwin should be the absent recipient of their nasty, judgmental disapproval. It infuriated him that he, too, still felt uncomfortable with Edwin. He wanted that feeling to go away. Why not be nice to Edwin?

"Why the hell do you want to invite him to dinner?" Preston snapped. "You don't even like him."

"I *do* like him," Joseph said. "I mean, really, why shouldn't he come to dinner? He lives here."

"As my mother's tenant," Preston interrupted. "In the basement."

"Precisely, Preston. In the *basement*. Don't you think it would be nice for him to crawl out of that hole and have a decent meal?"

"My mother's basement apartment is not a hole! And as for a 'decent meal,' Christ, he makes a good salary. Let him go out to dinner."

"I can't believe you. Look at this." Joseph gestured toward the piles of chopped vegetables. "There's enough food here to feed an army. What's wrong with sharing some of it with him?"

"What's wrong, Joseph, is that my mother has already invited guests for tonight."

"Who?"

"Some of the salon gals."

"Those bitches are coming to dinner?"

"Excuse me?"

"I am not sitting at the same table with those women." Joseph remembered lowering his voice so that Preston's mom, upstairs in one of her project rooms, would not hear.

"Bitches?" Preston fired back. "What the hell are you talking about? How dare you criticize my mother's guests? Last time I checked, *you* were a guest in this house, too."

"A guest? Really? So, I'm a *guest* here?"

"Who else do you think you are?" Preston demanded.

Joseph tore off his apron, threw it down on the floor, and stormed out of the kitchen. Up in the bedroom, his rage was at such a boil he hardly took note of what he was doing. He furiously repacked his weekend carryall, flinging Preston's stuff across the room. It was only then that he realized he had no transportation back to Lawrence. They'd come in Preston's VW. Still, he had to get out of the house.

Preston's mother was just emerging from her macramé room when Joseph bolted into the hallway, clutching his bag.

"Well, hello!" she called out cheerily. "You're in a rush."

"Excuse me" was all he said. The next thing he knew, he was hoofing it to the highway. An hour and two hitchhike rides later, he was back in Lawrence and planning how to get the hell out of Kansas.

❖ ❖ ❖

"Preston didn't return until the next afternoon," he told Donald. "I took some satisfaction in imagining how he was explaining my sudden departure to his mother."

They were in bed now, Donald idly glancing through a gardening magazine, Joseph with his hands cupped behind his head. It had gotten too dark for them to actually put in the pansies, but at least the bed had been prepared. Blessedly, Donald hadn't said anything about how they could have waited and bought higher-quality pansies in the morning.

"Preston and I didn't speak for the rest of that day or the next."

Donald closed the magazine and laid it on his bedside table, the "neat table," they called it. Joseph's was a jumble of books, music scores, bills, and a notebook of staff paper, where he jotted down ideas for new hymns he wanted to compose. Though he wasn't a Catholic anymore, and he never even prayed—who was there to pray to?—he still loved church music, especially the hymns.

Donald turned toward Joseph. "And when you finally *did* speak?"

"I told him I was moving out."

"Just like that?"

"Just like that. I mean, ending it was easy: all my stuff could fit into the trunk of my Oldsmobile. Took me an hour and I was gone." A guffaw escaped from his lips. "Preston was the one with serious stuff. He and his mother went antiquing every chance they got."

Donald placed a kiss on Joseph's cheek. "I think you both had some 'serious stuff' going on."

"Oh, Donald." Joseph snuggled closer. "I was so young, twenty-three that year. I didn't know what the fuck I was doing."

"You did the best ..."

"Don't say it!"

Later, after they'd turned out the lights, as Joseph listened to Donald breathing his deep, untroubled sleep—he hoped it was untroubled: why *hadn't* his husband eaten any of the pork?—he thought about whether he could have done any better during that year in Lawrence. Preston had not been an easy boyfriend, it was true. None of his boyfriends had been easy. Not Patrick, the narcissist; or Lee, with his aggressive law practice that kept him late at the office most nights. No, none of them had been easy. And in each case, his instinct had been to shut down, not wanting to look at what was really going on. That is, until Donald. With Donald, he was trying really hard not to go numb. And yet, how could you know, how could you ever know, if you were feeling everything there was to feel? What was he not seeing, he wondered, *even now*?

He shifted his body, trying to get more comfortable—sleep no longer came easily for him. Could he have done better that year with Preston? Could he have done better with Patrick or Lee?

Forgive yourself, Donald would tell him. *That was then; this is now.*

The events of the day paraded across Joseph's mind: the hasty breakfast before running off for a day of piano lessons; the swim at the gym (and lingering in the shower because his favorite swimmer, the Italian graduate student with the gorgeous body and the glorious dick, was there); the Vietnamese dinner with Donald, and the stories about Preston and his mom and Edwin Fleck. He wondered if maybe he'd been a bit in love with Edwin. Could it be that all his discomfort with Edwin was really a cover-up for some unrecognized attraction? Could it be that only now, forty-five years later, he was seeing that? Forty-five years from now, what would he come to see about his relationship with Donald? Except, of course, there would not be a forty-five-years-from-now. Not even close.

Outside, a police siren wailed, a fairly rare occurrence these days. Yes, gradually, almost without his noticing it, the neighborhood had changed for the better. This was the way of things, wasn't it: gradual, but inexorable, change. All those years ago, he had walked home every night, passing that anonymous bar—eventually, when he returned to Boston, he'd learned its name was Sporters—never going in, and then one night he had. And that had changed everything.

As the police siren faded, it struck him that maybe each and every day, there was a threshold he had to cross, a door he had to pass through, another discovery he had to make. Was anything ever finally settled? Would his feelings for Donald ever finally settle?

On the right side of the bed—he had slept on the right their entire fourteen years together—Donald had turned away. A gesture that Joseph knew signified nothing unfriendly, nothing he need worry about. Would *that* ever change—their sleeping arrangements? Who knew? Joseph hoped that when the big changes came, he'd have the courage to say yes to them, to walk through those doors, too.

He recalled how often, in the wee hours of a Topeka-visit night as he lay in bed with Preston, he would hear Mrs. Sedgwick padding about the house in her slippers, attending to her projects, watering her plants, puttering in the kitchen as she got ready to bake a cake or put a meatloaf into the oven. She had been so alive, so alert to everything. A woman who never slept.

At last, he felt himself getting drowsy, pulled into the oblivion of night. The *momentary* oblivion of night. Total oblivion would come one day, but not for a while, he hoped. It had come for Buddy, total oblivion, though Joseph hoped that keeping alive fond memories of Buddy counted for something. Was he afraid of death? He didn't think so. But maybe he was in shut-down mode about that, too.

And suddenly, he was praying. To no one in particular, perhaps only to the vast, indifferent universe—certainly not to God, that old God he'd given up on years ago. There, with the sweet fragrance of Donald's freshly laundered pajamas filling his nostrils, he sent up his silent appeal. *Please keep me awake,* he said. *Don't let me fall asleep. Even if it hurts. Even if it hurts.*

Sol y Sombra

The summer after my wife died, I tried to keep up her garden. Over the years, Marion had transformed the area in back of our house in Belmont into a leafy, flowery refuge. Hostas and lilies were her specialty—hostas for the shady parts of the garden, day lilies for the sunny areas. Marion majored in Spanish in college, a language she kept up all her life. She christened the garden *El Jardín de Sol y Sombra*, the Garden of Sun and Shadow. Marion was a perennially radiant person, positive about everything right through her diagnosis, illness, and death. Still, there it was: sun and shadow all in one little suburban plot, a reminder, I guess, that there are always dark places, even in the sunniest of lives.

That first summer after she was gone, I dutifully puttered about, weeding, pruning, even putting in a few new plants, but my heart wasn't in it. I was only doing it for Marion, to honor her memory and to honor the love she had lavished all those years on her special corner of the world. By August, my devotion to the project had waned. I was about to turn seventy-two. I felt old. Old and tired and lost. Without Marion's companionship, the garden didn't much feel like it was worth my nurturing.

But then another summer came, and I just couldn't bear watching the thing go to weed. At the very least, I felt that I should keep the garden looking presentable. So I hired a college kid to do the basics—just enough to make it look like it hadn't been abandoned. Brewster was an English major at Amherst College, spending the summer in Boston doing research for his senior thesis. He had grown up in Central Massachusetts, on an apple farm, so gardening was in his blood.

The first afternoon Brewster came to work, I was immediately charmed. His name somewhat suggests the quality of his appeal, a sort of old-fashioned, New England wholesomeness: dirty-blond hair, a plain but not unflattering face, neither tall nor short. I could picture him having grown up in one of those Federalist-era frame houses that still stand all over the Pioneer Valley: four-square, unadorned, honest, and quietly handsome.

And while he was hardly delicate—what boy who grew up on a farm is?—he exuded a surprisingly delicate gracefulness that was, I will confess, enchanting.

After I had explained what needed doing and he set to work, I retired to the kitchen in the back of the house to read the paper. Every now and then, from the window in the breakfast nook, I stole a glance at Brewster. He carried his body almost as if he were a dancer. And that scruffy head of dirty-blond hair, I saw that it was, in fact, a studied look, not quite as casual as I'd first thought. Even the loose-fitting tee shirt he wore that morning, emblazoned with a portrait of Shakespeare—well, the whole effect got me wondering. I know to be careful of stereotypes, but for the past several months, I'd been studying the mannerisms of gay men. I found that there's a fair accuracy in attributing certain traits to them—body carriage, hairstyle, high-culture references ... Not, of course, to every gay man, but enough that I'd begun to take note.

When he was finished in the garden that day, I invited Brewster in for a glass of iced tea.

"It's a beautiful garden, sir," he said, as we sat down at the kitchen table. I watched how he settled himself into the chair. It was not a farmer's way of sitting down.

I thanked him, gave him a capsule history of the garden, told me its name.

"It's an appropriate name, isn't it?" he said. "I noticed the mottled effect—the way the sunlight gilds certain areas while other areas remain shady."

"Mottled!" I chuckled. "You *are* an English major!"

"I like words," he said, slightly blushing.

I got up and went to the refrigerator. "Hungry? Would you like something to eat?" I realized I was behaving out of nervousness. Moving away from the table was, I hoped, a way to come across as casual, as being not too interested in him.

"No thank you, sir. My roommates and I are going out for pizza later on."

It had been weeks since I'd last gone out for a meal with friends. I wasn't exactly becoming a recluse, but I was shying away from social engagements. I was single now; my friends were all still coupled. Getting together with them made me feel like a charity case.

"Pizza. That sounds splendid," I said, wincing internally as soon as those words were out of my mouth. *Splendid!* I sounded like a caricature of the retired Boston pediatrician I was. Who uses words like "splendid" anymore?

"Your roommates," I asked, trying to steer the conversation toward less fuddy-duddy sentiments, "do they go to Amherst, too?"

"No," Brewster said. "Chloe goes to B.U. and Rachel's at Mass College of Art."

How much surprise registered on my face when I learned that he was living with two young women?

"We're subletting for the summer from one of Chloe's friends," he explained.

"Sounds like fun," I said, not knowing what I meant by that, but hoping he didn't take the remark as a male wink at his savoir faire in shacking up with two ladies.

"So far, it's been great, sir."

"Please call me Sterling," I told him.

❖ ❖ ❖

After Marion's death, my son Richard invited me to move in with him and Charlene. Their kids were all out of the house now; there was plenty of room. I thanked him, but turned down the offer right then and there. I told Richard I didn't want to be a burden, that I loved the old house in Belmont and that I was perfectly capable of taking care of myself. "Seventy is the new fifty," I told him, echoing my friend Raúl's motto. All of these things were true, but the real reason is that I wanted time to explore what a single man's life might be like. It was beginning to hit me that I'd never really had a single man's life.

Marion and I were very young when we met, seniors in college. She was my Spanish tutor that year. Somehow the college had screwed up when, during freshman year, they waived the foreign language requirement for me. Three-and-a-half years later, they informed me that my two years of Spanish in high school were, in fact, not enough to count toward fulfilling the language requirement. I had to do the equivalent of two semesters of college-level Spanish during the spring semester, or my diploma would be withheld until I completed summer school. I had plans to backpack through Europe after graduation. Nothing was going to keep me from a trip I'd been looking forward to for quite a while.

And so, I embarked on a marathon program to prepare for what the college called a "concept inventory" in Spanish. Marion was assigned to me by the Bureau of Study Counsel, a fancy name for the tutoring service. We started meeting in February, three evenings a week, to plow through the curriculum—verb conjugations including the present, past, and future subjunctive, the difference between *por* and *para, ser* and *estar*, lists of infernal pronouns, impossible prepositions, and gobs and gobs of vocabulary. After we were married, Marion used to tell me how very business-like I'd been—no flirting, no shooting the breeze, no anything but Spanish. Just before spring break, I took her out to dinner. I did not think of it as a date, just a gesture of thanks. Still, we had such a good time that, when we returned from vacation and resumed our lessons, we started going out more often.

Falling in love with her took me by surprise. Not because she wasn't attractive. Marion was attractive in every way imaginable. Beautiful, intelligent, funny, an excellent teacher, and that sunny disposition. There was nothing not to like about her. No, falling in love with her came as a surprise because I had never been in love with any woman before. In high school, I never even had a crush. At least not on a young lady. No one seemed to notice that I didn't go on dates. I was admired for my intellect, especially in science and math. My classmates used to call me "Dr. Bouchard" long before I ever thought of going to medical school. In those days—or maybe it was just my particular high school—a boy did not bring down suspicion on himself for not being girl crazy. It was a different time then.

Marion was my first and only sexual partner. For the first years of our marriage, we enjoyed a healthy sex life, and managed to bring two beautiful children into the world, Richard and his sister Karen. But by the time we were in our late forties, the ardor had waned, on both our parts. Our slackened sex life did not seem to bother either of us. We just didn't mind that much. At least we didn't talk about it. We still enjoyed sleeping together, cuddling, going to dinner dances, sitting in the living room over a martini before dinner. And watching our kids grow. That's where the ardor went, in the delight we took in the children. And then the grandchildren. We loved the roles we were allowed to play with the grandkids: babysitter, board-game partner, after-school chauffeur, take-the-kids-for-a-week grandparents. We also had our distinct roles: Marion was the one who bought books for the grandchildren; I functioned as a consultant in matters pediatric.

Our lives were rich. The stories our friends told us of their own carnal disgruntlements and guilt-ridden straying felt like tales from exotic places we had no interest in visiting. The name of our town, Belmont, means beautiful mountain, and it was from the pleasant heights of our agreeable marriage that we watched our lives play out along levelheaded, companionable paths. When Marion was diagnosed with cancer, we took it as another responsibility that we would meet, steadily, together.

❖ ❖ ❖

The next time Brewster showed up, the day was already swelteringly hot. Even though it was only ten in the morning, the temperature was inching toward the mid-eighties and the humidity was oppressive. Instead of jeans, he was wearing charmingly baggy shorts. An Amherst tee shirt and a pair of low-rise sneakers completed the ensemble. The sneakers were a sort of sea-foam green color, not exactly a match with his purple Amherst shirt, but on Brewster, the effect—if I may be permitted another fuddy-duddy word—was *fetching*.

This time, even before he got to work, I offered him a glass of iced tea.

"Tell me about your thesis," I invited as we sat at the kitchen table.

He seemed startled that I'd be interested.

"Oh, gosh. It's about amateur farmer-poets in New England during the early nineteenth century," he said. "People whose basic life was on the land but who occasionally wrote poetry and sent it in to the local newspapers to be published."

As he continued to talk about his project, his face began to open up with enthusiasm. "I'm spending a lot of time at the Massachusetts Historical Society. They've got a great collection of old newspapers."

He took a sip of his iced tea. Again, the delicacy of his movements—his fingers on the glass, the way he brought the glass to his lips—I thought about those by-gone New England farmers, snatching a few minutes here and there to put into words the thoughts and feelings that could not be expressed solely through the husbandry of the land. A bushel of apples was a beautiful expression of the soul, but apparently, these old Yankees had more to say, and only words—metered, rhymed words—could say it.

"You like doing research?" I asked.

"Yes, very much. I think it's fascinating digging up the past."

I laughed. "Digging seems to be in your genes, Brewster: digging in the dirt, digging in the archives."

Brewster laughed, too. "I never thought of it that way before. I guess you're right." He looked down at his empty glass. "Well, I'd better get going."

"Why don't you just work for an hour today?" I suggested. "It's brutally hot and only going to get hotter. I'll still pay you for three hours."

"Gosh, that's really nice of you ..." I heard the briefest pause, before he added, "Sterling."

❖ ❖ ❖

It was after Brewster had been working a few weeks that I decided to throw a fiftieth birthday party for my son Richard—a garden party in the very yard that Brewster had been so tenderly bringing back to life.

I asked him if he would care to bartend. It wouldn't be a big affair, I assured him, but if he wanted to bring along a pal to help out—or Chloe or Rachel, I quickly added—it would be fine with me. "I'll ask around," he said.

On the day of the party, he showed up with neither Chloe nor Rachel, but with a former high school chum, an Indian American boy named Deekshant. In their catering togs—black trousers and white, short-sleeved shirts—they were a handsome duo. As they went about setting up, I tried not to pay them any more attention than what might be expected of the host of a garden party trying to make sure everything was proceeding smoothly.

No sooner had the boys brought out the tables, filled a tub with ice, and helped me set up lawn chairs than my family started arriving, the ladies bearing salads, appetizers, and presents; the men toting six packs of beer and more bags of ice. It was a gorgeous late-July afternoon. The colors in Marion's garden were at their sun-dappled, *mottled*, best.

We were three generations of the Whiting-Bouchard family— Marion's and my generation; followed by the generation of our son and daughter; and finally, the youngest generation, the grandkids and their cousins. I had last seen the clan at Marion's funeral, so there was something poignant about our gathering again. At least, for me it was poignant. Everyone else seemed to have emotionally moved on. It was Richard's fifty years of life, not the end of Marion's, that they had come to bear witness to.

After the obligatory greetings, the family settled into its usual social patterns. My brother Tim and I caught up. Tim's wife and Marion's sister, the "old gals," as I jokingly call them, did likewise. Meanwhile, Richard's wife Charlene, Richard's sister Karen, and the other women of that generation—"the young gals"— plunked themselves down on lawn chairs with their wine coolers and did what they always do at these gatherings, trade friendly boasts about their kids' latest accomplishments. Charlene is the mistress of this game. You would think her three children had garnered every prize in the book. To be honest, I don't like my daughter-in-law very much: Charlene is brash and meddlesome and too sure of herself. She has three girls—two in college, one recently graduated—whose lives she tries to choreograph.

When my brother went off to get himself a hamburger, I just stood there, taking in the scene. I was doing that a lot that summer—just taking in the scene. The party was humming merrily along. The glorious weather, the garden, the happy flow of booze and conversations— everything was sparkly and tinkling and gay—that old, original kind of gay. It amused me to see that the youngest generation—all the cousins, both the girls and the boys—had gravitated toward Brewster and Deekshant. And why not? That's the prerogative of young people, isn't it—to be all over each other like a litter of puppies. What are they looking for in their polymorphous friendliness? Then again, what are any of us looking for when we go out of our way to meet new people?

I noticed that my granddaughter Becky was the only one of that generation not hovering around the catering table. At twenty-four, Becky is the oldest of all my grandchildren. She graduated a couple years ago from Mount Holyoke with a degree in political science. Summa cum laude. A smart cookie. Immediately after college, she went to work in the office of one of the state senators in Boston, doing research, writing policy statements and speeches, that kind of thing. "I told them right off that I wasn't there to make coffee and file papers," she told Marion and me when she got the job.

Becky has always been a stand-apart-from-the-crowd type. She's definitely not like her two sisters or her female cousins. She's both the smartest of the bunch and the least girly. In high school, she was on the debate team. She wrote an editorial in the school paper about why boys should be allowed to be cheerleaders. And, much to her mother's dismay, she went to the senior prom with the school's geeky math genius, a boy who played sousaphone in the marching band.

When she saw me looking at her, Becky sauntered over, bottle of beer in hand.

"Hey, Papaw. What's going on?"

Becky is beautiful, the lucky recipient of her parents' best features: her mom's silky chestnut hair and flawless complexion, Richard's height and blue eyes. During college, she put on some weight. In fact, by the end of her sophomore year, she'd gained almost thirty pounds. That's pretty much where it has stayed. Charlene is always harping on the extra bulk, but I think it looks good on Becky. She knows how to carry it off.

"I'm just thinking how happy I am that the whole family can be together," I told her. "On a far happier occasion than the last time we were all together."

She nodded her assent, a meditative seriousness momentarily darkening her face.

She was wearing shorts, which accentuated her thick thighs, and a loose-fitting, untucked linen blouse that showed off an amble bosom and some serious upper arm muscles.

"So, what's going on with you?" I asked.

"Usual stuff," she said. "Though work's a bit slow right now. The Senate's in recess, so I get some time to enjoy the summer."

"It's been a beautiful summer so far, hasn't it? A bit hot, but overall just beautiful."

"Yeah, my girlfriends and I have managed to get to the beach pretty much every weekend."

I've learned that when Becky says "girlfriends," she means her female friends—friends from college and work—not "girlfriend," as in the woman you're in love with.

She took a swig of beer, a fast, nervous-looking gulp. "We've been making the rounds of the beaches. Especially the ones on the North Shore. Crane's, up in Ipswich." Another nervous swig. "And Wingaersheek."

"Lovely places, I hear." I sensed there was more coming.

"A couple of weeks ago"—she was scraping the label on her beer bottle with a fingernail—"we went all the way to P'town."

"That's quite a distance to go for a beach," I said, putting as neutral a tone as possible into my observation. The last thing I wanted was to sound like Charlene. I let out a friendly chuckle. "And definitely not the North Shore."

"Yeah"—she paused momentarily, scraping harder at the label—"we didn't get home until really late. The traffic over the bridge was backed up for miles."

"It can get bad on a Sunday night," I confirmed.

"Last Sunday, we stuck closer to home. Carson Beach in Southie."

"Your grandmother and I went there a few times," I told her. Where was this going, I wondered, this catalogue of beaches.

"Cool. You never told me that."

"Well, there it is," I said.

"Yeah, so afterwards, we went out for beers." The label on her bottle was almost completely peeled away by now. "To one of the bars in Boston." She kept her attention on the ravaged label. "Actually, a gay bar."

The only response I could think of was, "Oh, and how was that?" I hated how grandfatherly my response sounded—corny and quaint and full of an old man's surprise at the things a young person will say. Which, of course, is just what it was.

"It was cool," she said, looking at me straight in the eye, then glancing down at her bottle again.

My God, I thought, *is my granddaughter telling me she's a lesbian?* And suddenly, lots of random facts about Becky's life fell into place. How had I missed this all these years? And why was she telling *me?*

"What was cool about it?" I asked, hoping this did not come across as a challenge.

"I don't know," she said, working hard now to seem as offhand as possible. "The guys were fun."

"Really?" It was now my turn to affect the offhand manner. "And you don't have fun with boys in normal bars?" I realized this was not the right way to put it. I am still learning that "normal" is not a normal word anymore. "I mean, ah, straight bars," I corrected.

"Papaw, I walk into a straight club and guys immediately start hitting on me." She laughed. "The big boobs, I guess." She took another sip of her beer. "You know what 'hitting on' means, right?"

"Yes, I know 'hitting on,'" I assured her, and followed that up with my standard grandfatherly chuckle. There are times when I think I have no response to the things my grandchildren—or *all* young people, for that matter—tell me other than to chuckle. My friend Raúl tells me to stop thinking of myself as a grandfather. It's good advice, but I'm still learning how. The first step, I guess, would be to excise the chuckle from my conversations with my grandchildren.

"And the boys in gay bars? What's so special about them?"

It was bizarre hearing myself ask this question, one I'd been posing to myself quite often during the past six months.

Becky laughed again, this time a relieved kind of laugh. "Well, to begin with, they're *gay,* Papaw. Which means you can actually have an interesting conversation with them. About interesting stuff."

This had not been my experience, limited as it was, but I held my tongue again.

Just then, Charlene wandered over.

"Hey, Mom." The way Becky greeted her mother, and then shot me a quick look, told me our conversation was over, at least for the time being.

"Well, you two look like you're having a nice catch-up," Charlene observed. I think Charlene has always been a bit jealous of my rapport with her eldest daughter. She can probably sense that Becky has been, for a long while now, my favorite grandchild. And the child that she, Charlene, least understands.

"Just shootin' the breeze with Papaw," Becky said.

"I just had the most interesting conversation with one of the catering boys over there," Charlene announced. "He goes to Amherst. And he told me that he took a course at Mount Holyoke last year."

"Cool." The tone in Becky's voice was chilly.

"You should go over and introduce yourself."

"*Because* ...?" Becky twisted the word in that way people her age do to indicate sarcastic befuddlement.

Charlene didn't pick up on the sarcasm.

"Well, I mean, you went to ..."

"Yeah, Mom. I went to Mount Holyoke; he goes to Amherst. He's—what?—three, four years younger than I am, and ..."

Charlene shook her head and sighed. "Becky, Becky, Becky." She looked at me, beseeching my understanding. All I could do was shrug my shoulders.

After Charlene left us—to go pester another one of her daughters, I guessed—I turned to Becky.

"Ah, your mother!" was the best I could come up with. There was so much more I wanted to say.

❖ ❖ ❖

I've mentioned Raúl, the guy who tells me to stop thinking of myself as old. I met him during the months that Marion and I went to Massachusetts General Hospital for her chemo treatments. Raúl's husband was also undergoing chemo. Breast cancer for Marion; pancreatic cancer for Alan. Each chemo session took several hours. Sitting in that waiting area, listening to time *drip, drip, drip* by, I tried to read. I did not want to make eye contact with the others sitting there. I did not want to see what was on their faces. But during the second visit, Raúl struck up a conversation with me. He was immediately forthcoming about the fact that he had a husband. When he said that, I offered my sympathy, as if it were the most normal thing in the world for a man to have a husband. Which these days, it is.

The next time we found ourselves in the waiting room, Raúl and I went to the hospital cafeteria for coffee. I told him a little more about Marion and me, and listened to more of his story. I watched myself playing a role: the sympathetic straight white male, totally nonjudgmental about his sexuality, showing interest and compassion, asking all the right questions.

The following week, when we had coffee again—this time at a little coffee shop on Beacon Hill— Raúl asked me if I were gay. Just like that.

I'm married, I told him. *I know*, he said, and stared right at me, hands folded in front of his coffee cup.

And that's how Raúl became the first person I ever told. Not in so many words at first. At first, I feigned surprise. *So why would you think that?* I asked. He smiled. *Just a hunch, Sterling.* That's what did it—it was like he knew me, which, in a sense, he did. Better than any other man I'd ever known. Better, I hate to admit, than Marion. I burst into tears.

I couldn't stop crying and kept apologizing. All these months of stress over Marion's cancer, I told him. The worry, the fear of losing her. My one and only sweetheart. The only life I knew. But I knew that the tears were about something else as well. And Raúl knew that, too.

A few weeks later, he and Alan invited us over for dinner. Good liberals that we were, Marion and I had socialized on a few occasions with other gay men—colleagues of mine or hers—but I'd never been in a gay couple's home before and never when the gay couple knew my secret. (Though now I wonder how many others had ever had a "hunch" about me but never said anything.)

It was an early dinner and we had agreed upon a time limit—two hours max—in deference to Alan and Marion's compromised health. Over that dinner, the three of them kept up a steady stream of conversation—how each couple had met, respective wedding stories, favorite vacations, favorite artists. (Alan was a curator at a small museum;

Raúl was a painter.) And then there was the topic of our children: Richard and Karen for us; two Welsh corgis, whose names were Lucy and Ethel, for them. In truth, I remember very little that was said that night. About all I remember is how animated the conversation was, how entertained—yes, I think that's the right word—how *entertained* Marion was. She laughed and carried on and drank more wine than I'd seen her drink in a long time.

"You were rather subdued," Marion remarked in the car driving home that night. "You didn't have a good time?"

I assured her that I'd had a fine time. "It's just that it's so weird, making new friends when ..." I couldn't finish the sentence. We drove the rest of the way home in silence, each with our thoughts.

The next morning, I fished out my old Spanish textbook and started relearning the language.

Six weeks later Alan died. I went to the memorial service alone. Marion was having a bad reaction to the chemo. It was at a church in Boston known for its outreach to LGBTQ people; the reception afterwards was at Alan's favorite watering hole—a bar called Score! in the South End. Raúl had rented the back half for the reception. The front half was still operating that afternoon as a gay bar. That's where I learned that "normal" is not a normal word anymore. The bar felt so normal in the old sense, just a bunch of guys enjoying a Saturday afternoon together. I tried not to gawk.

The following winter, Marion died. And three weeks after her funeral, I took myself back to Score! The exclamation point is part of the name. I wanted to believe in that mark, that promise of excitement. My heart was beating much too quickly.

The place was alive with guys drinking, chatting, watching sports on the screens over the bar. I desperately wanted a martini, but wondered if that weren't a bit too effete for the likes of a gay sports bar. I ordered a beer.

Not much happened that first night. I kept my eyes on the screens—basketball on one, hockey on another—afraid to make eye contact with anyone, and conjugating Spanish verbs in my head. The beer went down very quickly. I decided it was not a good idea to drink another. The roads were slippery; it was an unfamiliar drive back to Belmont. I counted it a victory just to have gotten myself through the door.

I held onto that empty beer bottle for fifteen more minutes, raising it to my lips from time to time to fake taking another sip, anything to force myself to stay. From time to time, I scanned the barroom, trying to take it all in—the kind of guys who came here, how they behaved, what the moves were. (Some were even drinking martinis.) I don't think I was the oldest gentleman there, though maybe I was. I've been told I look pretty good for someone who's now seventy-three. My hair is still thick, if silvery; I haven't got many wrinkles. Marion and I used to cut a good figure together.

❖ ❖ ❖

I'd ordered a big birthday cake for Richard. A Black Forest cake, his favorite. After we all sang "Happy Birthday" and Richard blew out the candles, Brewster and Deekshant took over. Brewster cut slices of cake—here, too, with that winsome delicacy of manner—and Deekshant poured the champagne.

I'd been drinking more than I should have that afternoon, but, hell, it was a birthday party, I told myself. The first really *happy* occasion I'd enjoyed since Marion died. Two beautiful boys were helping me serve. And my granddaughter had just come out to me. What a day!

The two of them, Brewster and Deekshant, went around with trays serving the guests. When Brewster offered me a piece of cake, I took the opportunity to strike up a conversation with him.

"One of my granddaughters went to Mount Holyoke. Her mother thought you two would hit it off."

Brewster laughed—a mixture of discomfort, embarrassment, and willingness to play along.

"Oh, gosh," he managed to say.

"Don't worry," I assured him. "I'm not here to act as a matchmaker."

"No, um, I mean, I'd be happy to meet her, Sterling."

The next words out of my mouth were totally unplanned. As I said, I'd been drinking too much.

"Well, the fact of the matter is," I said, starting up with that damn lordly tone again, "I'm not sure she'd be entirely interested in meeting you." I dropped my voice to a conspiratorial whisper. "You see, I think she's a lesbian."

"Oh, okay. Whatever."

"I assume that doesn't bother you?"

"Of course not, Sterling," he fired back. "A lot of my friends ..."

"I'm sure," I said. "The times are very different now, aren't they?"

"I think so."

"I *know* so," I told him, giving him a wink.

Brewster looked down at the tray of cake.

"I should probably keep passing this."

"Well then, off you go."

I watched him making his way to the others. He had a lovely ass. Questions were exploding in my head: Would I ever have sex with a man? Would I ever have sex with someone that young? Were Brewster and Deekshant lovers? And why in heaven's name had I told him that Becky was a lesbian?

❖ ❖ ❖

The day after the birthday party, I met Raúl. We went back to Score! On Sundays, they do a nice brunch. Our table was on the outdoor patio. We were surrounded by guys from the gay kickball league, several teams of them, each in their own distinctive jerseys and caps. Most were in their twenties and thirties. A few were older. Not everyone looked like an athlete. Yes, I was still taking lots of field notes.

I was lousy at kickball when I was in elementary school. Probably most of these guys were, too. That's one of the things I'm beginning to learn about gay men these days, how they can take up a former cause of shame—being a sissy, for example—and turn it on its head, make it something they can have fun with and celebrate. Gay kickball! Imagine.

Over omelets and drinks—a *virgin* Mary for me—I told Raúl about the party.

"I'm afraid I had a bit too much to drink and did something I now regret."

Raúl looked up from his plate. "Did you make a pass at one of the caterers?" He looked more amused than shocked.

"Worse," I said. "I outed my granddaughter to one of them."

"One of your granddaughters is a lesbian? You never told me that."

I laughed. "I didn't know myself. In fact, I'm still not sure. But what do you make of a twenty-three-year-old woman who went to a women's college and hangs out at gay bars because, as she says, the guys are more interesting?"

"I'd say she has good taste."

"Oh, dear. Have I jumped to conclusions?"

"Maybe so, maybe not."

"Her name's Becky," I continued. "Richard and Charlene's oldest."

Raúl laughed. "I definitely know who Charlene is."

"Well, Becky ... ever since she was a kid—fourth, fifth grade—there was something about her that was just different. She was always discreetly watching the world around her, as if she were assessing just how she would meet it. There was something almost noncommittal about the way she took things in, like she was trying to decide whether the manner—the *language* her pals and classmates used—was right for her."

Raúl was smiling at me.

"What?" I asked.

"You could be describing yourself, you know," he said.

I gave him a puzzled look.

"You were a watcher, too, Sterling. Don't you think? I mean I know you loved Marion, but all those years, weren't you also watching to see where and how you really fit in?"

"You think so?" I asked. I could hear the resistance in my voice. It was his word "really." Really fit in. But I had fit in, hadn't I? The marriage, the parenting, the career. "So you think I haven't *really* fit in until now?"

"I was a watcher, too," Raúl offered. "I always thought it was because I loved to draw and paint—always looking for a new picture to make—but there was something more going on. I was watching to figure out how a person like me could be in this world I found myself in."

I sat back in my chair and took in the scene on the patio. Raúl was right; I was a watcher and still was. And what I saw just then was a bunch of happy, raucous kickball players, their chatter loud and relaxed, and so liberated after the years of having to hold back expressing who they truly were. As a pediatrician, I'd learned a lot about the host of "challenges"—such a polite word in our profession—the pile of *shit* that gay kids have to face these days. Bullying, ostracism, depression, parental rejection, substance abuse, suicide. Half a century after I was a teenager—*more than half a century!*—gay kids were still struggling with how they would meet the world they were born into. Even here in liberal, deep-blue Boston. How amazing that, at least for this bunch of guys, that struggle seemed to have found a happy outcome.

"Do you think it's easier to come out now?" I asked Raúl.

"I think there's certainly more permission," he answered.

"Was Becky asking for my permission?"

"Maybe. But I think she was also giving *you* permission."

"Giving *me* permission?"

"To be more forthcoming with her."

I let that sink in for a moment before I spoke again. "You know, sometimes I think my life with Marion, as wonderful as it was, was a kind of holding pattern. A holding pattern that lasted a lifetime."

"It's not too late, Sterling. The holding pattern is over. You can give yourself permission now to spread those wings." He flashed me another grin. "You do realize that lots of guys are into daddies."

"I've already been a daddy," I told him. "I'd like to be something else."

"Then be it," he said. "Be whatever you want, Sterling."

❖ ❖ ❖

A week after the birthday party, I was out in the garden on another beautiful summer afternoon. It was Brewster's regular day to help me out. He was mowing the lawn; I was weeding. I have one of those contraptions that allows you to work on your knees but which you can also use to ease yourself up off the ground. Marion and I each had one. I hate the damn thing, but it's a necessity now. When Brewster finished mowing, I suggested we call it quits for the day and have our iced tea.

"You have a really nice family," he said, as we walked into the kitchen.

"Thank you," I said. "I'm glad you enjoyed them." Brewster went to fetch the ice tray out of the freezer. "And you have a very nice high school pal," I added. "It's nice how you've kept in touch even though you go to different schools now."

"We've worked hard to stay in touch," he acknowledged.

"You two hit it off with my grandchildren, I see."

"Yeah, they were cool."

I still have one of those old ice cube makers—the aluminum kind with the pull-handle that releases the cubes. Brewster dropped cubes into our glasses and poured the tea. I liked how he knew his way around the kitchen. It was beginning to feel like he was family.

"Did you meet Becky?" I asked.

"Becky?"

I could tell he was hedging.

"Becky," I repeated. "The one my daughter-in-law wanted you to meet because she went to Mount Holyoke."

"Oh, yeah. Well, actually, I didn't, but I think she and Deekshant kind of hit it off."

"Really?" As I raised my glass of iced tea to my lips, I did not take my eyes off him.

"Yeah," Brewster said. "In fact, I think they went to the beach this week."

"And after the beach, did they hit the gay bars together?"

I watched as Brewster tried to cover up his surprise.

"Um, yeah, I think they did."

"And did you join them?"

Brewster set his glass down on the table.

"Sterling, I know what you're thinking, but I'm not gay."

It was my turn to try to mask my surprise.

"Oh, I wasn't ..."

"Yes, you were, Sterling." Happily, the prick of resentment in his voice quickly gave way to amusement. "You're hardly the first person to make that assumption, Sterling. I mean, can't a guy love poetry without creating all sorts of ideas in people's minds?"

Oh, baby, I wanted to say. *It's not just that you love poetry.*

"I'm sorry," I told him. "It *was* an assumption. I apologize."

"No worries, there's really nothing to apologize for. I mean, I'd be proud to be gay, if I were gay." He shrugged his shoulders. "But I'm not."

We talked for another hour that afternoon. About how he'd had to fend off the attentions of Deekshant in high school and how it wasn't until the two of them had gone away to college that they'd become close again; about other boys at Amherst who'd come on to him; about Chloe and Rachel, with whom, yes, he had a strictly platonic friendship; and about his girlfriend at Amherst, Natalie, who was a physics major.

"She's from California, and has her heart set on graduate school at one of the big universities out there," he said. "I guess I could go anywhere after Amherst, but reading those farmer-poets has made me realize how much I love New England. Actually, it's been kind of a source of tension between us, Natalie and me." He paused. "Did you and Marion have a hard time deciding where to live after college?"

It dawned on me that Brewster was still operating under the assumption that I was straight.

"We were very young, Brewster. It was a different time. I was about to go to medical school, so there was no question that Marion would follow me. I know that sounds benighted and sexist and patriarchal, but that's the way it was in those days. When she died, I had to face some things about myself that I'd put on the back burner for a long time."

"You mean the patriarchal stuff?" he asked.

"I mean the gay stuff," I said. A momentary flicker of confusion clouded his face. "Brewster, I'm gay."

"Whoa!" he said. I looked him straight in the eyes, letting the information sink in. "Wow, Sterling, I didn't see that coming."

"You didn't?"

He shook his head. I could tell all sorts of recalculations were ticking through his brain.

"And you kept it from your wife?"

"Yes and no. I mean, I had those feelings, but I tamped them down pretty well. So in one sense, I wasn't keeping those feelings from her at all because those feelings were so deeply repressed. Besides, there were a lot of other things that kept me busy, that kept my mind off ..." I left the sentence unfinished. What were the words I couldn't speak? My mind off what? Men? Sex? The life I should have had? "A lot of things that, in fact, gave me quite a bit of joy."

Brewster nodded his understanding. But then he added, "When we left after the birthday party, Deekshant said he thought you might be gay. I said, *No way.*"

My immediate instinct was to be flattered—that Brewster had come to my defense—but then I realized that was all ass-backwards. What I should have felt flattered by was Deekshant's seeing the real me. And Becky's seeing the real me. Raúl calls that kind of thing "Gaydar." He says that gay people can just tell about each other.

"So, um ..." Brewster hesitated. I could tell he was full of questions.

"Ask me anything you want," I told him.

"I mean, I know you had a happy marriage and a beautiful family, but, I mean, do you feel like you missed out on anything?"

What could I tell this twenty-two-year-old college boy? That I felt I'd missed out on falling in love with someone like him? That I wished I'd grown up in another age? That I wished I hadn't had to pass a Spanish proficiency test, which had necessitated my taking tutoring lessons with Marion? That I wished Marion had not written love letters to me all that post-college summer while I was backpacking through Europe, two or three letters waiting for me at every American Express office I visited. That I wished that the Dutch boy I'd shared a room with in the pension in Florence, the one I got drunk with on cheap chianti, the one who tumbled into my bed, the one who apologized the next morning for "being so drunk he didn't know what he was doing," that *that* boy had not apologized, had not set up my own excuse: *Jeez, we were both so drunk, Geert. Let's just forget it, okay?*

"Do I feel I missed out on anything?" I repeated. "It's another yes-no answer. *Sol y sombra,* I guess. My life has brought me a lot of *sol,* Brewster. "A lot. But, sure, there's been some *sombra* now and then."

Reflectively, Brewster nodded his head again.

❖ ❖ ❖

There was so much I wanted to tell Raúl when we next had brunch at Score! I told him about coming out to Brewster and how wrong I'd been about his sexuality. I told him about Becky and Deekshant, how they seemed to have become beach-and-bar-hopping friends, and how I'd completely missed that Deekshant was the gay one, not Brewster.

I put down my fork. "You know," I told him, "all these mistakes, but somehow they've still left me feeling very excited. Eager to get on with my life. I'm done with speculating and second-guessing and wondering who's this and who's that. I just want to move on now." I smiled at him. "I want to do something more than just relearn Spanish verbs."

"That's great, Sterling. I'm happy for you."

"And what about you?" I asked. "Alan's been gone almost two years now. Are *you* moving on?"

"You mean aside from the occasional hookup? Well, I'm back to painting again. In fact, there's a gallery here that's going to mount a show of my new work next summer."

"Congratulations!"

"I think that's about as much moving on as I'm ready for right now."

I felt selfish asking him the next question, but I figured Raúl wouldn't mind.

"So hookups," I asked. "How does that work?"

Raúl let out a hearty laugh. "Beats me, Sterling! I'm out of practice. I'll tell you one thing, it doesn't happen here." He looked around the room and then back at me. "Think of it: a gay bar that's really just a friendly neighborhood sports bar. Man, have things changed." A smile came over his face. "How're your kickball skills? I'd say you'd have better luck meeting guys by joining a team, or singing in a choir, or, I don't know, taking an art class or something."

"Sounds like the kind of activities old people do."

"Take it from me, honey, taking a class beats wasting hours surfing the hookup sites."

I smiled. "You're the first person who's ever called me 'honey'! Not even Marion ever called me that."

"First time for everything, huh?"

There have been days—and nights—when I've wondered if Raúl and I might become lovers. But he's never given me the slightest indication that he's interested. Still, I'm grateful to have him as a friend. I hope he meets Becky one day. Maybe we'll even invite her—and Deekshant, too—to join us for brunch some Sunday. Maybe that's the life ahead for me, to be Becky's gay "uncle," so to speak.

"What are you thinking?" Raúl asked.

"The other day," I told him, "I suddenly remembered something from that semester I was learning Spanish with Marion. Just before I took the Spanish proficiency test, she and I met for one final review session. We were practicing verb conjugations. I was running through all the tenses, and the three moods—indicative, imperative and subjunctive. Marion stopped me. *I have a surprise for you,* she said. *The future subjunctive? You'll never use it. What!* I said. *Nope,* she said, *it hasn't been used in common speech since the seventeenth century. Then why?* I asked. *Why did you make me learn it?* I remember all she did was smile at me and say, *Oh, Sterling.*"

"I grew up speaking Spanish," Raúl said, "and I never even knew there was a future subjunctive."

"The funny thing is," I said, "there are days when I think I'm living in the future subjunctive."

Raúl laughed. "Are you telling me you're living in the seventeenth century?"

I recited the phrase Marion had taught me to remember the future subjunctive: "*Venga lo que viniere.* Let come what will come," I translated.

"*Venga lo que viniere,*" he repeated, his accent so much more beautiful than mine. "So there really is a future subjunctive. I was born in Mexico and never even knew that!"

We clinked glasses.

"*Venga lo que viniere,*" Raúl said again. He was clearly enjoying this bit of newfound knowledge.

"You think that's too much of an old-man's motto?" I asked him.

"What do you think? Raúl asked.

"I think it's a good motto for an old man about to embark on a new gay life," I said.

We toasted each other again.

Human Resources

Whenever a week goes by without a text message from Najib, Alan feels both anxious and relieved. Relieved because, as much as he would miss the sex—those fierce and furious two hours in a cheap motel room with this Egyptian half his age—there is no question that life without Najib would be deliciously uncomplicated. No more late-night rides up to Everett. No more sneaking past the motel clerk, even though this is one of those motels where late-night visitors seem to be the order of things. No more worrying about fucking Najib without a condom, despite Najib's assurances that he isn't hooking up with any other guys. No more love-making to the accompaniment of Grade B horror movies on the motel room television; no more coming home smelling of cigarette smoke; no more next-morning headaches, the after-effects of too little sleep and the Viagra that Alan takes before they meet. No more stories from Najib about his wife, his two beautiful children, and the girlfriend that he is fucking on the side. No more suggestions that they arrange a threesome, the two of them and the girlfriend. Uncomplicated? Man, life without Najib would be total bliss.

And yet, and yet, and yet ...

This is the mantra that unfailingly revives Alan's interest whenever he is about to call it quits. The mantra that tonight, to the accompaniment of his wiper blades set to high speed, keeps pounding in his head.

It's a Friday night—now Saturday morning—in early December, and Alan knows he should have turned off his cell phone before he went to bed, tuckered out from the week at work. He had planned to work on the renovations to his pantry this weekend, but he knows that he'll be exhausted by the time this get-together with Najib is over. The pantry will have to wait another week. Still, for all of the hassle, Najib is worth it. Just thinking about him gives Alan a boner.

When he left the house, it was already after midnight, and his housemate, Jerry, was still up, sitting at the kitchen table, in front of his laptop. Like Alan, Jerry is also sixty-three and unpartnered. He does something at a medical lab in Boston, something more than cleaning test tubes but less than actually running a research project. Most nights, Jerry spends scrolling through the Internet, sometimes reading scientific articles and sometimes trolling for guys. There are no secrets between them, especially when it comes to what Jerry used to call their "adventures." In his youth, Jerry was a pot-smoking, LSD-dropping hippie in San Francisco. He's had a life of adventures, adventures on the way to finding a boyfriend, a quest that has more or less frustrated him for over forty years. Recently, Jerry has been seeing a guy named Peter. Alan hopes this one won't fizzle out like all the rest. Jerry is so into the idea of a husband.

As soon as Alan bought his place, a nineteen-twenties bungalow in Mattapan, he realized it was too much house for him alone. Jerry was the first guy to answer his ad, and at their first meeting, they hit it off really well. He's got his quirks—Jerry, who wears a ponytail and likes to stroll through the house naked—but he's basically a good egg. And the nudity is consistent with Jerry's conviction that privacy of any sort is a bourgeois hang-up, especially between two gay roommates of a certain age. He used to tell Alan all the details of his adventures and expected the same of him. At first, Jerry's let-it-all-hang-out policy took Alan aback, but now he likes that he can leave the house at whatever hour of the night to go have an adventure of his own, and not have to explain to Jerry what he's up to.

Adventures, Alan muses. A funny word from a guy like Jerry, who is still hoping to find true love. Alan likes to think of himself as the *adventurous* one. That's what this thing with Najib has been. An adventure. And that's fine with Alan. Hooking up with Najib scratches the itch—boy, does it ever—and leaves him free to get on with his life, which these days is mostly about the house. *The house is my husband,* he once told Jerry. At his age, he thinks it's far too much trouble to go looking for a boyfriend, and certainly a husband. He thinks Jerry's life would be a lot less complicated if he'd just give up the quest, too. But, hey, everyone to his own thing.

Halfway to the motel, Alan turns on the radio and tunes it to the only rock station he can tolerate, one that plays the "oldies but goodies" from his youth. It's the kind of high-energy music that revs up his libido and wipes away any lingering doubts about what he's doing on this rain-slicked artery out of Boston headed for a sorry motel run by South Asians. He's bobbing his head now, tapping out the rhythm on the steering wheel. The wipers are going like crazy, hardly able to keep up with the driving rain. Outside, the temperature is mercifully above freezing, so he doesn't have to worry about skidding on ice. Still, he knows he should be careful. The speedometer says sixty-five. He slows down and turns up the volume on the radio.

❖ ❖ ❖

Each tryst begins with a beer and a cigarette. Alan doesn't smoke, but he loves taking a half-smoked cigarette from Najib's hand, buddy-buddy style, and drawing a puff or two, just for the pleasure of feeling the moisture of Najib's lips on the filter tip. He will nurse one beer over the course of the entire time they're together, while Najib will down the rest of the six-pack that Alan provides, his half of the bargain: Najib pays for the motel from a wad of cash he keeps in his pocket; Alan brings the beer.

Najib always leaves the motel room door ajar so that Alan can let himself in. When he arrives, Najib is always lying on the bed, stripped down to his bikini briefs, watching another horror flick. Tonight, the heater is on full blast, far warmer than it needs to be, but Najib is always complaining about how cold it is in Boston.

"Hi," Alan says.

"Hey," Najib mutters, not removing his eyes from the TV screen.

Alan takes off his coat, his scarf, his knit cap, and starts to undress. The routine has not varied much in three years. They will lie together on the bed—with its tacky, faux-Louis XIV headboard—drink beer, and talk above the TV, whose volume Najib keeps almost as high as the heater. Alan knows it's mostly just marking-time talk, the half hour and two or three beers that Najib needs to get the homo side of his libido going.

Sometimes, the talk is pretty perfunctory, stuff like the weather and how business went that week. Najib owns a string of lucrative donut shops on what the realtors now tout as the "near North Shore," but which Alan remembers from his youth as the shabby, working-class towns—Chelsea, Revere, Everett, Malden—just outside the city. It makes Alan feel old to realize that these days, Everett has become a place that someone might actually want to invest serious money in.

"Here's the beer," he says, setting it down on the night table on Najib's side of the king-size bed. The only time in his life that Alan has ever been on a king-size bed is in this motel room.

"Thanks," Najib says, still keeping his eyes on the TV screen. Alan takes a look: more of the same stuff Najib always watches. This time, it's grotesque, slimy creatures from outer space with vampire-like appetites. What so captivates Najib about these flicks? Is this kind of fare not available in Egypt? Then again, Najib has been in the U.S. for over ten years. Cheesy American culture is probably something he knows far better than Alan.

Najib reaches over, takes a beer, pops the tab, and quaffs down a long draft. Alan finishes getting undressed, down to his boxer briefs, and lies next to Najib, pretending to be interested in the movie. Najib hands him his half-drunk can and reaches for another for himself. Alan loves this, these quiet, unstudied moments of intimacy—drinking from the same can of beer, lying in bed watching a movie, even if it is such a dreadful one. They could almost be an old married couple, which Alan might even consider with Najib, though he knows two things: (1) that Najib will never leave his wife; and (2) that even if he did and they became boyfriends, Najib would probably start cheating on him just as he is cheating on both the missus and the girlfriend. No doubt about it: being boyfriends with Najib would be work, big time.

"My daughter taking piano lessons now," Najib says, his eyes still fixed on the gory mayhem on the screen. After ten years in the U.S., Najib's English is still not perfect. It's actually another thing Alan finds sexy about him.

Alan knows the daughter's name, Tracy, and that she is six years old, and that she loves her first-grade teacher. The son, Connor, is two-and-a-half. Alan is amused that Najib has given his children such American names. Or was it the American wife who named the kids? He almost hopes so, because she seems to have such little say in most of the decisions in Najib's family. She certainly has no say in how late he stays out on Friday nights.

"You have a piano now?" Alan asks.

"Electronic keyboard. Very good."

Najib's conversation is often pared down to clipped phrases. Unless he's talking about cars, which are his passion. Then he opens up. Alan doesn't know a thing about cars, but he loves listening to how Najib can go on and on, especially about BMWs, which are his favorites. Najib owns two of them. Apparently, you can make a lot of money owning a string of donut shops.

By the time he's moved on to his third beer, Najib is ready to "take a shower," his way of announcing that it's time to get on to sex.

"You wanna take a shower with me?" Najib asks. Alan is immediately aroused. He loves these surprise moments of affection, which Najib rarely doles out. At such times, Alan feels very old-fashioned. As the top, isn't he supposed to be the bold, cocky, take-charge one in these meetings? Certainly not the one who hankers after whatever intimate little scraps Najib will toss his way. Most nights, Alan has no idea what he's supposed to feel.

"Sure," he says, as matter-of-factly as possible.

Under the assault of warm water, Alan washes Najib's back and chest and ass, caressing his butt and then slowly working the tiny cake of motel soap into his crack, getting him ready for rimming and fucking. In his haste to get to the motel, he'd forgotten to take a Viagra, but he finds that tonight he doesn't need it. *Did I take my PrEP this morning?* he thinks in a panic. *Yes, yes. Relax.*

He embraces Najib from behind, pressing his erection onto Najib's ass, that luscious melon of a butt that Alan still can't believe is his for the taking. He lays his head against the nape of Najib's neck, just letting the water cascade over them. For a second, Najib permits this affectionate expression. Then he shrugs Alan away, turns off the water, and announces, "Let's go." Alan is still soapy under his armpits, but he says nothing. He doesn't want to interrupt the forward momentum of things.

Hastily toweled off, still half wet from the shower, Alan throws back the motel's hideous bed covers. Najib doesn't seem to care where they do it, but Alan likes the smell and feel of the clean sheets. Besides, he doesn't want to stain the bedspread with lubricant or semen. That seems like something even a seedy motel like this one shouldn't have to put up with.

He pushes Najib onto the bed, gets on top of him, and starts making out, which Alan has had to teach Najib to enjoy. Tonight, Najib is totally into it. He grabs Alan's head, pulling him closer. Hungrily, almost hostilely, their tongues explore each other's mouths. This is going to be one of the good nights, Alan thinks. And then he silently admonishes himself: *Stop analyzing. Just let go and keep your head out of it.*

Still, despite the passion they have already fallen into, tonight Alan can't quite turn off his thoughts. And what should enter those thoughts but William.

❖ ❖ ❖

William was a work colleague, forty years ago, during Alan's first year after college. Both of them were in the human resources division of a large Minneapolis dairy conglomerate. Unlike Alan, William was a native of Minnesota, from a Norwegian American farm family. Tall, ruddy, and wholesome, he wore flannel shirts and rimless glasses that accentuated his deep blue eyes. Alan liked that they had adjoining cubicles. He also liked that William had a luscious butt—a tight, round, farmer-boy butt—which Alan immediately noticed the first time they'd met.

One Friday night that first winter, a bunch of them went out for drinks, to a bar Alan hadn't been to before, over in St. Paul. Seven or eight of them, guys and gals, as the lingo went back then, all in their twenties. Over pitchers of beer and huge sandwiches of barbecued beef, they talked about the Vikings, about what city could lay claim to the best barbeque sauce, and how Ted Kennedy had just announced he would run against Jimmy Carter in the presidential primaries.

William, who, it came out, had been in DeMolay during high school, said he'd lost his respect for Kennedy after Chappaquiddick. Alan barely knew the story, but he was impressed by William's knowledge and his clean-cut, Protestant boys-club standards. In college, Alan had majored in Social Relations, a mixture of psychology, anthropology, and social theory, which left him with a muddled idea of his own convictions. He'd accepted the offer from the Minneapolis company because he needed a job and because the notion of helping fellow workers with their rights and benefits seemed like a good thing, the kind of thing a Social Relations major would do. The idea of living in Minneapolis, far away from East Providence, where he'd grown up, also appealed to him. That night at the bar, he felt as if he'd finally settled in, as if he belonged in this homey, beef-fed, barbecue-slathered land—a place that, when he arrived in September, had left him as bewildered as if he'd taken a job in Bombay or Beirut.

The evening merrily rolled along, the air twanging with the music of country western hits. Pitchers of beer kept arriving, and the conversation got sillier and sillier. By then, the guy doing most of the talking was Keith, a red-haired boy from Des Moines, who worked in another department, someone Alan had never met before. Though he didn't have much experience in this realm, Alan could tell that Keith was gay. There was something a little too clever and campy about Keith's banter.

Every time Keith said something funny, William would squeeze Alan's arm and burst out howling, as if to steady himself amid the raucous hooting that ensued. Except it had nothing to do with steadying himself. Alan knew this ploy. He'd tried it in college on the guys he'd been attracted to. In the boozy camaraderie that prevailed during pub crawls with his college buddies, he'd gotten away with a lot of tactile transgressions. By the time he graduated, Alan knew he wanted more, a lot more. And now William was touching him the way Alan used to touch his beer buddies back in college.

Around eleven, the last of their friends—Keith and the girl he'd driven over with—bid the two of them good night, Keith smirking and winking as he departed. Alan waited to see what William would do. But suddenly, Keith rushed back in to announce that it was snowing really hard outside and did William and Alan want to crash at his place, which was not far away? William immediately took charge, declining the offer. He told Keith that he and Alan had driven over from work together and that he'd rather get back to Minneapolis. *I'm telling you, hon,* Keith said, *it's coming down as fast as hotcakes off a griddle.*

William insisted that they'd be fine. All Alan could think of was that Keith had called William *hon.*

"One more beer?" William asked when Keith left. Under normal circumstances, this would have seemed foolish to Alan. The driving would only get worse the later they stayed, and more alcohol was not going to help the situation. But Alan was ready for something to happen with William, and when William punctuated the offer by taking off his glasses and flashing him a broad, farm-boy smile, Alan just couldn't turn him down.

It was close to midnight when they finally walked out to the parking lot. By now, the blizzard was raging. There were close to two feet of snow on the ground and it was still coming down hard. William grabbed Alan's arm and yelled above the howling wind: "No way I'm gonna drive in this stuff." Before Alan could ask what they were going to do now, William nodded over to a motel a block away, whose red neon sign—Heartland Haven—was flashing through the thick, swirling snowfall, a beacon of last resort. "What do you think?" he asked.

Alan was thinking a lot of things. How much had William choreographed all this? Who would make the first move once they got into the room? What would they tell their friends? For a fleeting moment, he even wondered if Keith had been aiming for a threesome back at his place.

William paid with a credit card, telling Alan they could settle up later. After that, everything went very fast, from the way William scribbled his signature on the charge slip, to their hustling along the outside corridor, heads bent against the wind and sleet, to the way he inserted the key in the door, pushed it open, and, hand on the small of Alan's back, guided him inside.

❖ ❖ ❖

Najib pulls away, refusing to make out anymore. He turns around and presents his freshly washed ass, which Alan obligingly devours with enthusiasm. Najib is a shaver. His chest, his bush, his asshole. Eating out Najib's slightly stubbly hole is another bit of the randy pleasure that Alan, after three years, still can't believe he gets into as much as he does.

But these ardors, too, continue only so long before Najib reaches for the tube of lubricant on the night table and passes it back to Alan, who, compliantly, squeezes a gob into his palm and slathers it all over Najib's sweet boy-cunt.

"Are you my bitch?" he asks.

"You know I am," Najib says. It's a call-and-response that has become a regular set piece in their repertoire of love-making dirty talk.

"You want this love stick, huh? Is that what you want?"

Najib, burying his head into a pillow, moans with pleasure, and then a whimper of pain as Alan enters him.

Bitch, boy-cunt, love stick: gradually over the years Alan has taken up the vocabulary of the porn star. In fact, the older he gets, the more comfortable he is spewing out this stuff. Romance is a thing of the past with him. This is what Najib wants—the raunchier the better—and Alan has learned to dole it out.

"Ouch! It hurts!" Najib tells him, then wriggles his ass so that Alan can achieve deeper penetration.

"You want me to pull out?" Alan taunts. "You don't like it?"

"I love it," Najib moans.

The glow from the television set is the only light in the room. Once, Alan had suggested that they turn the tube off, but Najib said he liked having the television on when they had sex. Alan is not sure why. Maybe all the horror-film pandemonium helps Najib tune out what he's doing—cheating on his wife, having gay sex, craving it. The motel's alarm clock reads ten minutes to two.

"Don't slow down!" Najib commands. "Fuck me."

This is the latest Alan has ever been to the motel. Usually, they end things by midnight, one at the latest. Nagib's excuses to his wife—about emergency repairs to the fry-o-lator or after-work drinks with his buddies—have worked in the past, but lately, she's been complaining about his late nights. Tonight, Najib seems to have thrown caution to the winds.

"Use more lube," he orders.

As Alan withdraws to slather up his cock again, he'd like to take a break. Not so much to catch his breath, though he could use a breather, but just to switch gears, go back to a bit of conversation again. He would like to ask about the wife. What is Najib going to tell her when he gets home? Or will he and Najib finally spend the whole night together? Has lust or love or mere reckless abandon so possessed Najib that he will finally forget about his wife and family just this once? It's a thought that instantly makes Alan even harder.

Forget it, he reminds himself. *This is all you get with Najib.*

"This is all you get" is another kind of mantra with Alan. All these years later, he is still doing HR work, but now in the human relations division of one of the large universities in Boston. He has never risen to the top of the pecking order, but it's fine with him. Life is less complicated that way. Learning to settle for what he can get has saved him a lot of disappointment.

❖ ❖ ❖

That night in St. Paul, as soon as William closed the door against the blizzard, he flipped off the light switch, turned around, and hurled himself at Alan, laying cold, wet kisses all over his lips. Alan hungrily reciprocated, devouring William's mouth, sucking on his tongue. He knew they were both a little drunk, but he also knew that this was the real thing, not some collegiate funny business that William would pretend was a woozy mistake when morning came.

In a room lit only by the lights from the parking lot, they began tearing off each other's clothes, breaking just long enough to remove their own shoes, socks, and trousers in furious eagerness to be naked together. William still had his underpants on when Alan flung him onto the bed, writhing and grinding against him, until finally he grabbed William's jockey shorts and ripped them off. He couldn't believe how ravenous he was. He'd been dreaming about this kind of passion— jerking off to thoughts about it—all through college, but now the intensity of his hunger was more than he'd ever imagined.

The wind kept howling outside, a savage accompaniment to their savage love making. William's ass, that gorgeous corn-fed bubble butt, soon became the object of all of Alan's desire. He maneuvered William into a position where he could caress it, kiss it, bury his face in it. The next thing he knew, he was sticking his tongue deep into William's hole.

William's DeMolay-nurtured scruples lasted about a minute, and then he submitted, letting Alan make love to his ass. *I want to fuck you,* Alan whispered. *Fuck me,* William moaned. But Alan was so dehydrated from all the alcohol he'd consumed that night that he couldn't generate enough saliva to make it comfortable for William. In the end, they jerked each other off. After he came, William immediately collapsed into sleep. Alan snuggled up next to him, breathing in William's warmth and wondering just what would have happened if they'd stayed at Keith's.

When he woke, it was close to noon. Across the motel room, William was dressed, looking out the window at the storm, which was still raging.

Alan panicked. Why was William dressed? Was he hankering to get away? But when William turned around, he flashed Alan a loving smile.

"Hey there!" he said. "Check out was at eleven, but there's no way we're getting out of here, at least not for the next several hours. There's more than four feet on the ground, and it's still coming down." He walked over to the bed and hovered over Alan, kissing him on the forehead. "I've paid for the room for another day. Guess you're stuck with me."

"Wonderfully stuck," Alan said.

"And I'm afraid your breakfast is the last Danish pastry in the hospitality lounge. That and some pretty dreadful coffee."

"Come back to bed," Alan said.

"Gladly."

William stripped (Alan saw that he was hard again) and crawled under the covers. For a few minutes, they watched coverage of the storm on TV. Then William said he had a surprise for Alan.

"I found some body lotion in the bathroom." He smiled. "Better than saliva, I think."

❖ ❖ ❖

"Don't come inside me," Najib commands. They have been fucking bareback for about three months now, but Najib is still scrupulous about this final detail, even though he assures Alan he's not letting anyone else fuck him raw. Alan hopes this is true, and it probably is. PrEP has a very good track record against HIV infection, but there are still STIs to worry about. Which is why Alan rarely hooks up with anyone else. Then again, these days, he can rarely find anyone else to hook with anyway. Even when he lies on the hook-up sites and says he's only fifty.

When they finish and Alan wipes off Najib's butt with one of the motel's dingy pink towels, Najib props himself up on the pillows, lights another cigarette, and increases the volume on the TV with the remote control. Alan snuggles up to him and tries to be interested in how the plot of the horror flick is unwinding.

"I gotta get home," Najib announces.

"You sure you're okay driving?" Alan asks. "You drank four beers."

Najib doesn't answer. He gets up and heads to the bathroom. Alan knows this ritual—it's to wash off any aromas of sex—but he has often wondered if Najib's wife is suspicious anyway, what with her husband arriving home so soapy-smelling. Najib closes the bathroom door and turns on the shower.

As much as Alan knows not to fall in love, he can't help wondering who Najib might turn out to be if he just stayed with Alan for one whole night, one night when his pro forma faithfulness to his wife didn't come into play. Every once in a while, during their love-making, or whatever one calls what they do together, Najib will touch Alan in such a way— squeezing his thigh, intertwining their fingers—that Alan thinks, *yes, yes. We could be boyfriends.* A pathetic fantasy, he knows. There are times when he thinks of himself as a pretty pathetic gay man for not being satisfied with just some random hot sex.

The horror flick on the TV is driving him crazy. He clicks it off with the remote. From inside the bathroom, even with the shower running, he can hear Najib talking on his cell phone. He's speaking Arabic. Has the wife called him? He's pretty sure she doesn't speak Arabic. Once, about a month ago, while Alan and Najib were at the motel, she called and Najib, commanding Alan to be quiet, spoke to her in English. *Never mind where I am,* he'd shouted. *Go to bed!*

The conversation ends. A few minutes later, Najib returns from the bathroom, toweling himself off. Still leaning against the pillows, Alan waits for him to say something about who was on the phone, even though he knows Najib is not going to bring this up.

As Najib starts putting on his underwear, Alan studies his body. He loves Najib's swarthy skin, his compact biceps, even the slight belly that has appeared over the past few months. Now that Najib has two kids, he doesn't get to the gym as much, but he's still solid and smooth and luscious. Alan can't understand how this Egyptian god could possibly be interested in him, who has never come close to looking godlike, *ever*. Even less godlike now, with his thin upper arms, flabby ass, and pecs that sag even with visits to the gym. What does this guy see in him? Najib has told Alan that he only likes older men, men who are exclusively tops. Alan is thankful that he fits both criteria.

"You leaving now?" Najib asks, now in his bikini briefs.

"I could stay overnight if you want me to," Alan says. "You want me to stay?"

"No," Najib says. "It's late. I gotta work in the morning."

"Gotta make the donuts, huh?" Alan chirps. He so wants to be friendly and supportive and understanding. He so wants Najib to once, just once ... well, what? *No way!* Najib once shouted when Alan suggested they meet for dinner. *I got too many customers around. They all know me.*

"Yeah, the donuts," Najib says. But he keeps standing there in his bikini briefs, not putting on the rest of his clothes.

Alan gets up. "I'll take a quick shower, too."

"Shower at home," Najib insists.

"Najib, it'll take two minutes," Alan protests. "Go, if you're in a rush. When I leave, I'll put the room key on the dresser. I know the routine."

"Be quick," Najib says. "I'm gonna have another cigarette." There is something in his voice that Alan finds weird.

Alan goes into the bathroom and takes a fast shower. He'd like to linger longer, but he wants to comply with Najib's command to be quick. When he shuts off the water, Najib is on his phone again, talking in Arabic.

"One of your donut shop managers?" he asks, coming out of the bathroom.

"Yeah," Najib mutters.

"Problems?"

"Get dressed," Najib orders. The tone of his voice is full of impatience. He flops on the bed, lights another cigarette, and presses the remote control, summoning back the grade-B horror flick, behaving as if Alan has already left.

❖ ❖ ❖

Driving home, Alan figures it out. Najib wasn't going anywhere. He was waiting for someone else to come by. The person on the phone. A man? A woman? Who knows? The rain has let up. It's just a dull drizzle now, though, because the temperature has fallen, the roads have become slippery. He slows down, both for safety's sake and in order to think.

Najib has always been honest about how insatiably horny he is. And while he tells Alan he loves the sex they have together, he has also been candid about how much he desires women, too. Alan doesn't care if he's hooking with a woman, but if it's another guy… He feels a stab of jealousy. And then he laughs. Man, oh man, jealous of what?

By the time he arrives home, it's well after three o'clock in the morning. But he's so revved up, by the evening's romp and now, too, by Najib's—he wants to call it "infidelity," but of course it's not that—so revved up by all of this that he can't relax enough to fall asleep. Lying there, under sheets and blankets that feel familiar and comforting, he rehearses the events of the night. And thinks about William again.

❖ ❖ ❖

He and William were boyfriends for three years. They moved in together that summer, under the pretext that sharing an apartment was cheaper. It was the beginning of the eighties and though gay pride had become a thing, neither of them was ready to tell their office friends that they were a couple. When he thinks about it now, Alan is sure they weren't fooling a soul, but everyone in the office played along.

Alan once tried to describe to his housemate Jerry what those three years with William had been like. *It was good*, he said. When Jerry didn't comment, he added, *But, yeah, a little dull. I married a wholesome DeMolay boy.*

The best part was the domesticity—cooking together, fixing up the apartment, watching TV on the sofa in the evening, the weekend drives into Wisconsin, and once all the way up to Canada, to go sightseeing and hiking. Alan's knees no longer serve him well for long hikes, but back then, he would happily trek miles with his boyfriend.

The worst part was also the domesticity. The unvarying routine of it. Nothing much changed, especially their sex life. William turned out to be a rather unimaginative bottom. He went about it like it was a farm chore. On nights when they fucked, Alan would flashback to that first time in the motel, when they'd used the body lotion, how passionate and exciting it had been. Now it was just something they did because they were a couple. Alan offered to bottom once in a while, but William said he wasn't into that.

Occasionally, on Saturday nights, they invited friends from the office over for dinner, the "guys and gals" they liked and who they knew weren't going to be freaked out that two men were entertaining them. The pretext was still that they were just roommates, roommates who liked to cook. They always included Keith, the red-haired boy from Des Moines, who could always be counted on to liven things up.

One weekend, two years into their relationship, William went to Chicago for a conference. He left on Thursday afternoon. That night Alan couldn't sleep. He kept fantasizing about having Keith over for dinner, just the two of them. All he wanted to do was talk to Keith, lay it out on the table—that he and William were boyfriends, but that it was hard sometimes, that ... Well, what else did he want Keith to know? He wasn't sure, which is why, the following morning, he invited Keith over for Saturday night.

❖ ❖ ❖

After his late-night hook-up with Najib, the next day is a wash. Alan sleeps until noon and then makes a stab at the pantry renovation, but the project feels overwhelming. Generally, house projects energize him, but he's been putting this one off for months. How to organize the space needs some rethinking. Lately, everything—the pantry renovation, his thing with Najib, those years with William—everything about his life seems to be calling for some rethinking.

Late in the afternoon, his housemate Jerry comes down to the kitchen with a bottle of wine, inviting Alan to join him for a drink.

"Hey, why not?" Happy to abandon the pantry, Alan sits down at the kitchen table. There's too much stuff on it—salt and pepper shakers, a napkin holder, a chipped Victorian sugar bowl, a ceramic colander full of apples, six or seven mismatched candle sticks holding the stubs of mismatched candles, a stack of plastic placemats, a tree to hang mugs on, a German beer stein with pencils and pens, a cellphone charger, a pill organizer. It's all Jerry's stuff. Alan would just as soon have a clean kitchen table, but he also recognizes that Jerry's clutter lends a certain domestic touch to their shared space.

"So what's the occasion?" Alan asks.

"I'm lonely," Jerry says, pouring each of them a generous glass of Pinot Grigio.

Jerry looks more than lonely, but Alan decides not to pry.

"So how was last night?" Jerry asks. He doesn't sound much interested. It's more of a conversation opener than a question with any real curiosity behind it.

"S.N.S.," Alan says, their shorthand for Standard Najib Stuff.

Jerry nods and takes a hefty sip from his glass.

In compliance with Jerry's no-bourgeois-privacy policy, Alan has always told him all the details of his motel-room capers with Najib. But there's something about Jerry's muted affect this afternoon that dissuades Alan from offering more than just this acronym about last night's romp. He senses he might be rubbing Jerry's face in something he'd rather not listen to. Instead, he tells Jerry his suspicions that Najib had another hookup in the wings after he left.

"What a surprise," Jerry sarcastically mutters and pours more wine for himself.

"Yeah," Alan agrees. "I wouldn't put it past Najib to have been cheating on me all along." He laughs. "Hey, all just part of the 'adventure,' right?"

"Yeah, *whatever*," Jerry echoes.

Man, Alan thinks, he does not sound in good shape this afternoon.

❖ ❖ ❖

The affair with Keith went on for three months before William found out. Alan was contrite, apologized profusely, said he didn't know what he was thinking, promised he would end it. When William suggested they see a couple's counselor, Alan agreed. In truth, he was already bored with Keith. If he and William were in counseling, it would be the perfect excuse to tell Keith he needed to take a break.

During the months they saw the counselor, Alan knew he was holding back from saying what was really on his mind. How could he say that he just didn't think William was the one anymore? In so many ways, William *was* the one. He was sweet-tempered, he was considerate, he had those beautiful Norwegian features and that scrumptious ass. He worked hard, he kept their household neat and running smoothly, he was the DeMolay boy who had grown up to be everything DeMolay boys were supposed to grow up to be. What was there not to like? But Alan was bored, as bored with him as he had so soon become with Keith.

Each of you say something that you want, the counselor prompted them during one session.

I want a life with Alan, William said. *A life where we grow old together.*

And how about you, Alan? the counselor asked. *What do you want?*

I want ... Alan began, but he couldn't say it. *I think I want more time to think about this relationship.*

They stopped sleeping together. Alan set up a day bed in the tiny second bedroom they used as an office. The phone sex lines were just coming into fashion then. He would call late at night when he knew William was asleep and jerk off with other guys. AIDS was becoming a huge thing, too, and he was terrified. It was a reason why he stayed with William another eight months. Secretly, he started working with a headhunter to find a new position in HR. When the job came up in Boston, he took it.

Sweet to the end, William wished him the best. *I hope you find what you're looking for in Boston,* he said.

After William, Alan had one more boyfriend, Carlos. Alan was in his thirties then; Carlos was twenty-three and everything William was not. "My crazy Latin lover," Alan called him. But after a while, a little too crazy. Carlos spent extravagantly—on clothing, on his car, on nights out at the clubs. He bought Alan a small diamond ring and a chihuahua. He insisted they go on gay cruises to nowhere. And he got jealous at the drop of a hat. Lying in bed at night, with Carlos passed out next to him, Alan kept hearing that old couple's counselor asking, *What do you want?*

Not this, he thought.

He started refusing to join Carlos at the clubs on Saturday nights. He'd stay home watching TV, hoping Carlos would trick with someone else. It would be fine, he thought. A short confrontation and it would be over—no long, drawn-out process of soul-searching with another couple's counselor. And that's pretty much how it happened.

Since then, and before Najib—"the twenty-five-year bachelor period," Alan calls it—there has been a succession of things with other guys. One-night stands, when that's what they were still called, and later hook-ups, when that became the word to use. A few guys wanted something more, but Alan just wasn't interested. In his many chats around the kitchen table with Jerry, Alan has rehearsed all the possible reasons why: fear of intimacy, boredom, lack of sexual compatibility. But it's more complex than that. Or simpler, perhaps. He's come to feel that he's just not good at relationships.

Maybe it's because I give everything I have at work, he once, half-facetiously, suggested to Jerry. *Human resources, you know. I'm always taking care of others' needs.*

Bullshit, Jerry told him.

❖ ❖ ❖

"Every once in a while, I think I should call it quits with Najib," he now tells Jerry as Jerry pours yet another glass of Pinot Grigio for himself. Alan hopes that switching to a more reflective tone might help to distract Jerry from his funk. "I mean, he can be so unpredictable. I never know when he's going to ask me to arrange a threesome"—Alan shakes his head—"or have someone cued up to take my place as soon as I leave."

When Jerry doesn't respond, Alan looks at the bottle. It's three-quarters empty. He looks at Jerry's stuff all over the kitchen table. He can't stand that kitschy beer stein and those awful plastic placemats.

"I mean, there are days when Najib drives me crazy, but, you know, it's reliable, hot sex, and, well, I even kind of like the guy."

Suddenly, Jerry is sobbing. With his elbows on the kitchen table, he lowers his face into the palms of his hands and bawls and bawls and bawls.

"Jerry, what is it?" Alan asks. "What's going on?"

"Oh, fuck, oh fuck!" Jerry says between gulps for air.

"What's the matter?"

Jerry raises his head. His eyes are red; tears streak down his cheeks.

"Peter," he manages to get out between the tears. "This guy I've been seeing." He composes himself just enough to add a self-mocking aside: "First one I haven't met on line in ages."

"Yeah, I know," Alan says. "You introduced me once." Even though the meeting was in passing, he can still picture Peter: fiftyish, good looking with gray hair and a swarthy complexion. And a good job, something in hotel management, he recalls. In many ways, a cut above many of the others Jerry has paraded through the house.

"He told me last night he didn't want to see me anymore." Jerry bursts into sobs again.

Alan tries to think what words might help. He's tired of hearing himself offer the consolation that they should be grateful for what comes their way. He knows that, right now, this piece of wisdom will fall completely flat.

"Jerry, I'm so sorry."

"I really wanted this one to work, Alan." And he collapses into more uncontrollable weeping.

Alan feels panic. This is new. In their years as housemates, even under Jerry's policy of no-holes-barred sharing, Jerry has never broken down like this. There have been other breakups, but Jerry has handled them all with aplomb. Alan sits there, letting his housemate have his cry. Should he touch him? They've never avoided physical contact, but they aren't exactly touchy-feely either. Meanwhile, Jerry just keeps sobbing.

"Why?" Jerry asks. "*Why?*"

He sounds so helpless, in so much pain. Nothing Alan can think to say seems adequate. It would be callous to tell him to get over it. *This too will pass*, he wants to say. It's the advice he's pretty much given himself all these years. But right now, with Jerry in so much distress, that, too, seems awfully trite. He realizes that at this moment, Jerry is utterly unreachable by anything he has to offer.

Jerry continues to weep, at times so beside himself with uncontainable grief that Alan fears he might start choking. He places his hand gently on his housemate's back, which is heaving in agony.

"Jerry, Jerry."

Jerry tires to speak. Nothing but strangled, mucus-clogged syllables come out.

"It's okay," Alan tries again. "It's gonna be alright, Jerry."

His efforts at consolation do nothing but trigger more sobbing. Not knowing what else to do, Alan starts gently massaging Jerry's neck, under his ponytail. It's rough to the touch and hot. Hot from emotion and too much wine.

As he continues to massage Jerry's neck, Alan remembers how relieved he felt when he broke up with Keith, with William, with Carlos. How relieved he's felt whenever he's ended it with any of the guys he's had more than a night or two with. Relationships are just too messy. Since Carlos, he has spent his life avoiding such complications.

Jerry composes himself enough to say that he knows he'll be alright, but then he breaks down again. "I was so hoping ..." His shoulders heave inconsolably.

"I know, I know," Alan tells him. But does he know? He can't imagine he will ever experience the kind of emotional turmoil Jerry is going through.

And then, as Jerry reaches for a paper napkin to blow his nose—that godawful cheap napkin holder!—Alan feels something else, something entirely new. For a second, just a second, but long enough to pack a wallop, he wonders if he could ever feel the kind of heartache—yes, that's the word: *heartache*—ever feel it as much as Jerry, the lucky bastard, is feeling it right now.

Faerie Wedding

When I was in London many years ago—many, many years ago—I hooked up with a guy. While we were having sex back in my hotel room, Sebastian suddenly remarked, "My, such a lovely cock." The way he pronounced "cock," in a high-toned Oxbridge accent, it sounded as if he were appraising a fine porcelain tea cup. The note of effete connoisseurship—it completely turned me off. I went limp.

I was twenty-two that summer and backpacking through England. My first few weeks in Britain were as chaste as my undergraduate years back in Boston. By day, with the help of a student Eurail pass, I visited the important places I thought I should see: Cambridge, Oxford, Canterbury, Stratford-on-Avon. At night, I ate lonely meals in tweedy, threadbare bed-and-breakfasts where my fellow guests were tweedy, threadbare couples in their sixties and seventies.

By the time my rail pass ran out and I returned to London, I was ready for something a bit more unbuttoned. Hidden deep in my suitcase, I'd packed a copy of a gay guide to Europe. The night I met Sebastian, I fished it out, found the name and description of a pub that seemed safe enough, and headed off, my heart racing. I thought everyone I passed on the street must know what I was up to.

I had only recently come out, and only to myself. Putting that cerebral knowledge into bodily practice was an experience I'd yet to have. I had lofty notions of what gay lovemaking would finally be like. As soon as Sebastian began chatting me up in the pub, I was hooked. After all, wasn't the attraction I immediately felt for him, this good-looking guy who was an art gallery dealer, certain confirmation that the two of us were on the threshold of becoming soulmates? And wasn't becoming soulmates what it was supposed to be about, this gay thing I was venturing into?

Our conversation, my first-ever with a self-identified gay man, was thrilling. When Sebastian told me that he'd gone to Cambridge

University, I gushed about how much I'd loved King's College Chapel and the punts on the river. When he told me that his gallery dealt mainly in eighteenth-century hunting pictures, I enthusiastically rattled off the names of the two eighteenth-century British painters I knew, names I'd recently gleaned from a visit to the National Portrait Gallery. In retrospect, my dorky observations must have left Sebastian impatient to get on with the real business he had in mind, which was to invite himself back to my hotel.

As we walked there, I debated whether I should tell him that this was going to be my first time with another man. It seemed only fair, in case I bungled something. But when, a block from the site where we would consummate our love, he took my hand and kissed me, it seemed the answer was clear: there was nothing to bungle. What we were about to do would need no preliminary discussion. Bedding Sebastian was not going to be a matter of technique; it would be about transcendence. I could hardly wait.

When I lost my erection, Sebastian asked me if something was wrong. Did I like to be blown some other way? Should he finger me? Lick my balls? Stick his tongue in my piss slit? His questions just made the situation worse. *Stop!* I wanted to cry out. His approach to lovemaking seemed so cold-blooded, so mechanical.

Nothing he tried worked. In the end, Sebastian apologized and said that perhaps he'd "best be getting along." I mumbled something about how it wasn't him: just the jetlag, I guessed, or too much to drink beforehand at the pub. Both were lies. But how could I possibly have revealed to him that, in fact, it *had* been his fault? He'd ruined everything with that crude remark about my cock and with all those clinical suggestions for a way to excite me again.

The next day, as I was touring Westminster Abbey, I kept replaying our disastrous evening in my head. How could someone who worked in an art gallery in Belgravia go about intimacy as if it were a paint-by-numbers kit? That afternoon, I threw away my gay guide to England.

I was born on April 4, 1949, the same day that NATO was founded. My childhood was a world of duck-and-cover nuclear attack drills under school desks; the Cuban missile crisis; Khrushchev declaring, "We will bury you." I've often wondered if all this dread contributed to my being so skittish about sex. The whole enterprise—this business that was supposed to be about grand and glorious love—it seemed so fraught with gracelessness, fear, and danger. Whatever the reason, it took me twenty years to get comfortable with the notion that sex could be fun, that it didn't have to be a matter of spiritual union. Over those two decades, there were two boyfriends, both of whom I seem to have picked because they were erotically unthreatening. Someone once quipped to me, "The English don't have sex; they have hot water bottles." On the contrary, I thought: Sebastian had been the randy one, while this American was the cold fish.

Sometime in my early forties, the second boyfriend decamped, leaving me for someone who, he said, had opened him up to "wider vistas." Was a relationship supposed to be like the Grand Canyon, I wondered. After two months of bewilderment and loneliness, I took myself to what, in those days, was known as Boston's gay bar of last resort, the Eagle. It was almost closing time when I met Ryan. I'd had a few drinks and my defenses were down. Ryan was considerably younger—in his twenties—and irresistibly sexy. Despite the Irish name, he was Azorean Portuguese. Swarthy skin, green eyes, a perpetual five-o'clock shadow.

For the three years we were together, though never as boyfriends, Ryan kept introducing me to new sexual kinks, stuff I'd never done—never even thought of doing. He had a girlfriend whose panties he always wore underneath his tight, ripped jeans. I was amazed to discover that this totally turned me on. I was amazed to discover that I loved to fuck and that I was, according to Ryan, "awesome" at it. I was amazed to discover how thermonuclear sex could be. *We will bury you?* Sure! Under a radioactive geyser of Ryan's hot cum.

Practically every time we got together, Ryan had another new proposal. The catalog of things he wanted us to try was inexhaustible: rimming, spit, frottage, bondage, water sports, threesomes, all sorts of role-play (daddy-son, of course, but coach-jock and state trooper-bad driver were two of his other favorites). And tons of sex-toy play as well. Fuck the "soulmate" shit, I thought. It was my time to be a slut.

Ryan was an auto mechanic who hoped to own his own garage one day. He lived with his girlfriend in one of the suburbs north of Boston. The girlfriend was a flight attendant and, therefore, conveniently out of town at least one night a week. For some maddening reason, even when she was on an overnight, he would never show up much before midnight, which meant that our fooling around extended way into the wee hours of the morning. The following day, I'd be a mess—tired, foggy-headed, and popping an erection every time I recalled what we'd done the night before. Fortunately, the company I worked for—we ran intercultural training sessions for big international firms—gave me very flexible hours. No one raised an eyebrow if I didn't stagger in until eleven. Apparently, our intercultural sensitivity included tolerance for unorthodox work hours.

For a little while, I was in love with Ryan. (Old habits die hard—I still thought we could morph our sex play into "something deeper.") But then, around the time I turned forty-five, I said to myself, *Screw it! Why give this up just because he's not going to marry you?* Sex with Ryan made me feel cutting-edge. It made me feel like I'd finally overcome all my hang-ups. Ryan helped to enroll me in a confederacy of carnal pleasure that I'd been squeamish about ever since my maiden foray into gay sex that summer in London. In comparison to the things I'd say to Ryan, Sebastian's "such a lovely cock" was child's play.

I told only three friends about Ryan. One congratulated me; another couldn't get beyond the idea that I actually loved it when he wore his girlfriend's panties. The third, my psychologist friend Kyle, asked me if I thought I was using Ryan as a way to postpone adulthood. "I'll get back to you on that," I told him.

When Ryan and the girlfriend moved to Bangor, I took it all in stride. After all, I'd always known it wasn't going to last forever (wasn't *that* a sign of adulthood?), and the extra sleep made life at work much easier.

For the next few years, I tried duplicating what I'd had with Ryan with various other guys. But now it was the early nineties; AIDS had become an issue. And I was beginning to look my age, which was a definite liability in hyper-collegiate Boston. If Daddy culture was a thing then, it somehow passed me by. For a while, an occasional foray into the Fens kept my sex life alive. But more and more, during those nights that I meandered through the reeds along the appropriately named Muddy River, my boredom with those fleeting, perfunctory encounters grew. I kept thinking of Kyle's question: was all this just a way to postpone adulthood?

The year of my fiftieth birthday—the year the Senate acquitted Clinton in the impeachment proceedings; the year Hungary, Poland, and the Czech Republic joined NATO; the year the UN designated as International Year of Older Persons—I decided it was time to give adulthood a try. I wasn't sure what that meant, but I thought it had something to do with acknowledging that my days of unfettered sexual sporting were over. As a recognizably "Older Person" now, I wanted to try a boyfriend again. More than a boyfriend, I wanted a husband. Legally, that wasn't yet possible, but the concept—a settled, domestic life (no, not tweedy and threadbare, but at least homey, comfortable, and comforting)—that life didn't seem like such a bad thing.

I turned again to Kyle, my psychologist friend. He and his partner had, by then, been together for something like twenty years. He said he thought integrating my sex life and my love life was the next right step for me.

"But how?" I asked.

"I can't tell you, Roger. Every person has to find their own path, but just don't turn it into a project. Relax with it."

My own path took three more years to find, three years of therapy, of singing in the Gay Men's Chorus, of volunteer work at the AIDS Action Committee, and lots of dating. In the end, I met George in the most innocuous way possible, around the communal table at Crumble, a South End café I used to hit in the mornings before work. There I was, minding my own business over a cappuccino and a sticky bun, thinking about the seminar I had to give the following week on Korean business etiquette. In came George, who sat down with his coffee, nodded at my pastry, and said something to the effect that he couldn't imagine surviving one of those sugary delights.

"It's a once-a-month indulgence," I told him, stretching the truth a bit.

George was in great shape. It looked like he hadn't eaten a piece of pastry in years. I guessed him to be about my age, fifty-four that year. A wholesome face, a kind face, a husband-material face. I couldn't tell if his quip about the sticky bun was meant as a bit of flirtatiousness, but I hoped so. I smiled.

It was September, in so many ways the loveliest month in Boston. The humidity of summer had broken; the hazy, milky skies of August heatwaves morphing into an intense, pure blue. I was in a fine mood that morning, ready to savor all that the season had to offer.

"You're here a lot," he said. It was then I saw that he had a gap between his two front teeth.

"As a matter of fact, yes," I told him, and smiled for a second time.

When he smiled back, I looked at that gap again. It was the kind of "flaw" that you could imagine falling for.

"I'm here most mornings, too," he said, "though usually just picking up a cup to go. This morning, I thought I'd get off the treadmill for ten minutes and actually enjoy my cappuccino."

I asked him what treadmill he was on.

"Podiatry," he said. "My father and grandfather were also podiatrists."

In all my years, I had never met a podiatrist. I'd certainly never been to one. What kind of response does one come up with when someone tells you that his family trade is working on people's gross, neglected feet? I tried for something witty, and said, "I suppose feet must run in your family."

George laughed. He introduced himself and we shook hands. His hand was super soft, a podiatrist's hand, I figured. Then his eyes strayed to the front page of the newspaper, which I'd abandoned on the table. The day before, Bush Two had addressed the U.N. on the "grave and gathering danger" of Iraq. I decided to lay my cards on the table.

"He is such an asshole. The guy just wants to be as tough and macho as his daddy."

This kind of anti-Bush talk was common fare at Café Crumble in those days, but you never knew when a Republican might wander in.

"So you don't think Saddam Hussein has weapons of mass destruction?" George asked.

"There's been no evidence to that effect," I declared.

George looked back down at the paper. "It's a dangerous gambit Bush is pursuing."

"More than dangerous," I said. "Potentially catastrophic."

George nodded his head reflectively. "I guess I'm the kind of person who's willing to wait a bit longer and see what the U.N. inspectors come up with."

Okay, I thought. *That's adult. I guess I can accept that.*

By the following week, George and I were dating.

❖ ❖ ❖

George has not been an easy partner. In the sixteen years we've been together, there have been—how shall I put this?—some "challenging" times? His best qualities are that he's honest, firmly knows his mind, has high ethical standards, is slow to express a negative opinion, and is scrupulous about billpaying. He keeps the car more immaculate than if we sent it to a detailer. He's the first in our neighborhood to shovel the sidewalk after a snowstorm. He still goes to church (tony Trinity Church in Copley Square) and serves on a couple of the parish's committees.

All this rectitude and polish—there are days when I admire it, days when I tolerate it, and days when it drives me fucking crazy.

Take our yearly vacation planning. We both like to travel. But we almost always get into a push-pull about the destination, a debate that George invariably wins. Mexico? I'll suggest. Too dangerous, he pronounces. Vietnam? Tropical diseases. Egypt? Big risk of terrorism. Same with Turkey, Israel, India. Last year, he even ruled out London. We ended up on a placid cruise down the Danube. I had a great time—a clear example of my benefitting from George's sober judgment and planning. Still, all the way from Regensburg to Budapest, I kept wondering what Turkey would have been like instead.

Buying our place involved a similar tug of war. I'd been hoping to stay in the South End, where I had a condo. He said that we should opt for a "neutral" neighborhood, one where neither of us had any past history. Okay, this seemed sensible, too. So, how about Charlestown, I threw out. George made a face.

"What?" I snapped.

"I'm not sure gay folks are welcome there."

"Last time I heard that was changing," I said.

Unconvinced, he shook his head: maybe yes, maybe no.

"Back Bay?" I suggested.

"Roger, I'm a podiatrist, not a brain surgeon! No way we can afford that."

He proposed Brighton. I countered that there were too many students there. He said there were lots of streets in Brighton that were family-oriented.

"You want me to move to Ozzie and Harriet Land?" I asked.

In the end, Brighton turned out to be another prudent suggestion on George's part: we got a lot more bang for our buck there.

Then there's been the business of renovating our Late Victorian fixer-upper. George's approach to projects—painting, wallpapering, redoing the floors, picking out appliances, insulating the attic—here's where his fastidiousness leaves me contemplating murder. Even something as simple as hanging a painting takes George hours as he meticulously eyes the placement, measures the distance along the wall, finds the exact midway point, levels and marks the spot, rechecks it, marks it again, then gently tap-tap-taps in the hanger, selected for just the right weight-bearing load. It's hard to imagine that he could possibly take as many pains with his patients' feet as he does with sticking a damn painting on the wall.

A month ago, I consulted Kyle. "This is feeling *way* too adult," I told him.

"Which part?" he asked. "That you don't always get your way?"

"It sometimes feels like I *never* get my way."

"I seem to recall," Kyle said, "that it was you who insisted on the house with the stained-glass windows and the turret. And how about the time George wanted to paint the dining room coral, and you insisted on yellow?"

"Name *one* more time I got my way."

"Is this about keeping score for you?" he asked. "Come on, Roger, tell me three things you like about George."

"Lots of things!"

"Three."

I drew a breath. "He's conscientious."

Kyle nodded.

"And his ethics are impeccable."

Kyle nodded again.

"And he likes Broadway musicals." I paused, then raised my voice in exasperation. "But only up to middle-period Sondheim!"

Kyle smiled.

"No, really," I insisted. "*My Fair Lady, The Music Man, Guys and Dolls.* And if I hear 'Send in the Clowns' one more time, I'm going to explode."

"It's a classic," was all Kyle said.

"Look," I wrapped up, "George is a very good person. Maybe even too good for me." I looked into Kyle's eyes, hoping for something more than that damn neutral look he always throws in my direction when we're having one of our talks.

"Roger, it's not about keeping score, and it's not about comparing. George isn't better than you, and he's not worse than you. You're two different people. Each of you brings many attractive—but, yes, different—attractive but *different* qualities into your marriage."

"Um, it's not a 'marriage,'" I reminded him.

"Should I call it a truce then?" Kyle joked.

"I've just never seen the need for us to get married."

Kyle smiled his enigmatic smile.

"Roger, it's not about keeping score, it's not about comparing, and it's not about need. In this day and age, no one *needs* to get married. You *choose* to get married, Roger. You choose to be in a relationship."

"I *have* chosen," I insisted. "It's just that sometimes that impeccable personality of his ... I don't know. It's just too much!"

"Impeccable personality?" Kyle echoed. "Do you think that maybe what you call his impeccable personality is really just your *idea* of who he is rather than who he actually is."

Smarty pants, I thought. Fucking adult smarty pants.

❖ ❖ ❖

A week ago, an invitation came in the mail for the wedding of a couple of casual friends of ours, Mateo and Cole. Mateo is one of my colleagues at the training company. Cole is our neighbor in Brighton. We knew neither of them well, but both had come to a dinner party we gave about three years ago. We'd had no intention of hooking them up romantically. They were just two interesting guys we thought would nicely round out our dinner table that evening. The fact that they were also both single, and both in their late forties, hadn't really factored into our guest list. But after dessert, having discovered that they were both into weed, they excused themselves to go outside for a smoke. When, a half hour later, they returned, I could see that something had been kindled.

It turned out that marijuana was not the only thing Mateo and Cole had in common. Earlier in their lives, both had had some experience with a group called the Radical Faeries, a kind of pagan, countercultural movement that, according to Mateo, was all about queer spirituality and the rejection of—to quote a phrase he often used—"assimilationist gay values." During the three years they dated, both of them reconnected with the faeries and together started attending their meet-ups again.

After these outings, Mateo would regale me with stories. He and Cole would drive to the country—Vermont, Maine, once even to Tennessee—for these faerie festivities, weekend events that included all sorts of countercultural rituals and consciousness-raising activities, often with a heavy layer of cross-dressing. I kept trying to pin down what, exactly, this movement was all about: free love? New Age spirituality? gender-bending role play?

Mateo said that George and I should come and see for ourselves.

I always declined, citing George's straightlaced attitudes, but the truth was this whole faerie thing sounded more than a little weird to me.

"*Weird?*" Mateo asked. "Dude, you and I do ICT, remember? Intercultural training. Think of the faeries as just another foreign culture."

I've done that kind of "foreign culture," I wanted to say. *Ryan was foreign culture.* But when the wedding invitation came, stipulating that it was to be a "faerie wedding," my interest was piqued.

"You aren't really thinking we'll go?" George asked when I showed him the invitation.

"Why not?" I said. Part of me wanted to confess that, whatever a faerie wedding was, it was hardly my cup of tea. But a combination of curiosity and, I'm embarrassed now to say, perverse pleasure in rubbing George's nose in something I knew would make him uncomfortable made me tell him we had to go. Such are the subtle dynamics that accompany a sixteen-year relationship between two men in their early seventies.

"Mateo's my colleague," I said. "He and Cole met each other at our house. I think it would be rude not to attend."

George shook his head. "A faerie wedding. Aren't they a little old for that sort of thing?"

I reminded him that Mateo and Cole were more than twenty years younger than we were.

❖ ❖ ❖

The morning of the wedding, a summer-perfect day in July, we drove out to a farm called "Uranus" in western Massachusetts. The place was owned by Mateo and Cole's friends Erik and Jay, who'd bought it for a song, all hundred acres, back in the eighties.

"How the heck did they ever find this place?" George, who was navigating, asked me. We had just turned off Route 2 and were headed toward a village called Tucker Hill. "It hardly even shows up on my GPS."

"I think that was the point," I said. "Erik and Jay wanted to be as far from civilization as possible. Mateo told me they used to be investment bankers in New York. On weekends, they'd come up here, poke around, go antiquing. Then they started getting into faerie stuff, and finally decided to chuck the whole corporate world and move to the country. I gather they tried to turn the farm into a faerie commune, but it never really took off. So now, they just open it up to events like this." I looked over at George, who raised his eyes.

It took us another half hour to find the farm, which had no street address. Nothing in Tucker Hill, Massachusetts, had a street address.

Even though it was only eleven, and the ceremony wasn't scheduled to begin until six, there were already several cars—from Audis and BMWs to beat-up, funkily painted VW buses—parked in a field near the farmhouse. It was a two-story clapboarded structure with a huge central chimney. I guessed it to be late eighteenth or early nineteenth century. Off to the left was an enormous barn, beside which stood a hay wagon festooned in rainbow bunting.

George fell silent as I parked the car.

"Well, here goes," I said. I hoped the extra dollop of chirpiness I'd thrown into my voice would distract George from what I knew he was focusing on: the farm met none of his standards for domestic upkeep. The clapboards needed a good coat or two of paint, the lawn in front of the house wasn't mowed, the gardens weren't weeded. It had been a hard-enough sell convincing George to attend this affair. The best I could hope for now was that he wouldn't be completely miserable.

As we got out of the car, a man with long, snowy-white hair and wearing a purple dashiki sauntered up to us.

"Hey, guys, welcome. I'm Erik, one of the hosts." When he held out his hand to shake, an excess of brass and copper bracelets jangled on his wrist. "You guys are?"

"Roger and George," I told him.

"Right, right!"

Erik, who had tied back his hair into a ponytail, was barefoot. His toenails were painted bright green. In the Bermuda shorts and polo shirts we'd worn for the drive out, I felt very square.

"You guys signed up for a single tent, right?"

I felt George shoot me a look. I had not told him about the sleeping accommodations. I'd hoped that a private tent for the two of us would go over better than the other option, the bunkhouse behind the barn.

We hauled our two canvas bags—very L.L. Bean, very monogrammed, very un-faerie—out of the car and followed Erik across the field, past the barn, and toward an encampment of tents in the back fields. Nearby, under a makeshift shower, two naked guys were soaping each other down. One of them had an erection.

"Do we have to stay overnight?" George whispered to me. "If we leave by nine, we'll be home before midnight. I'll drive. I promise not to drink a drop."

Another thing I hadn't told George: the wedding was alcohol-free. Drug-free and vegetarian, too.

We spent the next hour in our tent talking. George went through all five of Kübler-Ross's stages of grief: denial, anger, bargaining, depression, acceptance. His acceptance felt more like resignation. At noon, we were roused by the clanging of a chow bell. Erik stuck his head into our tent and announced that lunch was being provided for the guests who had arrived early.

On the lawn in front of the farmhouse, a picnic table had been set up on which were several bowls of salads: macaroni (it was whole wheat), quinoa, lentil, jalapeño-corn, strawberry-watermelon, and potato. There were loaves of freshly baked bread (whole wheat again) and pitchers of lemonade. I was dying for a glass of wine. A dozen men gathered around the table and started helping themselves. I recognized the two who had been showering. They were now wearing sarongs.

George and I filled our plates with food, then made our way over to an area of the lawn that had been spread with blankets. George began to head for an empty blanket, but as we passed one already occupied by two other guys, they invited us to join them. We introduced ourselves. George barely mumbled his name. Our picnic blanket mates were John and John.

"The Johns," the older of the two said. He looked to be about our age. "But don't worry, we're not potty poopers!" He laughed uproariously.

"He tells that joke every time he meets someone," the other John said. John the Elder was wearing a batik shirt and jeans. The younger John, who had quite the paunch, was in a sun dress.

"How do you guys know Mateo and Cole?" I asked, hoping to move the conversation away from bathroom humor.

"Through Erik and Jay," John the Younger said. "They're old friends from New York."

"This certainly is a far cry from Manhattan," George observed sourly.

I was grateful that he had decided to include himself in the conversation, even if he was being crotchety.

"And you guys?" George asked. "Have you chucked the New York thing, too?" Beneath the surface of this remark, I could hear his withering sarcasm. And maybe also a whisper of true curiosity.

"Neighbors down the road," John the Younger said. "We bought our place the same year they did."

"And your other neighbors?" George asked. "Do they, you know, accept you?"

"You mean, Do they call the morality police on us?" John the Elder asked. "Honey, this is Franklin County. The police have enough on their plate rounding up the stray llamas."

Just then, a guy walked by carrying a plate of food. He was naked except for several necklaces bouncing off his chest.

"This isn't a clothing-optional wedding, is it?" George asked. He sounded panicked.

"It's a clothing-any-way-you-want wedding," John the Younger said. He looked down at his sundress. "These are just our kick-back-before-the-ceremony frocks. John and I brought steampunk outfits for the wedding."

"Steampunk?"

I was glad George asked the question. I had no idea, either.

"You'll see," John the Elder said, a twinkling glimmer lighting up his pale blue eyes. "We made them ourselves."

❖ ❖ ❖

As the time approached for the ceremony, dark clouds began to move in. I overheard someone say that a front was coming through. Possible late afternoon thunderstorm.

George and I retreated to our tent to change. The wedding invitation had said "festive attire." Considering what I'd already seen some of the guys wearing, I was glad I'd convinced George that his Nantucket pink pants wouldn't quite cut the mustard at a faerie wedding. We'd gone out and bought ourselves a pair of flamboyant Hawaiian shirts and loose-fitting, white linen pants. Birkenstocks were our idea of festive footwear. When we emerged, I still felt under-dressed, but at least passable.

At six o'clock, with the skies getting darker, the chow bell rang again. Erik, now accompanied by his husband Jay, directed the guests to assemble on the front lawn. The majority—there were over sixty of us— were gay men of a certain age, fifties, sixties, seventies, and older. The array of wedding attire was as varied as the lunchtime salads, everything from modish tuxedos to outright drag. Sarongs, lots of sarongs. And caftans too. It was hard not to notice the contour of a dick or two underneath a few of the more diaphanous fabrics.

I spotted John the Elder. He was wearing a beautifully tailored Victorian waistcoat and breeches in royal blue and gold. On his head was a flamboyant blue top hat. Big, round, rose-colored sunglasses completed the look. So that was steampunk. And here came John the Younger. He was in a canary-yellow Victorian gown, complete with a tight corset pulling in his paunch. In his hand, he was twirling a frilly parasol. He'd tucked his hair up into a huge, feathered hat, topped by a white dove.

George must have spotted them at the same time, because he leaned over and whispered in my ear, "Exactly *whose* wedding is this?"

"Relax," I whispered back impatiently. It was a way to cover up my own mounting discomfort over this thing I'd gotten us into.

Once we had all assembled, Erik and Jay introduced Father Charlie, who would, they told us, officiate.

"'Officiate' only in the loosest sense of that word," Father Charlie explained. He was the youngest among all of us, maybe mid-forties. In bell-bottom jeans, a Mexican peasant shirt, and a beautifully embroidered clerical stole, he cut quite the figure. "This is really a commitment ceremony between Mateo and Cole, who have written their own vows. I'm not here to do anything but fulfill the legal stipulations of the Commonwealth of Massachusetts." He paused, looked up at the sky, and added, "And maybe put in a good word or two with the Goddess that she hold off the rain."

"That *they* hold off the rain!" someone corrected. Father Charlie blushed and bowed in humbled deference.

"He, she, they—we want you all to have a great time," Jay interjected. "This afternoon and into the night, it's all about celebrating Mateo and Cole and shedding your inhibitions." Again, he looked up into the sky. "Shedding your clothes, too, if this thunderstorm hits."

"Right on!" one of the guests called out.

"Whatever's the case," Erik finished, "Jay and I—and, of course, our wedding couple, Mateo and Cole—just want you to be your most authentic selves. Bring out all your radical faerie spirit."

"Faeries forever!" another person in the crowd shouted, and everyone cheered and snapped their fingers.

"So please form a circle," Father Charlie directed. Then, raising his voice, he shouted out, "And let the wedding begin!"

From behind the farmhouse, the boom of drums burst forth. Around the corner they came, a parade of loud, enthusiastic percussionists: bass drum, bongos, congas, tambourines. They were shirtless and wore baggy harem pants each in a different color of the rainbow.

Behind them came two giant papier-mâché puppets, at least ten feet tall, twirling and dancing to the beat of the drums.

"The Sun and the Moon," someone whispered in my ear.

Realizing I must have looked as clueless as I felt, I turned to see who my guide to the festivities was.

He smiled at me. "We faeries like to align ourselves with the energy of the universe," he explained. "There were supposed to be even more puppets—they're called *mojigangas*, Mexican puppets—but, well, the ones representing Pan and Dionysus ... they somehow never left Vermont this morning."

"Maybe they heard this was an alcohol-free event," I said, trying for both humor and gloom.

The guy smiled again. He was wearing a cheerful, goofy outfit that looked like it came out of Beatles-era Carnaby Street.

"Um, some of us forgot to read that part of the invitation," he said. "In fact, I think as the evening goes on, you'll discover that quite a few of us forgot to read that part of the invitation." He opened his jacket and drew out a pocket flask. "Kentucky Owl. Good stuff."

The parade continued. Next came a guy in a loincloth and beads. Cradling a large ceramic bowl, he dipped a pine branch into the bowl and shook it at us, spraying us with drops of water. He was followed by another guy, similarly clad, waving a large woven spray of smoldering sage.

"Oh, I get it," George whispered to me. "A high-church wedding." I was happy to hear a hint of amusement in his voice.

Last came Mateo and Cole. They were wearing paisley trousers, blowsy white shirts open to the navel, beads, and crowns of wildflowers. Holding hands and beaming, they entered the circle we had made. Father

Charlie followed them in. The drumming stopped and Father Charlie began to outline what would take place.

I had not been in the presence of a minister in years, not since I accompanied George to Trinity Church one Sunday early in our relationship. Church is not my thing, none of it—the ritual, the hymns, the prayers, the whole humbling yourself before an imagined Big Daddy, or gender-neutral Goddess, in the sky. I once asked George what he got out of it. *A chance to get out of my head for an hour every week,* he told me. Fair enough, I thought, but I never went back.

As if reading my mind, the friendly, Kentucky Owl guy whispered again into my ear: "He's a defrocked priest. When his bishop found out he was a faerie, he got axed."

Father, or ex-Father, Charlie invited Mateo and Cole to step forward.

Mateo spoke first, thanking us all for coming.

"Meeting Cole, falling in love with Cole, has been the biggest surprise of my life," he said. A few people laughed. "And the most wonderful. As some of you know, I was not—*not!*—looking for a husband." More laughter. "I thought my life was fine just as it was: a job I love, lots of time to travel ..." He paused and gave us a knowing look. "Lots of sex." Laughter again. And more finger snapping. It seemed to be a faerie thing.

Mateo took Cole's hands in his and looked him squarely in the eyes. "But this man has given me something so much better: he *sees* me like no one else ever has. And I see him. Fully. Completely. Unconditionally."

Cole laughed. "Not entirely true," he told us all. "Mateo *thinks* he sees a great cook in me. But he just wants to believe that so that he doesn't have to prepare dinner every night."

When the laughter and finger snapping died down, Father Charlie invited them to speak their vows.

To my surprise, Mateo specifically acknowledged that he wasn't promising monogamy but "something better," a total commitment to Cole's emotional and spiritual well-being.

As he continued speaking, I thought about what I might say to George if we ever got married. We'd never talked about the monogamy question. George's libido has always been, by and large, kind of flat; mine's a little friskier, at least it was during the early years of our relationship, when I occasionally strayed, mostly at the gym, which in those days still had communal showers. All that's changed now—no gang showers, no hanky-panky. Occasionally, I'll jerk off, thinking about those three years with Ryan, which seem like so much ancient history. But the truth is George's and my "marriage," or whatever it is we have, despite the occasional flare-ups, and all the times he drives me up the wall, well, it's not bad, sex or no sex. As good as I guess I can expect at my age.

❖ ❖ ❖

When Mateo and Cole finished their vows, and Father Charlie pronounced them husband and husband, we cheered and applauded. And, yes, snapped fingers. The earlier drizzle was becoming a more persistent rain. The drummers struck up again, and we all rushed into the shelter of the barn, where a table of champagne glasses (and non-alcoholic champagne) awaited us.

"How much longer do we have to stay?" George whispered to me.

"At least until they cut the cake," I said. I'll admit that part of me was hoping that would be soon.

Following a toast given by Erik and Jay, three musicians appeared, a violinist, a banjo player, and a bass fiddle. Although they'd been hired for the occasion and didn't seem to have bona fide faerie credentials, they seemed totally cool about playing for a bunch of men in "festive attire."

As they started up with their country tunes, several guys immediately got up to dance, including the Johns, who quickly became the center of attention, especially John the Younger, who lifted his yellow skirts and shook his fat, bustled booty like a shameless Victorian hussy. I glanced over to see how George was taking all this. He was clutching the top button of his Hawaiian shirt. My watch told me it was seven-fifteen. Maybe we really could leave by nine.

At the refreshment table, I picked up a couple of glasses of faux champagne and gulped mine down. It was terrible. When I turned around to give George his glass, someone was already pulling him into the dancing circle. He was shaking his head *no!* but the guy insisted.

At first, as if to get him into the swing of things, George's partner just held his hands and helped him to sway to the beat—the way the nursing home attendants used to try to engage my demented mom in a little recreational movement. Although he was pretty uncomfortable, George was giving it the proverbial good college try. What else could he do since he was on public display? If George is about anything, he's about good manners.

I continued to watch as his dance partner—holy shit! It was one of the formerly naked shower guys—coaxed George into ever more risqué moves: bumping hips, thrusting pelvises. To my amazement, George's good old college try began to give way to something a little more spirited. He was actually smiling! *What* had gotten into him? Had he found a flask of Kentucky Owl?

Soon, the two of them—George and Mr. Naked Shower Man—were in a tight embrace, crotches pressed against each other. I looked around, hoping to catch the eye of someone who would share my utter surprise. But no one else was reacting with anything but unrestrained good cheer. A seventy-year-old man in a luau shirt, bumping and grinding with a fifty-something guy in a sarong was, it seemed, perfecting normal behavior. As I watched them, I began to see George as something more than just the sixteen-year partner I shared a house and a bed with. He actually looked kind of hot.

Just then, a flash of lightning and then a deafening crack of thunder exploded overhead. Outside the barn, the skies opened up and the rain poured down. Inside, the music and the dancing continued.

"Would you like to dance?" I turned to see my Kentucky Owl friend holding out his hand in invitation. "I'm Conrad," he shouted above the noise.

"Roger," I shouted back.

"Come on," he invited and led me into the dancing.

Conrad wasn't so much into the bump-and-grind as Mr. Naked Shower Man. But he was fun—playful, good-natured, puckish even. As we danced, I occasionally glanced over at George. By now, he was totally taken up in the revelry. It occurred to me he might even be having more fun than I. I turned back to Conrad.

"I love your outfit! Beatles-era, huh?" It was one of those I-don't-know-what-else-to-say remarks.

He smiled and nodded his head in acknowledgment. The music, the storm, the hoopla—it was all too loud for us to carry on much of a conversation. Then again, conversation hardly seemed necessary. I hadn't danced in years. It felt delicious to move my body. I looked over at George again. Mr. Naked Shower Man was now squeezing his ass. Could George really be turning him on, or was this just standard faerie wedding protocol? Next thing I knew, George was squeezing Shower Man's ass in return.

The barn roof, which was in as bad repair as Erik and Jay's house, started leaking badly. From the rafters, rain dripped down on all of us. I saw John the Younger open his frilly parasol. Other guys just started stripping off their wet clothes. Conrad looked up, then back at me and smiled. He took out his flask and held it out, inviting me to take a swig. I shook my head, thinking that, if George had somehow gotten into the hooch, I would have to stay sober if we were going to drive home tonight.

By now, the dance floor was packed. Even the two *mojiganga* puppets were dancing, towering over everyone. No matter which way I moved, I kept bumping into other dancers, many near-naked by now. The rain kept coming down. In a matter of minutes, Conrad and I were soaked.

"Water sports!" he gleefully shouted at me.

I laughed and thought about the first time Ryan had proposed water sports. I'd gone along with it, but it was never my thing. This version felt like a lot more fun.

I glanced over at George again. His shirt was completely unbuttoned now, and he'd discarded his Birkenstocks. Mashing his beautifully manicured feet in the mud, he was shaking his booty like there was no tomorrow.

The next thing I knew, George and his partner had sidled up to Conrad and me. Mr. Naked Shower Man signaled that we should switch and handed George off to me, while he swept Conrad into a voluptuous embrace. Off they went.

"It's too bad about the rain," I said as George and I moved awkwardly about the barn floor. Once again, I could not think of anything else to say. It felt as if I were addressing someone I'd never met before.

"It doesn't seem to have put a damper on things," he said. There was a grin on his face that I can only describe as giddy. "Come on, take off your shoes," he invited.

In all our years together, I don't think George had ever invited me to take off any article of clothing. Off came my sandals. The mud under my feet felt luscious.

"I've never seen you like this," I told him.

"Maybe you haven't been looking," he said and shot me a lascivious leer.

Another flash of lightning, and the lights in the barn went out. We were plunged into near-total darkness. A cheer went up. It was as if the guests had been waiting for a signal to get even crazier. Hoots, howls, and whoops of delight filled the air. The music got faster and louder. Someone lit a cigarette lighter.

"Put it out!" someone else yelled. But whether because a flame was a hazard in a barn filled with hay or because the near darkness was wonderfully sexy, I don't know.

George was right in front of me, bouncing and grinding like I'd never seen him do before. I moved closer.

"Have you been hitting the booze?" I yelled.

George laughed. "Not a drop!"

The band continued playing, people kept bogeying. The next thing I knew, I wrapped my arms around George, holding on for dear life.

"Well, *hello!*" he said.

Once toward the end of our three years together, Ryan took me to Montreal, where he introduced me to a "back room," a completely dark orgy space in the back of a seedy bar. I remember getting groped and, not very enthusiastically, groping others, whom I could not see. I think that was the beginning of the end of things between Ryan and me. Ryan's love of kinky stuff was one thing, but utterly anonymous sex in a pitch-black room ... I couldn't get into it. But now this, whatever was going on between me and George suddenly felt very sexy.

"*Hello!*" I returned.

Aided by the little bit of twilight coming into the dark barn, we were looking into each other's eyes. He beamed at me. The gap between his teeth, which over the years I'd taught myself to ignore, now seemed irresistibly cute. And I told him so.

"So are you, Roger," he said.

And suddenly we were kissing. I'm not sure who made the first move, maybe both of us simultaneously. I pulled him closer. Rain poured down on us. I reached around and squeezed his buns, his soft, squishy, seventy-year-old buns.

Mmm, he murmured.

All around us, guys were dancing, embracing, kissing, fondling, stripping down. At least I assume they were. But I couldn't see. My face was pressed deep into my husband's neck.

"So, how do you feel about staying in the tent tonight?" I asked.

"Lovely," he murmured. "Lovely."

"It would be, wouldn't it?" I agreed.

Faulty Equipment

Every year, Leo dreaded the coming of November, the darkness and cold of another Boston winter, and every year, he was surprised by how outrageously brilliant the city could be in the final weeks before Thanksgiving. This year was no different. Riding the trolley out to the Longwood Medical Area on a sunny, early November morning, he took in the dazzling spectacle of color outside the car windows. The trees along Huntington Avenue were in their autumnal splendor—the chrome yellow of the ginkgoes and ailanthus trees, the flame red of the maples. It was an annual surprise.

Close to the trackway, the branches of younger trees grazed the trolley as it lumbered along. This struck Leo as a particularly European detail—trees planted along a trolley line—the flair and whimsy of it, so counter to American standards of efficiency, economy, and litigation-averse caution. He recalled certain neighborhoods in Utrecht, a city he'd lived in during the earlier years of his career as a violist. Quaint, scenic, brick-red Utrecht. A city he still missed all these years later. He would have stayed in the Netherlands, but when, in the early 90s, his mother was diagnosed with cancer, he had returned to Massachusetts to look after her. It was then he rediscovered Boston, though it took a while to readjust, to learn to live again in the American way, the *Bostonian* way.

The trolley continued along, trundling past the Museum of Fine Arts. Leo loved the car's gentle rocking; he loved the whole idea of public transportation. He'd grown up in an altogether ordinary blue-collar town some twenty-five miles north of Boston. Happily, North Billerica was on one of the commuter lines, the old Boston and Maine system back then, which had allowed him access into the city by the time he was fifteen. At first, it was the record shops and bookstores that beckoned him. Later, he discovered the art museums, the Public Garden and the swan boats, Beacon Hill, the Esplanade, the fruit and vegetable stalls at

Haymarket. "My little wanderer—*mon petit vagabond*—his mother, who had been born in France, called him.

Back in those days, the city had not yet undergone its transformation into "the new Boston," the Boston of urban renewal, of gentrification, of the first truly tall skyscrapers. It was that shabbier, more Old-World Boston that Leo had fallen in love with. By the time he was sixteen, he was standing in line for rush tickets to the Symphony. At those glorious concerts, under the gaze of the Greek gods and goddesses who looked down on him from their second-balcony niches, he felt so happy to have found his place in this city of culture and—his mother's favorite word—*finesse*. It was still *that* Boston that he loved, *that* Boston that always called to mind Utrecht.

Leo glanced at his watch: plenty of time to get to his appointment. In Holland, he had never been to a doctor's office. He was in his thirties then. No medical problems. Now, it seemed that every month there was another medical something or other he had to get to. Today, it was his urologist.

Across the aisle was a young man—no older than his mid-twenties—wearing earbuds and ripped jeans that showed off his knees to sexy advantage. His sneakers were untied, deliberately so, Leo guessed. My God, walking around like that on the uneven Boston sidewalks? A tumble could sprain a finger or, worse, fracture a wrist. And then where would *he* be? Not playing the viola, that's for sure.

The trolley arrived at Longwood. As he stepped down to the pavement—*gingerly,* Leo reminded himself—his mobile phone buzzed. The display indicated it was his brother Jack. By the time he went to answer, the ringtone had stopped.

Good, he thought.

Seven years ago, when he retired from his life as a golf pro, Jack had moved to Fort Lauderdale. That first winter, he invited Leo to come down. "Stay as long as you want," he offered. "I'll introduce you to the boys." The boys, Leo knew, were Jack's retired friends, gay men who, like Jack, had moved to Florida for the sun and the fun. Unable to think of anything he'd rather do less, Leo said there wasn't one week all that winter when he could get away. The excuse was real enough—he had concerts to play—but he had made it seem like he was booked solid.

"Then come in the spring," Jack had persisted. "Really, Leo, April in Boston? It's as shitty as February."

The only thing "shitty" about April, Leo wanted to tell his brother, was that the concert season started to wind down.

A text message appeared on the screen. *Pick up! Gorgeous morning down here. When r u coming for a visit?*

"How about never?" Leo said aloud.

The differences between them had become obvious by elementary school. Jack, three years older, had had a hard time learning to read, loved the rough and tumble of recess kickball, refused to practice the musical instrument, trumpet, that he was assigned in fourth grade. Meanwhile, Leo was reading chapter books by the time he was six, got picked last in kickball, and was named concertmaster of his grade-school orchestra. *Jack le magicien, Léo le médecin,* their mother used to say, a reference to the magic that Jack pulled off in any sport he put his mind to and her hoped-for career for Jack's brainy, bookish brother. All through their school years, Jack called Leo "Lemon Drop" because Leo couldn't catch a ball to save his life.

By his senior year in high school, Jack had risen to golf team captain and was crowned Prom King. So popular was he that, when he failed senior English, the high school administration quietly agreed to hand him a blank diploma as he walked across the stage, provided he make up the credit in summer school. Meanwhile, Leo, who had been studying the violin since fourth grade, had switched to the viola and, by his senior year, was good enough to play in one of the North Shore's best community orchestras. "Miss Viola" replaced "Lemon Drop" as Jack's moniker for his brother. Leo would fire back, "Jack the Jerk," but those insults never stuck.

From the trolley stop, it was a ten-minute walk to the urologist's. Ten minutes with nothing better to do than return Jack's call, Leo supposed.

❖ ❖ ❖

"You should have FaceTimed me," Jack said as soon as he answered. "I'm sitting around the pool. Some gorgeous men here."

"I'm sure," Leo said. "So, what's up, Jack?" He hoped his brother heard the impatience in his voice.

"What's up is I have a proposal." Leo kept silent. "What are you doing for Thanksgiving?"

"Invited!" Leo fired back. A little too fast, he knew. "My friends Harry and Joseph in Dorchester."

"Never heard of them," Jack said. "But they'd squeeze me in, no?"

"Jack, I can't invite you to someone else's Thanksgiving!"

"Why not? It's the classic American holiday. The one time in the year when everyone, even Republicans like me, are welcome at the table."

The crack about being a Republican was a joke. *Sort of.* Jack had voted for both Bushes and even, unaccountably, Bob Dole, but switched to Obama in both the 2008 and 2012 elections, before sitting out the 2016 election because, he said, he couldn't stand either candidate.

"Jack, you haven't been to Boston in forever, not since Mom's funeral. Why all of a sudden this interest in leaving your glorious Fort Lauderdale and coming here?"

"Duh, because I haven't been to Boston in forever? Because I haven't seen you in forever? Leo, I'm your brother. Since you never come see me, I decided I should come see you."

"Okay, okay," Leo conceded, "but just not Thanksgiving. Look, I'm outside right now. When I get home, I'll check my calendar and let you know a good weekend to come." He hoped *weekend* would send the message that that was all the time he was offering.

"What's the matter with the calendar on your phone?" Jack asked.

"I keep a *paper* calendar, Jack."

"Leo, get with the program."

"The program I'm on suits me quite well."

"Dude, you've been playing that program forever."

"Look, I'll call you when I get home."

"Okay. But don't call after eight. I'll be out with the boys."

"I'm sure you will," Leo said and ended the call.

❖ ❖ ❖

The urologist said that all of Leo's tests looked normal. The medications were having the desired effect: shrinking his prostate, lowering his PSA, allowing his "stream" to flow more smoothly.

"Any leakage?" he asked. "Accidental trickles?"

"No," Leo said.

"Well then." Dr. Chowdhury turned away from his computer screen, where he'd been typing notes. "No need to see you for another six months." He gave Leo a smile that indicated their business was done for the day. It was supposed to be encouraging, but Leo felt dismissed. He had been in the office only five minutes.

"There's one more thing," Leo ventured. "I'm glad the medications are working, but they're not doing much for my libido. I mean, I've lost most of my sexual desire and I can barely get an erection. When I do manage"—he hesitated—"to, um, masturbate, I don't have an ejaculation."

Dr. Chowdhury nodded. "That, unfortunately, can be one of the side effects of *both* of the medications you're on." He shrugged his shoulders. "Of course, if you're not aiming to have children, it's not really a problem, is it?"

At that moment, Leo wished he had more of his brother Jack's chutzpah. Having children is not the issue, he wanted to scream; being able to get a hard-on is. Being a sixty-six-year-old gay man who'd still like a sex life is!

"No, I'm not planning on having kids," he said, coughing up a feeble chuckle to acknowledge Chowdhury's pathetic attempt at humor. He *hoped* it had been an attempt at humor.

The last time he'd hooked up with someone, he'd only managed a partial erection, even after a full dose of Viagra. "No problem, daddy," the guy said and jerked off all over Leo's chest. Three minutes later, he was gone. That was eight months ago. Since then, Leo hadn't had sex with anyone.

"But what if I took myself off the medications?" he asked.

"Yes, your testosterone levels would rise," Dr. Chowdhury granted, "but then your prostrate would become enlarged again. Your PSA would probably go up, you'd be getting up several times at night to pee, and you'd run the risk of having to be catheterized again." He gave Leo a look that said, *Is that what you want again?*

"And if I went off *one* of the medications?" Leo bargained.

Chowdhury turned back to the computer screen and scrolled down, looking for something. "You've been on these medications for a year. I'd like to see your numbers after six more months before we think about changing anything."

"Not before next April?" Leo forlornly asked.

Chowdhury turned back and fixed Leo with an unflappable gaze. "Next May," he corrected.

❖ ❖ ❖

It was such a beautiful morning that Leo decided to walk back to his place on St. Botolph Street rather than take the trolley home. His route took him down Avenue Louis Pasteur and then along the Fenway and the quiet, reedy Muddy River. It was one of Leo's favorite walks, another European moment in this most European of American cities. Passing the Venetian palazzo that was the Gardner Museum, he recalled the first time he'd ever gone there. Another wonderful discovery during his high school days. Even more than the artwork, he'd loved the Sunday afternoon chamber music concerts in the museum's dark, grand Tapestry Room. He wondered now if anyone had ever cruised him while he'd been there, a teenager on a solo outing to the Gardner. Recently he'd heard that a lot of that used to go on there. If so, he'd missed it.

A sudden breeze ruffled the trees, dislodging a cascade of leaves from their branches. They drifted to the ground. His thoughts were drifting, too—back now to his years at the Boston Conservatory, the place where he'd become a professional musician and a young gay man. Those had been heady times—the thrill of mastering the viola; the thrill, too, of discovering his sexuality. But until he met his first boyfriend, Leo hadn't been very experienced. Music had pretty much been his life up to then. Though there was one bar, Sporter's, at the foot of Beacon Hill, where he'd occasionally pick up a guy when the itch for carnal release became stronger than his devotion to working through more etudes by Hrimaly and Wohlfahrt. Most times, he only stayed long enough to drink a beer and moon over guys. Even back then, what he'd wanted was a boyfriend, not a one-night stand.

Then, in the spring of his senior year, he met Viggo. Viggo was a musical theater major. That semester, he was in the Conservatory's production of *Brigadoon*. Leo didn't care for musicals. He'd only gone to the show because friends were going. But from the opening number, he was hooked. The music, the singing, the high-spirited dancing. It surprised him, how much fun it was. Which is what he needed in those final months of music school—a shake-up, something to take his mind off the scary, post-graduation future.

As the show unfolded, his attention kept going to a blond chorus boy in a feathered tam and pleated kilt, who, every now and then, when he kicked up his legs, revealed a delicious glimpse of a well-filled-out dance belt underneath his plaid tartan. Whenever the boy was on stage, Leo couldn't take his eyes off him. He read through the list of chorus members in the program and when he came to Viggo Olsen, he thought to himself, *That has got to be him. He looks like a Viggo.*

The following Monday, they ran into each other in the second-floor men's room of the Conservatory building. Leo screwed up his courage to say how much he'd loved the show. Viggo smiled and thanked him. His gaze went brazenly to Leo's crotch. Leo kept talking. It was a way to cover up his nervousness. He told Viggo how he'd never much cared for musicals, but that *Brigadoon* had completely won him over; how surprised he was to see that there was even a viola part in the score; how he'd loved the girl who played Fiona. "And the dancing," he added, "especially you."

A few days later, Viggo showed up at a chamber music recital that Leo was playing in. As soon as he walked on stage, Leo saw him sitting in the second row. He didn't look at him again until the applause and the bows. Then he flashed Viggo a broad smile. At the reception, they made plans to get together. The next evening, over hamburgers at a late-night eatery in Copley Square, they talked about the show, their majors at the Conservatory, where they'd grown up, and when they knew they were gay.

"I am so glad I came here," Leo told him, meaning the Conservatory, this place of musical *finesse*, but also of gay freedom, gay openness.

Viggo grinned. "Do you think you'd be just as glad to come over and see my room tonight?"

During that last month of their senior year, Leo felt all his boundaries being stretched. He learned to love Broadway musicals (Viggo had an enormous collection of Original Cast LP recordings), learned to disco dance, to smoke pot, and to eat Viggo's luscious dancer's ass.

"What's the next thing we're going to add to your repertoire?" Viggo asked one night after a steamy two hours of lovemaking.

"Anything you want to teach me," Leo said.

"Tie you up?" Viggo asked.

"Um, okay," Leo said, hoping his hesitancy wasn't obvious.

Viggo was turning out to be more of a livewire than he'd bargained for. But he loved this new person he was becoming, less buttoned up, and more—a *little* more anyway—adventurous. When they graduated, the two of them moved to Manhattan together. Leo loved the idea that they had become boyfriends. Viggo said, "Why do we have to put a name to it?"

They lucked out on a great apartment on West 103rd Street—cheap, cheap, cheap back then. Viggo waited tables and auditioned for shows. Leo landed a job with a chamber orchestra. Their hours were erratic, especially Viggo's. He often didn't fall into bed until two or three in the morning, complaining that hanging out with other half-out-of-work singers and dancers was what one had to do in order to keep your name and your face out there.

During their first year in New York, Leo rose to be principal violist in the chamber orchestra, and Viggo began getting gigs in off-Broadway shows. Leo's parents visited once to hear him play and to catch a show at Radio City. When they asked to see his apartment, Leo told them it was not worth the trouble of a long subway ride or expensive cab fare all the way uptown. There were too many other things he wanted them to see in the city, he said. He considered coming out to them, but squelched the notion. He didn't think they could handle the news.

There were other things that Leo hadn't wanted his parents to know about either. The apartment had been broken into, their neighbors down the hall were dealing drugs, Viggo was gay-bashed in Central Park. And the two of them weren't having much sex anymore. A few weeks after his parents' visit, Leo found out that Viggo was seeing someone else, someone he'd met while cruising the Ramble. From then on, the word they used to describe themselves was "roommates."

When he returned to Massachusetts, Leo was twenty-four. For the two months he stayed at his parents', they pestered him about when he was going to "find a nice girl."

"What about Jack?" Leo fired back. "He's twenty-seven, and he hasn't found a nice girl either." (Jack was working at a country club outside Pittsburgh that year.)

"*Ah, tu connais ton frère,*" their mother said, always ready to make excuses for Jack. "Jack's just not as serious as you are, Leo."

But then she sprang a surprise on him: Jack was moving back, too. He'd found a job as a golf pro. "At one of those *de luxe* country clubs in Newton." She laughed. "You can be sure he'll find a nice young lady there!"

The honking of a flock of Canada geese shook Leo out of his reverie. Near the little bridge that spanned the Muddy River, an old man was tossing out breadcrumbs. The geese came running over to him, squabbling over the scraps. Scattering the last of the bread, the man began to walk away. The geese clambered after him for a few seconds before they gave up and returned to pecking at the grass.

As soon as they sense you don't have the goodies anymore, they're no longer interested, Leo thought.

He'd sometimes cruised this area at night. The darkness helped to disguise his age, and there was always some action to be had. But he'd never much cared for it—the fast and fleeting encounters, the group scenes, the coked-up guys wandering around, sometimes completely naked, in the reeds. The last time he'd ventured down here, the place was dead, another victim of the online hook-up culture, he figured. As dead as his libido. That night, he'd returned home feeling like a eunuch—castrated, emasculated, desexed—a eunuch trying to remember why sex had once been so important.

He walked past the geese and crossed the bridge.

There were days, he had to admit, when he welcomed the shutdown of his sex life. His practicing had become more focused; his sleeping at night more peaceful. He didn't wake up with a woody anymore, and that didn't much trouble him. Would he feel the same six months from now when he went back to see Dr. Chowdhury? How awkward would it be to tell his urologist that he'd just as soon stay on those testosterone-blocking medications after all? Socrates once quipped that the compensation for growing old was the diminishment of his sex drive. Leo thought Socrates might have had a point. He guessed Jack would not see the point at all.

❖ ❖ ❖

Coming out to Jack had been an accident. A year after the two of them had moved back to Massachusetts, they bumped into each other outside Buddies. Back in those days, the line of guys waiting to be admitted into the popular gay club used to trail a block down Boylston Street. Leo had joined the line, trying not to look like the kind of person who joins a line of guys trying to get into a popular gay club. But that night, he was lonely, horny, and exhausted from a three-hour rehearsal for a summer festival of baroque opera. As much as he hated discos, he figured that as a single gay man, joining the line to get into Buddies was what he was supposed to do.

Just then, someone grabbed his arm.

"Leo! Holy shit!" It was Jack. "This is too freaky, man. I mean ... but, yeah, I've been wondering about you for years." Jack threw the cigarette he was smoking onto the sidewalk and turned to the guys he was with. They were all about Jack's age and all dressed in jeans and muscle shirts. "This is my little brother, Leo."

Jack's friends nodded their hellos, then turned back to the conversation they'd been having.

"Wow," Leo said, just as astonished. "Wow. My *brother*, my brother the *jock?*"

Jack laughed. "Um, in case you didn't know, jocks can be gay, too. Ever heard of Dave Kopay?"

"Of course," Leo said, trying to recall who this Dave Kopay guy was.

The line moved forward. Leo suggested they go have a coffee or a drink somewhere else. "Somewhere where we can hear ourselves think."

He'd been to Buddies exactly twice and hated it both times. The incessant, pounding music made it impossible to carry on a conversation.

"Leo, relax," Jack said. "Why can't we talk inside? I'm here with my friends. I can't just up and leave them."

The line moved forward, their IDs were checked, and they were admitted. Jack made a beeline for the bar, got them each a beer, and shouted into Leo's ear that he'd be right back, he just wanted to say hello to someone he knew. Leo watched his brother hustle off, looking as confident in this element as the debonair ladies' man he had been in high school.

The music was terrible. Leo had a classical music-loving friend, Louis, who complained that all baroque music sounded the same. But to Leo's ears, it was disco music that was unfailingly monotonous. In the morning, he was going to regret coming here—the way his clothes and hair would reek of smoke and the worry about what the decibel level was doing to his hearing.

Still, he had to admit that there were some hot-looking guys in the club. Blonds like Viggo were still his preference, though just last week he'd tricked with a Black guy, Curtis, who had cruised him on the trolley. After sex, Leo had given Curtis his phone number, but six days later, still no call. He took another sip of beer.

Even through the ear-punishing music, he could still hear, in the concert hall of his mind, the sumptuous music from the opera they'd been rehearsing that afternoon. It was Handel's *Giulio Cesare.* Leo thought each aria was a masterpiece. So often in baroque music, the viola part was there just to fill in the harmony, but every now and then, Handel gave the violas a luscious few measures that made playing that instrument completely worth it. Back in seventh grade, when his violin teacher had suggested he switch to the viola, Leo had been disappointed. But he had learned to love the deep, sonorous, throaty sound of the larger instrument, one his fingers had adapted to quickly.

"Hey, Larry," someone called out to him. When Leo turned, it was Curtis.

"It's Leo," he corrected.

"Leo, Leo—right," Curtis said. "What's going on, man?"

"I'm actually here with my brother," Leo said, more affably than he felt. He looked around to see if he could spot Jack. "I literally had no idea he was gay until I bumped into him tonight."

"Crazy, man. Crazy." A leer blossomed on Curtis' face. "He as hot as you?"

Leo hated that he was still smiling at Curtis. Just then, Jack sauntered up, a smirk beginning to bloom on his face, too.

It's not what you think, Leo wanted to say. Instead, he introduced them. Jack and Curtis hit it off immediately, so well that they ended up going home together that night.

The next afternoon, Jack called to ask what was up, and did Leo want to go with him and his buddies to Provincetown that weekend?

"Is one of these 'buddies' Curtis?" Leo asked.

Jack laughed, but didn't say. Leo made an excuse why he couldn't go.

"No problem," Jack said, "there'll be plenty more weekends, Little Bro."

Leo supposed he should be thankful that Little Bro had replaced Lemon Drop and Miss Viola. Still, for the rest of that summer and into the fall, he kept coming up with excuses why he couldn't hang out with Jack. He knew that his brother thought this one thing they finally had in common made up for all the differences between them. But Leo didn't think so. There were lots of ways to be gay, and Jack's way—the clubbing, the vapid friends, the breezy tricking, the expensive weekends in Provincetown—that way was not his. When, the following spring, Jack moved to North Carolina, his next country club stint, Leo was relieved. He figured the invitations would stop. For a while, they did.

❖ ❖ ❖

Back in his apartment on St. Botolph Street, Leo stretched out on the sofa. He guessed there was no avoiding hosting Jack. He looked around the living room, trying to imagine what Jack would think of his place. It was small and dark, sunlit only in the morning. The walls were lined with bookshelves; piles of music sat on his baby grand piano. The furniture was overstuffed and decorated with probably too many kilim pillows. On the one wall without bookshelves, Leo had hung two paintings—a bright abstract, all pinks and reds, done by his second boyfriend, Marty, who was a dentist by trade and an amateur painter on the side; and a small landscape from somewhere in Holland that he'd picked up for a song during his years in Utrecht. The rest of the wall was covered with antique etchings of some of his favorite baroque composers in ornate gold frames.

Marty had been the post-Viggo boyfriend, the boyfriend of Leo's thirties. They were together five years, until Marty announced he was opening his own dentistry practice in the suburbs. "I'm not sure I want to leave the city," Leo told him. He couldn't imagine going back to the suburbs, even one that was decidedly more sophisticated than North Billerica. In fact, their relationship had run its course. The irony was that, in many ways, Leo had had with Marty exactly what he wished he'd had with Viggo.

A few months after they ended it, Leo decided he needed a fresh start. Which is how he'd gotten to Utrecht. On a tip from a Conservatory friend, he flew there, auditioned for a position with a baroque band, and landed the job. In no time, he fell in love with Utrecht. He loved his new chamber orchestra, loved how cheerful and welcoming the Dutch were. He made some gay friends, who took him to Amsterdam, showed him the gay sites and introduced him to his first bathhouse. The unbridled sex that took place in the darkrooms and gloryholes, in the labyrinthine corridors and cramped little cubicles, boggled Leo's mind. And excited him. At least for a while.

He went to the tubs a few more times, allowing himself to settle for what the bathhouses had to offer. Occasionally, he would throw caution to the wind and have unprotected sex. Afterwards, he would suffer remorse and anxiety until he could get to a health clinic to get tested for HIV. "You're at less risk because you're a top," his friend Cornelis told him. Sometimes that fact relieved him; more often than not it didn't.

Eventually, he stopped going to Amsterdam altogether. The risk, but mostly the disappointments, weren't worth it. Instead, he settled for the occasional beer—and the occasional pick-up—at one of the gay watering holes in Utrecht. But he never developed the knack for keeping something going. He wasn't sure why—a combination, he guessed, of cultural disconnect, his busy concert schedule, and fizzling chemistry after a few dates. Instead, he threw himself even more into music making—the chamber orchestra, his viola students, and a church *kamerorkest*, where he played Bach and Buxtehude cantatas on Sundays. When he returned to Boston to take care of his mother, Leo had just turned forty. Three of his classmates from the Conservatory were dead. Viggo was one of them.

The third and last boyfriend was Jonathan, the one Leo thought was finally *the* one. He was a tree surgeon, at forty-two still lithe and fit enough to scale his clients' maples, oaks, and beeches. After three months of dating, they decided they were boyfriends and agreed on a monogamous relationship. But within a year, Jonathan said he wanted to open things up. Reluctantly, Leo agreed to a regular third—*regular*, he insisted. Just one, no playing around. The guy's name was Connor. He was in his mid-twenties.

Meanwhile, in the early music orchestra he played with, Leo was three times featured as a soloist, once in the Telemann viola concerto, once in the J.C. Bach, and once in the Mozart Sinfonia Concertante. He didn't understand how he could be so devoted to the sublimity of classical music and, at the same time, so embroiled in the complications, the *baroque* complications, of this threesome. He didn't want Connor-and-Jonathan. He only wanted Jonathan. Occasionally—and this scared him—he only wanted Connor.

After a year, Connor disappeared. Jonathan took it hard. At which point, Leo realized that their threesome had actually been a twosome all the while, with Leo merely tagging along for the ride. He decided he wanted out—out of threesomes and out of this marriage. He told Jonathan he hoped they could still be friends. Jonathan said he hoped so, too.

For a while, Leo returned to the bar scene. Then he found the men-seeking-men site on Craigslist. That scene was basically Utrecht all over again: his musical life still took precedence; the chemistry with these guys was generally off; and another kind of cultural disconnect prevailed. The few who showed any interest in seeing him again were bi-sexual guys—with girlfriends or wives. They kept contacting him, and Leo kept succumbing, even though he knew these assignations had about as much chance of turning into something significant as the Red Sox had of surviving their annual August slump.

The year he turned fifty, the old boyfriend—now friend—Jonathan threw a big "Half Century" birthday party for him. Jack, who by then had moved to a golf club in Savannah, came up for the celebration. His contribution to the festivities was to arrange for a male stripper to entertain. Several of Leo's straight friends from the chamber orchestra were there. They seemed amused by the strip show. Leo was mortified.

At the birthday party, Jack told Leo about his latest "boyfriend." Number Fourteen or Fifteen by Leo's count. Whenever he thought of Jack's boyfriends, Leo always put ironic quotes around the word. These guys fell in and out of his brother's life like ... well, like Canada geese swooping down onto a scattering of bread ends before rushing off elsewhere. And Jack, he seemed so mellow about it all. In comparison to his brother, Leo felt he was kind of a failure as a gay man. From faraway Utrecht, his friend Cornelis agreed. *You're too much into the classical Three B's,* Cornelis emailed one day. *Leo, embrace the Gay Three B's: bars, bushes and bathhouses.*

But try as he did, the Gay Three B's just weren't his scene. Meanwhile, Jack kept moving farther and farther south. After Savannah, it was Jacksonville, then Orlando, then Fort Myers. Periodically, he would report to Leo how great his life was. The weather, the country clubs, the parade of boys. Finally, he moved to Fort Lauderdale, his retirement Shangri-la. He sent Leo photos of his new place: pastel everything, a huge living room-cum-bar, lots of sea-shell artwork.

From the sofa, Leo stared at the painting that Marty, the dentist boyfriend, had given him. He tried to recall why, all those years ago, he'd thought Marty was boring. My God, if they'd stayed a couple, they'd be celebrating forty years together now.

He heaved himself up and called Jack. When Jack didn't pick up, he left a message suggesting the second weekend in December. He deliberately chose his busiest weekend, a weekend when he was playing two concerts.

❖ ❖ ❖

The Friday of Jack's visit, an early winter blizzard dumped twenty-one inches of snow on Boston. Jack's flight was canceled. He arrived the next afternoon, carrying three pieces of luggage: a leather backpack, an aluminum suitcase, and a Louis Vuitton weekend travel bag.

"You're going to be here twenty-four hours, right?" Leo asked.

"Nice to see you, too, Little Bro."

It was four o'clock, already dark outside. Leo offered Jack a glass of wine.

"I'll take a Coke, if you've got one."

"I don't have any Coke. How about orange juice?"

"Only if it's from Florida," Jack quipped. He plopped down on the sofa. "So, what's this concert going to be like?"

"Baroque Christmas music," Leo called from the kitchen. "You don't have to come if you don't want to."

"Of course, I'm coming. You got me a ticket, right?"

"Yes, for tonight." He returned with Jack's orange juice. "I figured it would be cutting it awfully close for your return flight if you came to the Sunday afternoon concert." *Please*, he thought. *You* are *leaving on Sunday!*

Jack took a sip of juice and looked around the apartment. "Cute place, Leo."

"Thanks."

Jack motioned over to the pink-and-red painting. "Where'd you get that?"

"An old boyfriend."

Jack kept studying the painting. "That guy ... what was his name? Marty, right? The dentist. He used to paint."

"Wow, how'd you remember all that!"

"Is it such a surprise that I'm interested in my brother's life?" Jack said.

"Okay, but that was decades ago."

"Hey, what can I say? Mom and Dad had great memories. It's in the genes, Leo."

Is it also in the genes, Leo wondered, *to have an enlarged prostate?* He sat down on the piano bench.

"So how's life in Florida?"

"Livin' my best life." Jack slouched down into the sofa. "Don't know why you won't come for a visit."

"I know, I know. It's just that I'm super busy." Leo directed his gaze around the living room, hoping the clutter would be more convincing than his words. "I've just got a ton of gigs right now."

"Ton of gigs," Jack echoed. "You ever gonna retire?"

Leo wriggled his fingers at his brother. "As long as these fingers stay nimble and I can read the notes, I don't see why I should. I still play every day."

Jack smiled. "Yeah, I still play every day, too."

"Golf?"

"Guys."

Wearily, Leo shook his head.

"Oh, come on, Leo, I'm joking. I know you write me off as a hoe, but I've actually gotten into doing some interesting fund-raising work down there."

Jack launched into a story about the night he dressed up in nothing but a jock strap and harness, and sold tickets to the guys at the bar for a fundraising event for transgender rights. He pulled up his sweater, exposing his stomach. "Not bad for sixty-nine, huh?" He slapped his belly.

Leo had not seen his brother's stomach in half a century, not since the days their parents would take them to Wingaersheek Beach. In the brief glimpse he got, he saw that Jack was in surprisingly good shape.

"A jock strap and harness? Jack, I'm having a hard time picturing ..."

Jack pulled out his smartphone. "I got photos. You wanna see?"

"No!"

Jack shrugged and repocketed his phone.

"Got myself a great personal trainer last year. That's the only reason I had the balls to parade my ass around that bar."

"I try to get to the gym a few times a week," Leo said, "but, well ... not enough hours in the day."

"All depends on what you're committed to," Jack said.

"Yeah, well, it's always been music for me, you know." For a moment, the conversation stopped. "So, look," Leo asked, rising from the piano bench, "you want to rest up before we head out to the concert?"

"No, I do not want to *rest up*. Jesus, Leo, I just got here, we haven't seen each other since Mom's funeral, and you're already putting me to bed?"

"Sorry, sorry. I thought you might be tired."

"I napped on the plane. And, in case you hadn't heard, Fort Lauderdale and Boston are in the same time zone."

"Okay, Jack, I was just trying to be a good host." The conversation stopped again. Fifteen minutes had gone by since his brother's arrival. Leo wished he had poured himself a glass of wine. "So, tell me about this fundraiser." He sat back down at the piano. "You put on a jock strap and paraded around the bar?"

"*And?*" Jack prompted.

"And raised money for transgender rights. I heard you, Jack. I think that's great." Jack stared at him, not saying a word. "Look, I'm sorry I haven't come to visit you in Florida."

"Could have fooled me."

"Jack, you've got to cut me some slack right now. I'm a little on edge."

"On edge about what?" The sarcasm had disappeared from Jack's voice. "The concert?"

"No, not that. Other stuff."

Jack cocked his head: *You gonna tell me?* he was asking.

"We'll talk about it later," Leo said.

"Ah, Leo's famous 'later'! Like next-year-I'll-come-see-you-in-Florida later?"

"No," Leo said. "Like after-the-concert-over-dinner later."

❖ ❖ ❖

The concert went well, though during the second half Leo realized he had forgotten to take his prostate medication. By the final movement of the Corelli Christmas concerto, he thought his bladder would burst.

He and Jack went out to dinner at a nearby French bistro in the Back Bay. On the way, they had to negotiate sidewalks that were snow-piled and slushy.

"*This* is why you should come visit me in Florida," Jack said. Leo didn't respond.

At the restaurant, they were seated and given menus. Leo suggested they share a bottle of wine, but Jack said that he had quit drinking.

"Since when?"

"Five years ago."

"Were you drinking a lot?" Leo delicately asked.

"'A lot' doesn't begin to describe it."

"I never knew," Leo said, and immediately he wished he hadn't. He was relieved when Jack didn't say the obvious. "You don't mind if I have some wine, do you?"

Jack said he didn't mind at all, and Leo ordered a bottle, quickly pointing out that he wasn't planning on drinking the whole thing. In Massachusetts, he said, it was now possible to take home an unfinished bottle of wine.

"Same in Florida," Jack told him. "We're more progressive than you think, Leo." He asked the waiter to bring him a club soda and lime. "So, I enjoyed the concert," he said. "A lot more than I thought I would. I could hear you playing."

Leo chuckled. "That's what Mom always said whenever she came to one of my concerts. I used to tell her that she shouldn't have been able to do that, that the idea was for each group of strings to blend. No one instrumentalist should stick out. She used to insist that she could hear me anyway."

"Mom was very proud of you, Leo. Even though she was sad that you chose to be a musician and not a doctor, she was always proud of what you accomplished."

The waiter arrived with the wine and Jack's club soda.

"*Merci*," Jack said, flashing a smile at the young man, who was French and cute. As the waiter twisted the corkscrew into the bottle of wine, he returned Jack's smile, and then—an equal opportunity flirter—turned to Leo and smiled at him. Leo wondered if he was just covering up for the fact that he was straining to pull out the cork. Cork finally pulled, wine poured, bottle settled into an ice bucket, the waiter told them in his thick French accent that he'd be back in a few minutes to take their order.

"Don't be gone too long," Jack said. "*No bow-coo long.*"

Leo swirled his glass and sniffed. The thought crossed his mind that it might be inappropriate to exhibit too much pleasure in the wine. He took a sip and put down his glass.

"What are you thinking about having?" It was the first thing he could think to say to break the silence.

Jack looked up from the menu. "Well, since I'm in Boston, maybe the mussels?"

"They're cooked in white wine, you know."

"Leo, the alcohol boils off." Jack set down his menu. "Look, I'm doing really well. You don't have to worry about me."

"I'm glad to hear that, Jack."

"Really well," Jack repeated.

The waiter returned, smiled again at both of them, and asked if they would care to order. Jack chose the mussels; Leo the trout.

"And maybe to start," Jack added, "we could share the beet-and-goat-cheese salad? I mean my brother and I, not you and I." He grinned at the waiter. "What do you think? Would that be a nice opener?"

"*Parfait, monsieur,*" the waiter said.

"Are you going to flirt with him all evening?" Leo asked after the waiter had left.

"Depends on how long the restaurant stays open," Jack said.

"He's a little young for you, no?"

Jack let out a chortle. "Oh, man, you should see some of the couples down in Fort Lauderdale!" The smile suddenly disappeared from his face. "Leo, I'm having fun. It's just play. Will you fucking relax?"

Leo took another sip of wine. "You think I don't know how to 'play'? Is that it? I know how to play." He would have liked to reel off a catalogue of the guys he'd hooked up with. But that kind of playing, little as he'd ever done it, was all past history now. "Jack, it's just that our lives have gone in very different directions. I think we should acknowledge that."

"Acknowledge," Jack said, throwing the word back at Leo like a rejected garment that didn't fit. "What I 'acknowledge,' Leo, is that you walk around with this stick-up-your-ass superior attitude. You think your 'direction' is better than mine: Boston, classical music, voted for Hilary Clinton. That's what you're really saying, isn't it?"

"No, that's *not* what I'm saying!" Leo heard his voice getting louder. "What I am saying," he continued, *più piano* now, "is that I like my life just fine. Just as it is." He paused just long enough to wonder if he believed this. "I'm not ranking our lives, Jack. I'm not calling my life superior to yours. I'm just pointing out that they're different."

"Different," Jack mused. He took a sip of his club soda before he spoke again. "Leo, do you remember the night I ran into you at Buddies. Damn, how many years ago now?"

"A lot of years ago."

"I was so happy to see you that night. To discover that my little Lemon Drop brother and I finally shared something in common."

Leo nodded.

"But all that summer," Jack went on, "you kept turning down my invitations to hang out. I didn't get it."

Leo began an explanation, but Jack cut him short.

"It's okay, Leo. I finally understood what was going on. I embarrassed you."

"No, you didn't!"

"Yes, I think I did. You were on another path—classical music, dreams of going to Europe ..." Jack chuckled. "I still haven't been to Europe."

"It's not too late."

"Just listen, Leo! This is not about me regretting not going to Europe. I don't regret anything in my life."

The waiter brought over the beet salad. His demeanor had suddenly become sober. Leo wondered if he'd overheard the earlier heated exchange.

Silently, Jack spooned some of the salad onto Leo's plate and then served himself. Leo nodded his thanks, happy for the distraction of food. "*Bon appétit,*" he said.

"You, too," Jack said. Leo watched his brother take a bite. "Mmm, very good."

"I thought you'd enjoy this place." Turning the conversation in the direction of their mutual pleasure in good food was a relief.

"Yeah, it's nice. The kind of place I figured you'd take me to."

"A little too *soigné*?" Leo asked.

"No, it's really nice, Leo. I'm happy you brought me here."

For a minute, they ate in silence. It was Jack who finally spoke.

"So, you promised me an after-the-concert big reveal. What had you so on edge this afternoon?"

"No big reveal. Just some medical issues."

A look of alarm came over Jack's face. "Fuck, what?"

"Enlarged prostate."

"That all? Christ, Leo, don't scare me like that. Half the guys in Fort Lauderdale have enlarged prostates."

"Well 'that all' hasn't been much fun. I mean the medications I'm taking, they've pretty much wiped out my sex drive." Leo studied Jack's face, looking for his reaction.

Jack chuckled. "Didn't know you wanted a sex drive!"

Leo smirked.

"But, yeah," Jack continued, "I hear that complaint a lot down in Fort Lauderdale." The teasing tone had been replaced by sympathy.

"My doctor tells me my tests are normal," Leo said. "Some fucking 'normal.'"

"Sucks, huh?"

"Sucks."

"Somehow, the prostate bullet missed me." Jack considered what he'd just said and laughed. "One of the only bullets that's missed me."

Leo cocked his head.

"Being a drunk," Jack explained. "And ..." He pushed a piece of beet salad around his plate, then looked up. "And being HIV positive."

"What! Jack, no."

"Hey, it's okay. I've been on the cocktail for fifteen years. I'm undetectable."

"Fifteen years. And you didn't tell me ..."

Jack interrupted. "When was I going to tell you, Leo? During one of your many visits to see me?"

"Jack," Leo began, "I'm ..."

"You're what, Leo? Sorry? Look, it happened. I was in my early fifties when I tested positive." He shook his head in amusement. "Like, who the fuck tests positive in their early fifties?"

Leo put down his fork. "So, you're okay?"

"More than okay. I'm healthy, and I love my life down there. I've got a great group of buddies, a great support group, I still golf, and I love my volunteer work for transgender rights."

"Yeah, where'd that come from?" Leo asked.

"Why not? It's as good a cause as any, right?" Jack smiled. "And, no, in case you're wondering, I'm not transitioning. But I have two friends who are. Both in their fifties."

"Wow."

"Yup, it's quite a world down there, Leo." Jack leaned forward, curiosity blooming on his face. "So, tonight, when that guy soprano started singing ..."

"Countertenor."

"Yeah, countertenor. I thought he, she, they were transgender."

Leo resisted the urge to laugh. "No, just a particular kind of highly trained voice. Back in the eighteenth century, they used to castrate boy sopranos before their voices changed so that they'd keep that high register."

Jack winced. "Ouch!"

The waiter came by, still sober-faced, and took away the salad plates.

"Mr. Flirtation seems to have lost interest," Leo observed.

"They come and they go," Jack said.

Leo took another sip of wine. "So I've noticed, but, I have to say, Jack, you do have this amazing talent for picking up ..."

"What? Diseases?"

"Boyfriends."

"Why do I think that's not meant as a compliment?" Jack asked.

"Just an observation."

The waiter returned, setting down their entrées.

"May I get you gentlemen anything else?" he asked.

"Another smile, perhaps?" Jack proposed.

Taken aback, the waiter complied, smiling at both of them.

"That was bold of you," Leo said after the waiter had left again.

"Bold? Look, Leo, it's not always about 'picking up boyfriends.' Sometimes it's just about being friendly, you know." Jack picked a mussel from out of his bowl, brought it to his lips, and sucked the flesh into his mouth. "Delicious." Leo watched as Jack used the now-empty shell to spoon up some of the broth and slurp it down. "Really delicious."

Leo smiled. His brother did have an amazing appetite for pleasure. After a minute, Jack stopped eating.

"Do you remember when your violin teacher made you switch to the viola? When was that? Seventh grade?"

"Seventh grade," Leo confirmed.

"You were heartbroken. Do you remember that?"

"Well, I don't know if 'heartbroken' is quite the word. Sure, I was disappointed."

"You were *heartbroken*, Leo. I can't believe you don't remember that. One night in our bedroom, I heard you crying. You didn't want me to hear, but I did. The next morning, I told Mom."

"You *what?*"

"Yeah, I wanted her to do something so you wouldn't be so unhappy."

Leo's eyes widened. He had no knowledge of any of this.

"Mom reassured me that you'd eventually come around and make the best of it, that you'd learn to love the viola." Jack tried to make eye contact, but Leo picked up his knife and fork, anything to avoid the intimacy in Jack's face. "I remember that so well," Jack continued, "because Mom's words actually hit me hard."

Leo looked up. "How?"

"Leo, you still don't get it, do you? Because I needed to learn that there was a 'best' in *me* that I could make something of. I felt like such a nobody in comparison to you."

"What!"

"You were my dweeby little brother who was so good at so many things."

Leo laughed. "And you were my obnoxious jock brother who was so good at so many things!"

Jack shrugged. "Hey, I just took what few talents I had and ran with them." He looked hard at Leo. "I'm still playing by those rules, Leo. Fuckup that I am, I am still trying to make the best of what I've been dealt."

"You're not a fuck-up, Jack."

Jack looked at him, searchingly.

The waiter came by, took the wine bottle from the ice bucket, and poured more for Leo. As he returned the bottle to the bucket, he shot Leo a quick smile, then bowed and went away.

"Oh, my God," Jack whispered. "Bro, he's totally into you."

Leo shook his head, brushing off the suggestion.

Jack cut him short. "Leo, let it happen!"

"Nothing was happening there, Jack."

Jack looked at him again, this time with greater insistence. "You know, you *really* need to come to Fort Lauderdale."

"Because?"

"Well, for starters, because you'd have *fun*. Because the guys there can give you some tips on—how should I put this?—on how to play with that damn faulty equipment of yours."

Leo wondered if, by "faulty equipment," Jack meant his prostate or his personality.

"You know," he said, "if you want to talk about making the best of things ... when Mom got diagnosed with cancer and I moved back to Boston, that, Jack, *that* was making the best of things. I mean, I didn't want to leave Europe; I didn't want to quit playing with my sweet Dutch orchestra. Holland may well have been the happiest time of my entire life. I loved everything about the country, especially Utrecht. Not just the quaintness of it—the medieval architecture, the canals, the way everyone rode bikes—but the whole Dutch attitude toward life." He looked at his brother to see if he was following. "I know I'm romanticizing, but that's how I felt."

Jack nodded.

"When I came back to Boston, I felt so out of synch with this city. My God, Massachusetts even had a Republican governor that year! It all felt so alien."

"But you did end up loving this place, didn't you?" Jack asked. "I can't imagine you anywhere else, Leo. This is your city."

"Yes," Leo agreed.

"So how'd that happen?"

"I guess I learned to stop comparing the two places. Utrecht was Utrecht, and Boston was Boston. The more I stopped thinking of Boston as 'not-Utrecht,' the more I came to appreciate what *was* here, what was always here, what I'd first fallen in love with in this city."

He took another sip of wine. There was more he had to say.

"Mom was undergoing chemo that year. Every week, I'd go up to North Billerica to have dinner with her and to help Dad around the house." He paused, thinking, *Okay, time to finally let this out.* "And I, I was so angry at you, Jack, for being—where at that point? Hilton Head? Savannah?—for being so far away and not coming up to lend a hand."

Jack kept listening.

"I'm not sure I ever 'made the best' of that," Leo said. "Your absence. I used to picture you on those damn manicured golf courses, doing nothing but hobnobbing with rich Southern country club types."

Jack nodded his head. "Yeah, I probably should have visited more often. It's just—I don't know—I guess I just couldn't face seeing Mom so sick. I did call her every week—you know that, right?"

Leo shook his head. He'd never heard that before.

"I did," Jack said. "I did, Leo."

For a moment, each of them returned to eating. Jack was the first to look up.

"'Rich Southern country club types'? Jesus, Leo, you can be such a fucking snob sometimes. You've never been south of, what, Philadelphia? I mean, pay attention to your own damn words: the South is *not* Boston; country clubs are *not* concert halls. They're just different, Leo. That's all."

Leo put down his knife and fork, leaned back in his chair, and sighed. *Snob?* It was hardly the sum total of who he was. But his brother had named something real enough about him, something that all his life he had resisted putting a name to. Reluctantly, he nodded his assent.

"Yeah, I guess." He chuckled. "Like maybe ever since sixth grade, huh?"

A chuckle from Jack now, too. "How about like maybe ever since *third* grade?"

"Ouch."

Jack picked up his water glass and held it out to toast. "Here's to that little third-grade snob. May he ..."

Leo picked up his wine glass and clinked. "May he ..." He started to laugh.

The couple at the next table turned to look.

"We're celebrating," Jack explained. He turned to Leo. "Leo, what are we celebrating?"

"Beats me," Leo said. And then, for the sheer whimsy of it, he told them, "We're celebrating faulty equipment. May he learn to love his faulty equipment!" The two brothers clinked glasses again.

The couple, a straight man and woman, smiled, the man warily; the woman all set to join in the fun.

"Ha!" she exclaimed, "tell me about faulty equipment!" and let out a cackle. By the way they were dressed—blazer and rep tie for him; expensive, slightly restrained couture for her—Leo pegged them as Beacon Hill types.

"Jocelyn," the woman said, reaching over to shake hands. Like her husband, she was pleasantly overweight. She wore a big diamond ring and an expensive hairdo with lots of blond highlights. They looked to be in their late thirties. "This is my husband Bob," she said.

More handshakes. And further information: they were celebrating, too. Their tenth wedding anniversary. The kids, Terry and Anna, were at home with the babysitter.

"And what's *your* baby's name?" Jocelyn asked, motioning to Leo's instrument case, which he'd set in an empty chair at their table.

Leo smiled, then made eye contact with Jack. "Lemon Drop."

"Lemon Drop!" Jocelyn exclaimed. "Lemon Drop!"

"Jocelyn," Bob entreated, laying his hand on her chubby arm.

"Oh, honey, come on. It's our anniversary."

A bottle of champagne was nestled in a wine cooler by their table. Jocelyn picked it up. "Empty," she pouted and told Bob to order another. "You look like fun guys," she said. "You boyfriends or just two dudes away from their wives for the night?"

"Brothers," Leo said. He started to say that they'd pass on the champagne, but Bob had already put in the order.

When Jack explained that he didn't drink, Jocelyn caught the waiter's attention. "And bring this gentleman a bottle of your best sparkling water."

They spent the rest of the evening talking and trading stories. Jocelyn even joined in flirting with the waiter, whose name, he revealed, was Marcel. When he next came around, he presented them with a complimentary *mousse au chocolat*.

❖ ❖ ❖

"Fun people," Jack said as he and Leo made their way back to the apartment. The night had turned cold, a wind was blowing.

"Yeah," Leo said abstractedly.

Jack turned to him. "What?"

"I'm just thinking about how I never would have started talking to them if I hadn't been with you."

"Why not?"

"Because I can be 'such a snob,' right?"

Jack looked at him. "You know what snobbery is? It's deciding who someone is before you even get to know them." He paused. "I had a golf coach once ... Shit, it's freezing! Let's move faster."

"What about the golf coach?" Leo asked as they hustled down Newbury Street.

"He said that deciding in advance how the game's gonna go—like you already assume your opponent is better than you, or you've played this course before and you know the turf—it doesn't really get you anywhere, does it? You have to throw yourself into the game and play it out right then and there, not in your head."

"Weird," Leo said, "back in my conservatory days, I had a teacher who said almost the same thing. She used to tell me, 'Whenever you play a familiar piece, play it as if you're discovering its beauty for the first time.'" He stopped in the middle of the block and turned toward Jack. "Do you know how many times over the years I've had to relearn that lesson?"

"It's kind of what it's all about, isn't it?" Jack said. "Learning the same lessons over and over."

"But I hate that," Leo said, as they started walking again. His breath sent out misty plumes of condensation into the frigid air. He stopped up short again. "I hate it." And suddenly, the glittering beauty of Newbury Street hit him—the warm, sparkling lights in the restaurant windows, the Christmas wreaths on the lampposts. Even the piles of snow seemed pretty. "Like every year I have to learn again how beautiful Boston can be in the damn winter. It drives me crazy."

"Drives you crazy? Why?" Jack asked. "Because you're human?" They started walking again. "Get used to it, Leo."

Christ, it really was freezing, Leo thought. Freezing and wintry beautiful. He crooked his elbow around Jack's and pulled him in close. It occurred to him that this was the first time in decades that he had touched his brother in anything like an affectionate manner.

"Lots to get used to, huh?" he asked.

"Welcome to the club," Jack said.

Number Six

When I was a sophomore in high school, our European history teacher taught us a mnemonic to remember the fate of Henry VIII's six wives: "Divorced, Beheaded, Died; Divorced, Beheaded, Survived."

To this day, I don't know why Mr. Fallon thought this was a necessary piece of information to imbed into our memories. Perhaps all he wanted was to spice up what was—even he must have known this—a dull course, fraught with too many names and dates, wars and treaties, conquests and councils. I was sixteen years old and had my own world-rattling turmoil to deal with. It did not take much—a girl trying to flirt with me, a boy's enigmatic smile, the perfect body of another boy under the showers in the locker room—to throw me into a tailspin. That year, I felt it all: love, confusion, shame, despair, anguish. In short, all the many emotional disturbances that cause an adolescent boy to suffer a heavy heart, nations to go to war, and kings to rid themselves of inconvenient wives.

Over the long stretch of time since Mr. Fallon's class, I, too, have enjoyed the delights and suffered the discontents of a succession of partners. Five, to be exact. If, however, I needed a mnemonic to tally them up, it would be much simpler: "Survived, Survived, Survived, Survived, Survived." By which I mean, either they survived me, or I survived them. This seems cold and heartless. I do not mean it that way. But I have come to see gay partnership as a precarious business, a study in attraction—often, a far too hasty attraction—followed by the inevitable unraveling. Five unravelings in my case, each one as terminal as a beheading.

A quick catalogue:

Number One was Wayne, the college boyfriend. "Wayne and William!" our friends would call out whenever they encountered us together on the St. Olaf campus. We met in the handbell choir and, well, bells started ringing shortly thereafter. We were both nineteen, both new to gay romance, both utterly caught by surprise at how intensely we felt about each other. Within a few months, I was keeping a photo album of our life together: a life defined by the kinds of diversions one could licitly enjoy at a Lutheran college in Minnesota, but also by the occasional secret, less licit pastimes we managed to pull off on those rare occasions when we could slip away from campus.

I suspect that one or two of our friends knew we were a couple, but most just thought we were buddies—handbell buddies, study buddies, water polo buddies—with cutely alliterative names. Wayne and William. I know of couples who met in college and are still together. Not Wayne and I. We had too much growing up still to do. Things began to unravel during our final semester. The snapshots in the scrapbook became fewer and fewer. A week after graduation, Wayne went into the Army. I moved to the Twin Cities.

Next was Alan. We met in Minneapolis, where he and I worked for the same dairy company. Alan had just graduated from college. I was two years older than he and picked up right away that he was gay. We lasted three years. After Alan cheated on me, we went into couples counseling. I was willing to work hard to stay together. But when Alan told the counselor, *I think I want more time to think about this relationship*, I realized that I had to let him go so that he could work out his commitment issues. Ironically, several years later, we both ended up in Boston, but to this day our only contact has been the annual exchange of a Christmas card, signed, nothing more.

Number Three was Chad, the rebound from Alan. I was still in Minneapolis when I met him, still working for the dairy company. My parents, whom I saw almost every Sunday for dinner, figured out that Chad was more than a friend. (They soon figured out that Alan and Wayne had been more than just friends, too.) They worked the guilt-and-shame angle on me very effectively. In truth, I took on the guilt and shame very effectively. After two failed relationships, I couldn't shake the suspicion that maybe Mom and Dad and their Lutheran God were right: that my love for Chad, for Alan, for Wayne was just some confused aberration, a "phase" I was going through. Poor Chad, he tried mightily to argue me out of my misguided, tortured theology, but in the end, miserable and wracked with turmoil, I left him. And then went straight.

Long enough to date a few women, the last of whom, Ellen, I followed to Vermont, where she and I tried raising llamas.

When I fell into unrequited love with Thad, our farm hand, I realized that my feelings for men—and the notion that I wanted to go through life with a guy both in my bed and by my side—those feelings were stronger, *realer,* than anything. Ellen tried to understand, but it was hard for her. We remained business partners until she met her current husband and he bought out my share of the farm. We, too, still exchange Christmas cards.

For a while after that, I kept the books for a big marble quarry in Dorset. These were the days before the Internet and all the hookup sites, but I managed to meet guys at the few gay bars Vermont in the eighties had to offer. None of these guys became anything more than bar friends or one-night stands. Until a weekend trip to Boston. It was there I fell in love again. First, with the city. All of it—the harbor, the museums, the narrow streets and ancient brick homes on Beacon Hill, the North End with its Italian cafés and restaurants, the Swan Boats, the sailboats on the river, the many, many gay bars! I started going down to Boston every chance I got. When a guy I met at one of those bars—a one-time sex partner who became a friend—started talking to me about careers in financial planning, I thought, *Well, why not?*

By the time Frank, Number Four, came along, I was doing very well in a money management company. Frank was everything that a gay man like me—late-thirties, a Boston convert from the Midwest, newly wealthy—was supposed to want. Frank, my vivacious, globe-trotting boyfriend, who loved to make a big splash everywhere he went. He was handsome, sophisticated, and very well-connected in the gay community. We became a much sought-after couple. There were days when I couldn't believe that I—this midwestern dairy guy turned llama farmer turned quarry accountant—was now living on Beacon Hill, making more money in one year than my parents had made in ten, and seeing my photo about once a month in the society pages of the gay and straight papers.

But for all our fabulousness, something wasn't right between us. Frank used to needle me about how "undiscriminating" I was. That was the word he used: undiscriminating in the restaurants I enjoyed, undiscriminating in the movies I liked, and, most of all, undiscriminating in my choice of friends.

You like everything and, worst of all, everyone! he would scold, an unpardonable fault in his book. According to Frank, it was important—indeed, *de rigueur*—to be more selective and to maintain a general air of coolness. *Otherwise,* he said, *you come across as too run-of-the-mill.* (I think that meant "too Midwestern.") For Frank, who had been president of his final club at Harvard, maintaining his reputation as an A-List Gay was an almost religious obligation. To do that, one had to be scrupulous about who to let into one's orbit. Only certain people, only certain restaurants, only certain vintages.

Frank was the boyfriend I *literally* survived. We both tested positive for HIV on the same day; a year later, Frank was dead. His funeral, at the spikey Anglican Church of the Advent on Brimmer Street, was an event worthy of Frank's social stature. High Mass, incense, the change ringers doing a full peal of six bells that took almost an hour after the service.

The night after the funeral, alone in our townhouse on Louisburg Square, I told myself: "You can keep getting better, or you can get bitter." I opted for better.

It was several years, and several changes in my medication later, that I met P.J., Number Five. I was forty-three. He was twenty-eight. By then, I was on the cocktail and undetectable. From the beginning, I was upfront with P.J. about my status; he said he was cool with that. The chemistry between us was pyrotechnic. I think the danger, as minimal as it was, turned him on. The two-thousand-square-foot apartment on Louisburg Square turned him on, too.

Apart from his cute, boyish looks, P.J. was everything Frank would have hated. He'd grown up on the wrong side of the Cape Cod Canal, in decidedly unfashionable Wareham, never finished college, and was a clerk in a sportswear store at the South Shore Mall. He drank too much, smoked too much, never saved a dime. We rented a house in Provincetown for the entire summer we were together. P.J. quit his job so he could be there full-time. For money, he waited tables. I thought this was a good career move for him.

It must be obvious that P.J. was another mismatch, but my perennial optimism about people, my "undiscriminating" embrace of men, led me to find in P.J. a personality I thought I liked. For a while, I described him as "buoyant," "animated," "fun." The complete opposite of uptight Frank. My friends called him a mess.

At the end of the summer, the restaurant closed, and P.J.—golden, ravenous, messy P.J.—decided that what I was offering him was not what he wanted. In truth, I don't think I could have said what I was offering him other than a chance to be the trophy boy on my expensively tailored arm. He was my shortest-lived boyfriend: less than a year.

My friends told me that P.J. was a riddance well worth celebrating. They told me I was a catch and that there were plenty more years ahead. My "best years," they said.

For a while, I tried making them my best years. I sold the Louisburg Square apartment, and with the proceeds—obscenely huge—bought a modest condo in Jamaica Plain and a small year-round place in Provincetown, to which I escaped every chance I had. I never went back to the clubs that P.J. and I used to frequent.

For me, Provincetown became about something else—something that I'd loved even that summer P.J. and I were together, but which I'd neglected. It became about the light on the bay, the muted rocking of the fishing boats in the harbor, the gentle lay of the land and the rolling dunes, where, late in the afternoon, I'd wander, sometimes giving myself over to the beauty of the beach grass, sand and sunlight, and sometimes giving myself over to the men who were cruising there. I met some guys and even dated a few. Nothing clicked. I guess I was grieving, though I wouldn't have been able to pinpoint exactly what it was that I was grieving. A lot, I guess.

To celebrate my fiftieth birthday, I decided to take myself to Vietnam. I went alone. Something—the last vestige of my Lutheran upbringing, perhaps—whispered to me that I needed to change my life. I had only a foggy idea of what that meant, but I got it into my head that my life needed a course correction, one that a trip halfway around the world might bring about. Still, expensive habits are hard to break. I booked a room at the best hotel in Hanoi, where I signed up for yoga classes and treated myself to a massage every afternoon.

But once I took myself outside the extravagant cocoon of the Hotel Metropole, the flurry and hubbub of Vietnam's capital totally won me over. An attractive blend of French colonial, Chinese, and Southeast Asian architecture. I loved the helter-skelter motor scooter traffic, the rickety-looking construction projects, the posters and banners in Vietnamese with its intriguing clusters of pronunciation and tone indications: squiggles, dots, circumflexes, question marks. I loved the cheek-by-jowl street vendors, everyone hustling to make money. Every day, I'd venture out to visit another requisite attraction: the Ho Chi Minh Mausoleum, the Imperial Citadel, the Confucian Temple of Literature, the Fine Arts Museum, the Military History Museum.

Of all the sites I saw, it was the Old Quarter that kept drawing me back. I'd wander along those ancient streets, each one named after a craft that had once been practiced there: Silver Street, Tin Street, Paper Street, Fish Sauce Street. I poked into art galleries, antiques markets, teahouses, shops that catered to stamp collectors. I strolled around Hoan Kiem Lake, occasionally stopping for an ice cream or a shoe shine. The lake's jade-green water and the leafy trees ringing the shore worked their peaceful magic on me. When I crossed the red wooden footbridge onto the island with its sweet little Temple of Jade Mountain, the chaotic bustle of the city completely faded away.

It was there that I met Trúc. He smiled at me; I smiled back. We introduced ourselves. His English was good. We made pleasant conversation for a while, and then I suggested we go for tea. He led me to a tea shop where, on squat stools, we sipped tea, ate *bánh rán*, and let our knees touch.

"How old are you, William?" he asked.

I considered lying, shaving off enough years to make the difference in our ages—I'd guessed him to be in his late twenties—less stark. But I told him the truth.

For the next week, we were inseparable. Trúc took time off from work and became my bedmate and my guide through the city and into the countryside. We traveled on his motor scooter, me in back, my arms wrapped around his impossibly thin waist. Our last night together, he stayed all night with me at the hotel, weeping in my arms.

We spent a year trying to get him a visa, but nothing worked. And then I stopped hearing from him. I suspect he must have eventually smiled at someone else on that magical island in the middle of Hoan

Kiem Lake, maybe a fellow Vietnamese, or maybe a foreigner whose country had easier entry rules. Trúc came so close to becoming Boyfriend Number Six, but we never managed to pull it off.

Two years later, I got out of the money management racket and started working for a sustainable energy organization. I couldn't bear the thought that all the carbon my country was pouring into the atmosphere was helping to fuel more powerful monsoons in Southeast Asia. While I wasn't making anywhere near what I used to make, I was happy to be giving my life to something that finally seemed important. Something that would, in a modest way, help to save the planet. To save humanity. I thought about those beautiful, green rice fields in Vietnam, and the small boys who, like little Buddhas, would ride on the backs of water buffalos, gently navigating the narrow paths between tracts of precious, fragile farmland.

❖ ❖ ❖

So here I am, sixty-five years old, but not ready to retire, neither from sustainable energy work nor from the search for Number Six. Would old Mr. Fallon, who, it now seems obvious to me, was gay, would he be proud of me for hoping that my Catherine Parr, if you will, might yet come along? Number Six, the one I do not want to relegate to the "Survived" pile; the one with whom I'd like to journey together through—how I hate to say it—*old age*. But what are the odds? It's been sixteen years since P.J., fifteen years since that trip to Vietnam. The prospects are not encouraging.

Still, whenever the opportunity comes along, I'm game to go on a date. Last week, I arranged to have coffee with a guy I'd met on one of the gay dating apps. We'd texted back and forth, traded a few photos (the kind that are "safe to be opened at work"), agreed it would be nice to have coffee and see "what happens." Bennett gave me his number and I called to arrange our rendezvous. His voice sounded raspy, but in a sexy kind of way. I told him I'd meet him at the northeast corner of Clarendon and Newbury. He started to laugh.

"You really were telling me the truth when you said you'd grown up in Minnesota."

"Of course. What do you mean?"

"No true Bostonian would use compass points to give directions! I mean, the North End is *east* of the West End; and north of the South End is East Boston!" He laughed again. "I've lived here all my life but haven't a clue which way northeast is. Okay, maybe the Back Bay, but nothing else here runs in neat, straight lines." He laughed again. "This is the least *straight* city in America."

This made no sense to me. A week after I moved here, I knew north from south. But I liked his joke about "least straight city in America."

"Well, I guess I can figure it out," Bennett said. "Northeast corner of Clarendon and Newbury. See you there." He laughed again.

Two days later, a mild day in late March, Bennett and I met. As we shook hands, I tried not to look like I was studying him. (I'm sure he was doing the same with me.) I had a vague idea of what he looked like from the photos he'd posted on the dating site, but the real test is always in the face-to-face meeting.

Bennett was an inch or two taller than I, a bit over six feet. He had a head of thick gray hair nicely barbered. His eyes were the color of the Boston sky that day, a kind of washed-out, late-winter gray. There were deep creases in his cheeks, which looked like he'd shaved just before our meeting. A hint of cologne—nothing overpowering, English leather, I think—lingered about his person. The sad, gray eyes and the creases made him look like he'd been through a lot. For a moment, I wondered if he was HIV positive, too. (In our initial phone conversation, I'd told him about my status, but all he'd said was a cautious and ambiguous "Okay.")

We set off for The Thinking Cup. It's a cozy café below ground level on Newbury Street, a place for a quiet tête-à-tête. Good coffee, great biscotti, old-fashioned café tables. Bennett, who was a few years older than me, told me it had been a café forever.

While he was putting in his order at the counter, I stole another look at him. Under an L.L. Bean windbreaker, he was wearing a black turtleneck and turmeric-colored, wide-wale corduroys. He'd driven in from one of the tony western suburbs. The look—it was tastefully expensive—made sense.

I've hardly ever seen the suburbs. Within a year of my move to Boston, I gave up my car. Unlike Minneapolis, unlike Vermont, here you can get around without one. And though the transportation system extends into the burbs, I don't see much reason to go there. When I fell in love with Boston, it was with the *city*—its density, its hodgepodge of neighborhoods, languages, races, rivalries, sports teams, social classes. I fell in love with the urban grit and glory of this City on a Hill. This livable alternative to New York, this bluest of blue metropolises—I've found a home here. What, I ask myself, can Wellesley or Wayland or Wakefield give me that Beantown doesn't?

As we settled down with our cappuccinos, Bennett opened up the conversation: "You know, back when I was in college, this place was called the Florian." He shook his head. "*That* was a great café. Now, I don't know—the ambiance just isn't what it used to be back then. So much has changed since the good old days. You know what I mean?"

"A lot has changed, hasn't it?" I hated falling into this too-easy, nostalgic look back at the past. I wanted to move forward ... into the Land of Number Six. Bennett's candidacy was already looking lackluster. My friend Arthur—he lives a few doors down from me—says I shouldn't try to force things. Okay, I thought, let's not foreclose on this one yet.

Bennett looked around and nodded toward the far wall. "There used to be a large map of Switzerland on the wall over there. Whoever or whatever Florian was, I think it had something to do with Switzerland. Never did find out."

"A fair number of people in Minnesota have Swiss heritage," I volunteered. "Not as many, of course, as have Scandinavian heritage."

As if I hadn't said a thing, Bennett twisted around. "The bathrooms used to be over there. I wonder where they are now. And the cashier." He turned back and nodded to the front of the café. "She used to be up on that raised area by the door. For all the times I came here during college, I don't think she ever smiled at me once."

"You have a great memory," I said.

My compliment washed right over him; he continued on his nostalgic roll. "The Florian used to be open until midnight. Ha! Just try to find a coffee shop open past eight nowadays."

"Well," I began, straining for something to say.

"Around ten o'clock, after studying, I'd ride my bike all the way down Commonwealth Avenue from Boston University. I'd stay until they closed, reading science fiction or my model railroading magazines. I had a steel-frame bike. Cost me seventy-five bucks new. Can you imagine buying a new bike today for seventy-five bucks? That bike lasted me all through college and graduate school."

It looked like we were headed for a long stroll down memory lane. It's only natural, I suppose, telling stories about the past, about how things used to be, about how much things used to cost. Over the last few years, I've heard more than my fair share of these stories. And I guess I've done my fair share of telling them, too. Bennett's reminiscences, they were just one more variation on a theme a lot of us old guys lapse into: the gay bars that are gone, the cruising areas that are gone, the gay bookstores and newspapers and theater companies that are gone. And, of course, the guys who are gone.

My neighbor Arthur says that we are the first generation of out older gay men. He thinks this is a wonderful state of affairs. "We are working out how to age as proud, Baby Boomer gay men," he declares. (Arthur rarely "says"; he prefers to declare. Even to his husband Andy.) I love being an out, proud, older gay man, but surely there's more to it than lamenting the passing of things we once loved.

"Do you still ride a bike?" I tried.

"Gosh, no," Bennett gasped. "Once Loring and I got together, that stopped. As a kid, he never learned how to ride and wasn't interested in learning."

"Who's Loring?"

"My husband ... well, partner. We never got married. He died five years ago."

"I'm sorry to hear that."

"He was a wonderful guy." Bennett momentarily turned his attention to his cappuccino, stirring it so that the spumy valentine the barista had left floating on the surface dissolved into a wispy cloud of milkiness.

"We were together thirty-five years" he said, continuing to stir.

"Wow, that's amazing. What was your secret?"

He looked up. "Secret?"

"To the longevity."

"Oh, you know, the usual factors. Loring and I had a lot of common interests—crossword puzzles, model railroading, collecting kachina dolls. We used to take a trip to the Southwest every few years in our camper. It was a towable. An Airstream. Now *that* was a great camper."

"You enjoyed traveling?"

He took a sip of his cappuccino.

"As long as we could do it by car or train. We were both terrified of flying"—he chuckled—"another thing we had in common, so we never went to Europe, or any place like that."

I considered offering an expression of condolence, but something held me back.

"We only traveled in the summer, because we both taught Sunday school at our church. Separate classes, of course. I suppose the minister knew we were a couple, but, well, we didn't flaunt it. After Loring had a stroke that left him partially paralyzed, we really got into jigsaw puzzles. That was something he could do with his one good arm."

For the next half hour or so, Bennett continued telling me about his and Loring's life together. I heard about the display cases they had built for the kachina doll collection, the once-a-year outing to Fenway Park (always a Red Sox-Yankees game), and their passion for model trains— "Lionel," Bennett emphasized, "not American Flyer"—and how their layout kept expanding until it took over the entire basement of the house in Westwood.

The stories spilled out in an *Oh, and then ... oh, and then* stream of recollections. Bennett seemed oblivious to the notion that maybe he should occasionally ask me something about myself. I was dying to look at my watch, but didn't have the heart to do so.

"It sounds like you two had a very full life," I offered.

"Yes. Plus, we were lucky," he said. "We met just as the AIDS thing was starting up. So that, you know, kind of protected us."

All through his monologue, I'd been trying to show Bennett I was interested, but at that moment, I let my face go neutral. It was the subtlest way I could think of to remind him that I'd earlier revealed I was positive. He didn't notice.

"You two never fooled around on the side?" I asked.

He gave me a look that was somewhere between surprise and affronted. "Of course not! Never."

I flashed back to my sexual history with "The Five." Toward the end, Wayne and I strayed—randy college kids that we were, eager to sample the field. Alan cheated on me. Chad and I tried a few threesomes. As for Frank, he was never into monogamy, and I went along because it seemed radical, a protest, as he liked to say, against "the hetero thing." And P. J.—well, most of our time together was that summer in Provincetown. I would come down on Friday night, eat dinner at his restaurant, then wait at home for him to wander in around one, two if he decided to hang with friends at Spiritus after his shift. I knew he was hooking up a lot, but he was good about not straying on weekends when I was there.

Something perverse in me wanted to challenge Bennett about his certainty that Loring had never strayed, a gentle, half-joking prodding: *Oh, come on, you think in thirty-five years, he never fooled around?* But then, without warning, Bennett finished his cappuccino and announced, "Well, I guess I should be going."

It was such an unexpected remark, totally out of the blue, the kind of thing a friend might say after a casual get-together, not something that someone you've agreed to meet "to see what happens" is supposed to say. For a split second, I was stunned, until I realized this was actually a kind way to signal that we were both off the hook. Apparently, I hadn't passed muster, even though I'd hardly been given a chance to properly "audition." My amazement dissolved into relief.

We shook hands, traded perfunctory observations about how it was nice to meet. Neither of us said anything about getting together again.

On the sidewalk, I tried for a lighthearted parting: "Now you're sure you know which way west is in order to get home?"

"Oh, all I have to do is get on the Pike," he said. "I was in the seventh grade when they extended it to Allston. I wrote a report about it. Mine got the award for the best report in my grade."

❖ ❖ ❖

I took the Orange Line home. It was late afternoon. When I got off at Stony Brook, the sky had gone from washed-out, late-winter gray to almost-dark. The temperature had dropped at least fifteen degrees since my afternoon with Bennett. In the chilly gloaming, I wasn't quite ready to go home to an empty house.

Arthur and Andy's house is just a few doors down from mine. I knew that Arthur would still be at work, but Andy, who's a tree surgeon, never works past three. He was probably already making supper. When he answered the door, the aroma of cooking (something with a lot of curry in it) wafted down from their apartment.

"So," Andy asked as we mounted the stairs to their condo, "how was the date?" There was a slight giggle in his voice. I love these guys dearly, but they've been together forever. My endless search for another mate strikes them as slightly amusing, as if I were pursuing a rigorous sport—football or wrestling—that someone my age should have dropped years ago.

"In a nutshell? A flop."

"Oh, dear."

We walked into the kitchen and I took a seat at their table while Andy resumed the magic he was performing at the stove.

"I don't know, maybe it's me, but all he did was talk about the past. We walk into the café, and immediately he launches into how it was so much better a place when he was in college. And from there, all downhill: the life he used to have with his husband, the trips they didn't take because they both were afraid of flying, the fucking report he wrote in the seventh grade that won a prize!"

"Sounds dreadful."

"I mean, he's a sweet-enough guy. I suppose he's still grieving the loss of his husband. But, Jesus, that was five years ago. Why the fuck did he agree to go on a date if all he wanted to do ..."

I checked myself. It was obvious: all Bennett wanted to do was talk. The poor guy had no intention of ever taking our "date" any farther, let alone replacing thirty-five-year-long Loring with anyone else.

"I guess Number One was enough for him," I said.

"Taste this." Andy held out a wooden spoon that he had dipped into the pot on the stove. Gingerly, I sipped the hot sauce.

"Delicious!"

"Thai green curry. We're eating vegetarian tonight."

I don't know why, but that simple sentence caught me off guard. I started tearing up.

"You okay?" Andy asked. He took back the spoon that I was holding out to him, as if even holding that utensil was more than I could handle right then. "William?"

"'We're eating vegetarian tonight.' Will I *ever* say something like that again? *We're* eating, *we're* going to Provincetown, *we're* buying a new rug, *we're* getting married."

Andy handed me a paper napkin and I blew my nose.

"I mean, it's been sixteen years. Is it too much to ask that ... Okay, so some guys *never* even have one boyfriend, and I've had five. Maybe I'm supposed to be content with that."

Andy handed me another napkin. Before he met Arthur, he studied Buddhism in Japan. His love of trees, his love of Asian cooking, his serenity in the midst of my fits and crying jags—this is Andy.

"I've fucked up five times, and I'd like a chance, just once, Andy, not to fuck up again."

"Ouch! Fuck up? That's awfully harsh, no?"

"It's just how I feel sometimes."

"You certainly didn't fuck up with Trúc."

"Trúc? What, for a *week*? And then that awful year of trying to get him here?"

Andy just looked at me, waiting for something.

"What?" I snapped.

"'And Eternity in an hour.'" He paused. I had no idea what he was talking about. "Your namesake," he explained. "William Blake." He turned back to the pot on the stove. "William, darling"—he was deliberately affecting an off-the-cuff manner, his eyes on the sauce— "from the way you've told it to us—a *dozen* times—that week with Trúc was one of the most transcendent moments in your life."

"Moments, Andy! *Moments*."

He looked up from the pot. "So, the Japanese have this concept. I've forgotten how you say it in Japanese, but it's the awareness that everything is ephemeral. That nothing lasts forever. They've actually developed a whole aesthetic around the deliberate cultivation of the sad passing nature of life."

"You want me to be sad? For the rest of my life?"

Andy put down the serving spoon and, with sassy theatricality, put his arms akimbo.

"Girl! I'm trying to show you that there's sad and then there's sad."

I furrowed my brow.

"There's wallowing in poor-me sad; and then there's the oh-wow-life-is-so-beautifully-fragile sad. Get it?"

I have never—and this is a point of pride with me—wallowed in self-pity. About anything. And certainly not about my HIV status. *Better, not bitter* is something I remind myself of every day.

"Am I wallowing?" I asked.

"Well, I'm not exactly hearing, 'Life is so beautifully fragile' from you."

"What you're hearing is, 'I'm halfway through my sixties and I'm wondering what the rest is going to be like.'"

Andy sat down at the table. "William, there's not a day that goes by that I'm not aware that this thing I have with Arthur, it's not forever."

"And that cheers you?"

"It makes me grateful."

"So, you want me to be grateful for the five boyfriends I've had and shut up?"

"Why don't we just concentrate on the 'be grateful' part?"

Two soggy napkins sat on the table between us. I stared at them, letting Andy's words play in my mind. Except for the light over the stove, the kitchen was in almost-darkness now. It was nice—the early evening duskiness, sitting across the table from my friend, the aromas of Thai green curry wafting around the kitchen.

"You want to stay for dinner?" Andy asked. "There's plenty. We've invited Fred from downstairs to join us."

"Sounds nice, but I've got something else going on this evening."

"What 'something else'?" I must have looked sheepish, because he pursued: "Are you going on *another* date tonight?"

"Sort of."

"You actually lined up another date on the heels of the one this afternoon! What if Bradley, or Bennett, or whatever his name was had worked out?"

I shrugged my shoulders. "I would have said, 'Let's get together soon,' and left it at that."

Andy's assumption that I had another date lined up delivered me out of what I knew would have been a far worse reprimand. The fact was I'd arranged to hook up with some guy I'd met on Grindr.

"So, you're playing the field?"

"Why is that an issue for you?" I challenged. And then, to ease up on the testiness, I added, somewhat coyly, "Just think of it as an efficient use of the precious little time I have left."

"Efficient." He giggled, then returned to whatever was happening in the pot on the stove.

❖ ❖ ❖

The guy who was supposed to drop over to my place— "Right after I get out of work at eight," he'd texted that morning—never showed up. It was such a common experience for me that I could not take it personally. *Whatever*, my younger colleagues at work say. Whatever, indeed.

But here it was, eight o'clock on a Friday night, and I had an entire evening free. For a brief moment, I considered hitting up Grindr again. But tonight, a hookup felt about as exciting as memorizing more names and dates for one of Mr. Fallon's history quizzes.

Survived, Survived, Survived, Survived, Survived.

Besides my five boyfriends, another thing that's survived is that photo album I began to keep when Wayne and I were together. With each subsequent boyfriend, I added a few more pages. The snapshots—in ever clearer, brighter, sharper resolution—tell the story of my life, or at least outline a certain aspect of my life, the high points of my romances and flirtations. Call me sentimental, but I have never been able to bring myself to chuck that album. Tonight, post-Bennett, post-Grindr no-show, I felt a need to spend some time with it again, something I hadn't done in quite a while.

I got into my pajamas, poured myself a light scotch, pulled the scrapbook out, curled up on the couch under a throw, and began paging through the album.

Graduation from St. Olaf's, 1979: there I am with Wayne, both of us in cap and gown, our arms around each other, buddy-buddy style, smiling at the photographer (who? my mother? our friend Sue?), each of us knowing it was over, not just our college years but our secret love affair.

Minneapolis, 1982: a dinner party that Alan and I gave. Around the table, three other guys, including Keith, the guy Alan was, still unbeknownst to me, having an affair with.

Minneapolis, 1987: Chad at my parent's farm, just before Mom and Dad, looking for all the world like Grant Wood's "American Gothic," figured out who exactly Chad was.

Vermont, 1989: Yes, even Ellen made it into the scrapbook. Here we were, posing on the outside of the llama corral, hay forks in hand, looking for all the world like a younger, hipper, happier version of "American Gothic." The shadow of the photographer—it must have been Thad—is falling between us. Thad-in-the-flesh made it into the scrapbook, too, though he had no idea how much I was pining away for him when I took that photo. Just one innocent shot: that final summer he worked for us. Dressed in jeans and a tee shirt, he is standing next to Mama Pacha, our favorite llama.

And before Frank, whom I met two years after I moved to Boston, there are several pages of guys I was ... well, what's the word we used back then? courting? dating? tricking with? I duly wrote their names in white ink on the black pages of that scrapbook. Hank, Richard, David, Najib, Kalin, Toby, Joe, Jemal, another Richard, Maxim. Goodness, I auditioned a lot of candidates for Number Four those first years in Boston. Why didn't any of them make the cut?

I turned another page: here were the Frank years. *Not tonight,* I thought: all those snapshots of us in tuxes, at events that increasingly bored me. I flipped through the many Frank pages, until, toward the end of the album, I arrived at the summer of P.J.—P.J. in his skimpy Speedo at Herring Cove Beach; P.J. belting out another show tune around the piano at the Crown and Anchor; P.J. as Marilyn Monroe riding a pink Cadillac in the Carnival Parade. Sun-spangled, sun-kissed, sun-and-peroxide-bleached P.J. What a difference from Frank, what a difference from any of the others.

The last page was devoted to Trúc, a page I could title "The One Who Should Have Been Number Six." I suppose Andy is right: as brief as my thing with Trúc was, he was, in a way, the most special. There were four photos on that page: Trúc on that red wooden footbridge, Trúc in front of the Temple of Jade Mountain, Trúc squatting on a little stool eating street food and smiling at me, and lastly, Trúc during our day-long excursion to Ha Long Bay. Sometimes I think I have unconsciously shied away from any other serious relationship because I am still holding a candle for him. Which makes no sense since we have completely lost touch with each other.

Not yet ready to go to bed, I flipped back the pages of the album. Here were the pre-Frank Boston boys again. I could still tell you stories about each one of them. The fun ones, the heartthrobs, the ones who just wanted to fuck, the one who wanted to move in after one date, the one who, after several dates, invited his friends over one night while I was there to check me out, as if I were a new suit he was considering purchasing.

What is it that determines why one guy becomes a boyfriend while another, just as appealing, never does? What weird chemistry bonded me to Frank or P.J., but not to Hank, Richard, David, Najib, Kalin, Toby, Joe, Jemal, the other Richard, or Maxim? Maxim, who worked in a used record shop and loved Russian classical music. David, the nurse at Massachusetts General Hospital, who, the day I went in for a gonorrhea test, whispered to me to meet him at Sporters that night. Jemal, the best kisser of any of them. Kalin, a great dancer; the first Richard, a cuddler; Hank, the best conversationalist. Why did I spend a year trying to get Trúc over here and not give more than two dates to Joe?

The shortcut answer is "chemistry." But there are days when I wonder if the chemistry could have gone another way if only some particular catalyst had been present or absent: the weather, the guy's choice of clothing, the way they fucked, the way they pronounced certain words, the stories they told about being afraid to travel in an airplane. How many Number Sixes have I failed to recognize because one little element was missing or, for that matter, was too irritatingly present?

Too many names and dates, I used to say of Mr. Fallon's class. There are days when my own history seems just as crowded with too many names and—*ha!*—too many dates.

I closed the album, tossed off the throw, got up, and switched off the lamp. Walking in the dark to my bedroom, knowing the way as surely as I know north from south in Boston, I had a weird, momentarily disorienting thought: hadn't some of these guys—well, maybe not Toby, who didn't like to kiss; or Najib, who kept pushing me to do threesomes with women—but hadn't the rest of them, in some way, been my lovers, too? What crazy calculus had led me to assign numbers only to the Fab Five? Hadn't every one of the others also been for me a person I'd cared for in some way, made plans with, shared my life with, however briefly, however fleetingly? No, I had not set up housekeeping with any of them, but was that going to be the litmus test by which I determined who had been ... what? a lover? a romance? a significant person? someone to whom I accorded the honor of being an Official Boyfriend?

Under the covers—it was a cold night, the kind when it would be nice to have someone to cuddle with—I began to whisper: *Survived, Survived, Survived ...*

But I cut myself off. There was another way to measure it, a truer way:

Loved.

Loved.

Loved.

I could picture Arthur shaking his head and saying, "*Loved*, William? Get real, girlfriend. They were tricks." And I would insist:

Loved.

Loved.

Loved.

Loved ...

Yes, even Toby, who didn't like to kiss; even, bless him, Najib.

The Walker

When Tavish's balance got a little too iffy—in the last couple of months, he'd fallen twice on his way to the bathroom—his doctor suggested a walker.

"Sure," Tavish said, feigning delight. "I'll take one who's twenty-five and built like a football player." He paused, giving Dr. Marshall a tongue-in-cheek grin. "Oh, you mean one of those metal contraptions!"

Dr. Marshall shook his head in tongue-in-cheek disbelief. He had been Tavish's primary care physician at the gay health clinic for fifteen years.

"Yes, Tavish, one of those metal contraptions. At least for the middle of the night when you get up to pee. The M.S. is progressing faster than I, or your neurologist, expected."

Dr. Marshall was in his mid-forties, and good-looking in the way that gay men in their forties who ate right, exercised regularly, and had inherited a lucky set of genes were good-looking. (Christ, Tavish thought, these days, *every* man in his forties, gay or straight, looks good to me.)

He tried to picture himself using a walker. He knew this had been coming. The cane, prescribed a year ago, had only been a stopgap.

"You know I can't stand that neurologist," he said.

Dr. Marshall gave Tavish no sign of empathy. "We can find you another neurologist, if you'd like."

"But that won't change the prognosis, will it?" Tavish asked, a bit too hostilely.

"No, it won't."

"Well then, how long before I'm in a wheelchair?" He studied Dr. Marshall's face again, hoping his physician would reassure him that a wheelchair was not yet in the offing. But Marshall gave him no sign of encouragement.

"To be honest, Tavish, I think you'd have more options in a wheelchair. The walker will help you around your apartment, get you to the bathroom, that sort of thing. But with a wheelchair—and the neurologist agrees—you'll have more mobility, especially outside. Look, if you'd be more comfortable getting another opinion ..."

Tavish managed a snicker. "I want another life, doc."

"At this point, it's still your call," Marshall said. "There's no immediate need for a wheelchair."

"But sooner rather than later, right?"

"Yes, I think so." Dr. Marshall paused before delivering what Tavish knew was supposed to be brighter news. "There are some terrific new models out there these days. Very comfortable, safe, equipped with all sorts of nifty features."

"Ha! Nifty features! Like a pocket for my condoms, lube, and Viagra?"

Dr. Marshall indulged him with a faint smile. "Tavish, this does not have to curtail your sex life, if that's what you're worried about." His reassurance sounded both professional and perfunctory.

"My sex life. Ah, yes, my fabulous sex life."

A year ago, he was still hooking up. A few regulars, nothing serious, but guys who loved older men and would text Tavish whenever they needed a daddy. But then he started using a cane, and pretty soon his libido had fizzled. Dr. Marshall had told him there was no correlation between the two events. Tavish wasn't convinced.

"So, what do you think?" he asked. "Is there a cohort of guys out there who get into sex with men in wheelchairs?"

"You aren't going to be in the wheelchair all the time." Dr. Marshall made direct eye contact with him. "We can get you some counseling, too. I mean, if you need to ..."

Tavish cut him short. "If I need to what?" The anger was back in his voice. "Vent my outrage?"

"Well, yes, but I'd like to think that counseling might help you find something more than outrage to express."

Tavish stared at Dr. Marshall, trying to decide what face to show his physician—scorn, indifference, pleading.

"I'll pass on the counseling, doc. Just the main course: one wheelchair."

Marshall nodded. "So we're doing this?" he asked.

"I love the way you say *we*," Tavish said, smirking at Dr. Marshall's baby blues. "Yes, *we* are doing this."

❖ ❖ ❖

Three weeks later, the wheelchair arrived, delivered by the medical equipment people to Tavish's tenth-floor condo downtown.

"Just in the nick of time," he quipped as the deliverymen began assembling it in his living room. "I'm supposed to go for a *walk* today." He looked out the windows, which faced the Boston Common. It was a bright March day, temperatures in the low fifties, the radio had said. He had not been out of his apartment since his last visit to the doctor.

The men explained how to use the wheelchair, its special features, its braking mechanism. Tavish listened without enthusiasm. He had no intention of "driving" the thing himself. An agency he'd contracted with was sending a companion who would take him on his outings.

When the men left, Tavish sat on the sofa, staring at the wheelchair. Amid the Hepplewhite furniture, the oriental carpets, the yew wood display cabinet with his collection of Chinese blue-and-white porcelain, the thing was an eyesore. He'd never been so grateful for the second, unused bedroom, his junk room. That's where he'd store it.

Two hours later, John, the concierge, rang to announce the arrival of "your assistant from the agency." There was a whisper of skepticism in John's voice.

"Send him up," Tavish instructed and hobbled over to the door with his cane. Or was it *her*, he wondered. In his world of diminishing expectations, he hoped that wishing for a male attendant was not too much to ask. He opened the door, which faced the elevator, and waited to see who would appear.

When the assistant got off the elevator, Tavish was taken aback. *He*— praise Jesus!—was practically a kid, somewhere in his early twenties. And heavenly. Olive skin, dark curly hair, luscious pouty lips. Tavish resisted beaming at the lad. Instead, he held out his hand in a gesture of formal courtesy.

"Hello, sir," the young man said, shaking hands. "I'm Danny Magliano. But you can call me Mags."

"Mags?" Tavish asked, studying the kid's black-olive eyes and five-o'clock shadow. He was wearing a trim Celtics jacket, which emphasized his magnificent torso. Still, as delectable as he was, the kid looked like the kind of straight townie who, almost forty years ago, had sent Tavish to the emergency room when he was attacked walking home from Buddies.

"Yes, sir. Mags. When my family moved to Charlestown—that's where I'm from—no one knew how to pronounce Magliano. They said MAG-liano. The Mag part stuck. Mag. Mags." He shrugged his glorious shoulders.

"Come in," Tavish invited. He was feeling wobbly on his feet and wanted to sit down. "Charlestown, huh? I grew up right next door, in Everett." He listened to how ingratiating he was trying to sound. "They sure would have known how to pronounce your name there. The place was full of Italians back then." He motioned to the sofa—"Please, have a seat"—before easing himself down into his wingback chair. The kid sat down. He seemed oblivious to Tavish's handsome décor.

"Man, when I was growing up, Charlestown kids and Everett kids did *not* get along," the boy reported.

"They didn't in my day either," Tavish said. Holding his cane in front of himself for extra support, he gave the lad a quick appreciative examination. "So, is that what I should call you? Mags? If you don't mind, I'd prefer calling you Danny."

"Okay, Danny's cool."

Nestling further into the sofa, Danny splayed out his legs. To Tavish's disappointment, the kid's jeans were loose, so whatever his goody basket contained remained a mystery. One of the guys in Tavish's bridge group had once called him a randy old queen.

Randy, yes, Tavish retorted. *Queen, on special occasions. But old? Never!* Everyone had laughed. They were all well past sixty.

"Well, there's the contraption," Tavish said, nodding over to the wheelchair. "Fresh off the assembly line. I'm christening her Nellybelle."

"Nellybelle?"

"Roy Rogers' jeep." Danny sat there, not reacting. "You do know who Roy Rogers was, no?"

"Um, that guy on TV with the kids' show? The one with the sweater and the puppets?"

"No. *Roy* Rogers was the Rogers *before* Mr. Rogers."

"Oh, okay," Danny said obligingly.

Tavish was annoyed by the boy's deference. He reminded himself not to check out the kid's crotch again.

"Well then, Mr. Danny Magliano, shall we be off?"

Danny gave him a thumbs up. "Perfect pronunciation."

"I've studied Italian," Tavish told him. "I once had a hopeless crush on an Italian."

"Can't beat the Italian ladies," Danny said.

"Yes, so I'm told."

Danny offered to help him get into the wheelchair, but Tavish shooed him away.

"I'm not *that* handicapped," he barked. With his cane, he pushed himself out of the wingback and shuffled over to Nellybelle. "Voilà. A new Olympic track record."

Danny laughed.

"So, let's give this a whirl." As he tried to sit down in the wheelchair, his legs began to wobble. Danny immediately came to his aid, supporting him under the arms as Tavish lowered himself in.

"First time," Tavish explained. "I'll get the hang of it." He let out a deep sigh. It was a relief to have made it into the chair, and an exasperation to have needed help for such a simple operation. A frustration, too, that the only touches he'd receive from this lovely young man would be the ones that came from professional assistance. "Mind getting my beret?" Tavish asked. "It's over there on the desk in the hall."

He watched as Danny went to fetch his cap, checking out the kid's tight ass, which was as mouth-watering as the rest of him. Danny returned and handed him the beret, a dark olive one that Tavish had picked up one summer in France.

"Were you a Green Beret, sir?"

Tavish let out a loud guffaw. "When you get to know me better, you'll understand just how absurd that question is."

"Okay," Danny said. It seemed to be his word of choice whenever he wanted to express compliance. There was another awkward moment of silence. "Would you like a blanket over your legs, sir? It's a little chilly out there."

The image of a blanket-swaddled invalid popped into Tavish's mind.

"Oh, I suppose. There's a lap rug on the sofa over there."

Danny went over to the sofa and picked up the soft woolen throw, another overseas purchase, this one bought in Scotland many years ago.

"I didn't know these were called lap rugs," he said.

"Stick with me, kid. I'll teach you plenty."

"Okay."

❖ ❖ ❖

They took the elevator down to the lobby. As Danny wheeled him out onto Tremont Street, Tavish looked across the street to the Common. When he moved here, ten years ago, he'd loved how close he was to this beautiful, historic park with its fountains and tree-shaded benches, the elegant Ionic-columned bandstand, the Soldiers and Sailors Monument, and the Frog Pond, which the city froze every winter for skating. Across the way, Bulfinch's State House, with its gold dome, rose on Beacon Hill.

Every weekday morning, he used to walk through the Common and over to Charles Street, where the real estate firm he worked for was located. Until he retired two years ago, he'd been with Kent and Company his entire working career. The firm, one of those cold-roast-beef Boston companies, handled tasteful, expensive properties in what Mr. Kent called "the better parts of town." It was the kind of company that had resisted the adoption of modern technology until they couldn't any longer. Tavish's desk, a mahogany monster with claw-and-ball feet, had been equipped with nothing but a phone, a blotter, and a Rolodex. His retirement had been prompted by three turns of events: his age, the onset of the M.S., and the fact that he couldn't get the hang of the new computer system that Mr. Kent's son, who took over the business, had installed.

Tavish had done well at Kent and Company. His years there had allowed him to go, as he liked to say, "from rags to riches." When he first started out, a year after college, all he could afford was a shabby rental apartment in the North End, a neighborhood he'd chosen because of all the hunky Italian guys who used to hang out in front of the cafés. But as he got the hang of the real estate business and his commissions rose, Tavish had been able to move to a nicer place, on one of Beacon Hill's leafy, Federalist-era streets. Six years later, he bought his unit from the owner, who was converting the building to condos. In the next few years, he managed to buy and sell more properties, turning each one over for several times what he'd paid. When he moved to his condo on the Common—a necessity because he needed an elevator—he was a comfortably wealthy man.

"Where do you want to go, sir?" Danny asked.

"To the gym," Tavish grunted. Behind him, he could sense Danny's puzzlement. "I'm kidding! Just turn left. Head for the Theatre District."

As they made their way down Tremont Street, he looked up at the new construction going on all around. This neighborhood, on the edge of the old Combat Zone, was being completely transformed. Glitzy high-rises everywhere. Back when he'd started out at Kent and Company, the Combat Zone had been nothing but seedy dives, porno stores, strip clubs, and a few hustler bars. There had also been a slightly more reputable gay club—was it called Feelings?—a dark, secretive kind of place where a slow-turning mirror ball cast desultory spangles of light onto the go-go boys who gyrated above the shadowy dance floor. Tuesday nights, after choir practice, a few of them would walk across the Common to Feelings—or was it Suspicion? or Heartache?—where he would order his usual, a rusty nail, and wish, wish, wish that the blond tenor named Compey would do more than friendly-dance with him.

Feelings, or whatever the place had been called, was gone. The porno stores and strip joints were gone. The entire Combat Zone had been erased from the map of downtown. Gone, too, the larger gay world that over the years Tavish had enjoyed—the nicer clubs and discos, the blocks that were good for cruising, the Beacon Hill brunches and weekends in

Ogunquit, the dreams of a lasting relationship. The years had marched on—astoundingly, forty-one with Kent and Company—and here he now was, loomed over by glass skyscrapers and towers. It was not the Boston that he had fallen in love with. *Towers!* Assholes like Trump put up towers, ugly monstrosities that shouted at you with boorish vulgarity.

As Danny pushed him down the sidewalk, Tavish studied the reaction of the pedestrians. Some averted their eyes, others seemed curious—a gentleman in a houndstooth jacket, silk ascot, flannel slacks and a beret being escorted by a magnificent, if somewhat gauchely dressed, young man.

They got to Boylston Street. "Cross over and head to Elliot Norton Park," he directed.

"Where's that?"

Tavish craned his head over his shoulder.

"You *are* from Boston, right?"

"Ah, this is kind of new territory for me, sir."

"Please stop calling me *sir*," Tavish snapped. He turned to face forward again. "Just keep going. You'll see it." Danny pushed on. "So, you grew up in Charlestown?" Tavish put more friendliness into the question.

"Actually, I'm originally from the North End."

"Ha! The first place I ever lived, right after college. Hanover Street. Believe it or not, the place I rented had a bathtub in the kitchen. You know what condos in the North End are going for now?"

"I do. My parents lost their apartment when the owner sold the building. They offered my dad first dibs, but no way *that* was going to happen."

"Sorry to hear that."

"It's okay," Danny said. "Dad kind of wanted out of the North End anyway. He said it wasn't like the old days anymore."

"Nothing is like the old days anymore," Tavish grumbled.

"We moved to Charlestown, into the projects, when I was ten."

"I assume you went to Charlestown High?" Tavish heard himself trying to put together the kid's story.

"Yup."

"And you've been with the Agency since you graduated?"

"I did a semester at Bunker Hill Community College."

"Just a semester? You didn't finish?"

"No."

"Why not?"

They had reached the park.

"This it?" Danny asked.

"Yes. Head for that bench over there. We'll sit for a minute." He laughed. "Well, *you'll* sit a minute. He chuckled. "I'll be Jimmy Stewart in *Rear Window*."

"Who?"

"Never mind, just wheel me over there." Danny parked the wheelchair by a bench, locked the wheels, and sat down. "Do you know who Elliot Norton was?" He did not wait for an answer. "An important theater critic. Elliot Norton reviewed *plays*. Hell, he helped shape those plays."

"I've never been to a play."

"No, neither had I when I was your age." He was trying, he knew, to convey a sense of their common background. Tavish envisioned the two of them going to see a show together one day. What would Danny like— a musical? a comedy? Shakespeare?

The boy pulled a pack of cigarettes out of his jacket pocket. "Mind if I smoke?"

"Those things'll kill you. But be my guest. It's your life."

Danny shook out a cigarette from his pack, pulled a Bic from his pocket, and tried to light up. The late March breeze was brisk and he couldn't manage it.

"Here," Tavish said, cupping his hands around the lighter. "Try now." When one of his fingers touched Danny's hand, he let it stay there until the cigarette caught.

"Thanks." Danny took in a deep drag, held it, turned his head away from Tavish and exhaled. "I'm gonna quit."

"That's what they all say." Tavish looked into Danny's eyes, pretending this bit of intimacy was merely to impress a point on him. "When I was your age, I smoked, too. Back then, everyone smoked. Couldn't not smoke. Hell, every time you walked into a bar, you were inhaling cigarette smoke, whether you were smoking or not. I quit when I was thirty." He paused. "How old are you anyway?"

"Twenty-three."

Tavish tried to think of some witty remark, something clever about being so young, but nothing came to him. He'd once been good at that sort of thing, the clever quip, the amusing witticism. It was a knack that hadn't been natural with him, but that over the years he had developed. All gay men of his generation—at least the kind of gay man he had aspired to be—had honed this kind of verbal dexterity. It was a signal that you were quick on the uptake, someone who could hold your own in whatever situation came your way, a cocktail party, a fancy dinner, intermission at the opera. But nowadays, he just couldn't come up with snappy retorts. *Twenty-three.* What could you possibly say to that?

Grand. That's what his dad would have said. It was the all-purpose expression of approval Tavish's father had used his whole life. *Grand.* One of those expressions from the old country that Da had never abandoned, even though he'd come over when he was only eight. There were days when, despite his father's drinking problem, Tavish missed the bastard.

"You're sixty-eight, right?" Danny asked.

"How did you know that?"

"The Agency. They gave me a brief description."

"Description?" Tavish chuckled. "What else did they tell you about me?"

"Not much. Just about the wheelchair and stuff."

"Ah, yes, *stuff.*"

Danny tossed his cigarette away.

"Do you want to keep going?" he asked.

"Sure. Just stick to the speed limit, kid. And mind, there are no ashtrays in this Mercedes."

Danny laughed. *Well then,* Tavish thought. *Maybe I do still have the knack.*

They crossed the park and headed for Bay Village. There was a rainbow flag displayed in one of the windows of Jacques, the drag bar.

Tavish wondered if Danny knew what a rainbow flag meant. Halfway down Piedmont Street, he nodded over to the left.

"There used to be a popular club here." No response from Danny, who just kept pushing the wheelchair. And just as well, Tavish thought. Too many more details and he'd have been venturing into risky conversational territory. "It was called the Napoleon."

"Okay," Danny said.

They moved on, down Arlington Street and into the South End. There were even more ghosts here than in Bay Village. On this block, Tavish's first boyfriend had lived, a guy his age who had also aspired to the soigné life. And on Shawmut Avenue—in those days, as dangerous as the Combat Zone—that's where he'd cheated on that first boyfriend. And on Dwight Street, where Compey, the blond tenor, used to live. The last he'd heard of Compey, he was living in Ohio, doing what, Tavish had no idea.

"So what happened that you didn't finish at Bunker Hill?" he asked. They'd gotten as far as Peters Park. A man was practicing his backhand returns against the handball wall.

"I had a kid," Danny said. "I had to drop out to take care of the baby."

"You were not married, I take it?"

"No. The mom was my girlfriend. Well, sort of my girlfriend. That didn't work out either."

"So I've heard," Tavish said. When Danny didn't respond, he craned his neck around. "Things not working out. It's a song I know well."

Danny wheeled him over to a bench and sat down.

"And the child?" Tavish asked.

"She's two-and-a-half now. I have her weekends."

"And you can support her on this job?"

"No way! No, man, I have three jobs. This, plus I help out at my dad's shop. He's a glass cutter. And weekday nights, I wait tables. An Italian place back in the North End."

"Good food?"

"It's pretty good."

"I'll come sometime. They're wheelchair accessible?"

"I think so."

"I've never said that before. 'Wheelchair accessible.' It doesn't exactly trip off the tongue, does it?"

❖ ❖ ❖

At each outing, they took the same route, through Elliott Norton Park, down Piedmont Street, and into the South End. At first, Tavish did most of the talking. He told stories about growing up a working-class Irish kid in Everett, his scholarship to Holy Cross, his ascent in the real estate world. He talked about his bridge group.

"It used to be a larger club, twelve of us, but now we're just four old duffers."

"Duffers?" Danny asked. It sounded as if he was testing out the word.

"Old guys," Travis explained.

"Okay."

By their third or fourth outing, Danny began to open up. And started to ask questions, too.

"Do your children ever wheel you around?"

"What children?" Tavish said curtly. "I never had kids."

"What about your bridge guys?"

"What about them?"

"Do they take you for walks?"

"Christ no! First of all, some of them are older than I. And second, they're too hoity-toity to push a wheelchair." When Danny didn't say anything, Tavish apologized. "I hope that didn't come across the wrong way."

"No, it's okay."

Tavish looked at him. "Seems like everything's 'okay' with you."

"I dunno," Danny said. "Maybe."

They were on Piedmont Street again.

"That former club I told you about? The Napoleon Club?" Tavish twisted around. "Very swanky. At least, we thought so. Piano bar, coat-and-tie, that sort of thing. In the old days, they didn't even serve beer.

Just cocktails. Very piss-elegant." He craned his neck so as to make eye contact with Danny. "Posh, classy," he explained.

Danny nodded, but said nothing.

When they got to Frieda Garcia Park, Danny wheeled him over to a bench, locked the wheels, and sat down. The day was warm enough that people were eating their lunch outdoors, some on benches in the park and some across Stanhope Street at Flour Bakery. Tavish noticed a quartet of gay men horsing around on the park's climbing structure. He resisted checking to see if Danny was watching them, too.

"So, am I the only person who takes you on walks?" Danny asked.

"I'm afraid so." Tavish looked over at him and grinned. "Guess you're stuck with me, huh?"

Danny let out a short, nervous laugh. Tavish saw that one of the gay men was looking at them, and then leaned over to his buddy and whispered something. The buddy looked over at them, too.

On their way back to the condo, Danny brought up the club.

"So, did you pick up women there?"

"Danny, it was a *gay* club!" Danny didn't react. "You cool with that?"

"Sure."

"You ever been to a gay bar?"

"Of course not! I'm straight."

Tavish laughed. "That's what they all say!" He turned around. "That was a joke, Danny."

"I know."

❖ ❖ ❖

On the next outing, as they were sitting in Elliott Norton Park, Tavish opened up about his former hook-ups.

"We called it 'tricking.' One night, I tricked with a Black kid—this is when I was still living in the North End—brought him back to the apartment."

"He rob you?" Danny asked.

"Christ, no!" Tavish glared at him. "It might surprise you to learn that most Black people—like most *Italian* people—are not criminals." He let out a sigh. "Just listen and stop making assumptions. So, the next day, my landlord—she was a nosy old bitch—she made it very clear that I couldn't have any Black friends visiting me. I got the hell out of that apartment and out of the North End as soon as I could."

There was more to the story about why he'd moved away from the North End, but he decided not to bring it up. The fact was, he had wanted a better address. "Better address," at least at Kent and Company, always meant those neighborhoods described in their property listings with words like "charming," "quiet," "historic," and "gracious." What he'd wanted, in fact, was to become like old Mr. Kent—with his beautiful suits and ties from Brooks Brothers, his Friday afternoon subscription to the Symphony, his membership at the Union Club on Park Street. What he'd wanted was to become a discreet, gay version of old Mr. Kent. And in fact, it had pretty much worked out that way. Tavish had become the kind of Bostonian whose name appears on the patrons list of a few select philanthropies, including his gay health clinic, the opera, and the Boys and Girls Club. In the last several years, the names of pairs of men— husband and husband—would show up on these lists, but Tavish's name was always alone.

It could have been otherwise, another story he did not tell Danny. When he was in his early thirties—after he'd given up pining after Compey—he'd had another boyfriend, Matthew, who was the antithesis of all his other friends. "Mr. Not-Mister-Kent," Tavish affectionately called Matthew. Matthew was, as the saying went back then, a hot ticket. In his late teenage years and into his early twenties, he'd been a drag queen performer at a club in Chicago. He moved to Boston to be with a boyfriend who hadn't worked out. But the runaway freight train that was Matthew didn't let that setback stop him. By day, he cleaned houses; at night, he waited tables. Somehow, he also found time to do some occasional drag work. When he and Tavish met—Tavish's friends had hired him to entertain at Tavish's fortieth birthday party—Matthew was twenty-seven.

Their affair lasted three years, during which time Matthew moved in with Tavish and enrolled at Mass College of Art, which Tavish paid for.

He had hoped that Matthew would settle down, become an artist or an art teacher. When they broke up—Matthew moving to Miami to be with another older man—Tavish vowed *never again*.

Danny's stories were about other kinds of disappointments: too short to make the basketball team in high school, too many brothers to have his own bedroom, too poor to go to cooking school, which was what he really wanted to do.

"You'd like to be a chef?" Tavish asked. During this particular conversation, they were in the Public Garden, sitting by the pond. Danny had never seen the Swan Boats.

"I like to cook."

"Whom do you cook for?"

"I used to love to cook for my mom and dad. Mom's dead now—she died a couple of years ago, right after the baby was born—and Dad kinda became uninterested in things."

"He's depressed?"

"I guess. I don't know. We don't talk much. With his hours and my hours, we hardly even see each other. Sundays. Sundays we see each other. He's home, and I have the baby. Well, she's not a baby anymore."

"What's her name?"

"Stella."

"Stella," Tavish repeated. "That's a pretty name."

"We named her after Stella Bennett."

Tavish shook his head.

"She's a singer," Danny explained.

Tavish laughed. "Unless this Stella Bennett sings Cole Porter or opera, I'm afraid I wouldn't have heard of her."

"Yeah, she doesn't sing that kind of stuff."

"And your Stella? Does she sing, too?"

"Well, she's learning 'Twinkle, twinkle.'"

"I'd like to meet her someday."

Danny looked startled. "I don't think the Agency allows that."

"And who's going to tell the Agency?" Tavish asked.

❖ ❖ ❖

The next time Danny came, he brought a casserole.

"Stuffed manicotti," he said. "I made them myself. They're already cooked; you just have to heat them up."

Tavish was speechless. As pleasant as their wheelchair outings had been, he had not thought they'd gotten chummy enough for Danny to bring him a gift. He hoped the plate of food was not charity, like some sort of Meals on Wheels delivery.

"But what do I owe you for this?" was all he could say.

Danny made a face. "Just enjoy them," he said. "There's enough for two. Maybe you can invite one of your bridge buddies over."

"This is very sweet of you, Danny." As soon as it was out of his mouth, Tavish regretted using the word "sweet."

"I didn't know how spicy you liked your tomato sauce, so I made it kinda mild. Not too much salt either."

Tavish laughed. "I have M.S., not high blood pressure."

"I'll put them in the refrigerator," Danny said. "You can give me the dish the next time I come." He went to the kitchen.

"Wow, your fridge is pretty empty," Danny said when he opened the refrigerator door.

Tavish wheeled himself over. "I don't seem to have much appetite these days. I have yogurt and cereal for breakfast, maybe some crackers and cheese for lunch. A piece of fruit." He stopped there. He didn't want to reveal that dinner was almost always out of a can—lentil soup, chicken soup, clam chowder. "Sometimes I order takeout for dinner."

"There's something funky growing in this." Danny held out a plastic container.

"That's hummus. Throw it out." He watched Danny looking for the expiration date. "Forget it! Just throw it out," he ordered.

"Three hundred degrees for about twenty minutes," Danny told him, tossing the container of hummus into the kitchen trash can. "If you microwave it, take off the aluminum foil."

"I know, I know! Jesus, you sound like my wife."

"You had a wife?" Danny asked, his brow furrowed in confusion.

"Of course not!" Tavish snapped. "It's a goddam expression."

❖ ❖ ❖

On his next visit, Danny brought a quart of bolognese sauce and directions on how to serve it over pasta. Next it was a lasagna, then a plate of meatballs and gravy, an eggplant parmesan.

"You shouldn't do this!" Tavish kept protesting, though secretly he was tickled. The food was always excellent. *Why are you doing this?* he wanted to ask, though he didn't. He was afraid Danny would say, *Because you're an old man in a wheelchair.*

After each of their walks, Tavish would ask Danny to join him for supper, but the boy always declined. He had other things to do, he said: another client to wheel, a delivery for his father, or a turn taking care of his daughter when the ex-girlfriend had something to do in the evening.

"You bring me so much food. It lasts for days," Tavish told him one afternoon. It was the middle of June now. They were taking their walks late in the afternoon to avoid the heat of the day. But Tavish had also finagled it so that he would be Danny's last client of the day. He kept hoping Danny would stay for dinner.

"Why don't you share it with your buddies?" Danny asked. "I made enough for all of you this time."

"They're not that kind of buddies."

But Danny wanted to know more: how long had they known each other, how had they all met, and did they ever do stuff together besides play bridge?

"I mean ..." He seemed flustered. "Don't you guys ever, like, hang out together, go out to eat? Stuff like that."

"Rarely. To tell you the truth, one of the guys, Neal ... I'm actually not very fond of him. And the other two, well, they're married. One of them is quite old. Getting out for an evening of bridge is his big activity each week."

"Wow, married."

"You have heard, I hope, that we have same-sex marriage now in this country?"

"Yes, Tavish." Danny took off his Red Sox cap and lightly bopped him on the head with it. "I've heard of same-sex marriage." It was the first time he had ever addressed Tavish by name.

❖ ❖ ❖

Three days later—it was a Saturday night—the bridge gang came over. In the past, they would take turns hosting: one month at Tavish's, the next at Neal's place on Commonwealth Avenue, and then the next month at Monroe and Richard's on Worcester Square in the South End. But now, with Tavish having a hard time getting around, especially at night, they'd agreed to meet every month at his condo.

In the past, they would play several rubbers, but these days, the bridge evenings had become more of an excuse to drink some good scotch, catch up, and finish the evening with dessert.

As the evening was winding down, Tavish told them about Danny's gifts of food.

"He likes to *cook*?" Neal asked. "Exactly how straight is this escort of yours?" He took a healthy sip of his scotch. "One club."

"Two diamonds," Richard countered.

"He's my walker, not my escort," Tavish said. "And you're barking up the wrong tree." He pretended to study his hand but was silently fuming at the way Neal could never let a straight man just be a straight man. "Danny has—or *had*—a girlfriend. Three clubs. And they have a baby."

"Ah!" Neal snorted. "Like that proves anything."

Everyone looked at Monroe, waiting for him to bid.

"Your turn, Monroe," Tavish prompted. There had been some discussion between Tavish and Monroe's husband Richard about whether Monroe could still keep up with the game. In his day, he had been the best player among them, but his concentration was failing. Monroe was the oldest of their quartet, eighty this year.

"What's the bidding so far?" Monroe asked.

"Tavish bid three clubs," Richard told his husband.

"I mean, really, Tavish," Neal said. "These young 'bi-curious' types, or whatever they call themselves these days. Jesus, they'll fuck anything. Or let anyone fuck them."

"Don't be crude," Tavish scolded.

Neal, who had one of those WASPy last names that let you know he came from old money, was by far the wealthiest among them. He sat on the board of several cultural institutions in the city; belonged to three gentlemen's clubs, which he'd unsuccessfully fought to keep all-male; and flew to Thailand every winter, where he had a house and a houseboy. He and Tavish had become friends decades ago when Tavish thought it was important to hobnob with people like Neal in order to establish himself among Boston's upper crust. But, over the years, the charm had worn off. Tavish was relieved that their acquaintanceship now only extended to these bridge nights.

"Monroe, darling, your bid," Tavish prompted again.

Monroe looked up. "Richard, help me out." He passed his cards over to his husband.

"Bid three diamonds," Richard whispered, handing the cards back to Monroe.

When the bidding finished and play commenced, Tavish resumed the story.

"Danny's quite talented in the kitchen. The other day, he brought me a plate of gnocchi. They were superb. He told me that he'd wanted to go to cooking school but couldn't afford it."

"My God, you aren't thinking of paying his tuition, are you?" Neal asked. He got up, went to the liquor caddy, poured himself more scotch, and pirouetted to face Tavish again. "Because that would be very foolish." As he sashayed back to the card table, out came his reasons: Tavish had tried that once before, with Matthew, the would-be artist, and look where that had got him? And he hardly knew Danny. How did he know whether the kid could even make it through cooking school? And pretty soon, just wait and see, he'd be asking for child support money, too.

"And would you like to advise me, Neal, on whom exactly I should give my money to?"

"Relax, Tavish, relax," Richard broke in. "Neal's just suggesting that maybe you should take a little more time to think this through."

"Think *what* through? There's nothing to think through. All I said was the kid had once hoped to go to cooking school."

He was baffled, and miffed. He had absolutely no intention of giving Danny money. Did these guys think he was that much of a fool? He slapped a card on the table. "Play!"

The game resumed. He and Neal won another trick.

Monroe suddenly piped up: "But what would be your motives?" Tavish realized that Monroe was several seconds behind the rest of them in following the path of the conversation.

"I have no motives because I have no *designs* on him!" Tavish snapped. He hated raising his voice at poor, foggy Monroe, but he wanted the whole direction of the conversation to stop.

"Well, that's a surprise," Neal said. "Because every other word out of your mouth this evening has been Danny, Danny, Danny."

"Look, Neal, I am as attracted to handsome young men as you are, but I don't go flying off to Thailand to pay them to sleep with me." There, he'd said it. It was a sentence he'd been wanting to deliver for a long time.

"The only thing I pay Anuman for is to look after my house, I'll thank you to know."

"Ah, look after your house? Is that what we're calling it these days?"

"Guys, guys," Richard interrupted, "I think this conversation has gone far enough."

"Well, then, maybe it's time for dessert," Tavish said, happy to have an excuse to wheel himself away from the table. "Cannolis tonight."

"Did your lovely Danny make them, too?" Neal asked.

"No!" Tavish lied.

❖ ❖ ❖

The following Monday, Danny showed up with Stella. "Her mom's up in New Hampshire today," he explained, holding the child in his arms. Her face was turned into Danny's shoulder. "She had to see a lawyer. Some business about the ex-husband."

"Ex-husband!"

"Yeah."

"Before you, or after you?"

"After." Danny seemed embarrassed to venture the next detail. "They only lasted six months."

"She sounds like bad news."

"I'm not sure I was such great shakes either, Tavish."

"Danny, quit it!" Tavish looked him directly in the eyes. "Will you stop selling yourself short? I mean, you have to start believing in yourself."

The look that came onto Danny's face—was it contrition, anger, pain?—Tavish didn't care. He pressed on.

"You have to start believing that you're capable of achieving something."

Stella began to squirm. Danny set her down on the floor, and she ran to the liquor caddy.

"Juice!" she called out.

"That's not juice, Stella," Danny said, running over and pulling her back.

"Juice!" she demanded.

"There's some cranberry juice in the refrigerator," Tavish told him. He turned to the girl. "Cranberry juice?" He had not spoken to a child in decades.

Danny picked her up. "Do you mind holding her while I get it?"

"If you think this wheelchair can bear the extra weight." It felt good to return to a bit of lightheartedness, even though there were things lingering between them that needed to be addressed.

Danny lifted Stella onto Tavish's lap. Remarkably, the little girl did not make a fuss.

"Well, hello," Tavish said, touching the tip of her nose. "What's your name." Stella lowered her eyes. "Is your name Mary?"

She looked up and giggled. "No."

"Is it Susan?"

More giggles. "No."

"I know! It's Henrietta!"

The girl squealed. "No!"

Danny came back from the kitchen with a small glass of cranberry juice. "Tell Tavish your name."

"My name is Stella."

"Stella! What a pretty name! And what a pretty girl!"

Stella giggled again, as if the idea that she might be pretty was silly. She wriggled out of his lap and walked over to Danny, holding out her hands for the glass of juice.

Danny looked over at Tavish. "Can she sit on the sofa while she drinks?"

"Of course."

"I'm just afraid she might ..."

"Danny, if she spills, she spills. Things can be cleaned. Or thrown away. Lord knows this place could use a good cleaning out. Too much stuff I don't care a wit about anymore."

Danny guided Stella over to the sofa, got her seated, and handed her the glass. "Take it with both hands now," he told her. "That's it. Be careful."

Tavish watched as Danny did his fatherly duties. The boy seemed so capable. Why couldn't he see that in himself? Stella carefully took a sip.

"Like father, like daughter," he said. Danny gave him a quizzical look. "She's like you, Danny. Very careful, very dutiful."

"Tell that to my dad," he said. "The other day, I broke a really expensive pane of glass at the shop."

"That's because you don't give a"—he glanced at Stella—"you don't give one *gosh darn* about the glass business, Danny. You're an artist. An artist with food. That's where your creativity lies, not in putting up old window frames."

Danny sat down next to Stella. "Remember when I told you I used to go to Bunker Hill, and you asked me why I didn't finish?"

"Because you had Stella."

"That's not the full story."

Out it came: he'd gone to class one evening drunk, started mouthing off to the professor, and when the professor suggested that Danny not come to class inebriated, Danny had gotten out of his seat, sworn at him, thrown a punch that fortunately missed, and stormed out of the classroom. He shrugged his shoulders. "End of college."

Tavish listened. And thought about his own father, dead at fifty-two.

"Do you think you have a drinking problem?"

"I went to A.A. for a while. But I don't know. Those touchy-feely groups aren't for me."

"Those touchy-feely groups save lives, Danny."

"You think I'm an alcoholic?"

"I have no idea. But going to class drunk is, you have to admit, not normal behavior."

Danny looked down at Stella.

"Tell me," Tavish continued, "have you ever come here when you'd been drinking?"

Danny's head shot up. "Hell no!"

"Thank you." Tavish let a few seconds go by before he spoke again: "My father drank. Heavily. In and out of detox. He died when I was twenty-seven."

"I'm sorry."

"It's one reason behind"—he looked around the apartment—"behind *this*. The life I made for myself. I hated that my father never got out of Everett, hated that he'd never made anything of himself."

He looked at the two of them—father and daughter—sitting demurely on his sofa. His dad had been timid, too. Not an ounce of ambition in him. Just penitence and guilt after each bout of drinking. He studied Danny's face, hoping he would not see penitence and guilt there, too.

"Tavish, you're staring at me," Danny said.

"Sorry."

"What are you thinking?"

Tavish closed his eyes and pictured his second bedroom, empty except for a pile of stuff he'd never use anymore: his expensive luggage, the shelves stacked with dozens of travel guides, a treadmill he hadn't been on in years, and boxes of stuff whose contents he had no idea about.

Things can be thrown away, he'd told Danny. What a hypocrite he was, holding onto so much crap himself. And not only all that junk, but so many memories, too—the happy ones and the ones that now made him cringe. So many notions about who he was, what he had achieved, about who he was supposed to be, and about what he couldn't, *shouldn't*, do anymore.

He opened his eyes.

"So, I'm thinking," he began, ignoring the voices in his head—old Mr. Kent telling him to invest conservatively; John, the concierge, dubiously announcing that his "assistant" had arrived; Dr. Marshall and his wheelchair advice—all those voices of caution, caution, caution. "I'm thinking that you should bring Stella here more often."

Danny winced. "I don't know, Tavish. Like I told you, it's against Agency policy."

The still louder voice in Tavish's head was Neal's, telling him what a fool he had been to take in Matthew, pay for his tuition at Mass College of Art, try to set him on a better path. *Never again*, Tavish had vowed.

"So I'm guessing that the Agency wouldn't take too kindly to my inviting you and Stella to share this apartment with me. Move in."

Danny's eyes widened. "Okay," he said, drawing out the word as if to draw more words out of Tavish.

"And I'm thinking about what the guys in my bridge group would say if I did that."

"Okay."

Tavish laughed. "And I'm thinking that the way you keep saying 'okay' just might mean that you don't think I'm totally crazy."

"Daddy, more juice?" Stella asked, holding up her glass.

Danny bent down, moving his head attentively toward his daughter's. "You have to ask Tavish, Stella."

She sent an inquisitive gaze toward him. Tavish smiled and asked her if she wanted more juice.

"Use your words, Stella," Danny prompted.

"Yes."

"What else, Stella?"

"Please," she said.

Tavish looked up at Danny. "*Please?*" he inquired, impressed by Stella's good manners. "I'd say you're raising her quite well."

"Thank you."

"I mean it," he said.

"Her mom doesn't ..."

"I think you've told me enough about her mom," Tavish said. He was eager to get back to the proposal he had broached. "So, if you were to decide to move in, we would continue with the good manners, but"—he looked up and shot Danny a stern scowl—"I will absolutely put my foot down on her asking me for permission to drink juice." A look of alarm covered Danny's face.

"No," Tavish reassured him. "You see, it will have to be *your* refrigerator as much as mine. We're not going to set up a boarding house here."

Danny smiled. "Okay," he said.

"Okay," Tavish echoed. "So, now, what are *you* thinking?"

Danny burst out laughing. "I'm thinking you're going to get pretty tired of my cooking."

"Try me," Tavish challenged.

"So you're serious?" Danny asked.

"More serious than I've been about anything in a long time," Tavish told him.

At that moment, all he could think of was how pleasant it would be when the three of them—he and Danny and Stella—could go to the theater together.

Zigzag

Because of the pandemic, my friend Raúl's art opening was postponed. And then the Dorchester gallery where his show was to take place almost folded. For a while, it looked as if Raúl's big moment would never happen. But finally, two years after he'd been invited to mount a solo exhibition, he had his debut. Raúl had just turned fifty-five. "Much too old for a painter's first major show," he said, though I knew he was thrilled all the same.

Raúl and I became best friends in high school, which means he's been my best friend for close to forty years. When the gallery finally gave him the go-ahead, there was no question that I would pitch in to do whatever he needed to make his show a success. For starters, I volunteered to handle the publicity. There's hardly a gay paper in Boston anymore, but I got him a pre-exhibition profile in a local gay glossy, another in the *Globe*, and a big piece in the *Journal* in Providence, where Raúl had gone to art school. There were even a couple of interviews on the radio. *My Gay Life / Mi Vida Gay*, he called the show. "A gay Mexican American Chagall," the pre-show profile in the *Globe* called him. We couldn't have paid for what that kind of a plug is worth.

But as the event date drew closer, Raúl was convinced that, despite all the great publicity, no one would come. "Well, you can at least count on a crowd of two," I teased. "Tripp and I will be there."

"*Please,*" he begged, totally unresponsive to my attempt at humor. "Just come early. I'm already having nightmares about standing there, all alone, waiting for someone to show up."

He was so jittery that I was persuaded to take over choreographing the whole affair, not just seeing to the publicity but arranging the food and serving as the greeter at the door.

"Make sure there's a guestbook," Raúl said. "And I'd also like everyone to wear a name tag. I'm going to be so nervous—I know I won't be able to put names and faces together."

"Name tags it is," I assured him, even though I had never heard of such a thing at an art opening.

"And the food! *Real* food, Eddie, not popcorn and a glass of cheap wine."

We settled on hiring a pair of caterers who were known for their Mexican fare. I'd never heard of them, but Raúl swore their food was excellent.

"Their empanadas are the best. And wait till you try their margaritas," he said. "Oh, and I told them to make sure to have seltzer for the non-drinkers," he added.

It was such a thoughtful gesture, Raúl's acknowledgment of Tripp's sobriety. Over twenty years now.

❖ ❖ ❖

The opening was to run from four to seven on the first Saturday in April. True to April in Boston, when the day came, it was one of those classic awful days in our city's "cruelest" month. A heavy rain began just after noon and showed no signs of letting up. Except for the slightly milder temperature, it might as well have been February.

Raúl called me at one o'clock. "¡*Chingado clima*!" he wailed.

"What are you talking about? This is just the kind of weather that encourages people to get out and do something." I did not believe my own words but hoped he would.

Raúl, Tripp, and I got to the gallery at three o'clock. It was located on Dorchester Avenue, in an innocuous block of storefronts and light industries. Somehow, the gallery owner had thought he could make a go of it there. And somehow, he'd kept it from going belly up during the pandemic.

In the days leading up to the opening, Raúl had hung the show with the gallery owner, whose name was Jayden, but he'd kept me away. I'd only seen a few of his paintings while he was working on them, nothing more. So when I walked in and saw the entire show beautifully hung on the gallery's tasteful white walls, I was bowled over.

The comparison with Chagall was fair enough, though for me Fellini immediately came to mind. Each of Raúl's paintings—there were over two dozen—was crammed with Mexicans of all stripes jostling each other in a joyous, orgiastic dance of life. Here were campesinos, artisans, and mariachi musicians, bullfighters, drunkards, and coffee pickers, soccer players and peasants on their burros. Aztec and Mayan gods, a skeleton wearing a sombrero, a Virgin of Guadalupe. There were gangsters, tortilla makers, teenagers in American sports gear, young lovers, and *charros* on their horses. There were political demonstrators and policemen beating them back; blowhard politicians and old *abuelitas* wrapped in colorful rebozos.

On closer examination, there was also, somewhere in each canvas, at least one gay reference: a male couple dancing, a drag queen, a street-corner hustler. And somewhere, amid this riot of bodies, Raúl always inserted himself. You could tell it was Raúl by the palette and brushes the figure was holding and by the piled-up shock of thick black hair. At fifty, Raúl has yet to sprout any gray hair. His sensational good looks have always been one of the reasons why I love him so much.

While Raúl went over to confab with Jayden, Tripp and I stood there, taking it all in. I was dazzled. And delighted. How much he deserved this success—my high school pal who'd been through a lot in the last few years, not only the agonizing postponement of his show but, before that, the death of his husband, Alan. Taking in all the paintings, I saw—and *felt*—just how much Raúl loved his native country. Just how much he loved life, how much he loved *his* life, in all its crazy, diverse, soulful, queer Mexican American jumble.

Soon, the caterers arrived, dripping water all over the gallery's polyurethaned plank floor. I went into manager mode, showing them where to set up the chafing dishes and the bar. The aroma of empanadas began to fill the air. The bustle of the caterers and the savory smells gave me hope that the dreary day would yet be saved. Tripp helped me set up the greeter's table. Next to the guestbook, we arranged a pile of name tags and marker pens. Jayden came over and set down a large vase of white canna lilies. When he'd gone, Raúl came over.

"Oh, God," he whispered to me. "Those flowers are going to remind the reviewers—if any even bother to come—of Diego Rivera! I'm fucked."

"Relax," I told him. "Go eat an empanada."

But as the minutes ticked by, I started to fret, too. Every few minutes, I checked my watch: three-twenty-seven, three-thirty-six, ten to four. Would anyone come? At four o'clock, it was still only the six of us: Tripp and I, Raúl, Jayden, and the two caterers. I was beginning to think Raúl was right: no one was going to show up. A few minutes after four, our first visitor arrived.

"Sterling!" Raúl called out from across the room.

So much for his not remembering anyone's name. Feeling slightly foolish, I handed the guy a name tag and a marker. "Raúl would like everyone to wear one," I explained.

I watched him print his name: *Sterling Bouchard*. I'd heard Raúl talk about Sterling, how he'd met him in the hospital: Sterling accompanying his wife and Raúl his husband Alan, both of whom were there for their weekly chemo sessions. When Alan died, Sterling went to the funeral. Later, after Sterling's wife died, he came out as a gay man. Raúl had been there to show Sterling the ropes.

Raúl bounded over, put his arm around Sterling's shoulder, and gave him a kiss on the cheek.

"Thank you for coming!" he said.

"Of course!" Sterling said. "I wouldn't have missed this for anything." He surveyed the room. "Amazing, Raúl."

Raúl looked around as well. "I honestly never thought it was going to happen, Sterling." The two fell into each other's arms and held their embrace for a long moment.

And so the party began. The jitters of the last few hours were gone. I leaned into Tripp, my head on his shoulder. Tears began to fill my eyes.

❖ ❖ ❖

Raúl was the one Mexican kid in our New Jersey town. The day we met, in the first chemistry class of the year, he told me, in near-perfect English, that his family had moved from Mexico that summer so that his father could begin a post-doc program at Rutgers.

"Your dad doesn't want to be a doctor anymore?" I asked.

"*Hombre,* do you really not know what a post-doc is?" He looked at me like I should turn in my American citizenship card.

I was a smart kid, but neither of my parents had gone to college. "Post-doc" was not a term I'd ever heard before. I went into defensive mode: "Excuse me, *hombre,* but I know what 'post' means, and I know what a doctor is."

"*Doctorate*, dude, post-*doctorate.*" I remember how Raúl began to study my face. "Look," he said, "we're supposed to pick lab partners today. You want to be mine?"

"Sure," I said. "Why not?"

He smiled, the first smile he'd given me.

"Yeah, why not?" he echoed, the smile turning into something that looked like mockery.

A month later—a month during which we became not only lab partners but tennis buddies and art club co-presidents—Raúl came clean about that first day: he told me he had been searching my face for evidence of something more than bluffing. What he was really looking for, he said, was evidence that I was gay. He and his family had been in New Jersey since July, and he'd yet to meet another gay boy.

We were both sixteen that autumn, but Raúl, who'd gone to a fancy private school in Mexico City, was already well-versed in the art of gay love. So well-versed that, apparently, he'd only needed one look at me— the kid who had just begun to identify what he was feeling for other boys—and knew he'd found a *compañero.*

"You really could tell?" I asked him. It was a Friday afternoon. We were seated opposite each other in a booth at the local soda shop, having our by-then customary end-of-the-week sundae. My heart was racing. I'd kept this part of myself hidden from everyone, but Raúl had seen through my mask. And now he was telling me that not only was it okay that I was queer but that he had similar feelings.

"Could I *tell?*" He laughed. "Eddie, what couldn't I tell?" He leaned his body over the table and lowered his voice. "I could tell that"—he held up one finger—"you hadn't a fucking clue what a post-doctorate was"—another finger—"that you were a pretty cool dude anyway, and"—a third finger—"that, yes, you were a *maricón.*"

Maricón, I thought. I'd heard other words for that life I still wasn't sure about—some neutral, some playful, some ugly. Here was another one, one Raúl seemed to wear with pride.

"That was some pretty fast detective work," I teased.

He grinned. "Maybe that's why I got a ninety-seven on last week's chem quiz, and you only got a ninety-one?"

Later that afternoon, Raúl introduced me to sex, a blow job and some kissing up in his bedroom. That was as far as it went. A one-time thing. We never became boyfriends. I would have liked—liked *a lot*—for him to become my boyfriend, but he was already too advanced along the path of gay love to find me, a rookie, of much appeal. Besides, he went for older guys, he told me. "And I don't mean the seniors at this lame high school," he added. He must have seen, once again, the incomprehension on my face, because he sighed and launched into an explanation.

On Saturday mornings, he would take the train into Manhattan for advanced art classes, after which he would cruise one or another of the city's art galleries or museums until he was picked up—"by an older gentleman," he always emphasized—and taken to bed somewhere in Manhattan. "Upper West Side apartments are so *chingón,*" he told me.

His stories titillated me, alarmed me (AIDS seemed to be the only topic in our sex ed class that year), and made me deliriously envious. I'd watch him flirt with the girls during the passing periods between classes He was an authentic Mexican Don Juan. With his swarthy good looks, black olive eyes, and piles of pomaded hair the color of a raven's wing, Raúl was a stunner. Two or three of our female classmates were in love with him. And while he never let these flirtations advance to the dating stage, still he managed to avoid suspicion because the girls (as well as the guys) at our school figured he was merely showing the kind of restraint a Latino foreigner was expected to show these flowers of American maidenhood.

Meanwhile, now that my own maidenhood, so to speak, had been given up to Raúl, I found myself paying closer attention to the boys I was attracted to. There was one in particular, Whit Shevlin, I was totally moony over.

"Don't waste your time," Raúl told me when I confessed my captivation. "He's so straight you could use him as a meter stick."

"Yardstick," I teased.

Raúl shook his head in disgust. *"¡Gringos!"*

❖ ❖ ❖

"Hi, I'm Joseph," our next visitor said, holding out his hand. "This is my husband Donald. Are you Raúl?"

I said no, explained that I was Eddie, Raúl's friend, and nodded over to where Raúl, Sterling and Tripp were standing in front of one of his canvasses.

"We live practically down the street," Joseph said, "but we've never been to this gallery before. Actually, it was kind of hard to find."

"Worth the search, I hope."

"We were going to work in our garden today, but"—Joseph spread out his arms like a wet cormorant ruffling his wings—"well, no gardening today."

The husband laughed. "Every year I remind Joseph that the beginning of April is a little too early for gardening.'"

"And every year"—it was Joseph's turn to laugh—"I ignore him."

They seemed like a sweet couple, typical Dorchester homesteaders. I welcomed them, asked them to sign the guestbook, and gave them name tags to fill out. "Please help yourselves to some food and enjoy the show."

I watched them head off. When I turned back, a trio of guys was waiting to sign in. They introduced themselves: Richard, Daryl, and Sam.

"We read the article in the *Globe* last week and it sounded interesting," the one called Daryl said. He handed the marker over to another one. I watched him print his name, *Sam*. The third one, Richard, had already wandered off, to look at the art.

"Where are you guys from?" I asked, looking from Sam to Daryl.

"South End," Sam said. "Worcester Square."

"That's a beautiful street."

"So we're discovering," Daryl said. "We only just moved there." He looked around, found the third one, who was already talking to Raúl, and nodded over to him. "It's actually Richard's townhouse. His partner, Monroe, died in December. COVID. Next thing we know, he invited us to move in with him."

"It's a *wild* story," Sam added.

"Not now, Sam," Daryl admonished. He looked at me. "But, yeah, it is. Totally wild." And then back at Sam, chuckling: "Even wilder than mixing William Morris and Moroccan, right Sam?"

Our making chitchat was holding up the next guys who were waiting to sign in.

"Well, thank you for braving the weather and coming. Please ..." I gestured toward the buffet. "The empanadas are really good."

"Empanadas, art, and ... Oo! Are those margaritas I see?" Daryl took affectionate hold of Sam's arm and pulled him toward the refreshment table.

A bunch of Raúl's friends followed, five guys whom I'd met on a few occasions. One—his name was Rick—was wearing an absurdly large Mexican sombrero. But his complexion and features were about as Mexican as St. Patrick's. Raúl often referred to these guys as the "gay caballeros." They were all somewhere in their fifties and sixties, and despite the fact that they were dripping wet, they looked like they were ready for a good time. Maybe too good a time. I could tell they'd already been drinking.

As much as Fellini had made it into the paintings, it seemed as if he'd had a hand in the guest list, too.

❖ ❖ ❖

A week after we finished our junior year in high school, Raúl took me to my first-ever Gay Pride parade. It was in Manhattan, a place he was, by then, quite familiar with. He led me to the Village, so packed with people that I could hardly move. I couldn't believe what I was seeing—floats with half-naked men dancing to the music of Cyndi Lauper, Prince, and Madonna; bare-breasted lesbians on motorcycles, drag queens. I couldn't believe what I was doing—shouting, chanting, dancing in the streets, kissing strangers. Couldn't believe what I was feeling, which was so big, so euphoric, so liberated that I wanted to tell my parents as soon as I got home that I was a proud gay boy.

As it turned out, I didn't come out to them, not then and not during my senior year, during which I kept hoping that Raúl would become my boyfriend. The following September, Raúl went off to the Rhode Island School of Design, and I to Connecticut College, where, after a semester, I changed majors from art history to English, went to my first-ever gay dance, got (and gave) more than a blow job, found a boyfriend, and, in June, finally told my parents I was gay.

That first boyfriend, Colin, was a couple years older than I. In retrospect, I think I was subliminally trying to walk in Raúl's shoes. I loved how worldly Colin was. He knew about things I didn't know. He introduced me to theater and fine dining. He introduced me to fucking.

Despite the switch to English, art remained my first love. All through college, I kept going to museums and galleries. I'd take the train to New York and, of course, to Providence, where I'd meet Raúl for an afternoon at the RISD Museum or a trip together up to Boston.

The weekend after Colin and I broke up—it was the spring of my sophomore year—I fled to Providence, where I poured out my grief to Raúl. (I'm sure I thought my heartbreak would finally win him over, would make him see how much more desirable I was than any of his older gentlemen.) He said all the right things, none of which made any difference. I could not imagine how I was supposed to go on ... without Colin, without Raúl. Of course, I did go on, passing all my courses, continuing to look at art, and, to my surprise, finding another boyfriend. Junior year, I started writing art reviews for the college paper. That got me a summer internship in Provincetown—"not to be confused with Providence," Raúl always joked—where I wrote about the local art scene and put out press releases for an important gallery. Midway through that summer, the new boyfriend broke up with me. This time, I did not seek out Raúl's solace. Instead, I went dancing at the A-House.

After we graduated, Raúl and I backpacked through Europe together, five glorious weeks of living on bread, cheese and wine, and hitting as many museums as we could. Five weeks, during which I had to keep reminding myself not to fall in love with him. It was in the Uffizi that he met Alan, a thirty-five-year-old art historian. For the next twenty-four hours, I did not see Raúl. When he finally resurfaced, he was madly in love. I assumed it would be nothing more than a summer fling, but when we all got back to the States, he and Alan moved in together.

That's how Raúl came to settle in Boston. Meanwhile, I'd already landed a job writing for the Hartford *Courant*. For the next two years, he and I saw each other only a few times, two years during which Raúl did a master's degree at the Museum School and he and Alan bought a condo in Charlestown. At the beginning of the millennium, when the *Courant* let me go, I moved to Boston. A week later, I got a job teaching English at a community college, began writing art reviews for a couple of alternative papers, and found another boyfriend, Tripp. *The* boyfriend. The guy who finally took Raúl's place in my heart.

❖ ❖ ❖

By five o'clock, the gallery was humming. The food was a big hit, but an even bigger hit was Raúl's paintings, which our visitors raved about, lingered over, and contemplated buying. I watched the Dorchester couple—Joseph and Donald—consulting each other. It looked like they were deliberating between two of Raúl's canvasses. I sent Tripp over to tell Raúl to chat them up.

People kept coming in. One was an old guy named Harry, who told me he'd given Raúl some painting lessons back about twenty years ago.

"I lost track of him, but I always knew he had talent." Harry looked around. "Damn, this is really good work. I guess he needed to get away from me to really develop." He let out a chortle and turned to the man he'd come in with. "A lot of people would say that about me, right, Vardan?"

Vardan tittered. He was considerably younger than Harry. I couldn't tell whether they were lovers or only friends. Today, none of that seemed to matter. The opening was as promiscuously festive as Raúl's paintings.

Harry introduced me to Vardan. As we started to shake hands, a loud and brazen laugh cut through the amiable buzz in the room. We all looked in the direction from which it came.

"Oh, Jesus!" Harry said. "*He's* here."

"Who?" Vardan asked.

"His name's Rick. Rick Something. Look at him in that ridiculous sombrero! Figures. He's such an asshole. A year ago, he commissioned me to do his portrait. At every sitting, he kept telling me I'd gotten it wrong: 'too saggy in the cheeks,' 'too puffy under the eyes.' A pain in the ass, is what he was. Come on, Vardan, I need a drink."

When they moved off, assiduously avoiding Rick, I turned my attention back to my duties as greeter. Until now, all our visitors had been men of a certain age, no one much under fifty. This did not surprise me. No matter what cultural events I happen to find myself at these days—the symphony, the theater, a book reading—the gay men who show up tend to fall into that demographic. That's not been my experience elsewhere: in Chicago a few years ago, I was surprised to see a lot of younger gay men at the opera. Same in New York and San Francisco. But here in Boston, the so-called "Athens of America," all the gay Athenians seem to be the age of Socrates. Why that is, I don't know. Maybe the younger ones are too busy making money, or establishing their pedigrees, or revising their Grindr profiles. These kids don't even *know* that Boston was once the Athens of America.

So it was a surprise to see two young men waiting to sign in. One of them looked like he was still in college. I guessed them to be a couple.

"Hi!" the younger one said, a beaming, confident smile on his face. "I'm Duncan. Are you Raúl?"

"Just his humble servant. Raúl's over there."

I asked them to sign the guestbook and fill out their name tags.

Duncan took charge, handing one of the markers to his friend and repeating what I'd just said as if the friend were hard of hearing. It was a cute, if awkward, moment. I guessed they were a very new couple.

As they printed out their names, I studied the friend's face. He seemed familiar. Where did I know him from? When they stuck their name tags onto their jackets—Duncan and Philip—I suddenly recognized him. Philip was the goofy Sunday bartender at Cru/Cuts, a South End restaurant Tripp and I sometimes go to. The kind of kid who, when he shakes a cocktail, simultaneously shakes his ass. Almost at the same moment, Philip recognized me.

"Hey! You're ..."

"Eddie."

"Wow, small world."

"You know Raúl?" I asked.

The boyfriend took over: "Neither of us do, but the show sounded interesting."

"It's a great show. I hope you enjoy it," I told them.

"So look," Philip chimed in, "next time you come to the bar, I'll treat you to a drink."

"'I'll admit,'" I said, putting on my best Bette Davis imitation, "'I may have seen better days, but I'm still not to be had for the price of a cocktail.'"

"'Like a salted peanut!'" Duncan finished the punchline. We both laughed.

A puzzled look came over Philip's face.

"Margo Channing?" Duncan prompted. "*All About Eve?*" Philip shook his head, still clueless.

I decided to move on to less intellectually taxing fare: "So, how'd you guys hear about Raúl's show?"

Duncan took the lead again. "There was a piece about it in the *Crimson*," he said. "The Harvard student newspaper."

"I did the publicity for this show, but I never thought about contacting any student newspapers. How do you suppose they heard about it?"

"The *Crimson* has its ways," Duncan said, a mixture of pride and amusement in his voice.

"You're at Harvard?" I asked.

"I'm a junior there. Double majoring in French and art."

"Smart boy." I avoided making eye contact with Philip.

Duncan blushed. Under the gallery's track lighting, his hair, which was curly and golden, and very wet from the downpour outside, shone as brightly as his self-assurance.

"I'm probably going to do my honors thesis on colonialist influences in the art of francophone cultures, mainly Haiti and French Guiana. So naturally, Señor Martínez's show interests me: I mean, Mexican art is also about the intersection of colonial and Indigenous cultures. So I thought I'd check it out, see if there are any points of similarity with the art I'm including in my thesis.

His use of "Señor Martínez"—respectful, academic, a bit pretentious—was charming.

"Are you looking specifically at *gay* art?" I asked.

"Well, not exclusively," Duncan said. "But"—he tossed an affectionate smile at Philip— "how could I *not* look at gay art!"

"Then I think you'll find a lot in Raúl's show that'll interest you." When I smiled at him, I realized I was flirting. Except for the time when Tripp was drinking heavily, those last six months before he got sober and I was easing my pain by hooking up with other guys, I have never been unfaithful to him. Of course, I'll flirt, but that's as far as I'll take it. But Duncan ... *whew!* Cute and smart and self-confident. I figured he was one twink who would know that Boston was once the Athens of America.

"So what did the *Crimson* say about Raúl?" I asked.

I knew I was shutting Philip out of the conversation. Ever since I'd been going to Cru/Cuts, I'd seen him as a bit of an airhead.

"They said that anyone interested in modern queer Mexican art should get on the Red Line and check out his show."

"Harvard Square to Fields Corner. A convenient direct line." It was a stupid observation. The kind you make when you're flirting. *Easy, Eddie,* I told myself. "Well, have a look around," I invited, still ignoring the BF, "and help yourself to some food. The empanadas are terrific."

As Duncan and Philip moved into the gallery, the eyes of many of the other guests fell on him. It was as if Alcibiades had just walked into Socrates' dinner party. Duncan made a beeline for Raúl and began chatting him up. Philip went for the food and the margaritas.

I sat back at the greeting table and made a count of the number of guests we had: over twenty-five. For a rainy day in April, this was doing well. For a gallery opening, this was doing quite well. Raúl, surrounded by well-wishers, was beaming. Jayden came up to me.

"First sale!" he whispered. "The couple from Dorchester. They got a good one, too."

I made a clinched-it gesture with my hand.

In front of Raúl's largest canvas, Duncan was drawing his share of admirers, bees hovering around a delectable blossom. Philip, who was standing in front of the bar area, had attracted his bevy of fans as well. Some of them, it was clear, knew him from the bar.

As I started recapping the markers and gathering up the peeled-off paper backings to the name tags, two more guests arrived. The afternoon's litany was repeated once more: Was I Raúl? No. How did they hear about the show? The *Globe.*

"I used to paint," the one whose name tag said Christopher told me. "I'm in awe of talented people, and, well, the piece in the *Globe*—'a Mexican American Chagall'—he sounds awesome."

"He is," I said, turning to include Christopher's partner, whose name tag told me he was Mitch.

"Christopher will tell you that I don't know much about art, but"— Mitch gave the room a quick survey—"even I know this is amazing."

"Take a closer look," I invited. "And remember, they're all for sale." Off they went.

I'd yet to have any food, so I headed over to the buffet table and made a small plate for myself. Philip turned to me.

"The food is amazing." He took a sip of his margarita. "And the drinks. Sriracha-mango margaritas!" He looked at the other guys he'd been talking to. "I've gotta introduce this flavor at the bar." They nodded their approval, then wandered off, leaving the two of us to ourselves.

"You're the guy whose husband always orders a club soda and lime, right?" he asked.

"Great memory."

"That's what a good bartender has to have."

There was a pause. Even at Cru/Cuts, he and I had never had much conversation.

"So, how did you and Duncan meet?" I asked.

Before Philip had a chance to answer, we were distracted by an angry outburst coming from the other end of the room. I turned in the direction of the row. Apparently, Raúl's friend Rick, the one with the sombrero, had said something that Duncan had found insulting.

"Exactly how many times have you even set foot on the Harvard campus?" Duncan was grilling him in a voice that brought a hush to the room. "You know I am so fucking sick of people assuming they know all about *Harvard men*." He twisted the phrase sarcastically in a way that told me he was quoting something Rick had said. "You do *not* know Harvard men, dude, and you do not know me, so please keep your assumptions to yourself."

Raúl rushed over to try to ease the tension. I decided I should go to Raúl's side and see if there was anything I could do. Philip wandered over, too.

Raúl began to apologize to Duncan on behalf of his friend, who was standing there, a boozy, stony-faced glare on his face.

"I was trying to explain to this ... this *gentleman*," Duncan said, "that I came here because I'm interested in how Indigenous and European art traditions intersect." He glared back at Rick. "I'm sorry if you think that's 'the kind of thing only a Harvard man would say.' There are at least thirty colleges and universities all over this city and I dare say there's at least one student at each of them who's probably interested in the same thing."

"*I dare say*," Rick muttered under his breath. He'd arrived two sheets to the wind, and it was apparent that since then he'd had a few too many of the caterer's margaritas.

"Do you have a problem with my boyfriend's language?" Philip asked.

"Okay, okay," Raúl intervened. "Let's all calm down." He turned to Rick. "I'm honored, Rick, that this young man"—he turned directly now to Duncan—"that *you* have taken such an intelligent interest in my work."

"I love your work, sir."

"And so do I!" The speaker was the old guy, Harry, the one who'd once given Raúl some lessons. He was probably the oldest guy in the gallery, maybe eighty, but the intensity in his voice was robust. The crowd parted to let him approach. He looked at Duncan. "And your thesis, young man, it sounds fascinating. Art is always fed by many influences, isn't it?" Now he shot a scornful look at Rick. "All in the service of truth. Even if the truth is not *pretty*. Right, *Ricky*?"

The silence in the room was chilling. Just when I wondered how this would end, another guy spoke up.

"And I'd like to be the first to buy one of these terrific canvasses." It was Richard, the one who'd come in with Sam and Daryl.

"*Second*!" one of the two guys from Dorchester corrected. "Sorry, but we've already bought the first one."

Everyone laughed and cheered. This good-feeling exchange immediately defused the tension in the air. Rick held out his hand to Duncan.

"I apologize," he said. "My dad was a janitor at Harvard, so ... well, he didn't exactly have a lot of happy stories about his interactions with Harvard students."

Duncan nodded his head. "Yeah, unfortunately, some of those students are still there. But I'm not one of them."

They shook. Everyone applauded, then went back to the conversations they'd been engaged in.

I patted Philip on the shoulder. "That was good of you to speak up."

"Hey, I have to listen to my fair share of assholes at the bar," he said. "Usually, I hold my tongue. But not today, not when it's my boyfriend who's being attacked."

"So, how *did* you two meet?"

Philip laughed. "At the bar. Duncan and his Harvard friends came in on his twenty-first birthday. We got chatting and ... well, I generally don't go for twinks, but Duncan doesn't act like a twink."

"So I've observed," I told him.

"I have no idea where it's going, but for now"—Philip shrugged his shoulders—"hey, we're both really enjoying each other. I mean, I *never* would have come to this show if it weren't for him." He laughed. "And Duncan would never have taken his spring vacation in Fort Lauderdale this year if it weren't for me."

I was so wrong to have written Philip off. No, none of us has any idea where any of this is going. Twenty-three years ago, would I ever have predicted that Tripp and I would still be together?

"I wish you two all the best," I said.

"I appreciate that," Philip replied.

"And next time Tripp and I come into Cru/Cuts, I'll be looking for that sriracha-mango margarita."

"And a club soda and lime for your husband."

I gave him the thumbs up.

"So," I said, "I've never asked you before, but what do you do when you're not bartending?"

Philip looked directly into my eyes, a look that said—or was I imagining this?—that he wanted me to take him very seriously. "I work for an environmental sustainability company."

"Wow. That's awesome."

"It *is* awesome." He shot me a teasing smile. "More awesome than— what did Duncan say?—*All About Eve*?"

As if on cue, Duncan walked over and put his arm around Philip.

"And we're gonna download it tonight."

"You'll love it," I told Philip.

"Hey, I've loved everything this guy has shown me so far."

The two of them exchanged a glance that was pregnant with suggestion.

"You ready to go?" Duncan asked.

"Up to you, babe."

"Yeah, let's go. I'm coming back on Tuesday to tape an interview with Raúl." He'd dropped the "Señor Martínez" line. He shook my hand. "We didn't get much of a chance to talk, but Raúl tells me he could never have pulled this off if it weren't for you."

"That's nice of him to say, but he's the one who painted these awesome paintings."

"And you're the one," Philip interrupted, "who was a good enough friend to manage the thing." He peeled off his name tag, stuck it on my chest, and gave me a quick kiss. So did Duncan.

❖ ❖ ❖

The great Catalan artist Joan Miró was once asked what accounted for the changes in his style over the decades, for the apparent sudden rejection of one style for another.

"Not a rejection," Miró insisted. "It's a continuation, but it happens in another way." His artistic path, he explained, had always been a straight line, but one nourished by all the things that came before. And then he clarified: "What *looks* like a zigzag is really a straight line."

I've never forgotten those words. When I think about it, all the zigzags of my own life—my closeted high school years, the late coming out, the drama with various boyfriends, the falling in and out of love with Raúl, dropping my art major, the twists and turns of my professional career, the years when Tripp was drinking excessively—somehow, all those zigzags have turned out to be the straight line of my life, a life I am very grateful for.

And not just my life. Raúl, what a circuitous path he's walked all these years: the move from Mexico to the U.S., those many afternoons in high school when he was in and out of men's apartments in Manhattan, trying to make a go of it as a serious artist, his husband Alan's death, the postponement of his show. In fact, when I think about it, every guy who came here today must have traveled, must *be* traveling, a road that looks anything but straight (and, oh, I joyfully embrace the pun). Raúl's friend Sterling, who came out in his seventies; the trio from Worcester Square with the wild story they'd yet to tell me; Sombrero Rick and his gaggle of gringo friends; young Duncan, so confident, so sure he already has it all figured out; and the new boyfriend, the bartender, whom I was so sure I had all figured out. Every last one of us—we're all traveling paths that look like a zigzag and that I can only hope will make coherent sense in the long run.

I looked around the gallery. The party was winding down. The caterers were consolidating the few remaining empanadas into one chafing dish. Margarita glasses—Raúl had insisted on real glass, not plastic—were strewn on every available tabletop. I caught Jayden's eye. He gave me a thumbs up and nodded over to Sterling Bouchard. *Another sale,* he whispered.

Tripp wandered over.

"Eddie, you totally pulled this off," he said.

"*Raúl* totally pulled this off."

"But you got the word out. I met someone who drove up all the way from Providence to see the show. And there's a reviewer here from *El Planeta*."

Raúl came over, placed himself between us, and put his arms around both of us.

"Thank you, guys."

He looked exhausted, and elated.

I patted him on the back. Was this the big break that Raúl had been waiting for? Where would all this hoopla lead? Wherever things went—for him, for me and Tripp, for any of the guys here—one thing I knew for sure: those zigzaggy journeys would somehow get each of us to the place we were supposed to be.

Just then, the trio from Worcester Square joined us.

"I hope you'll enjoy the painting you bought." I made sure to look at all three of them. My first thruple? Who knew?

"We love it," said the one with the name tag that said Sam.

"So, someday," I prompted, "you're going to have to tell me that 'wild' story about how all three of you ended up living together on Worcester Square. I lived there briefly when I first moved to Boston."

"We'll have you over for a drink," the one named Daryl said. He turned to Sam. "That's how it all started with us and Richard and Monroe, isn't it?" He chuckled, then turned back to me. "Yes, a very wild story. Be careful: when you get invited for a drink with Sam and me, anything could happen!"

"I'm ready," I said and put my arm around Tripp's waist. Tripp, so aptly named. The man I've journeyed with these past two-plus decades. The man who has sometimes stumbled, the man I've sometimes stumbled with. I squeezed him tight. In my head, all I could think was, *zigzag, zigzag, zigzag.*

Acknowledgments

I am very grateful for the criticism and feedback I have received from friends who also happen to be excellent readers and writers: Jim Farley, Gil Noam, Larry Weinstein, Rosemary Davis, Leslie Acoca, Janet Rodgers, Reed Woodhouse, Susan McCully, David Eberly, and Steven Ralston.

I also want to thank three friends, Karen Ward, Joe Caruso and the late Dermot Meagher, for giving me accurate and helpful information about technical details in some of these stories. To David Bjork I owe copious thanks for stories and details about the Radical Faeries.

Thanks to Greg Kruszewski for help with the Polish in one story; and Kevin Chao for help with the Arabic in another.

I also wish to thank the editors of the literary magazines who previously published some of these stories: *Night Picnic* ("The Hazardous Life"); *Saints + Sinners Anthology* ("Big Boy"); and *Prairie Schooner* ("Sol y Sombra").

To my editor at Rattling Good Yarns Press, Ian Henzel, I owe, once again, many thanks for his faith in my work, his close and insightful reading, and his utmost professionalism throughout the process of bringing out this book.

Finally, deep and heartfelt thanks go to two dear writer friends, without whose help this book would never have been finished: Penny Noyce, who hosted me on numerous occasions at her home in Bremen, Maine, and whose astute reading of some of these stories improved them greatly. And Dale Mitchell, who read most of these stories and sent me copious and detailed notes on how to make them better and, even more important, doled out generous praise and encouragement when I needed it most.

About the Author

Philip Gambone is a writer of fiction and nonfiction. His first collection of short stories, *The Language We Use Up Here,* and his novel, *Beijing,* each garnered enthusiastic critical praise.

Phil's book of interviews, *Something Inside: Conversation with Gay Fiction Writers*, was named one of the "Best Books of 1999" by *Pride* magazine. His *Travels in a Gay Nation: Portraits of LGBTQ Americans* was nominated for an American Library Association Award. His memoir, *As Far As I Can Tell: Finding My Father in World War* II, was named one of the Best Books of 2020 by *The Boston Globe.* He is also the editor of *Breaking the Rules: The Intimate Diary of Ross Terrill.*

Phil has contributed important essays, reviews, features pieces, and scholarly articles to numerous journals including *The New York Times Book Review, The Boston Globe, Provincetown Arts, Italian Americana, The Gay & Lesbian Review Worldwide, The Harvard Crimson,* and *American National Biography.* His longer essays have appeared in a number of anthologies, including *Hometowns, Sister and Brother, Wrestling with the Angel, Inside Out, Boys Like Us, Wonderlands,* and *Big Trips.*

He is a recipient of fellowships from the MacDowell Colony, the Helene Wurlitzer Foundation, the Massachusetts Arts Council, the National Endowment for the Humanities, and the Massachusetts Historical Society.

Phil taught high school English for over forty years and college-level writing at the University of Massachusetts, Boston College, and, for over twenty-five years, in the Department of Continuing Education at Harvard, where his courses in expository and fiction writing earned him several awards.

Currently, Phil writes a weekly column, "The Writer in Mexico," for the online magazine *Lokkal* in San Miguel de Allende, Mexico.